$3.95

The **DRAGONLANCE**® Saga
Three Million Copies Sold!

WASHOE COUNTY LIBRARY
31235008605623

0-88038-382-8

Tales · Volume 2

KENDER, GULLY DWARVES and GNOMES

New Stories Including an Exciting Novella

by Margaret Weis and Tracy Hickman

"Wanna Bet?"

"**W**ait!" Dougan cried, raising one hand, the other grasping the handle of a burning red warhammer. "I say we leave everything up to chance. I offer you . . . a wager!"

The Graygem appeared to consider; its light pulsed more slowly, thoughtfully.

"A wager?" murmured the women dressed in tiger skins. Feathers were in their hair, and they carried stone-tipped spears in their hands.

"A wager," said the black dragon in pleased tones, settling its wings to the floor.

"A wager!" Palin muttered, wiping his sleeve across his sweating brow. "My god, a wager is what started all this trouble!"

Dougan stroked his beard. "These young men," he said to the women, pointing at Tanin, Sturm, and Palin, "for yourselves. Freedom for the Graygem."

"We agree to the stakes," said the dark-haired beauty, after a glance at the Graygem. "And now, what is the wager?"

Dougan appeared to consider, twirling his moustache round and round his finger. His gaze happened to rest on Palin and he grinned. "That this young man" —he pointed at the mage— "will throw my hammer in the air and it will hang suspended, never falling to the floor."

DRAGONLANCE® TALES

Volume Two

KENDER, GULLY DWARVES, AND GNOMES

©Copyright 1987 TSR, Inc.
All Rights Reserved.

This book is protected under the copyright laws of the United States of America. Any reproduction or other unauthorized use of the material or artwork contained herein is prohibited without the express written permission of TSR, Inc.

Distributed to the book trade in the United States by Random House, Inc. and in Canada by Random House of Canada, Ltd.

Distributed to the toy and hobby trade by regional distributors.

All DRAGONLANCE characters and the distinctive likenesses thereof are trademarks of TSR, Inc.

DRAGONLANCE, DUNGEONS & DRAGONS, and ADVANCED DUNGEONS & DRAGONS are registered trademarks owned by TSR, Inc.

First Printing, July, 1987
Printed in the United States of America.
Library of Congress Catalog Card Number: 87-90084

9 8 7 6 5 4 3 2 1

ISBN: 0-88038-382-8

All characters in this book are fictitious. Any resemblance to actual persons, living or dead is purely coincidental.

TSR, Inc.
P.O. Box 756
Lake Geneva, WI 53147

TSR UK Ltd.
The Mill, Rathmore Road
Cambridge CB14AD
United Kingdom

3 1235 00860 5623

DragonLance®

❧ Tales Volume 2 ❧

Kender, Gully Dwarves, and Gnomes

Edited by
Margaret Weis and Tracy Hickman

featuring "Wanna Bet?"
by Margaret Weis and Tracy Hickman

Cover Art by LARRY ELMORE
Interior Art by STEVE FABIAN

TABLE OF CONTENTS

FOREWORD

"*Tas? Tasslehoff Burrfoot!*" we shout sternly, peering down the road. "Come back with our magical time-traveling device, you doorknob of a kender!"

"I'll come out," shouts Tas, "if you tell me some more stories!"

"Promise?" we ask, peering behind bushes and into ravines.

"Oh, yes. I promise!" says Tas cheerfully. "Just let me get comfortable." There is a tremendous sound of rustling and tree-branch cracking. Then, "All right, I'm ready. Go ahead. I love stories, you know. Did I ever tell you about the time I saved Sturm's life—"

Tas goes on to tell *us* the first story in this new anthology set in the world of Krynn. "Snowsong," by Nancy Varian Berberick, relates an early adventure of the companions. Sturm and Tanis, lost in a blizzard, have only one hope of being rescued—Tasslehoff Burrfoot!

"The Wizard's Spectacles," by Morris Simon, is a "what-if" story. Tas always *said* he found the Glasses of Arcanist in the dwarven kingdom. But what if . . .

A storyteller tells his tales not wisely but too well in "The Storyteller," by Barbara Siegel and Scott Siegel.

"There's a lesson you could learn from that!" we yell to Tas, but he ignores us and goes on to relate "A Shaggy Dog's Tail," by Danny Peary. It is a kender favorite, undoubtedly passed down from generation to generation although Tas, of course, swears that he knew *everyone* involved *personally!*

Next, we hear the *true* story of the demise of Lord Toede in "Lord Toede's Disastrous Hunt," by Harold Bakst.

The minotaur race is the subject of "Definitions of Honor," by Rick Knaak. A young knight of Solamnia rides to the rescue of a village, only to discover that his enemy threatens more than his life.

"Hearth Cat and Winter Wren," by Nancy Varian Berberick, tells another of the Companions' early adventures in which a young Raistlin uses his ingenuity to fight a powerful, evil wizard.

"All right, Tas!" we call. "Will you come out now? We really *must* be going!"

"Those were truly wonderful stories," yells the kender shrilly from his hiding place. "But I want to hear more about Palin and his brothers. You remember. You told me the story last time about how Raistlin gave Palin his magic staff. What happens next?"

Settling ourselves down on a sun-warmed, comfortable boulder, we relate "Wanna Bet?", Palin's very first adventure as a young mage. And certainly *not* the type of heroic quest the brothers expected!

Still sitting on the boulder, we are somewhat startled to be suddenly confronted by a gnome, who thrusts a manuscript at us. "Here, you! Tell the *true* story about the so-called Heroes of the Lance!" the gnome snarls and runs off. We are truly delighted to present for your enjoyment, therefore, "Into the Heart of the Story," a "treatise" by Michael Williams.

"Now, Tas!" we call threateningly.

"Just one more?" he pleads.

"All right, but this is the last!" we add severely. "Dagger-Flight," by Nick O'Donohoe, is a retelling of the beginning of *Dragons of Autumn Twilight* as seen from a weird and deadly viewpoint—that of a sentient dagger!

"Tas, come out now!" we shout. "You promised."

Silence.

"Tas?"

No answer.

Looking at each other, we smile, shrug, and continue on our way through Krynn. So much for kender promises!

SNOWSONG

Nancy Varian Berberick

*T*anis let the hinged lid of the wood bin fall. Its hollow thud might have been the sound of a tomb's closing. Hope, cherished for all the long hours of the trek up the mountain, fell abruptly dead. The wood bin was empty.

A brawling wind shrieked around the gaping walls of the crude shelter, whirling in through the doorless entry and the broken roof. The storm had caught Tanis and his friends unaware at midday. Far below, in the warmer valleys, the autumn had not yet withered under winter's icy cloak. But here in the mountains autumn had suddenly become nothing more substantial than a memory. Esker was a day and a half's journey behind them, Haven was a two-day trek ahead. Their only hope of weathering the storm had been this shelter, one of the few maintained by the folk of Esker and Haven as a sanctuary for storm-caught travelers. But now, with the blizzard raging harder, it seemed that their hope might be as hollow as the empty wood bin.

Behind him the half-elf could hear Tas poking around the bleak shelter, his bright kender spirit undaunted by the toll of the journey. There wasn't much to find. Shards of crockery lay scattered around the hard-packed dirt floor. The one narrow table that had been the shelter's only furnishing was now a heap of broken boards and splintered wood. After a moment Tanis heard the tuneless notes of the shepherd's pipe that Tas had been trying to play since he came by it several weeks ago. The kender had never succeeded in coaxing anything from the shabby old instrument that didn't sound like a goat in agony. But he tried, every chance he got, maintaining—every chance he got—that the pipe was enchanted. Tanis was certain that the pipe had as much likelihood of being enchanted as he had now of getting warm sometime soon.

"Oh, wonderful—the dreaded pipe," Flint growled. "Tas! Not *now!*"

As though he hadn't heard, Tas went on piping.

With a weary sigh Tanis turned to see Flint sitting on his pack, trying with cold-numbed hands to thaw the frozen snow from his beard. The old dwarf's muttered curses were a fine testament to the sting of the ice's freezing pull.

Only Sturm was silent. He leaned against the door jamb, staring out into the blizzard as though taking the measure of an opponent held, for a time, at bay.

"Sturm?"

The boy turned his back on the waning day. "No wood?"

"None." Tanis shivered, and it had little to do with the cold. "Flint," he called, "Tas, come here."

Grumbling, Flint rose from his pack.

Tas reluctantly abandoned his pipe and made a curious foray past the empty wood bin. He'd gamboled through snow as high as his waist today, been hauled, laughing like some gleeful snow sprite, out of drifts so deep that only the pennon of his brown topknot marked the place where he'd sunk. Still his brown eyes were alight with questions in a face polished red by the bite of the wind.

"Tanis, there's no wood in the bins," he said. "Where do they keep it?"

"In the bins—when it's here. There is none, Tas."

"None? What do you suppose happened to it? Do you think the storm came up so suddenly that they didn't have a chance to stock the bin? Or do you suppose they're not stocking the shelters anymore? From the look of this place no one's been here in a while. *That* would be a shame, wouldn't it? It's going to be a long, cold night without a fire."

"Aye," Flint growled. "Maybe not as long as you think."

Behind him Tanis heard Sturm draw a short, sharp breath. If Tas had romped through the blizzard, Sturm had forged through with all the earnest determination he could muster. Each time Tas foundered, Sturm was right beside Tanis to pull him out. His innate chivalry kept him always ahead of Flint, blocking the wind's icy sting, breaking a broader path than he might have for the old dwarf whose muttering and grumbling would never become a plea for assistance.

But for all that, Tanis knew, the youth had never seen a blizzard like this one. He's acquitted himself well, and more's the pity that I'll have to take him out with me yet again, the half-elf thought to himself.

A roaring wind drove from the north, wet and bitter with snow. The climb to this fireless shelter had left Tanis stiff and aching, numb and clumsy with the cold. He wanted nothing less than to venture out into the screaming storm again. But his choices were between sure death in the long black cold of night and one more trip into the storm. It was not, in the end, a difficult choice to make.

"It won't come to that, Flint. We're going to have a fire."

Flint's doubt was written in the hard set of his face. Tas looked from the wood bin to Tanis. "But there's no wood, Tanis. I don't see how we're going to have a fire without wood."

Tanis drew a long breath against rising impatience. "We'll get wood. There was a stand of pine trees along our way up. No doubt Sturm and I can get enough from there and be back before nightfall."

Tas brightened then. Now there would be something to do besides spending a long cold night wondering what it would feel like to freeze solid. Shrugging closer into the warmth of his furred vest, he started for the doorway. "I'll come, too," he announced, confident that his offer would be gratefully accepted.

"Oh, no." Tanis clamped both hands on the kender's shoulders and caught him back. "You're staying here with Flint."

"But, Tanis—"

"No. I mean it, Tas. The snow is drifting too high. This is something that Sturm and I will do."

"But you'll *need* my help, Tanis. I can carry wood, and we're going to need a lot of it if we're not to freeze here tonight."

Tanis glanced at Flint. He thought he might hear a similar argument from his old friend. He forestalled it with a grim shake of his head, and Flint, recognizing but not liking the wisdom of Tanis's decision, nodded agreement. With a dour sigh Flint went to gather up the splintered wood that had once been the shelter's table.

"It's something," he muttered. "Sturm, come give me a hand."

Alone with Tas, Tanis went down on his heels.

Mutiny lurked in Tas's long brown eyes. There was a stubborn set to his jaw that told Tanis that the only way he'd get the kender to stay behind would be to give him a charge that he considered, if not as interesting, at least as important as the task of gathering fuel for a fire.

"Tas, now listen to me. We don't have many choices. I've never seen a storm like this one come up so suddenly or so early. But it's here, and tonight it will be so cold that we will not survive without a fire."

"I know! That's why—"

"No. Let me finish. I need you to stay here with Flint. It's going to be a dangerous trip out for wood. The tracks we made only a short while ago are gone. I'll barely be able to find the landmarks I need to get back to the pines. I have to know that you'll both be here if we need you."

"But, Tanis, you'll *need* me to help with the wood-gathering."

The offer, Tanis knew, was sincere . . . for the moment. But as clearly as he might see through a stream to the sparkling sand below, that clearly did he see the mischievous kender-logic dancing in Tas's brown eyes. Tas had no fear of the killing cold, the battering winds. The prospect of the journey back to the pines held only joyous anticipation and a chance to satisfy some of that unquenchable curiosity that had brought the kender to the crumbling edge of many a catastrophe before now.

Well, I'm afraid! he thought. And it won't hurt for Tas to know why if it keeps him here.

"Tas, the best way to make certain we don't survive this night is to scatter, all four of us, all over this mountain. That will be the fastest way to die. We're going to be careful. But Sturm and I have to be able to depend on you two being here just in case one of us needs to come back for help. Understand?"

Tas nodded slowly, trying to ease his disappointment with the sudden understanding that Tanis was trusting him, depending on him.

"And I can count on you?"

"Yes, you can count on me," Tas said solemnly. Privately he thought that staying behind, no matter how virtuous it made him feel right now, might be just the least bit boring.

Despite the cold and the bitter wind chasing snow in through the open doorway, Tanis found a smile for the kender. "Good. Now why don't you give Flint a hand, and tell Sturm that we should be leaving."

For a moment it seemed to Tanis that his charge wouldn't hold. He saw the struggle between what Tas wanted to do and what he'd promised to do written on his face as easily as though he were reading one of the kender's precious maps. But it was a brief war, and in the end, Tas's promise won out.

Sturm emptied both his and Tanis's packs. He took up two small hand axes, tested their blades, and prepared to leave. Tanis, preferring his bow and quiver if danger should arise, left his sword with Flint.

"I won't need the extra weight, I think," he said, handing the weapon to the old dwarf.

"Tanis, isn't there another way? I don't like this."

Tanis dropped a hand onto his friend's shoulder. "You'd be alone if you did like it. Rest easy; it's too cold out there to keep us gone long. Just keep Tas safe here with you. He promised, but . . ."

Flint laughed grimly. "Aye, *but.* Don't worry. We'll both be here when you get back." A high squealing, Tas at the pipe, tore around the shelter. Flint winced. "Although whether both of us will yet be sane is another matter."

With grave misdoubt Flint watched Tanis and

Sturm leave. Tas sidled up beside him, standing close to the old dwarf. He called good luck after them but he didn't think that they could hear him above the storm's cry.

"Come along, then," Flint growled. "No sense standing any closer to the wind than we have to. We might as well find the best kindling from that wood. When those two get back they'll be fair frozen and needing a fire as quickly as we can make one."

Tas stood in the breached doorway for a long moment. The white and screaming storm quickly swallowed all trace of Sturm and Tanis. Already he had begun to regret his promise to stay behind.

I could find those trees straight off! he thought. For Tas, to think was to do. He tucked his pipe into his belt and stepped out into the blinding storm. The wind caught him hard, and he laughed from the sheer pleasure of feeling its bullying push, hearing its thundering roar. He hadn't taken many steps, however, before two hard hands grabbed him by the back of his vest and dragged him back inside.

"No, you *don't!*"

"But, Flint—"

The fire in the old dwarf's eyes could have warmed a company of men. His face, Tas thought, certainly shouldn't be that interesting shade of red now that he was out of the wind.

"I only want to go a little way, Flint. I'll come right back, I promise."

Flint snorted. "The same way you promised Tanis to stay here in the first place? That lad is a fool to put stock in a kender's promise." He glared from Tas to the storm raging without. "But he *can* put stock in mine. I said I'd keep you here, and here you'll stay."

Tas wondered if there would be a way to get around the old dwarf standing between him and the doorway.

Well, there might be, he thought, considering a quick run under Flint's arm. Grinning, he braced for the dash, but then caught the darkly dangerous look in Flint's eyes and decided against it. There was, after all, his promise to Tanis, spider-web thin but still holding after a fashion. And he could, he supposed, manage to pass the time trying to find the magic in his pipe.

It was going to be, each thought, a very long, cold afternoon.

Under the sheltering wings of the broad-branched pines the storm seemed distant, deflected by the thick growing trunks and the sweep of a rising hill. Deadfalls littered the little stand. Tanis made right for the heart of the pines where the snow was a thinner mantle covering the ground and the fallen trees.

"Gather what you can first," he told Sturm. "It will be easier if we don't have to cut any wood."

It had taken longer than he had hoped to reach the pines. Though he could see little difference in the light under the trees, he knew from some sure instinct that night had fallen. The driving snow was no longer daytime gray, but brighter. Only an hour ago the sky had been the color of wet slate. Now it was an unreflecting, unforgiving black. It *felt* like a night sky for all that Tanis could see no moons, no stars. The air was as cold and sharp as frozen blades.

They worked as fast as awkward hands would permit, filling their packs with as much wood as they could carry. Carefully used it would be enough to keep them from freezing in the night.

Tanis shoved the last of the wood into his pack, lashed it tight, and looked around for Sturm. He was a dark figure hunched against the cold, kneeling over his own pack.

"Ready?" Tanis called.

Sturm looked around. "Aye, if you'll give me a hand getting this on."

It was the work of a few moments to help Sturm with the heavily laden pack. "Set?" Tanis asked, watching the boy brace and find a comfortable balance.

"Set. Your turn."

The half-elf clenched his jaw and bit back a groan as Sturm settled the burden on his shoulders. "Gods," he whispered, "if I could wish for anything, it would be that I were a pack mule strong enough to carry this with ease!"

For the first time that day Sturm smiled, his white teeth flashing in the gloom beneath the pines. "It is an odd wish, Tanis. But were it granted, I promise I would lead you gently."

Tanis laughed and, for a moment, he forgot the cold. Sturm's smile was like the sun breaking from behind dark clouds, always welcome for coming so seldom. At the beginning of the trip Tanis had wondered about the wisdom of taking the youth along. It had been Flint, to Tanis's surprise, who had urged that Sturm be included in the party.

"You argue his inexperience," the dwarf had said, "but I'd like to know how he's to come by any if he spends all his time in Solace."

It was, Tanis thought at the time, a telling point. But he had not been swayed until he heard in Flint's careful silence the echo of memories of another inexperienced youth: himself. That was no argument against which he might win. In the end he had been persuaded to include Sturm among the party. It was, after all, to have been a brief trip, with no diversions.

And Sturm, to his credit, did not rail against the hardships of the unlooked-for storm, but accepted the challenge and deferred, with a solemn and graceful courtesy that contrasted oddly with his youth, to Tanis's leadership.

Well, we've certainly been diverted now, the half-elf thought, settling his pack and stamping numb feet in the snow in a vain effort to urge into sluggish circulation the blood that surely must be near frozen.

"Come on, Sturm. The sooner we get back, the happier we'll all be. Tas's promise to stay behind will only hold for so long. Were you inclined to gamble, I'd wager you anything you like that though we've a long trudge ahead of us, it is Flint who is beset with the worse trial."

When they stepped out into the rage of the storm again, Tanis thought that were wishes to be granted he would forsake a mule's strong back and ask instead for a dog's finely developed instinct for finding home. The wind had erased any tracks they'd made coming into the stand.

Flint glared out into the night, thinking, as Tanis had, that this was to have been an easy trip. It had been a journey of only a few days to reach Esker. The wealthy headman of the village had welcomed them eagerly and been well pleased with the pair of silver goblets he'd commissioned the previous summer. The goblets, with their elegantly shaped stems, gilded interiors, and jeweled cups, were to be a wedding gift for the man's beloved daughter. Flint had labored long over their design, obtaining the finest jewels for their decoration and the purest silver for their execution. His client had been well pleased with them and not inclined toward even the ritual dickering over their cost.

Aye, Flint thought now, they were beauties. And like to cost us our lives.

The weird, atonal wailing of Tas's shepherd's pipe

keened through the shelter, rivaling the whine of the storm, drawing Flint's nerves tighter with each moment that passed. It never seemed to find a tune, never seemed to settle into anything he recognized as even remotely resembling music.

"Tas!" he snapped. "If you're bound to fuss with that wretched thing, can't you at least find a tune and play it?"

The piping stopped abruptly. Tas got to his feet and joined Flint near the door. "I would if I could. But this is the best I can do."

Before Flint could protest, Tas began to play again. The awful screech rose in pitch, splintering his temper, never very strong where Tas was concerned, into shards as sharp and hard as needles of ice.

"Enough!" he snatched the pipe from Tas's hand. But before he could fling it across the shelter, the kender leaped up and caught it back handily.

"No, Flint! My magic pipe!"

"Magic! Don't tell me you're going to start that again. There's no more magic than music in that thing."

"But there is, Flint. The shepherd told me that I'd find the magic when I found the music. And I'd find the music when I wanted it most. I really do want it now, but I don't seem to be able to find it."

Flint had heard the story before. Though the circumstances and some finer details varied from one telling to the next, the core of the tale was always the same: a shepherd had given Tas the pipe, swearing that it was enchanted. But he wouldn't tell the kender what the magical property of the pipe was.

"You will discover its use," he'd supposedly said, "when you unlock the music. And when it has served you, you must pass it on, as I have to you, for the magic can be used only once by each who frees it."

Like as not, Flint thought, the instrument had been acquired the same way a kender comes by most anything. A quick, plausible distraction, a subtle movement of the hand, and a shepherd spends the next hour searching for his pipe. He probably should have counted himself lucky that half his flock hadn't vanished as well!

"There's no magic in this," Flint said. "More likely there's a flaw in the making. Give over now, Tas, and let me wait in peace."

With a sigh that seemed to come straight from his toes, Tas went back to where he'd been piping. He dropped onto the frozen dirt floor and propped his back up against his pack. In his head he could hear the song he wanted his pipe to sing. In some places it was soft and wistful. Yet, in others it was bright, almost playful. It would be a pretty tune, a song for the snow. Why, he wondered, couldn't the pipe play the music?

The blizzard raged, shaking the walls of the little shelter. Night now held the mountain in its freezing grip. It occurred to Tas that Sturm and Tanis had been gone much longer than they should have been.

Likely, he thought, drifting with the memory of the tune he heard but couldn't play, it only *seemed* that the waiting was long. Probably Tanis and Sturm had only been gone a few hours at most. It would take them that long to get to where the trees were, find the wood, and fill their packs. He was certain, though, that if he'd been with them, it wouldn't take nearly that long to get back. And three could carry more wood than two. Tanis's reasons for extracting his promise seemed less clear to Tas now. He wished he had gone with them!

It might have been the cold that set him to shivering deep down in his bones. Or the sudden strange turn that the storm's song took. Whatever it was, Tas found that his music had faded and left him.

The wind roared and screamed. The snow, falling more heavily now than it had in the afternoon, was like a gray woolen curtain. Frustrated, Tas laid aside his pipe and went to stand by the door.

"Doesn't the wind sound strange?"

Flint did not answer, but stayed still where he sat, peering out into the storm.

"Flint?"

"I heard you."

"It sounds like . . . I don't know." Tas cocked his head to listen. "Like wolves howling."

"It's not wolves. It's only the wind."

"I've never heard the wind sound like that. Well, once I heard it sound *almost* like wolves. But it was really more like a dog. Sometimes you hear a dog howling in the night and you think it's a wolf but it's not because wolves really do sound different. More ferocious, not so lonesome. This does sound like wolves, Flint, don't you think? But I've never heard of wolves hunting in a blizzard unless they were *really* starving." Tas frowned, remembering a story he'd heard once. "There was a village way up in the mountains in Khur that was attacked by wolves in a blizzard. I didn't see it. But my father did, and he told me about it. He said it was really interesting the way the wolves came down after dark and stalked anything that looked like good food. And he said it was *amazing* what wolves consider good food when they-'re starving—"

"Will you hush! And while you're at it, stop imagining things that aren't there!" Gritting his teeth against his anger and the fear that the kender's tale of starving wolves and blizzards fanned, Flint climbed to his feet. He was stiff and aching with the cold. "If you must do something, come help me start a fire."

"With what, Flint?"

"With those old boards and—" Flint thought of the blocks of wood in his pack. He sighed heavily, regretting the loss of his whittling wood. "And whatever I have in my pack."

"All right." But Tas lingered at the doorway. It *was* wolves howling, he decided firmly, and not the wind. In his mind's eye he could see them: big, heavy-chested brutes, gray as a storm sky, eyes bright with hunger, fangs as sharp as the blade of his own small dagger. They would leap across the drifts and slink through the hollows, pause to taste the air with their noses, howl in eerie mourning for their empty bellies, and lope on again.

His father had also told him that the big gray wolves could be almost invisible against a snowy sky. Lifting his head to listen, he thought the howling was closer now. He wouldn't have to go very far to get just a quick glimpse of the beasts. Forgetting his promise to Tanis, forgetting the uncooperative pipe, Tas decided that he simply had to see—or not see—the wolves.

Checking to be sure that Flint was not watching, Tas grinned happily and slipped out into the storm.

"Tanis!" He was but an arm's length behind the half-elf yet Sturm could see Tanis only as a vague, dark shadow. He hardly heard his own voice, bellow though he did above the wind's scream, and he knew that Tanis had not heard him at all. He caught Tanis's arm and pulled him to a halt.

"Listen!" Sturm shouldered his pack to an easier perch on his back and moved in close. "You're not going to tell me again about how that's the wind, are you? Those are wolves!"

They were indeed. The fiction of the wind had been partly for Sturm's sake, partly for his own. Tanis abandoned it as useless now. "I know! But we have to push on, Sturm! We can't let them get between us and the shelter!"

"Run? You want us to run?" The thought of fleeing from danger sent a spasm of disgust across the youth's face. Beneath that revulsion, though, was an instinctive fear. It was not hidden, Tanis saw, as well as Sturm might have hoped.

Tanis's humorless laughter was caught by the wind and flung away. "I do! But the best we can do is slog on. There is no shame in this retreat, Sturm. We're no match for a pack, and Flint and Tas won't appreciate our courage at all if they have to consider it while freezing to death."

Though carefully given, it was a reprimand. Sturm recognized it and took it with considered grace. "I'm not accustomed to flight, Tanis," he said gravely. "But neither am I accustomed to abandoning friends. Lead on."

Sturm, Tanis thought, seeking his bearings, you're too solemn by half for your years! But, aye, I'll lead on . . .

And that was another matter. How far had they come? Tanis could no longer tell. He was storm-blind now, hardly able to keep his eyes open for the merciless bite of wind-driven snow and ice. The bitter wind had battered at their backs when they'd left the shelter. As long as it roared and screamed in their faces, clawing at their skin, tearing at their clothing, he could be fairly certain that they were moving in the right direction. He did not like to think what might happen should the storm suddenly change direction.

Likely someone would find our bones in spring and wonder and pity. Putting aside the grim thought, Tanis hunched his shoulders and bowed his head before the storm's blast, protecting his eyes as best he could.

His legs were heavier and harder to move with each step. His neck and shoulders ached beneath his burden of wood. And the wolves were howling closer.

It only *seems* a never-ending journey, he told himself as he waded through still another drift. Before the night was much older they would be back at the shelter. Then the storm could tear across the mountains, then the wolves could howl until they were hoarse. It wouldn't matter. Tanis could almost hear Flint scolding and grumbling about two young fools who couldn't come right back, but must linger to catch their deaths in the storm. Beneath it all would run Tas's chattering and incessant, never-ending questions. Their miserable burdens of fuel would feed a crackling fire to thaw hands and feet they could no longer feel.

Thinking to share the encouragement with Sturm toiling silently behind, he turned, squinting into the blinding snow.

"Sturm! Soon!" he shouted.

Sturm looked up. Ice rimned his hair, long streaks of white scored his face where the cold had bitten. "What?"

"Soon! We're almost—"

It might have been instinct that made Tanis slip immediately out of his pack and reach for his bow and quiver. Or it might have been the look of wide-eyed horror on Sturm's face. He never heard the wolf's roar, or the slavering snarl of its mate. He only felt the heavy weight where it caught him behind the knees and drove him with all the force of its hundred pounds face first into the snow.

His bow was beneath him, his dagger still sheathed at his belt. Fear raced through him like a hot river. He shoved his chin tight to his chest and locked his hands behind his head, protecting his neck and throat. The wolf's hot breath, stinking of its last kill, gagged him. Powerful jaws snapping, unable to reach his neck or throat, the wolf fastened on his shoulder, worrying at the thick cloth of his cloak, tearing through it and his leather tunic to lay his flesh bare to dripping fangs. Its eyes were gleaming green fire, its mouth a roaring crimson maw.

Bucking and kicking, his mind empty of all thought but survival, Tanis heaved onto his back. His head still low, he freed his hands and found his dagger. The wolf rose up, scrambling to regain position, belly exposed for an instant. Tanis gripped his dagger hard. The icy air stung in his lungs. He thrust upward with all his strength. The blade drove into the wolf's belly to the hilt. Gasping hard, he dragged until he struck breastbone. The beast fell away, dead as it hit the snow.

Shuddering, locked for one painful moment in the rictus of fear, Tanis lay on his back. Sweat froze on his face, nausea churned in his belly. His breath, ragged and hurting, sounded like the pumping of a bellows. Dark blood pooled, steaming in the freezing night.

Behind and above him another wolf roared. That challenge was followed swiftly by deadly snarling and then a shocked scream of pain. So horrible was the sound that Tanis could not tell if it had come from the lungs of man or beast.

Sturm! Coppery, musty, the stench of fresh blood filled the air. Tanis scrambled to his feet. The storm wind blinded him, tore at him. He couldn't see!

Though he'd always wielded his blade well in practice bouts with a confidence seldom disappointed, Sturm had only blooded his sword once and that against a human opponent whose moves could, to some extent, be gauged. Could he have gone against a wolf who would charge in under a sword's reach with the desperation of a predator starving?

Sliding in the freezing snow, Tanis ran to where he imagined the scent of blood was strongest. He crashed to his knees and, cursing, regained his feet.

"Sturm!" he howled. He thought in that moment that no blizzard wind could sound a cry as desolate. "Sturm! Where are you?"

Tanis found him sitting in the snow, bending over drawn up knees. The second wolf lay sprawled behind him, its head nearly severed from its neck. Beside it, slick with rapidly congealing blood, lay Sturm's sword. Tanis slid to his knees beside his friend. The rest of the pack had to be nearby! They had to get out of here!

"Sturm, are you hurt?"

The boy braced and straightened. The leather of his tunic had been shredded by the wolf's fangs. A trail of blood and ragged wounds whose edges were even now freezing white showed Tanis where fangs had raked from collarbone to breast. His hands trembling, the half-elf tried to gently separate leather from freezing blood. A hiss of indrawn breath, Sturm's only protest against the handling, made Tanis wince for the pain he caused.

"A moment, lad, just a moment longer. There." The leather came away, and Tanis heaved a long sigh of relief. The wound was ugly and long. But though he had dreaded to see the white glare of bone or the dark shadow of exposed muscle, he did not. Working with hands made awkward by the cold, Tanis tore thick strips of cloth from his cloak and made a bandage.

"If we can bless the cold for anything, it's that it will prevent you from bleeding overlong. Can you move your arm?"

Sturm lifted his shoulder, tried to reach. He managed a grim smile. "Yes," he said, his voice rough with the effort not to groan. "But I'll not be lifting a sword for a time."

Tanis shook his head. "The gods willing, you won't have to. Sturm, we have to go on. Those two cannot have been hunting alone. Can you walk?"

For an answer Sturm got to his feet. He stumbled a little, but righted himself quickly. The hard gleam in his eyes told Tanis what he needed to know. But when he made to reach for his pack, Tanis stopped him.

"No. Leave it. We have to get out of here. It will only slow us down."

"Tanis, we need the wood."

"*Damn* the wood!"

"Tanis, no! The need for fire is still the same. And without a guard fire, won't we have to face the rest of the pack at the shelter? I can drag the wood."

Sturm was right. Tanis snatched up his pack and shouldered it with a snarled oath. He retrieved Sturm's sword, wiped it clean on his cloak, and helped the youth to scabbard it. An arrow lay ready against the bow's string. Don't rush! he told himself. Get your bearings now!

But that was not so easily done. The wind no longer pushed from any one direction, but seemed to bellow and thunder from all four. Tanis cast about him, searched the snow to see if he could tell by the tracks where he'd been standing when the wolves attacked.

There was no sign.

"Which way, Tanis?"

"I—I can't tell. No, wait. Up, we were moving up the hill." He squinted into the wind. "There! That way."

Behind them, silent phantoms in the night, the rest of the wolf pack moved in to do a starving predator's grisly honor to fallen comrades.

* * * * *

Flint roared curses into the screaming wind. That wretched, straw-brained Tas! If there was a god of mischief and deviltry, he would be no god at all but a kender! He'd not turned his back for a moment! But a moment, he thought bitterly, was all it took to send Tas out into the snow. What had he been off after? Tanis and Sturm? Likely not. That would have been too sensible a motive to ascribe to a kender.

"Tas!" he shouted, flinging up an arm to protect his eyes against the wind's teeth. "Tas!"

The surest way to die, Tanis had said, was to scatter all over the mountain. "Well and fine, and here we are," Flint snarled, kicking furiously at the snow drifting past his knees. "Scattered all over the mountain. If I had half the brains I curse that kender for *not* having, I'd leave him out here to freeze as a warning to the rest of his empty-headed kind."

Then he heard, mourning above the wind, the howling of the wolves he'd thought to deny. Fear shivered through the old dwarf. They were close now. He hunched his shoulders against the wind.

Wolves! Aye, and likely hungry enough not to turn aside from stone-headed kender or young idiots who can't hie themselves back from a simple wood-gathering trip in decent time. . . .

"Tas! Where *are* you?!"

The snow erupted right at Flint's feet. Scrambling for balance he slipped, tried to catch himself and, tripping over a snow-mantled boulder, tumbled into a drift.

"Flint! Wait! Flint! Where'd you go?"

His long brown eyes ablaze with laughter, his face bright with merriment, Tas leaped into the drift, narrowly missing Flint's head. Tugging and pulling, then shoving and pushing, he got the dwarf righted and on his feet again.

"Flint, it's a little cold for playing games, don't you think? Look at you, I can't find your beard for the snow!" His impish laughter skirled high above the wind's roar. "What are you doing out here, Flint? I thought you said we were to wait at the shelter. You know, you're really going to be sorry later. There might not be a fire, after all, and you're so wet you'll freeze solid. You should have stayed inside."

There *were* words, Flint thought later, to express his fury. And a pity it was that he could not have found them when he needed them; they would easily have melted the last inch of snow from the mountain.

"*I* should have stayed inside?" Flint took a quick swipe at the kender's head, missed, and slipped to his knees. "*I* should have stayed?" He flung off the hand that Tas offered him and climbed to his feet again. "I'd not be out here at all if it weren't for you!"

"Me?" Tas's eyes went round with surprise. "You came out after me? But I'm fine, Flint. I just went out for a look. I thought I might be able to see a wolf. Or not see one. They say they're almost invisible against a storm, you know." His eyes darkened for a moment with disappointment. "But I didn't see any. Or I didn't *not* see any. I'm not sure which. And I didn't get very far. You know, Tanis was right. You can hardly see where you've been out here. You certainly can't see where you're going. On the whole," he decided, reaching out a tentative hand to help Flint dust the snow from his back, "I'd really rather be inside where it's warmer."

The logic was too tortuous for Flint to follow, and he was too cold and wet—nearly frozen to death, he thought furiously—to work it out now. He turned and stamped back toward the shelter, growling and cursing.

Cold, but undaunted, frolicking like a half-grown

pup taken to play, Tas scampered ahead. "You'll feel better once we get inside," he called back. "It's not much warmer there, but it is drier. And I've been thinking about my magic pipe while I was out looking for the wolves. I think I'd be able to find the music if I tried just a little harder."

Oh, fine, Flint thought, trudging stiffly behind, the dreaded pipe! It wasn't enough that he had to contend with blizzards and promises to people who haven't the sense to come in out of a storm, with brainless kender and wolves. No. On top of all of that had to be laid a "magic" pipe.

When he stumbled, shaking and wet, into the shelter he saw Tas sitting crosslegged and absent-eyed, hunched over his pipe. The high, tortured wailing that had tormented Flint all afternoon filled the air, rising almost loud enough to compete with the wind and the wolves' howls.

"The dreaded pipe," he sighed.

He returned to his task of coaxing a fire from the broken boards and fine, smooth blocks of his whittling wood. It would barely be enough to thaw his frozen clothing. It would not be enough to light the lost back to safety.

Tanis negotiated the gently descending slope as though it were a vertical cliff face, and slid to a ragged halt at the bottom. Sturm skidded past him, overbalanced by his pack, and dropped to his knees in a drift that seemed to swallow him to the shoulders. Tanis helped his friend to his feet. His stomach lurched in fear when he saw a dark red spot of fresh blood on Sturm's bandage.

"Don't stop!" he cried above the wind's scream. "We've got to go on!"

"Aye, Tanis, we do! But *where*? We're lost!"

They were. Or they might be. Tanis didn't know any more. He was fairly certain of his direction. This hollow was familiar, more filled with snow and drifts, but still familiar. Or was that only hope, the last thing inside him that hadn't frozen yet? He could not see ahead the length of his arm. Had they come to the shelter? Had they passed it? He couldn't think, and he did not see anymore how it mattered. Now it only mattered that they keep moving.

The deadly lethargy of freezing had been dogging them with patient tenacity. To give in now to aching limbs, to sit down just once to rest, to ease the burning of their lungs, the fire licking behind their eyes, would be to die.

And we'll not freeze to death an arm's length from that damned shelter! Tanis vowed.

But Sturm went down a few moments later and did not rise. He tried, foundered in a drift, and fell back. For a moment fury blazed so bright in his brown eyes that Tanis could see it despite the blizzard's concealing curtain.

He dropped to his knees beside his friend, shouted and tried again to pull him to his feet. He could get no purchase in the drifted snow, no grip with his frozen hands.

"Tanis, no."

How could he have heard Sturm's whisper above the wind's scream? Or was it that he read the protest in the boy's eyes?

"Tanis . . . take the wood . . . go."

"No! We'll rest. Just for a moment. We'll rest." There was more danger, he knew, in resting than in going on. The very wind that tore at them now would carry the scent of fresh blood to the wolves who must be trailing behind. But he, too, was not accustomed to abandoning his friends.

Tanis went down on his knees again in the snow and drew Sturm as close to him as he could, hoping to protect the boy from the worst of the piercing wind. Just for a moment, he promised himself. Just until Sturm can recoup.

So gentle is the paradoxical warmth that suffuses a man just before freezing, so entrancing, that Tanis did not recognize it for what it was. He only wondered briefly that he had enough body warmth left to feel, then closed his eyes wearily and forgot to open them.

The note, coming suddenly amid the squeaks and protests of the pipe, startled Tas. It was soft, gentle, and reminded him of the sigh of a mourning dove. He moved his numb fingers over the holes, drew another breath, and found the note again. And then he found another, higher, and a third, lower. Almost it was a tune, and Tas caught the change. He tried again.

There was a rabbit in the storm. Caught away from its burrow, too young to know that it must dig into the snow for its insulating warmth, it scurried this way and that, as though it might outrun the cold. Home! screamed through the rabbit's veins with the frantic pumping of panic-driven blood. Home! But home, a burrow snug and warm, smelling of good brown earth and the comforting odor of safety, was too far away.

Tas heard the rabbit's frightened squeak above the faltering tune he played. How could he have heard the rabbit's cry? He didn't know, but he squeezed his eyes tightly shut, let the pipe fall silent, and lost the image and the sound. Before he could think of absurdity, before he could decide that the pipe had nothing to do with the rabbit, he hunched over it again and continued to play.

There was a deer, its antlers almost too heavy with

the snow's burden to bear. There was a mountain goat, foundered in a drift, its bleating protest wailing and lost in the biting wind.

Tas drew a sharp breath, knowing that the deer would soon go to its knees in surrender, that the mountain goat would thrash and surge against its snowy restraints and surely break a leg.

If his attention was a vagrant thing, his heart was a kind one. Poor rabbit! he thought, poor brave deer! He wanted, as much as he had ever wanted anything, to go out to find them, to show them a way out of the storm. He wanted this more than he'd wanted anything before. More, even, than he'd wanted to find the magic in his little pipe.

In Tas's mind there was something dark and still. It was a man—it was Sturm! And beside him knelt Tanis! They might have been ice sculptures so cold and motionless were they.

Though it was no doing of his—and yet perhaps it was—a long ache of sadness drifted through Tas's music when he realized that they might be dead. Like the rabbit or the deer or the mountain goat, there was no way to tell where they were, near or far, no way to find them and help. There was only the pipe. He played, then, with all his heart and trusted to the magic that it would not be a song of farewell.

There was a rabbit in the doorway. Ears aslant, pink nose twitching, it paused for a second beneath the slight overhang of the roof as though asking permission to enter. Where he sat before a fire dwindled to meager embers and dying coals, Flint saw the ice frozen on its back, the snow clumped between its toes. Part of him sighed for pity, and part decided he must bid his wits goodbye.

And behind him the horrible squealing of Tas's pipe

settled gently into a sweet, low song.

The rabbit moved then, hunched forward, and fell onto its side, eyes wide as though it could no more believe that it now waited a foot away from the old dwarf than Flint could.

The storm, Flint told himself, it's only seeking shelter. . . . Easier to believe that than to believe that his wits had frozen solid around some mad dream. Moving slowly, he reached his hand out to the rabbit. He had not Tanis's way with animals. That lad could call a bird to hand, silence a chattering squirrel in the tree with a whisper. Or so it had often seemed to Flint. But the rabbit accepted the old dwarf's touch and quivered only a little.

He gathered up the little creature in both hands, felt the quick race of its heart, and moved his thumb carefully over its broad feet. The snow fell away. Under the warmth of his hands the ice melted from the rabbit's back.

"There," he whispered, amazed. He turned the rabbit back toward the door. "Off with you."

But the rabbit did not, as Flint had expected, dart away in fear. It paused in the doorway, seemed for a moment to consider the storm, and turned, bounding back past Flint and into the shelter. Flint saw it scamper into the shadows behind him and vanish into the darkness. Tas, still bent over his pipe, looked up only briefly to laugh.

Puzzled, Flint turned back to the door and gasped. Looming like some dream beast was a rough-coated mountain goat. To the left of the goat, its antlers heavy with snow, a dark-eyed deer waited.

Dipping its antlers—courteous beast, Flint thought and so thinking abandoned his sense and logic—the deer stepped into the shelter. The goat, as though hanging back to await the passage of mountain royalty, entered last.

Nothing Flint had ever seen was brighter than the delight shining in Tas's eyes. His pipe still in hand, the kender leaped to his feet, ducked around the deer, patted the goat, and scurried to the door.

"Flint! Look! Do you see? I brought them here!"

Flint shook his head. I can't be seeing this! he thought, stubbornly. And I'm not!

"It's the pipe! It's the pipe, Flint! Listen!"

Again that enticing, gentle song. Behind him Flint heard the thick flap of wings. He ducked only in time to miss being struck by a wide-eyed owl. Two white-bellied mice darted past his feet, saw the owl, and dove screaming behind Tas's pack.

"Tas! Stop!"

"No, Flint! It's the magic! They heard it! I wanted them to hear, and they did."

Magic? Flint turned this way and that, and everywhere he looked he saw what he knew he shouldn't be seeing. Sputtering protest, stammering questions, he received no answers from Tas.

The kender was on the floor again, bent over his pipe, his eyes squeezed shut in fierce concentration. He'd brought the rabbit and the deer. The mountain goat had heard and found him. And two mice and an owl. Soon, surely, his song would bring Tanis and Sturm.

Numbly, too stunned to know where to look first, Flint clapped his hands to his ears. After a moment he closed his eyes because there was a deer pawing at the frozen dirt floor, an owl preening its wings in the rafters, and a goat nibbling delicately at the straps of the dwarf's pack. He felt something soft and warm touch him and looked down to see the rabbit asleep against his foot.

He'd never heard that one of the first signs of freezing was a wild slipping away of the wits. But he imagined that it probably was because he still could not believe that what he saw was real.

Get up, the words whispered. Get up! Come back, they urged. Come back! Lies, they sighed. The cold is telling lies! Like dreams of a blazing hearth seen through frosted windows, the words wandered through Tanis's mind. Gently they coaxed and encouraged. Beneath the simple words danced the light, bright notes of a shepherd's pipe. Behind the tune, beyond the words, flickered images of a place where the cold had no power to touch him.

The wind, he thought, pulling away from Sturm. Or just my sanity slipping away . . .

But there was no wind. Its howl was silenced. And when he lifted his face to the night sky he no longer felt the snow's deadly kiss. Beside him Sturm moved, slowly, but with the deliberate care of a man marshalling strength.

"Tanis, do you hear?"

"The wind—it's died down."

"Aye," Sturm agreed, as though it had only just come to his attention. "That, too."

Tanis looked at him in surprise. "You hear music?"

"Yes. It sounds like a shepherd's pipe. . . ." His words wandered away, lost in surprise and sudden realization. "Tas's pipe, Tanis! We must be near the shelter!"

Tas's pipe! But that poor, crippled little instrument, the "dreaded pipe" Flint called it, had never given Tas music this sweet. And yet, what other could it be? Tanis climbed wearily to his feet and helped Sturm to rise.

"We'll follow it," he said. "No, leave your pack. If the shelter is that close, I can come back for the wood. And I've still got mine."

Home, the music sang, *come home.* . . .

Snow ghosts! The spirits of the storm-killed. Or so they would have been called in the faraway mountains of his homeland. Flint watched the eerie blue race of breaking clouds across the white mantle of the snow. He shivered, more from the memory of an old legend than from the cold. Behind him Tas's pipe faltered, then fell silent.

In an odd little exodus, as soon as the snow had stopped falling, moments after the wind finally died, Tas's strangely assorted menagerie of storm refugees had filed past him into the night. Still, even after the last creature had left, Tas had continued to play, hoping that Tanis and Sturm would hear the pipe's music, feel the call of its magic.

Magic! Flint thought now. The word felt bitter and hard in his mind. He told himself that he never had believed. Some wild coincidence, some quirk had led the animals to the shelter. It hadn't been, after all, any of the pipe's doing. Though he could still feel, in memory, the frightened race of the rabbit's heart against his palms, and later the confiding warmth of it where it lay against his foot. Nonsense! The poor little beast was too exhausted and frozen to care where it finally collapsed. He refused to remember the deer and the goat, the mice or the owl. He sighed and kicked at the blackened embers of the fire. We can go out and look now, he thought. He would not allow himself to think further. He did not want to consider what they must find.

"They're home." Tas's voice was oddly hollow.

Flint turned slowly, the skin on the back of his neck prickling. "What did you say?"

The kender's face was white, etched with weariness. But his eyes were bright with some pleasure or satisfaction that Flint did not understand. "They're home, Flint. They're back." He put his pipe aside. Wobbling to his feet, he went to stand beside the dwarf. He was tired, but it was the best tired he'd ever felt.

Flint peered out into the night. Two shadows intersected those pouring across the gleaming snow. They were darker and more solid than that weird blue flow. Snow ghosts?

Shivering, the old dwarf squinted harder. Not yet! he thought triumphantly. Not yet, they're not! But one of them was staggering, leaning on the other.

Flint grasped Tas's shoulders and hurried him back inside the shelter. "Stay here, Tas. *Stay here.* They're back!"

Tas smiled and nodded. "Of course they're back. I *told* you they were. They heard the pipe, they felt the magic—Flint! Where are you going?"

Yawning mightily, forgetting Flint's warning to stay inside the shelter, Tas retrieved his pipe and jogged out into the snow.

As he had for the past two mornings, Tanis leaned against the door jamb, smiling at the winter sun as though hailing a well-met friend. Beside him Sturm gingerly lifted his pack.

"You're certain you are well enough to travel?"

The youth nodded once. "Yes." He was pale yet, but the dressing covering his wound had come away clean with its last two changings.

"You did well, Sturm."

Sturm's solemn eyes lighted, then darkened. "No. I almost cost you your life, Tanis. I couldn't go on, and you stayed."

"I did. It was my choice. And," he said quickly, forestalling further protest, "it was a choice, at the time, of freezing with you or a few yards farther on. Where you did well was in another place altogether."

"I don't understand."

"You are a good companion, lad, and one I would not hesitate to travel with again."

Plainly Sturm still did not understand. But he took the compliment with a notable absence of youthful awkwardness.

In the silence fallen between them Tanis heard the beginnings of an argument between Tas and Flint that had become all too familiar these last two days.

"There was no mountain goat," Flint growled.

But Tas was insistent. "Yes, there *was*. And not only that, there was a deer—"

"There was no deer."

Grinning, Tanis went to join them.

"Flint, there *was*! You saw them. And the field mice, and the owl. And what about the rabbit, Flint? It slept against your foot all the time."

This time Flint made no firm denial. "Kender stories," he snorted. He glanced sidelong at Tanis and veered sharply away from the subject of magic pipes. "Are you certain Sturm is ready to travel?"

"So he says, and I think he is."

"I'd like to check that bandage once more."

Tas watched him leave, then reached over to finger a broken pack strap that had been giving the old dwarf trouble. "Look, Tanis."

"Frayed, but it should hold with repair."

"No. Look. It's not frayed. The goat chewed it."

"Yes, well . . ." Tanis smiled and quietly relieved Tas of Flint's small whittling knife. "Fell out of the pack, did it?"

Tas's eyes widened innocently. "Oh! I guess it did. Good thing I found it. Flint wouldn't have been happy to leave it behind. But what about the pack strap?"

"It looks frayed to me." He patted Tas's shoulder.

"Come on, now. It's time to go."

"I don't know why no one believes me, Tanis."

Tanis wished then, for the sake of the wistful hope in the kender's voice, that he could believe in the magic pipe. But it sounded too much like all of Tas's fantastic stories. Some, doubtless, were true. But Tanis had never been able to separate those from the soaring flights of imagination that Tas passed off as adventures.

"You know," he said kindly, "enchanted or not, your piping saved our lives. If we hadn't heard it, Sturm and I would have died out there."

"I'm glad it did, Tanis, I really am. But, still, I wish someone would believe I found the magic. I don't know why Flint won't. He saw the deer and the goat and the mice and the owl. And the rabbit *was* sleeping against his foot."

That rabbit, Tanis realized then, was not among the things that Flint denied. In matters of magic, that might be, where Flint was concerned, considered avowal.

When he looked up again Tas had gone. Rising to join the others, he caught sight of something small and abandoned on the floor. "Tas, you forgot your pipe." He picked it up and then saw words carved into the wood that he had not seen before.

Find the music, find the magic.

"Did you carve this?"

Tas did not turn. "Yes," he said, reluctantly. "I have to leave it."

"But, Tas, why?"

Tas squared his shoulders as though firming some resolve. But still he did not turn. "Because the shepherd said that it could only be used once. That's why I can't get the pipe to play that song again—or any song. I've used the magic." He took a deep breath and went on. "And he said that once I found the magic I had to pass the pipe on." He paused and then he did turn, a scamp's humor in his long brown eyes. "It's going to be a long winter. I'm going to leave it here for someone else to find."

Suddenly, as sharply as though he was yet there, the half-elf saw himself crouched in the snow, too aching and exhausted to move. He felt again the bitter whip of the wind, the life-draining cold. He heard, very faintly, the coaxing tune that had called him back from freezing. Maybe, he thought, seeing the earnest belief in the kender's brown eyes. Maybe . . .

But no. If there were any magic in the shabby little pipe at all, it lay in the fact that Tas, that inveterate and inevitable collector, could be induced to believe that he must leave behind a pipe he swore was enchanted.

Tanis grinned again. That, he supposed, was magic enough for one pipe.

The Wizard's Spectacles

Morris Simon

Nugold Lodston shook a gnarled fist at his youthful tormentors.

"Get away! Pester somebody else! Leave me alone!"

The old hermit shielded his face with his forearm from another flurry of pebbles amid the laughter of the dirty street urchins and their audience of amused onlookers. He despised these trips into Digfel and longed for the quiet solitude of his cave on the banks of the Meltstone River.

"We don't want your kind in Digfel, you old miser. Go home to Hylar where you belong, and take your worthless gold with you!"

The aged dwarf squinted in the general direction of the adult voice. His eyesight was terrible, even for his four hundred years. A blurry outline of a heavy human figure loomed in front of him, barring his way into Milo Martin's shop. It was obvious that he had to either push past the abusive speaker or retreat through his delinquent henchmen without buying winter provisions.

"Remove your carcass from my path, and take your ill-bred issue with you!" Lodston shouted. Several of

45

the spectators laughed at the old hermit's taunt. The blurry-faced speaker leaned closer, revealing his florid cheeks and filthy, tobacco-stained mouth to the dwarf's faded eyes.

"You heard what I said, scum! Get out of Digfel before I feed your scrawny bones to my dogs!" blustered the fat townsman. Lodston smelled the odors of stale wine and unwashed human skin even before he could see the man's quivering red jowls. He grinned and gestured toward the beggar children.

"If those are your mongrels, you ought to be more careful when you mate. You'll ruin your bloodline!" Lodston sneered and shook his quarterstaff in the drunk's face, which was darkening with rage as the catcalls grew louder.

"You gonna let him talk to you like that, Joss?" someone goaded the drunk.

"Kick that uppity dwarf in the teeth, if he's got any!" yelled one of the urchins.

The drunken bully sputtered a curse and raised a beefy hand. In the same instant, Lodston muttered a single word with his bearded mouth pressed against the smooth shaft of his heavy staff. The stick of rare bronzewood glowed suddenly with an inner light and began to vibrate in the hermit's hand. The old dwarf seemed almost as surprised as everyone else by the force within the enchanted weapon and nearly dropped it. He clutched its shaft more tightly, feeling its inner power throbbing as it lifted itself in the air above the bully's head.

Suddenly the staff descended repeatedly, faster than the eye could see, upon the head of Nugold Lodston's assailant. It appeared to the astonished onlookers as if it were a drumstick in the hands of a practiced drummer. Each blow landed with vicious force and accuracy, producing lacerations and bruises on the startled

---

bully's scalp and face.

"Run, Joss! It's a magical staff! He'll kill you!"

The bully's eyes were blinded with his own blood from the wounds on his forehead. He backed away from Lodston's flashing staff, his hands raised in front of his face to ward off the unerring blows of the enchanted weapon. To the hermit's failing eyes, the scene was a muddled image of fleeing shapes as the street emptied. Digfel was a superstitious town, especially in the rough section where Milo Martin kept his store.

"Get in here, Nugold, before they come back!"

Martin's rotund figure was standing in the doorway of his shop. He was gesturing frantically for the hermit to come inside. The staff had already lost the aura summoned by the ancient command word, but the merchant's bulging eyes were staring greedily at it.

The hermit grunted a minor dwarvish epithet to himself and pushed past the excited shopkeeper into the store. Smells of candlewax, oil, and soap mingled with those of wood smoke, spices, and leather—the comfortable and familiar odors of Martin's General Store. Lodston came to Digfel no more than four or five times a year, and this was one of the few places he liked to shop for provisions. Digfel was a rowdy human mining town on the outskirts of the dwarven mountains, steeped in fears and prejudices dating to the Cataclysm. Milo Martin's shop had a reputation as a brief haven amid the turmoil of the times, perhaps because Martin himself was such a tolerant man. The jolly but enterprising little merchant sold his goods to anyone with iron coins in his pockets, whether dwarf, human, or elf. Only kender, those notorious shoplifters, were unwelcome in his store.

"You old fool! Don't you know you can't fight all of those bumpkins by yourself, with or without a magic staff?" Milo's gentle reprimand was undercut by an excited sparkle in his crisp blue eyes. The merchant was thrilled at the promise of something new to talk about at the Pig Iron Alehouse. He was also bursting with curiosity about the mysterious bronzewood stick that seemed to have a life of its own.

"Bah!" spat the dwarf. "You humans think that you know everything. My people mined these mountains before you farmers learned how to grow your nause-ating vegetables. We dig more than potatoes out of the dirt, I'll tell you that much!"

Martin nodded judiciously, although he knew that the old hermit's dwarven pride was only momentary. Lodston lived alone because he had alienated his own people as much as he had the humans in Digfel. The merchant wanted to divert the conversation toward the staff. He certainly did not want to provoke a long-winded discourse on past dwarven glories and present human frailties.

"That's a fascinating quarterstaff, Nugold," he probed. "If you tell me how you came by it, I might pay good iron ingots for it. I've been needing a fine old stick like that!"

Lodston's bearded mouth curled in a sly smirk. Martin's face was a mere blur to him, but the silkiness in the wily human's voice betrayed his usual greed.

"How much?" he demanded quickly, cocking his head at the shopkeeper's fuzzy features.

"Enough to pay what you owe me, and maybe for this trip as well—*if* the staff is worth that much," Mar-tin added shrewdly.

"Oh, it's worth ten times the trash you sell in this place," vowed the dwarf. "I got it from an elven wiz-ard!"

If the hermit's vision had been sharper, he might have recognized the immediate frown on the shopkeeper's face as a look of disbelief.

"There aren't any elves in Hylar! No elf I've ever met would have anything to do with a dwarf!"

"There's one who would, all right, and he lives in my cave!" Lodston retorted defiantly. The hermit pulled a small keg of pickled fish closer to the fireplace and sat on it. He clutched the magical staff in front of him as if he were guarding it from the merchant's covetous gaze. Then he reached into a pocket and handed Martin a crumpled piece of parchment.

"He wrote down what we need. You fetch all those things while I rest my legs, and I'll tell you the strangest tale you'll ever hear in this ugly town of simpletons."

Milo Martin's frown deepened as he grabbed the list from the hermit's filthy fingers. He expected to see a barely literate scrawl, and was astonished when he recognized the fine penmanship of a scholar on the crude parchment. Each character was fashioned with elegant swirls, while the spelling and phrases were archaic.

"'Balls of twyne, a sette of three;

"Grinded millett, so fyne as to pass through a tea sieve;

"Twin hyves of honey, with compleat combs for the waxxe . . .'"

It was obvious that the old dwarf hadn't written the list. Martin doubted if the hermit was literate at all, and he was positive that those gnarled hands and failing vision would be incapable of such careful strokes of a nib.

"This is quite a list, Nugold," he admitted. "I might not have it all. Tell me about this 'elven wizard' who lives in your cave while I gather whatever I can to suit you and your guest."

"His name's Dalamar," the dwarf began. "I found

him on the riverbank last month, half-starved and out of his head. I knew he was strange, because of his white skin and long hair as jet black as his sorcerer's robe. 'This ain't no human,' I says to myself. Then I drug him into my cave and made him a bed by the fire. When he woke up, I thought he'd be afraid, but he was just as calm as he could be. He acted like he knew where he was, and like he knew me, too. Even called me by name, he did!"

Milo Martin paused with some candles in his hand. "Black hair, you say? Not just dark?"

"Nay!" Lodston replied irritably. "I said black, and I meant it! It be black as soot, and his skin like white linen, so white that it shines like a full moon in a night sky."

The merchant stroked his chubby chin, considering the dwarf's words. "Well, if he's an elf as you say, I'd guess that he was from Sylvanesti. I've heard that the eastern elves look like that, but I've never seen one of them."

The dwarf nodded excitedly. "That's it!" he exclaimed. "Sylvanesti is where he said he was from! You beat all I've ever seen with those wild guesses, Milo!"

The shopkeeper shrugged. It was no guess, but he decided to let the hermit believe that he possessed such an unpredictable skill. People were more reluctant to cheat someone who could "outguess" them.

"Go on with your story. Tell me about the staff," urged Martin as he turned toward his shelves to collect more items on the list.

"Well, he asks me right off if I found his box. When I tell him not to fret about some box after I save him from drowning, he doesn't say anything. He just stares at the fire for a long time. Then he gets up and heads for the door. 'Wait!' I calls. 'You ain't fit enough to walk!'

'Come to the river with me,' he says in this strange voice. It was like his words were stronger than I was! Before I knew what I was doing, I was up to my ankles in mud, helping the elf find this staff and that danged box."

"What kind of box?" Milo Martin had stopped gathering items from the list and was leaning against his counter. His curiosity had grown too great to bother hiding.

"A little wooden chest bound with brass strips," Lodston replied. "I carried it back to the cave after we found the staff. When we both was dry and warm again, he told me his name and said he used to be a wizard for some king named 'Lorac.' "

The name meant nothing to Martin. The enthralled shopkeeper motioned for Lodston to continue.

"Dalamar said he got into some kind of trouble back at this Sylvanesti place for changing his robes from white to black or something like that. Said he had to leave before the king killed him. When I told him I didn't think a king'd worry that much about the color of a man's clothes, he just smiled and laid his head back against the hearth."

Martin knew very little about magic and wizards, but he did know more than old Lodston. The shopkeeper's pudgy face flushed as he flaunted his superior knowledge of matters arcane.

"Idiot! Don't you even know the difference between white-robed and black-robed sorcerers? You ever heard of an evil elf, much less an evil elven wizard?"

"Evil?" demanded the hermit. "You mean like Joss out there and his scum-brained kids?"

"No!" Martin growled. "I don't mean simple pick-pockets and drunks. If you'd ever got out of that cave of yours, you'd know that some dark force is sweeping over Krynn, and it sounds to me like your new buddy is part of it!"

The shopkeeper's crisp eyes clouded. The normally jolly and mercurial man seemed suddenly over-whelmed with melancholia. "I thought Digfel was too little to get involved in this thing," he muttered sadly. "I thought everybody would leave us alone as long as we supplied them with steel for their swords and spears."

"What in Reorx's name are you mumbling about?" Lodston demanded.

"I'm talking about that guest of yours!" Martin replied angrily. "He and his evil friends will bring the war to Digfel!"

"War? What war? I don't understand what . . ."

"Go on with your story," the shopkeeper urged, interrupting the dwarf's flurry of questions in a calmer voice. The hermit's naive ignorance of the outside world was incorrigible. Martin could barely explain the sinister events of recent years to himself, much less to the reclusive dwarf.

"Harrumph!" snorted Lodston. He was too old and battle-weary to listen to human war stories. Vivid memories of *the* war still lingered in his aged brain, the war which had forced the mountain dwarves from their traditional homes.

"Well, as I was saying," he continued, "Dalamar's been wandering around in the west ever since they threw him out of this Sylvanesti place. He said he had to take some kind of 'test' at Wayreth to be a wizard, and it made him sick. I asked him if his stomach hurt, but he just said I wouldn't understand if he told me. He was up at Solace when a Seeker priest tried to kill him. So he made this raft and sneaked away on the river just before they came to burn him as a witch."

"Are they after him now?" Martin demanded quickly. Digfel had been free of the Seeker insanity, and he hoped that Lodston's refugee would not attract the zealous witch-hunters to this rough but quiet corner of Krynn.

"You got me there," Lodston replied. "I think they lost his trail during the storm that wrecked his raft. Nobody'd ever believe that he could have drifted this far downstream, all the way through the Qualinesti woods. I told him I'd hide him from them maniacs till he was well enough to take care of himself. He didn't thank me or anything, just rolled over and went to sleep."

"Did you search his belongings while he was sleeping?" Milo Martin asked eagerly. The opportunistic shopkeeper was imagining what he would have done under the same circumstances.

"What am I, a kender?" cried the insulted dwarf. "Anyway, I didn't need to snoop. He showed me what was in his box."

The hermit paused to retrieve a blackened clay pipe from beneath his fur cloak and gestured toward the tobacco jar on the counter.

"How's about some of that weed, the kind you sprinkle with honey wine? And maybe a little ale and biscuits to go with it," he added as Martin fetched the tobacco. The hermit might have been nearly blind, but he knew when he had hooked a listener on a story. The shopkeeper thrust a foaming mug of freshly brewed stout at the dwarf, who waited until his pipe was well-fired before accepting it. He was enjoying tempting Milo Martin's curiosity.

"Ahhh!" exclaimed the hermit, wiping ale from his mouth with a sleeve.

"Get on with it!" demanded the impatient shopkeeper. "What was in the chest?"

"Scrolls and books!" Lodston replied in a coarse

whisper. "Dozens of them! And a pair of funny old glasses with wire rims."

"What was on the scrolls?" cried Martin.

"Spells, I reckon," growled the dwarf. "How should I know? I can't read!"

The shopkeeper's pudgy face clouded. "Then how do you know they were magic?"

" 'Cause I saw Dalamar using one to see the future!"

Martin said nothing for several moments. His eyes were wide with imagination as he speculated to himself about the value of such a treasure—if the old dwarf was telling the truth.

"It was a couple of nights ago. We just ate some fish stew and bread. I'm sitting by the fire smoking some wild tobacco, nothing like this stuff, when Dalamar puts on them glasses. He unrolls a piece of parchment like it was holy and stares at the fire for a long time before he starts to read it. I ask him what he's doing, but he acts like he don't hear me."

Lodston took a long swig of ale and a few more puffs of the fragrant cured tobacco before resuming his story.

"Dalamar reads the words out loud, but they's in a language I never heard before. The words had a lot of 'ssss' and 'ffff' sounds that ended in 'i's or 'o's. You ever hear somebody talking like that?"

"No!" blurted his impatient listener. "Forget the language! What happened then?"

"Settle down, and let me finish the story! There was this light, kind of a white glow like moonshine, that got stronger with every word he read. It was coming from the scroll, but it spread all over his body. By the time he finished reading them words, it got so bright in my cave that it hurt my eyes to look at him."

"How long did it last?" Milo Martin asked breathlessly.

"I reckon not more than two or three minutes after he stopped reading," said the hermit. "Soon as it was gone, he stands up and heads for the door. He steps outside and looks around the cave, like he's checking the ground for footprints or something. 'What are you doing?' I asks him. 'What was that bright light in there?'

" 'They're not here yet,' he says.

" 'Who's not here?' I asks him, but he just comes back inside and sits by the fire again. That's when I looked at the scroll he was reading."

"Well? What did it look like?" Martin prompted.

"Nothing," the dwarf answered. "There was nothing on it at all. Dalamar wrote that list on it this morning!"

The startled shopkeeper dropped the parchment onto the counter as if it were a hot coal. Then he retrieved it and studied the writing more carefully. He even held it near a candle to see if the heat would reveal hidden characters of any kind. Regardless of the events at the hermit's cave, the "magic scroll" was now nothing more than a grocery list.

"See what I told you?" said Lodston. "The spellwords are gone. All I know is that whatever he saw last night scared him."

"Why do you say that?"

"Because he didn't go right to sleep. He made a sign with some ashes on the inside of the door and then bolted it like he thought somebody was going to try to break in. In the morning, he gave me that list and told me to get the stuff in a hurry. He handed me his staff and said I needed to take it with me; that's when he whispered the secret word in my ear to make it work."

"What secret word?" demanded Martin, his eyes riveted to the enchanted weapon.

"None of your business," replied the dwarf, "and I

can't give you this staff. It's the elf's, not mine. Now give me those goods, and let me get back to the cave before dark. I don't know why he wanted all this stuff, but he told me to hurry."

"You promised me . . ."

"I never promised you anything, Milo Martin!" countered the hermit. "But if you want me to tell Dalamar that you wouldn't loan him the things on that list . . ."

"All right, all right!" growled the cautious merchant. Martin was angry with himself for letting Nugold Lodston trick him into another extension of his credit, but he was also hoping to find a way to acquire much more than just the staff.

"Tell this Dalamar that I want to meet him," the shopkeeper said in a calmer voice. "I have a few business ideas that may interest him. Knowledge like this can be a valuable piece of merchandise. I know of several people who would pay fortunes to get a single glimpse of the future."

"Like you?" Lodston snorted sarcastically. He collected the provisions in a bulky sack and headed for the door.

"Don't forget to tell him what I said!" Martin called as the hermit stumbled into the empty street without looking back.

Lodston's "cave" was actually an abandoned dwarven gold mine. For centuries before he was born, the hermit's people had tunneled into the mountainside near the Meltstone River, enriching both themselves and the local human merchants with great amounts of the yellow metal. When iron ingots replaced gold and silver as the most precious substance on Krynn—to make weapons of steel—the rich Hylar dwarves near Digfel became paupers. Only a handful of the sturdy miners remained in human towns in the foothills of the dwarven highlands, becoming blacksmiths and armorers. Human prospectors took their place as miners, but of iron ore rather than softer metals such as gold and silver.

Nugold Lodston chose to remain in the Hylar hills, making cheap golden toys and baubles for local children. He cherished the gleaming metal more than he had ever loved anyone, dwarf or human. He also could not bear the tedium of toiling over a blistering iron forge to produce weapons and tools of burnished steel. Humans craving such products of the dwarven metallurgists regarded Lodston as a traitor, one who had critical skills but refused to use them. Even the few of his own race left in Digfel spat on the ground whenever he passed, a sign of ultimate rejection among the Hylar dwarves.

"Dalamar! Come help me!" the hermit called from the trail by the river. "I've carried these things far enough already!"

Lodston waited, staring up the riverbank toward the entrance to the mine shaft, but there was no sign of movement. Then he noticed that the door was ajar. The worried elf had slammed and barred the thick portal behind him seconds after Lodston had left for Digfel. Why would Dalamar be leaving the door open now?

Dropping the heavy cloth sack on the sandy trail, the old hermit broke into a doddering run up the hill to his cave. He sensed that some terrible event had befallen the elven sorcerer even before he saw the footprints in the dirt outside the shaft entrance. There were scores of boot marks with low heelprints in the soft earth, as well as the tracks of several large hounds. The dwarf dropped closer to the ground to focus his failing sight on the muddy threshold where the searchers had entered his home. Four large symbols had been drawn in black soot on the timber over the gaping door, but the illiterate hermit could not understand the inscriptions.

"Dalamar!" he called softly, hesitant to push the door. In his nightmares, unseen evils always lurked within silent doorways like this one. "Are you in there?"

Only the constant sound of the river below the shaft broke the ominous silence. Lodston finally mustered the courage to squelch his imagination and kicked the door open wide enough to peer into the antechamber of the ancient mine shaft.

It was empty. The fire was still warm, and a lamp had been lit beside the small table. There were no remnants of death and dismemberment, as he had expected to see—not even a sign of a struggle. The door leading into the abandoned network of shafts was bolted securely on the antechamber side. Dalamar and his box of scrolls had vanished, perhaps taken without a struggle by the strangers with the dogs. The enchanted staff in Lodston's gnarled hands seemed to be all that remained of his strange guest.

The hermit scrambled down the steep bank in the failing light of dusk and retrieved the sack of provisions. When he returned to the mine shaft, he slammed the door and slid the heavy wooden bar into place to guard it from whomever had come for the elven sorcerer. Then he threw another log on the fire and fumbled among the large ingots of gold in a basket beside the table for one to melt into a toy figure. He saw the end of a parchment case as soon as he moved the first bar of gold. It was one of the elf's scrolls!

"Ah! They left one behind!" he exclaimed aloud. The familiar echoes of his own voice inside the mine's entry chamber was a friendly, reassuring sound. Lodston's tension melted, giving way to excitement. The old hermit fumbled clumsily with the scroll case, finally managing to dump the neatly rolled white parchment into his filthy hand.

Trembling with anticipation, he pressed an end of the scroll to the table and unrolled it beneath the light of the lamp. There was a hasty line drawing at the top of the page, just above some undecipherable characters in Dalamar's flourishing script.

"Hey, that's me!" Lodston croaked, peering at the drawing. Sure enough, Dalamar had drawn a crude caricature of the hermit's profile. The bulbous nose and bushy eyebrows were unmistakable. Beside the face, the wizard had drawn his own spectacles, equally obvious because of their curious hexagonal lenses and wire rims. A dotted arrow led from the glasses to Lodston's profile, and a solid arrow from his eyes to the text below the drawing. Even a child could understand the simple diagram.

"He wants me to put on his glasses, but where are they?" muttered the hermit.

He began rummaging through the room, his excited imagination blossoming into full-blown frenzy. After searching inside, under and on top of everything in the sparsely furnished chamber, the only thing he discovered was the absence of his oldest cloak, a tattered, floor-length garment of crudely woven wool. He sat down heavily in the chair and stared once more at the elf's drawing.

Suddenly he knew where the glasses had to be. He whirled around toward the basket of gold ore and began tossing the heavy nuggets on the floor. The wire-rimmed spectacles were at the bottom of the pile, wrapped in thick goatskin and wedged into a crevice between two huge nuggets to protect them from the weight of the ore. Lodston thrust the wire rims around

---

his hairy ears and peered again at the parchment.

The black characters beneath the drawing began to swim and wriggle before his eyes. The motion was so distracting at first that Lodston felt a little light-headed and dizzy. Soon, though, the characters settled into firmer images, more in the dwarf's mind than on the scroll.

"I can't read," he muttered in amazement, "yet I know exactly what this says!" The elf's message in wizard-scrawl was brief but clear:

> *The Qualinesti mage has found me. Guard my scrolls and books with your life. If I fail to return within a month, you must take them to Ladonna, Mistress of Black Arts in the Tower of High Sorcery at Wayreth. You will find them behind the old door. Go into the tunnel and turn left at the fourth passage. Walk twelve paces and look up. My staff and these dwarven Glasses of True Seeing will repay you for your past and future kindnesses.*
>
> *Do not try to read the other parchments! Their power would destroy you and attract my enemies.*
>
> *Dalamar*

Lodston removed the enchanted glasses, only to see the magical writing encode itself again in his mind. He experimented with them a few more times, feeling the message swim in and out of his awareness each time he donned and removed the spectacles. He also noticed that he could see his surroundings perfectly whenever he was wearing the magical lenses.

" 'Glasses of True Seeing,' huh? Now that's some piece of sorcery!" he exclaimed aloud. "Healing an old dwarf's eyesight and teaching him to read secret spells all at the same time!" Lodston could not have known that the "healing" effects were accidental. The lenses, which some unknown dwarven wizard had used to fashion the enchanted spectacles, just happened to have the right angle of refraction to improve Lodston's failing vision.

The jubilant hermit unbolted the inner door and ran into the tunnels, following Dalamar's directions to the letter. At the twelfth step in the fourth passageway, he looked upward, using the lamplight and his wondrous new glasses to study the shadows of the ceiling. The small chest was wedged between the tunnel roof and a loose timber, just as the parchment had promised. He quickly pried it loose and scurried back to the antechamber to study his newfound treasure.

Lodston opened the unlocked lid of the chest and dumped its contents on the table in the lamplight. Dalamar's voluminous robe tumbled onto the rough wooden surface, forming a black cushion for dozens of small parchment cases and several slender books covered in purple silk and bound with leather straps.

"So he traded me his fine black robe for my old cloak, huh? Sorcerers might be brainy, but they're short on common sense," Lodston muttered to himself. The hermit picked up each scroll separately, weighing it in his hands and examining it with his powerful new spectacles. Still he saw nothing unusual about any of them.

"Why didn't he put labels on them?" mumbled the curious dwarf. "What good are enchanted glasses if there's nothing to read with them? At least they should have titles so I'd know what I'm guarding 'with my life.' "

For several minutes of agonizing temptation, Lodston stared first at the scrolls, then at the note from Dalamar. Finally, he snorted and started returning the cases, one-by-one, to the chest. He held the last one in his hand a moment too long, letting curiosity win the battle with judgment. With a muffled growl of surrender, he squinted behind the tiny glasses perched upon his huge nose and opened the scroll case.

Once again, the magical glyphs on the parchment writhed into a meaningful form, the words of an incantation in some unknown language forcing themselves from the dwarf's throat.

"*Drish fetts, drish fetts, lorgon trits,*" he heard his own voice pronouncing, but he could not understand what he was saying.

Lodston found it difficult to recall which of several things happened first at the instant he uttered the last syllable of the strange incantation. The scroll itself flared with a yellow light, then disintegrated into fine ashes in his hands. At the same time (it seemed) a huge sphere of orange flames formed itself from the yellow glow of the scroll and shot forward, away from the hermit. In a blinding, deafening explosion, the fireball struck the pantry wall with such stunning force that Lodston was slammed to the rock floor of the antechamber.

"Great Reorx!" he swore when he was able to stagger to his feet. The pantry, with its dirty dishes and utensils, plus some sacks of food, had been completely destroyed! The nearest corner of the ancient mine chamber was charred and bare of everything. The wooden shelves had disintegrated into smoking embers on the floor. Lodston looked at the pile of seemingly harmless scroll-cases in the chest and slammed its lid shut with a fearful cry.

"I won't touch another one of the damnable things!" he vowed in a ringing shout, as if he were promising the absent Dalamar that he would never disobey him again. "You and this 'Ladonna' can have these evil things to yourselves!"

The old dwarf's dreams that first night were filled with images of black-robed sorcerers who were fighting him with deadly magic. He had no way of imagining Dalamar's enemy, this "Qualinesti mage," but his mind constructed a spectral figure in a hooded white robe, the face hidden by the cowl except for terrible red eyes gleaming from its shadows. Lodston woke from his nightmare with a shudder and lay awake staring at the dying embers in the fireplace.

"What am I supposed to do if this mage from Qualinesti comes for your scrolls and books?" he cried in a hushed voice, as if Dalamar could hear and advise him. "I don't know anything about magic. I wouldn't even know which spell to read until it was too late. Why should I have to fight your enemy when you ran away from him yourself?"

The silence that followed his desperate cry for help offered no solace. Lodston fumbled in the darkness for the staff and the glasses. When he had found both magical items, he crawled to the door. The only thing he could do, it seemed, was leave this business to Dalamar and the mage from Qualinesti, whoever he was. He remembered stories from his childhood about the Kinslayer Wars between different elven clans and wondered fleetingly if that was the "war" that Milo Martin had mentioned.

"It's none of my business, any way you look at it!" he muttered at the door. Then he slid the wooden bar aside and stepped into the darkness outside his dwarf-made cave. By the silver light of the white moon, he could see the curious inscription on his front door which he hadn't been able to read before. The runes flowed together under the power of the Glasses of True Seeing, startling the hermit with their stark warning.

———

Death to traitors and to those who hide them! it read.

Lodston felt his skin prickle with fear as he read his own death sentence. He whirled around and probed the darkness with the aid of his new glasses, hoping to spot one of Dalamar's enemies in the thick shadows of the cliffside bushes.

"And death to you!" he shouted into the darkness with a shake of the quarterstaff. "This is my home! Leave me alone! I want nothing to do with elven squabbles!"

The old dwarf tensed himself, prepared to fight anyone who responded to his challenge, but the stillness remained unbroken save for the steady gurgle of the Meltstone River below him.

"Well, if magic's your game, then that's what you'll get from Nugold Lodston!" the hermit shouted into the night. With that burst of bravado, he darted back inside the mine chamber and bolted the door behind him. Then he opened the chest and looked at the mute wooden scroll cases. Finally he shut his eyes behind the wizard's spectacles and reached inside for another parchment.

He was more cautious this time. The gnarled fingers shook as he unfurled an inch or two of the scroll's top edge and examined its surface carefully with the aid of his enchanted spectacles. A single line of glyphs began to twist themselves into a meaningful phrase in his mind.

Tisnollo's Wondrous Incantation of Suggestion read the parchment's title.

Encouraged by the fact that nothing dangerous had happened, Lodston unrolled another few inches of the scroll and continued to read.

"To win powerful control over the thoughts and body of one's subject, the adept must focus his occult energies upon the . . ."

Aha! Wait until I spring this one on Milo! he thought gleefully. Lodston's childish excitement stifled his immediate curiosity. He re-rolled the parchment tightly and returned it to its case. Then he made a small mark on the polished wood with a charred stick from the fireplace. He couldn't write, but he might at least mark the scrolls to distinguish those which seemed safe from those which were more dangerous. Then he reached for another of the powerful parchments.

By sunrise, the would-be wizard had catalogued each of the scrolls into one of four categories: "tricks," which meant (he thought) harmless spells he wanted to use on people he knew, such as Milo Martin; "guard spells," which seemed to protect their caster from harm; "attack spells," whose titles suggested more aggressive results; and "unknown spells," whose results the untrained hermit could not predict even by reading and understanding the first few lines.

A sorcerer needs a sorcerer's robe, Lodston thought, delighted with the promise of new and unusual powers. He lifted Dalamar's black robe from the table and let it fall loosely over his head. A blend of cloying fragrances stormed his nostrils from the hundreds of hidden pockets which had contained the wizard's spell components and ingredients for herbal potions. The pockets were empty now, but residue of their exotic contents remained to perfume the silken fabric.

The hermit had planned to gather the voluminous garment at the waist to adjust its length, but the robe seemed to sense his shorter height. At the moment the light but strong fabric settled on his shoulders, Lodston felt Dalamar's power surging in the robe and spreading into his own body. The flawless stitches seemed to shrink closer together, drawing the garment's hem from the floor until it barely covered the dwarf's boots.

Suddenly, the dark elf's lingering dweomer flooded Lodston's mind with alien thoughts and impulses, confusing the dwarf with flashing images of fire, pain, and dark presences. Just as the psychic turmoil was becoming unbearable, it stopped. The powerful memories melted and receded into Lodston's aged brain, merging with his own dim recollections of the past. A wave of energy swept into his arthritic limbs, dulling their pain and moving him toward the door. The black-robed figure that descended the cliff and strode confidently toward Digfel bore little resemblance to the reclusive dwarf who made golden toys for children.

Four days later, the Pig Iron Alehouse was buzzing with gossip about Lodston and his guest from Sylvanesti.

"He must be an evil sorcerer, part of that trouble in the north," someone whispered.

"Nobody's ever seen him, but look at old Lodston!"

"I saw him reading a spell from a scroll!" claimed one witness. "He called up a lightning bolt and set the blacksmith's shop on fire, just because the smith spat on the ground when he walked past! Old Lodston always was an ornery cuss, but never that mean. I think that elf has cast an evil spell on him."

"Dwarves don't know anything about magic," scoffed a less superstitious townsman. "I heard that was some kind of family feud—something to do with the old gold mine. The hermit probably kept the blacksmith busy while the elf set the fire."

"I know what I saw!" protested the witness. "He had on some funny glasses and was reading from a piece of parchment when the lightning came right out of his hands just before the scroll blew up!"

"I heard Lodston tell Tidbore Ummer that his sheep were going to die, and they did—every one of them! Tidbore said the old fool told him he read the future from a magic scroll."

"That old gold-hound can't read!"

"Read? By Paladine, he can't even see!"

"Well, he can now! I heard that this elf is a healer, not a wizard, and that he made some glasses to heal the dwarf's eyesight," someone whispered.

There was a nervous titter as a flurry of gossip about healing spectacles spread among the tables.

"If that were true, the Seekers from Solace would be crawling all over us. A healer in Krynn? Don't be a fool!"

"To me, the biggest puzzle is why a dwarf would take up with an elf. They're supposed to hate each other, you know."

"That wouldn't be a special problem for Nugold Lodston. He hates everybody and everything, except gold, that is!"

"That's not any harder to believe than an elf in black robes, I tell you. If you ask me, it's got something to do with all that mess in the north."

"Maybe he and this Dalamar like something else about each other, if you know what I mean!"

The drunken insinuation cut through the underlying tension of the conversation, causing peals of laughter to fill the tavern. During the raucous outbreak of crude jokes about Lodston and Dalamar, a man clad in a rough wool cloak flipped the hood closer around his face. Then he tossed an iron coin on the table and left the tavern.

While the patrons of the Pig Iron Alehouse were debating over the nature of his relationship with Dalamar, Nugold Lodston was on the other side of Digfel, shaking his stick in Milo Martin's flushed face. Even his voice had changed in the last several days, developing an impatient edge and a curious clipped accent.

"You heard what we want! We'll expect delivery, as usual, before nightfall!"

"I can't do that, Nugold," Martin insisted. "My cart was in the blacksmith's shop when you . . . uh, when it caught fire. It'll be a week before I'm able to bring all this stuff out to you. Tell Dalamar it's not my fault!"

Martin looked away from the dwarf's angry gaze behind the curious hexagonal glasses. Though he had never met the elf, he now feared Lodston's guest. The powers which the elven wizard had bestowed upon his unlikely dwarven friend were more than the shopkeeper wanted to face. Hadn't they changed the irascible but harmless old hermit into a fearsome sorcerer with a more dangerous temper? Hadn't the elf somehow healed the dwarf's failing vision with the enchanted spectacles perched upon Lodston's huge nose?

"Well, bring it as soon as you get your cart fixed," growled the dwarf as he turned to leave Martin's shop. "Just remember what I said about the door, if you value your life!"

"I know, I know!" the man mumbled. "You and the elf have placed a curse on it. No thief in his right mind would try to steal anything from you or your new 'friend.' "

Lodston smirked behind his whiskers and stepped through the doorway onto the street. The curious little glasses perched on his thick nose sparkled in the late morning sun. The bully, Joss, interrupted a conspiratorial discussion with a pair of teenaged pickpockets and muttered a hasty warning. The unscrupulous trio darted into the shadows, away from Lodston's path. The hermit scowled in their direction, wishing he had a suitably vindictive spell to cast upon the fleeing threesome.

I've used all the scrolls I understand, he mused on his way home. I guess I'll just have to take a chance on a strange one, if I mean to keep these human clods on their toes.

When he reached the mine, Lodston headed immediately for the chest. He had already used all of the "fun" and "attack" spells and was ready to risk reading one or two incantations in his "unknown" category in order to strengthen his image in Digfel as a dangerous sorcerer. The hermit unrolled the first scroll he found with four black marks and began to read it.

Hapgammiton's Mode of Interplanar Gating

To summon other intelligences residing on other planes of existence, it is essential for the caster to prepare himself for five consecutive nights prior to uttering the incantation. Failure to purify himself beforehand will render the incantation either powerless or unpredictable.

Bah! I already knew it was unpredictable! Lodston thought. The worst that can come of it is that it'll fail. In that case, I can just pick another one. Undaunted, the amateur wizard skipped the rest of the page and began reading the ancient words at the bottom of the parchment.

His pronunciation and understanding of the forgotten elvish dialect had grown more accurate with each reading of Dalamar's scroll's. This time, his dwarven accents had dwindled to a mere trace, as had much of his original personality before it was dominated by the dark elf's spells and robe. Lodston intoned the ancient words perfectly, letting the scroll's dweomer fuse with the vestiges of Dalamar's power within his mind and body.

> *Margash joras nollen grath*
> *Grissit dorsi, grissit blude;*
> *Itel forna drilid shude;*
> *Margash nepps u hallem grath!*

> *Obey these words of power*
> *Watchers of the threshold, watchers at the gate,*
> *Unbar the guarded door;*
> *Obey the command of this servant of power!*

Beneath the dwarf's feet, the firm rock floor seemed to quiver as he spoke the final spellwords. Lodston's untrained concentration shattered completely when a thin stream of opaque light seemed to slice through both floor and ceiling of his sturdy artificial cave. The frightened hermit collapsed in a babbling heap on the floor, shielding his face from the intensifying light.

Suddenly the beam began to split, as if a doorway were opening onto a new yet darker dimension. Peering through his trembling fingers, Lodston saw moving forms just inside the opening, monstrous forms with scaly appendages and tentacles writhing and lurching toward the threshold produced by Dalamar's scroll.

The dwarf began to moan and crawled toward the door. Just as he was reaching for the bar, the stout wooden timbers exploded from some terrible force on the outside. The blast drove scores of thick splinters into the dwarf's head and chest and dashed him against the far wall with such force that he crumpled to the floor in a daze. The Glasses of True Seeing fell from his face into his lap, adding natural blindness to the old hermit's stupor. He could still see the gaping doorway because of the sunlight outside the entrance. He could also see a bulky figure clad and cowled in rough wool framed by the shattered sill.

"Idiot! What have you done?"

Dalamar's distinctive accent boomed in the small chamber.

"Dalamar!" the hermit tried to cry. "Help . . ."

"Quiet, you ignorant fool! I must try to undo what you've done before the gate widens!"

Blood from several gashes in his head blinded the dwarf even more. He was growing weaker and was clutching desperately to consciousness. Through the haze, he could barely see Dalamar marking the floor with a bit of chalk. Tentacled paws and stranger appendages were probing the air above the dark elf's head while he began chanting a singsong phrase over and over again from within the sanctuary of the hastily drawn pentagram.

For a moment it seemed that the horde of unearthly creatures Lodston had freed would swarm into the chamber and engulf the wizard. Yet he faced the monstrous beings with unflinching, intense concentration until the "gate" began to close. Then Dalamar raised both hands and his voice, crying the same phrase as loudly as he could. The final surge of energy was enough to dissipate the rest of the ethereal light. Silence and semidarkness enveloped the hermit's fading thoughts.

Dalamar glanced first at the dwarf and then at the crude table that held the open chest with his spellbooks and the remaining scrolls. The dark elf began removing the magical writings from the chest, examining each one for signs of damage.

"H . . . H . . . Help me, D . . . D . . . Dalamar," Lodston pleaded weakly. He crawled forward, trailing blood from his many wounds, until he could grasp the elf's ankle in his gnarled hand. "I n . . . n . . . need some w . . . w . . . water."

Dalamar pulled his leg firmly away from the hermit's clutching fingers.

"You'll need nothing in a moment or two, old dwarf," he told the hermit. "You will have peace, but you will have paid dearly for your disobedience. Already the dweomer of your bumbling incantations has spread northward to Qualinesti, if not farther. This quiet village will be drawn into the Dark Queen's war, thanks to you and your meddling. But you will have peace."

Dalamar watched in grim silence while Lodston's grasping fingers relaxed on the floor at his feet. Then he threw the hermit's crude cloak to one side and stooped to retrieve his black robe from the dwarf's body.

Milo Martin could see that something was very wrong the moment he arrived at the riverside trail leading to Lodston's gold mine. He left the sacks of provisions on the trail and picked his way stealthily among the bushes until he could see the darkened entrance.

Fragments of the heavy door were hanging from its sill by only one hinge. Some terrible force had blasted the thick portal inward, shattering it as if it had been an eggshell. The nervous storekeeper crept closer to examine the ground for tracks. The sandy soil was riddled with hundreds of footprints, tracks of boots with low heels, the kind commonly worn by elves. He also noted pawprints of large dogs, possibly bloodhounds used to track criminals. Satisfied that none of Lodston's visitors were still in the vicinity of the mine, Martin crossed warily to the gaping doorway. Then he called in a low, halting voice, as though he dreaded either an answer or no answer at all.

"Nugold! Nugold Lodston! It's Milo Martin, with your goods!"

Somehow the silence seemed more ominous than a reply might have to the cautious shopkeeper. He entered the murky chamber, stepping over the debris from what had been the door. The chamber had been ransacked, and the stench of rotten flesh nearly sickened him. Packages of food from his own store were broken and scattered everywhere. A fine layer of flour had settled throughout the antechamber, lending an eerie white cast to everything in the room.

Martin lit a lamp he found on a small table. Its light shone through the haze of flour which he had disturbed when he entered. At the rear of the room, he saw another shattered door leading into a pitch-black tunnel. Whatever force had blasted the heavy timbers of those doors was more than a mere battering ram. In fact, the inner door appeared to have been blown completely off its hinges.

The merchant was just starting toward the tunnel when his feet stumbled over something soft beside the table. He held the lamp closer and realized that it was the old dwarf's tattered woolen cloak. It was draped over something much firmer, something which was the obvious source of the stench in the small chamber. Martin lifted a corner of the filthy rag just enough to verify what he suspected. The old hermit's rotting body was lying inside some kind of mystical diagram with its bloated face staring vacantly at the ceiling. The head and chest were riddled with sharp splinters from the outer door, and the back of the scalp was badly gashed and bruised.

"What did they do to you, old friend? Where's your fine sorcerer's robe now?" Martin mumbled sourly, a few tears moistening his blue eyes. Despite Lodston's crankiness, the merchant knew that he'd miss the dwarf's trips to Digfel. "You were playing with fire when you let that elven wizard teach you magic!" he scolded the silent corpse.

Martin shook his head and turned away from Lodston's body. Being a practical man, he found an empty flour sack and began to rummage through the rubble, looking for anything of value which he might resell in his store. He found a metal cup and spoon in a scorched corner, as well as several half-finished golden figurines and a bit of cheap tobacco he could soak in wine to disguise its harshness. In the lamplight, he could see footprints where the searchers from Qualinesti had tracked flour into the mine. Just inside the mine passage, he could see a sturdy little chest lying empty on its side.

Whatever might have been in that box, magic or otherwise, belongs to the dark elf or his friends now, Martin thought grimly. Just as he was leaving, he noticed the light from the doorway glinting on something under the table, something made of metal and glass.

"Aha! The famous healing spectacles, I'll wager," Martin muttered. He wiped them free of flour and gore from the bloody floor, then balanced them on his nose. The thick lenses distorted his vision so badly that his head began to hurt almost instantly.

Humph! I don't know anybody in Digfel with eyesight bad enough for these glasses. What a waste of good workmanship! he thought. Still, some traveler might have a need for them. Martin frowned and removed the glasses, sticking them impulsively into one of his trouser pockets. Then he turned toward the failing sunlight outside Lodston's shattered door.

———

The Storyteller

By Barbara Siegel & Scott Siegel

*S*PINNER KENRO, YOU'RE UNDER ARREST!" ANNOUNCED
the dragonarmy officer, the point of his blade at my
throat.

I swallowed hard, hoping my bobbing adam's apple
wouldn't be sliced by the edge of his sword. Struggling
to keep my voice from quivering, I said, "I haven't
broken any laws. On what charge are you arresting
me?"

The officer, a human, his face a mottled mass of
burn scars surrounding dead, gray eyes, growled,
"You were warned, Kenro, to stop telling your stories.
The Highlord doesn't give second chances."

I was standing near the fireplace in the main room
of the Paw's Mark Inn. I had just finished telling one of
my tales to the assembled audience. How strange it
was to see them all in one place; the kender, with their
comically bright-colored clothes, stood out like stars
in a dark sky against the somber gray beards of the
fastidious dwarves and the earthy brown skin of the
ever-so diligent gnomes.

The dragonarmy officer seemed to pay them no
mind. I suppose he had little fear because his fellow

soldiers had entered the inn just behind him and had stationed themselves at every exit.

Out of the corner of my eye I saw the kender, Quinby Cull, strut forward. His face had turned red, and his cheeks were puffed out. Though Quinby was unarmed and half the size of the dragonarmy officer, he seemed thoroughly unafraid. I wish I could have said the same for myself.

"Spinner is our friend, and you've no right to arrest him!" declared Quinby.

"There's room for you in the Highlord's prison, too, kender," the dragonarmy officer said darkly.

Quinby seemed to mull that over before he innocently asked, "How much room is there in the Highlord's prison? I thought it was already full."

The officer pulled the edge of his sword away from my throat and stepped forward to threaten Quinby.

I grabbed the officer's arm. "He doesn't mean anything by it," I quickly said. "Leave him be."

Quinby had become a good friend since I arrived in Flotsam just a few short weeks ago. I had been disheveled and my spirit nearly broken until my long, meandering journey from the outskirts of Solace ended in this dark, forbidding city. I had traveled more than half a continent searching for an audience for my stories. And here, at last, I had found one. But more than that, I had found friendship. . . .

"Please," I begged, hanging onto the soldier's arm.

The dragonarmy officer slowly lowered his sword.

"It's all right, Quinby," I said. "I'll go with this soldier and get everything straightened out. I'm sure," I added with more confidence than I felt, "that I'll be free by morning."

A dwarf named Vigre Arch suddenly stepped up beside Quinby and said boldly, "I don't like this. You'd better stay here with us, Spinner."

The dragonarmy officer's eyebrows raised in alarm. Dwarves and kender in agreement? "The Highlord was right," he muttered.

"Right about what?" I asked.

"That you're a dangerous man. Enough of this talk. Let's go, Kenro, or I'll lop off your head right now. That'd put a quick end to your storytelling, now, wouldn't it?" he sneered.

Not having any choice, I started following the officer out of the inn. Both Quinby and Vigre Arch were shouldered aside, but there was a growing rumble among the crowd.

"Where are you taking Spinner?" one of the kender cried.

"We want another story!" shouted a dwarf at the far side of the room. "Let Spinner go!"

"Yeah! Let Spinner go," yelled a young gnome, taking up the cry.

Soon everyone in the room—except, of course, the dragonarmy soldiers—began to chant, "Let Spinner go! Let Spinner go!"

The kender, dwarves, and gnomes who crammed the inn had never joined together for anything—except to fight among themselves—and that had made it easy for the Highlord to rule. But the dragonarmy soldiers were seeing something that opened their eyes to a new and startling reality. The three races had united in my defense!

Frankly, it amazed me, too.

The angry crowd—they easily numbered more than two hundred—began to surge forward.

"Tell them to stop!" ordered the officer.

I saw the dragonarmy soldiers raise their crossbows.

This was madness.

"Listen," I said to the officer, "let me tell them a story. It will calm them down."

The soldier looked at the ugly mob and his nervous troops. He shrugged and then reluctantly said, "Make it a short one."

I held up my hands for quiet.

Everyone quickly settled down into an expectant silence. I was relieved. And so was the officer.

"I have to go with these men, but first let me tell you a simple tale to end this rather remarkable afternoon." I pointedly glanced at the officer who still had not sheathed his sword. He glared back at me.

I took a deep breath and began, "This is a story as old as time but as short as man's memory. It's a story of three orphans growing up in a city not unlike Flotsam."

"It's a sad story," sighed Vigre Arch. "I love it when Spinner makes me cry."

There was a sniffle in the audience as several dwarves began to weep in anticipation of my tale.

"Yes, it's a sad story," I said, "but there is a lesson to be learned in it. You see," I continued, "the orphans were starving, and they fought each other over every scrap of food they found. This was not a poor city, mind you, no. This was a city rich with power, wealth, and finery. Only not for our three little wretches. They were looked down upon, spat upon, and abused by the city elders."

The dragonarmy officer eyed me closely. His knuckles turned white on his sword handle.

I hurried on with my story.

"One day, the three orphans were at the edge of the city. And it was there that they came upon a Great Red Clarion, that fierce and magical bird that even some of the smaller dragons fear. If they could catch the Clarion and hold its magic in their hands, the orphans would never be laughed at or go hungry ever again.

"The Clarion's wing was broken, and it couldn't fly away. But its talons were sharp, and its beak made a formidable weapon.

"Here, finally, was a chance for the three orphans to make new lives for themselves, and all they had to do was work together to capture the magical bird."

I swept my arm out in front of my body and pointed at my audience. "But did they work together to capture the Clarion's magic? No!" I declared. "So hungry, so desperate, were these poor orphans that they didn't even think of joining forces. Instead, they fought each other over the Clarion. And while they fought, the city elders sneaked up behind them and captured the bird—and its magic—for themselves!"

"Oh, how could those orphans be so foolish and stupid!" cried Quinby.

"It's a terrible shame!" declared Vigre, agreeing with the kender. "The three orphans should have known better." The dwarf saw Barsh wiping tears from his eyes. He gently patted the leader of the gnomes on the shoulder.

The gnomes looked up to Barsh, not because he was the tallest of them, but because he was the greatest, most inspired of their inventors. Vigre, on the other hand, thought of Barsh as a hopelessly confused creator of useless, impossible machines. But at that moment, Vigre and Barsh were of the same mind.

Barsh turned to look up at his new friend, Vigre, and sobbed, "They should have designed a way to work together. Then they could have taken all the power and riches away from those cruel city elders!"

The dragonarmy officer who stood next to me hissed in my ear, "You're a clever one, Kenro, but I'm not deceived. I know what you're up to. End this story now, or I'll end your life, instead."

A storyteller is nothing if his tales don't have the

ring of truth. And this story had but one true ending. . . .

"My friends," I said softly, making them all lean forward and strain their ears to hear, *"the three orphans are here in this room."*

The officer began to raise his sword.

At the same time, however, the kender began shouting, "Where are they? I don't see them! Are they under the tables?"

"You doorknobs!" roared the dwarves, glaring at the kender in disgust. They knew what I was talking about. As for the gnomes, they became instantly agitated, but they all spoke so fast that no one could understand a single word they were saying.

The officer laughed at all three races. "The fools," he said. Then he prodded me with the tip of his sword. "Out the door, Kenro," he commanded.

I had come from a small woodland village and had never known the intoxicating effect of hearing a crowd chant my name. But Jawbone Jekson had. Now there was a man who could weave a tale. People would walk two days to reach our village in order to hear him. Their return trip, however, always seemed to go faster because their heads were filled with his wondrous tales.

When I was a child, I traipsed after Jawbone wherever he went. I learned his stories, his little vocal tricks, the way he moved his body at the climax of a tale. He took me under his wing and taught me still more. Jawbone was more than a teacher, he was a father to me—a father who told bedtime stories from morning till night. But I was never as good as he was, and no one wanted to listen to me when Jawbone Jekson could be called upon to tell his tales. Despite everything I had learned, I was unneeded, unwanted, useless.

It was clearly time for me to go off on my own, but I was afraid to leave. What if no one listened?

Late one night, Jawbone walked with me along the Patch River and—what else?—he told me a story. In his little tale I became a hero, a myth, a storyteller whose name lasted through the ages. As I listened, I could see myself standing high on a hill, the sun shining down on me, as hundreds—no, thousands—of people gathered below to hear my words.

Despite my terrible fears, I left my home and sailed into the unknown on a wispy cloud of Jawbone's words. Such was his storytelling power.

I traveled across Krynn, telling my own tales in little villages and towns with barely a tear being shed or a laugh being loosed. I thought myself a dismal failure. But then I came to Flotsam. There were no storytellers among the kender, dwarves, and gnomes. When they heard me tell my tales, it was as if the first dragon had taken wing. Their eyes opened wide, and they listened and stared with awestruck fascination.

Once, soon after arriving in Flotsam, I told a story in a tannery to a small group of kender in exchange for a meal. The tanner was crying by the end of my tale. One of his friends took me home to feed me. As I ate, he told me that the tanner's daughter had died during the last new moon. The father did not cry at the funeral, yet he clearly loved his little girl. "Why," he asked me, "could the tanner weep for the people in my story and not for his daughter?"

I wanted to say that I was such a wonderful storyteller that I could make a stone cry. But I didn't. I had no answer—until now. I remember that Jawbone once said that stories are the windows of life. They let everyone peek inside to see that they are not alone in their suffering. It's that knowledge that gives them hope when their world is bleak, makes them laugh when they see their own folly, makes them cry when tears are the only answer. Without that window, he said, the greatest emotions are sometimes never touched, never felt, and never shared.

Oh, how I wished Jawbone could have been there to see the huge crowd in the Paw's Mark Inn chanting my name. He would have been proud of me. I had opened a lot of windows.

I was brought before the Dragon Highlord. She had long, slender legs that were only partially hidden by her armor. And there were tantalizing glimpses of flesh above her breastplate. But it was her face, with blazing green eyes and high cheekbones, that riveted me in place. She was the kind of woman storytellers usually make the love interest of their tales. Perhaps that's the difference between stories and reality.

As I waited on my knees in front of her, the Highlord whispered something to one of her generals. All I heard was the name Tanis and an order to ready the dragons to attack a ship that had just left the harbor. She obviously wasn't planning on spending much time on my case.

"How do you plead?" she demanded, finally turning her attention toward me.

"Plead?" I asked. "How can I plead when I don't know the charge?"

Her full lips opened into a mirthless smile that revealed sharp, white teeth.

"The charge," she said with surprising gentleness, "is treason." Still smiling, she continued. "We need the kender, dwarves, and gnomes working day and night if we are to conquer Krynn. But now they shirk their jobs to come and hear you prattle on about nonsense. Your silly stories have turned them into hapless dreamers who stare into space and ignore their work."

"Please," I began, answering her smile with one of my own. "You must understand that telling stories is no crime. The imagination is part of the soul. Without it, my audience might as well be animals."

At that, the Highlord laughed. "Animals. Exactly. That's what those races are. And that's what they shall remain. Work animals. Now, how do you plead?"

I didn't know what to say. It is true I hated the tyranny of the dragonarmy, but I had never regarded my storytelling as treason. "Not guilty," I said.

"In the interest of justice," announced the Highlord as she rose to a standing position, "I have always given the people of this court a chance to defend themselves." The smile reappeared. "But I am the final judge of truth and falsehood. And you, Spinner Kenro, are guilty as charged."

I began to rise from my knees to protest, but two soldiers clamped their hands on my shoulders and held me down.

"I sentence Spinner Kenro to death by hanging," she proclaimed. "The sentence shall be carried out tomorrow morning at dawn. Be sure that his fate is known throughout the city. Our 'citizens' "—she sneered—"must learn what happens to those who lose themselves in dreams."

While awaiting my execution, I was thrown into a cell with a young half-elf named Davin. He was quiet and didn't speak a word. But I did.

I told him my story.

While I was telling him who I was, what I was, and what was to become of me, something miraculous was happening out beyond the prison walls.

Quinby Cull, that fearless kender, bravely crossed over into the dwarf section of the city and sought out

Vigre Arch.

"Did you hear about Spinner's sentence?" he demanded of the dwarf. Before Vigre could answer, Quinby declared, "We've got to help our friend. If he dies, there will be no more stories."

Vigre Arch dug his boot heel into the hardpacked ground before he finally said, "You know how I feel about humans. They aren't worth the skin they're packed into. You just can't trust them. But," he added, looking Quinby straight in the eye, "Spinner is different. He isn't like the other humans. And he certainly isn't like those dragonarmy soldiers. I like him just as much as you do. Maybe more."

Quinby sniffed. "That's ridiculous," he said. "I like Spinner more than you, and he likes me best of everyone."

"Does not," said the dwarf.

"Does so," countered the kender.

"Does not," said the dwarf.

"Does so," insisted the kender.

This debate might have gone on all night had not Barsh, the gnome, suddenly arrived in a rush.

"Spinner is to be hanged at dawn!" declared the gnome.

Quinby and Vigre stopped their argument and soberly nodded their heads. "We know," said Vigre.

"It's terrible," exclaimed Barsh. "If the Highlord kills him, there will be no more beautiful females who bring the dead back to life with a kiss, no more exciting chases through walls of fire, and no more great heroes who fight and die for freedom. How dull everything will be if he is killed."

Vigre Arch looked at these two creatures, the kender and the gnome, both of whom he and his people had never much liked. But just then he felt a kinship with them that stirred his heart. They had a common bond in their love of Spinner Kenro. And maybe that was enough to help them unite the way those three orphans in Spinner's story should have done. Vigre smiled to himself. It struck him as a funny coincidence that Spinner's story was so similar to their present dilemma. But he shrugged it off. There were more important matters at hand.

"What if we tried to rescue Spinner?" suggested the dwarf.

"What?" asked Barsh, not quite believing his ears.

"He said, 'What if we tried to rescue Spinner?'," repeated the kender helpfully.

"I heard him," said Barsh.

"Then why did you ask, 'What?'," questioned the kender.

Vigre Arch sighed deeply. Sometimes there was just no talking to kender.

"Never mind all that," piped up Barsh. "We've only got until dawn before they hang Spinner. Between now and then we have to find a way to break into the prison, free him, and spirit him to safety before the Dragon Highlord and her soldiers can stop us. Once he's free, we'll protect him and hide him so he can always tell us his stories."

"The Highlord won't like it," said Vigre.

"Since when do you care what the Highlord thinks?" asked Quinby.

The dwarf had to grin. "I never really have."

"Me neither," said Quinby.

"The same goes for me," added Barsh. "The Highlord is no friend of mine. But Spinner is. And I say we save him tonight!"

The three of them agreed that Spinner had to be saved. They shook hands on it and went immediately to work on a plan.

* * * * *

It fell to Barsh and his gnomes to quickly create a device that would help them scale the prison walls and open the gate. It was up to Quinby to rally every kender in the city to storm through the prison gates once they were open, then hold them long enough so that Vigre and his dwarves could race through the prison and return with Spinner Kenro safely in tow.

Word of the impending attack on the prison swept through the city. Every kender, dwarf, and gnome knew of the plans, and they all readied themselves for the battle to come.

The Highlord and her soldiers thought of these little people as foolish and simple, so they suspected nothing. But facing death was not foolish or simple. And everyone who prepared for the coming battle knew that he might never see the rising sun.

The life of Spinner Kenro, however, was worth the risk. Yet it was more than Spinner's life that they were fighting for. It was the spark of their souls, the light of their minds, the richness of their imaginations that spurred them on that memorable night. Somewhere inside each of them there was an epic tale bursting to be told and they sensed it, knew it, believed it, and were willing to die for it.

As the night wore on, hundreds of gnomes stumbled through the dark, windswept streets of Flotsam carrying heavy joints, long poles, and hundreds of tree branches still sprouting their leaves. These were the basic elements of their wall-scaling device which they carried past dragonarmy patrols who merely shrugged their shoulders at yet another gnome oddity.

Barsh's hastily conceived invention was quickly assembled in a big, empty barn just beyond the rear prison walls. Nearly a thousand gnomes had gathered there to put the finishing touches on the wall-scaling device, and they were anxious to put it to the test.

The invention, a huge, rectangular ladder, was as long as the entire southern wall of the prison. Two hundred fifty gnomes could climb it at one time. The tree branches attached to the top of the ladder were meant to camouflage the ladder as they approached the enemy fortress.

Just before dawn, the kender began arriving at the Paw's Mark Inn. At first they filled the main room. Then their numbers swelled into the garden in the back. Luckily, the garden was surrounded by trees and bushes that kept the small army of kender hidden from the dragonarmy soldiers who watched the streets.

Quinby Cull had given his fellow kender strict instructions to remain perfectly quiet. They knew that to do otherwise might mean death and the failure of their mission. And failure meant the end of Spinner Kenro. Nonetheless, Quinby heard little shouts of surprise, followed by titters and giggles, as his fellow kender constantly poked each other with their hoopaks, swords, and lances, curious to see if the weapons were in good working order.

Not far from the Paw's Mark Inn, in a hidden ravine dug deep into a hillside near the prison, Vigre Arch complained bitterly about the cold wind—and that wasn't all he grumped about. "How come we're out here?" he mumbled angrily. "Barsh and his gnomes are warm inside that barn, and Quinby and his kender are drinking and having a fine old time in the Paw's Mark Inn. It isn't fair! Maybe," he muttered, "we ought to just go home and get some sleep and forget this nonsense."

But Vigre didn't utter any such orders. He was proud of his people that night. And he was proud of himself. If their plan to free Spinner Kenro failed, Vigre vowed that it wasn't going to be because the dwarves didn't do their part.

It seemed, somehow, that the stars were moving more swiftly across the sky than usual. It was nearly time.

The gnomes were to lead the attack. But because the original idea had been Quinby Cull's, the kender was given the honor of giving the signal to start the battle. . . .

Quinby looked out the window of the Paw's Mark Inn. It had stormed all night, but the sky was beginning to lighten. It was now or never. He looked at his fellow kender and smiled with satisfaction. If he had been a painter he would have drawn the scene inside the inn so that he'd never forget it. Perhaps Spinner, when he was a free man, would tell a story about this glorious adventure. It occurred to Quinby that Spinner might even make him a hero in the tale. Wouldn't that be something? he thought. But then Quinby laughed at himself. How could a kender be a hero? he scoffed, shaking his head. Such things never happened. Yet, in his imagination, stoked by the stories that Spinner had told, Quinby Cull held on to the dream.

With those thoughts circling in his mind, the kender opened the door of the inn. He took a horn made of bone from his waistband and lifted it to his lips.

The shrill, piercing sound of Quinby's horn echoed throughout the silent city. Vigre heard it. Barsh heard it. And so did the dragonarmy guards who stood atop the prison walls.

The Highlord's soldiers rubbed the sleep from their eyes, wondering what that strange sound might mean.

It didn't take them long to find out.

Suddenly, they heard shouts and cries coming out

of the darkness. Then, illuminated by the torch light from the parapets, one guard saw the forest moving first one way, then another, and yet in a third direction.

"What magic is this?" cried the guard, staring at the gyrating woods.

Suddenly, a gnome popped his head through the front of the forest and shouted, "It's this way, you idiots!"

"We can't see!" a chorus of voices answered.

An entire squad of gnomes came forward and began chopping the branches off the wall-scaling device in full view of the startled dragonarmy guard. But even then, the Highlord's soldier had no idea what the gnomes were doing. At least not until the shrubbery was fully hacked away and the gnomes charged with their massive ladder.

When they leaned it against the prison wall, though, the top of the ladder soared far beyond the top of the battlements.

"It's the wrong way!" cried Barsh, exasperated. "Turn it down on its side!"

By this time, of course, the dragonarmy guard had yelled for help. As the correct side of the ladder finally settled down across the battlement, the Highlord's soldiers rushed to the rear of the prison. But the wall-scaling device was so heavy with gnomes climbing upon it that the enemy couldn't push the ladder away from the wall. And soon the gnomes were climbing over the parapets!

The first gnome to stand on the prison wall was Barsh himself. A tall dragonarmy guard swung a heavy broadsword at Barsh's head. The gnome ducked under the blade and dove at the feet of the soldier. As the guard prepared to swing his sword down on Barsh's back, the gnome pulled the soldier's legs together while another gnome whacked the enemy in the belly with a stick. The soldier lost his balance, falling off the battlement and landing with a heavy thud on the prison grounds below.

Barsh couldn't believe that he was still alive.

And not only was Barsh alive, but his fellow gnomes were swarming onto the parapet, overwhelming the small number of dragonarmy soldiers who had been on watch.

"To the gate!" cried Barsh, leading his people along the battlement to the front of the prison.

Even as they worked their way toward the gate, prison guards were racing out of their barracks to fight the intruders. If the gnomes couldn't get the gates opened quickly, they'd be destroyed by the powerful dragonarmy soldiers. It was only with the help of the kender as reinforcements that they had a chance of holding out against the fierce soldiers of the Dragon Highlord.

The kender, with Quinby Cull urging them on, had already begun their charge. The Paw's Mark Inn was just a short distance from the prison, and now the kender were racing like an angry wind toward the gate.

Quinby could see the battle unfolding up on the parapet. The gnomes were fighting furiously to reach the gate's pulley system. Quinby knew that if they failed, he and his kender army would be racing toward death.

He saw gnomes dying. A dragonarmy soldier pierced one of them in the chest with his sword. Another gnome was thrown over the wall. And still another had his head split open with an ax. But the gnomes fought on, gallantly pushing the prison guards away from the gate. Until . . .

"It's opening!" cried Quinby just as he and his army of kender were about to give up hope. Without having to break their stride, they surged under the rising metal gate and plowed right into a phalanx of dragon-army soldiers!

"Are we supposed to fight *kender*?!" demanded one of the enemy with contempt in his voice.

Quinby heard the soldier and, filled with fury, he shouted in return, "On this day you will not only fight kender, you will die at our hands!" The soldier thrust his sword's point toward Quinby's throat. But the kender nimbly parried, then lunged forward and stabbed the enemy clean through the heart.

Scores of kender and gnomes witnessed Quinby's bold declaration and even bolder swordplay. A great cheer went up when the dragonarmy soldier fell. For, in that moment, Quinby Cull had done more than simply kill one enemy. He had shown that the kender were a force to be reckoned with. He had given dignity back to his race. And he had shown that a kender could be a hero!

On the heels of Quinby's dramatic battle, the kender drove the better-armed and better-trained dragon-army force away from the gate as they fought for control of the prison grounds.

But the Highlord's soldiers quickly formed a new battle line. Their bowman sent one withering volley after another into the kender ranks. In their fearlessness, the kender didn't let the arrows stop them. Even with bloody shafts sticking in their stomachs, shoulders, and legs—many of them dying on their feet—the kender troops charged headlong into the dragonarmy lines. They swung crude swords and knives at the soldiers until their enemy was finally routed.

It was then that a shockingly small number of dwarves led by Vigre Arch came streaming through the open gate.

"Where are the rest of your people?" demanded

Barsh.

"You promised you would have an army of dwarves," echoed Quinby. "There are barely a hundred of you here. What's going on?"

Vigre took a deep breath and told them the bad news.

"Dragonarmy soldiers are coming this way," he reported. "We saw them from the top of the ravine. There must be at least two thousand of them marching through the city. We'd all be trapped in the prison if they got here before Spinner was freed. So I ordered most of our people to meet the dragonarmy soldiers in the street and fight them there. It was the only way to stall for time."

Barsh and Quinby turned pale. A ragtag group of dwarves didn't have a chance against two thousand crack dragonarmy troops. Vigre's people were going to be slaughtered. They must have known their fate, yet they were willing to sacrifice their lives for stories they would never hear. Truly, thought Quinby, this was the stuff of legend. He put his hand on Vigre's shoulder and said, "If I were a dwarf, I'd be proud on this day. Then again," he added, considering, "I'm not a dwarf."

Vigre looked at the kender trying to decide what Quinby meant.

"No matter what happens," Quinby went on, oblivious to Vigre's questioning stare, "your people belong in Spinner's stories. Not all of his stories," he hastily added. "Just one of them."

Vigre gave up trying to figure out the kender's intentions and simply said, "Spinner could make a fine, though tragic, tale of the battle in the city. So let's make sure that he lives to tell it. I'll take what's left of our force and fight our way through the prison till we find our storyteller."

"But there aren't enough of you," Quinby declared. "You're going to need help. I'll take some kender and go with you."

"And I'll come, too," volunteered Barsh. "I'll bring a small troop of gnomes along."

Vigre couldn't refuse. He knew they were right. There was no telling how many of the Dragon Highlord's soldiers were waiting for them inside the prison's labyrinth of cells.

"Come on," he said. "Spinner must be wondering what all the noise is about."

I was, indeed, wondering what all the noise was about. The night had nearly passed, and I waited for the dawning, resigned to my fate. My cellmate, Davin, had listened to me throughout the night, offering not a word of his own.

Then I heard shouts and screams filtering down to the depths of the filthy dungeon where I had been left to languish until my death.

"What's going on?" I called out to a dragonarmy guard who raced past the cell.

He ignored me.

"What do you think is happening?" I asked Davin. He shook his head.

The noise grew louder. It sounded like battle. There was the clash of steel on steel. There were howls of pain, boots running on stone, and shouts of . . . *my name!*

"Here!" I cried. "I'm here! This way!"

I couldn't believe my own senses. But yes, it was the voice of Quinby Cull calling out to me! Then I heard Vigre Arch. My mind was reeling when even that clever gnome, Barsh, made his presence known.

"It's impossible!" I exclaimed. And then I turned to Davin. "Do you hear them, or have I gone mad? Are

95

my friends really here to save me?"

My cellmate was about to answer, but then, instead, he shouted, "Look out!"

Too late. A prison guard had suddenly appeared at my cell and grabbed me through the bars. "I'll see you dead before they free you," he vowed. And then he lifted his dagger and plunged it toward my chest.

Davin was faster than I was. He lunged forward and grabbed the guard's wrist just before the knife could strike me. He twisted the man's arm against the iron bars until there was an audible crack. The guard screamed as the knife clattered to the floor. He ran in terror as Quinby, Vigre, and Barsh led a legion of their people toward my cell.

"Keys!" crowed Barsh, dangling them happily in the air.

"We took them from an officer at the landing," explained Vigre. "You're going to be free."

"We're glad to see you," said Quinby, standing back from the door with tears of joy in his eyes.

"*You're* glad to see me?" I cried in disbelief. "To be sure, it's the other way around!"

The cell door flew open.

"Come with us," said Quinby. "We came to save you. Now you and your stories can live forever!"

Spinner Kenro ended the long tale about himself with a flourish, his voice rising in a dramatic crescendo. His timing was impeccable. No sooner had he finished than a prison guard unlocked the cell door.

"It's dawn," said the Highlord's emissary.

Spinner took a deep breath and rose to his feet. "Sometimes," he said softly, "I half believe my own stories. There was a part of me that really thought my friends would come and save me. Do you think I'm foolish, Davin?"

I couldn't answer. I was crying.

Spinner had not slept. He had sat up against a wall, weaving his final story during the last hours of his life. And I was his only audience.

They hanged Spinner Kenro at daybreak.

Spinner died a great many years ago, but his memory lives on. For that night in the prison he opened the window of my soul. And though his voice was stilled, his gift was somehow passed to me. I've told many stories throughout the years as I've traveled across Krynn. But I never fail to tell this, the one, great, final story exactly as Spinner told it to me that night in the prison.

Oh, I know what really happened. Quinby, Vigre, and Barsh did try to save Spinner. But once they made their plans, Quinby forgot all about them—he was true to his kender soul; out of sight, out of mind. Vigre, ever distrustful of humans, had second thoughts about the entire enterprise. Meanwhile, Barsh and his gnomes did set about creating a huge wall-scaling device. The problem was that it was so big that they couldn't get it out of the building in which they had constructed it. It's still there to this day.

Now, you might say that the truth doesn't make a good tale. But that's not the point. There is a higher truth than the facts. And that truth reveals itself every time I tell Spinner's story. For as the years went by, the kender, dwarves, and gnomes of Flotsam grew to *believe* that they had saved Spinner. They have convinced themselves that on one cold, windswept night they joined together to make history, to reach greatness, to become heroes. And if they did it once, might they not do it again?

A Shaggy Dog's Tail

by Danny Peary

poem by Suzanne Rafer

WORD SPREAD like wildfire that Tasslehoff Burr-foot was in Spritzbriar. "I'm just passing through," he told the villagers as they rushed home to lock up their valuables. "But if anyone wants to hear some stories, I might just hang around a bit." Of course, everyone knew that as long as anyone would listen to the kender's improbable tales, he wasn't going anywhere. That's what worried the men and women of Spritzbriar. They knew that while they were safe-guarding those belongings they feared might wind up in the kender's pouches, their children would slip out doors and wriggle out windows in order to see the illustrious visitor.

As the boys and girls raced across the grassy field toward Prine Lake at the edge of the forest, they looked nervously over their shoulders, hoping their absences wouldn't be discovered until *after* Tas had spun a few yarns. Most had promised their parents to never again listen to his stories after even the bravest had had nightmares in the wake of his last visit. But

---

they'd grown tired of those cheery tales told by their mothers and grandmothers. Because kender weren't frightened of anything, Tas thought nothing of telling the children about bloody battles in war-torn areas of Krynn, vicious dragons, hobgoblins, or black-robed magic-users. The children found such stories well worth risking a night without supper.

The children who gathered at Prine Lake sat on the ground and formed a tight circle around Tas, with the oldest by his small, wriggling feet. Tas sat proudly under a mammoth vallenwood, propped like a king on a wooden stool so everyone could see him. He stroked his hoopak staff and grinned broadly, delighted his audience was so large. If only Flint could see him now.

While everyone waited impatiently, Tas took a meticulously carved flute from an elegant, woven-rope, yellow pouch that was strapped around his neck. As he brought it toward his lips, a young boy named Jespato intercepted his hand.

"My, that looks like my father's flute!" the boy exclaimed without suspicion.

"Your father's flute?" asked Tas innocently.

"It's been missing since the last time you were in Spritzbriar!"

The kender's childlike face flushed red. He examined the instrument. "Great Uncle Trapspringer! It *is* your father's flute! Good eye, boy! Now I remember: I took it for safekeeping. It was sticking out of his pouch, where any thief might have snatched it."

"His pouch disappeared at the same time as the flute," said the boy. "It was *yellow*, just like the one you've got around your neck!"

Tas grinned sheepishly. "Of course, *this* pouch is older and more worn than the one your father carried," he said, failing to remind Jespato that it had been some time since he'd been to Spritzbriar. "But please give *my* pouch to him to replace his missing one." Tas pulled the strap over his head and handed the pouch and the flute to the young boy. He forced a big smile.

Jespato looked at Tas with great respect. "My father will surely change his opinion of you when I give him your present. Imagine: he said you're the type who'd snatch candy-bubbles from children!"

The kender's face turned even redder. "I was just borrowing them," he replied with deep embarrassment as he reached into a red pouch and retrieved a dozen multi-colored candy-bubbles. The children around him checked their pockets and were startled to discover they were empty. Tas sadly returned the tasty treats, saying weakly, "I didn't want anyone to have his appetite spoiled."

Tas would have enjoyed playing that nifty flute, but he was cheered by the children's willingness to share their candy-bubbles with him and by the sight of eager faces around him, anticipating his story.

"Are you going to tell another whopper?" asked a young, curly-haired boy who sat to his left.

"I . . . I never tell whoppers!" Tas insisted, a bit indignant.

Everyone groaned. They knew better.

A little freckle-faced girl stood up and asked politely, "What will your first story be about, sir?"

There was a definite trace of mischievousness in the kender's big brown eyes. "Revenge!" he barked with such force that the startled little girl plopped over backward.

Everyone else slid forward.

* * * * *

"Revenge! I want revenge!" Gorath's threatening words resounded through the little shack, causing all the pots and pans to rattle and the rickety furniture to creak. His angry, blood-shot eyes doubled in size, and the veins on his temple were ready to burst. "Revenge, I want . . ."

This time his words were stifled by a large wooden spoon that was being forced into his gaping mouth. The spoon carried an ugly mound of undercooked slug stew. A stream of steaming, foul-smelling gravy dribbled down his chin and drenched his long black beard. Gorath groaned.

"Oh, so sorry, darling," said Zorna. Using her long, bony fingers, she managed to push most of the gravy back into Gorath's mouth. The huge man nearly gagged. "There, there," said the tiny old woman, her teeth clicking with every word. "You don't want to lose a drop, do you, darling?" Her shrill, scratchy voice was irritating, but there was no mistaking it was full of love. She wiped her shriveled hands on her shabby black robe. "After what you've suffered, darling, a meal is just what you need."

"Stop calling me *darling*, you old hag!" growled Gorath, spitting stew across the room. "You don't even know me!"

"But I do love you!" Zorna protested softly, her feelings hurt. "And I'll cook, and clean, and care for you for the rest of your life." She brushed away a tear, wiped her dripping nose, and smiled lovingly. "We'll have such a happy time together."

This thought horrified Gorath. He tried to rise, but he couldn't budge. All he could move was his head. That's why he could offer no resistance when Zorna again stuffed slug stew into his mouth.

Gorath couldn't believe his terrible luck. He had been the most decorated and feared human officer in the dragonarmy. In the war campaigns against the Que-shu, no one had razed more villages, slaughtered more enemies, or enslaved more women and children than the mighty Gorath! For amusement, he had broken men's backs with his bare hands and held beautiful women prisoner in his tent, forcing them to do his bidding. But now he suddenly found himself paralyzed from the neck down and the prisoner of an old lady who kept him strapped to a chair in her gloomy, windowless shack in the Forest of Wayreth. What an indignity!

He thought back to when his bad fortune began.

Was it yesterday morning or early afternoon when he awoke from a drunken stupor to find that Meadow had fled his tent? He was so stunned by her brazen act that at first all he could do was scream, "Revenge! I want revenge!"

No wonder her escape troubled him so much. With her long, flowing black hair, alluring green eyes, slim figure, and delicate features, Meadow was the loveliest female he had ever abducted during a raid of the Que-shu tribe. Moreover, she had already lived longer than any of the previous women he'd captured, although he had worked her endlessly and beat her mercilessly.

In Gorath's twisted mind, Meadow had actually *betrayed* him by running away and deserved to be punished severely. Gorath never forgave anyone for what he believed was a wrong action against him. In the past, he had sworn revenge on dragonarmy soldiers he suspected of talking mutiny behind his back, friends he suspected of trying to steal his women, and even his brothers, who he suspected of plotting his death so that they could confiscate his goods. Now all those men lay in their graves. At last, Gorath's lone companion had been this woman he held captive. How dare Meadow desert him and leave him completely alone!

Pulling in his huge belly, his head pounding, Gorath knelt to examine the heavy chain that had kept Meadow attached to an iron post even when she slept. It had been severed by a sharp weapon, probably a sword. Meadow had an accomplice, another person who had betrayed him!

Gorath reasoned that the trespasser had been Starglow, the tribesman for whom Meadow had pined during her torturous term of captivity. The barbarian smiled slyly. It would give him great pleasure to kill Starglow while Meadow looked on. He sheathed his sword. "Revenge! I want revenge!" he thundered as he stormed from the tent.

The lovers' trail led north toward Solace. It was easy to follow because they were traveling on foot and were too hurried to attempt deception. Without stopping to rest or water his horse, Gorath rode at full gallop over rocky roads, treacherous mountain paths, and overgrown trails where sharp spines ripped into his steed's flesh. The poor beast finally collapsed under Gorath's great weight, unable to endure the punishing journey or its master's whip any longer. Gorath cursed and reviled the animal, but rather than putting it out of its misery, he left it to die in the wilderness.

He proceeded on foot, feeling meaner with every step. He thought how much he'd enjoy strangling Starglow with his mighty hands or piercing his enemy's heart with his sword while Meadow screamed helplessly. Maybe he would stab her as well, or make her drop to her knees and beg him to allow her to be his slave again. How he would make her suffer! Gorath shouted: "Revenge! I want revenge!"

As the sun sank low in the west, Gorath discovered that Meadow and Starglow had veered east, thereby avoiding Solace and well-traveled roads on their way back to their own village. Gorath followed blindly although he had to travel over unfamiliar terrain. He wasn't one to worry about the possible consequences of acting so impulsively, especially with thoughts of revenge dancing on his dizzy brain.

Soon the mighty warrior stood facing the Forest of Wayreth.

Gorath had heard eerie legends throughout Krynn about Wayreth and how it often played tricks with the minds of those who dared pass through. "They think I'll be too frightened to follow," said Gorath, attempting to laugh. "But Gorath is scared of nothing!" Nevertheless, before taking another step, he peered through the trees on the perimeter of the strange forest. He was relieved that it seemed peaceful inside, even inviting.

Suddenly a dozen dark-colored birds floated down from the nearest tree and circled above him. They taunted him in song:

> *Is this the mighty Gorath, hovering like a child*
> *At Wayreth's edge, afraid to move*
> *Belittled, bewitched, beguiled?*
>
> *You have killed with brutish strength and nary*
> *once did grieve*
> *Yet your mind is not so strong*
> *Thus easy to deceive.*
>
> *So, dare you enter Wayreth, knowing not which*
> *paths to tread*
> *And seek revenge you think is sweet? . . .*
> *Better turn around instead!*

The warrior nervously yanked his sword from his

scabbard and thrust it wildly into the air. "Get away, you silly birds!" he demanded, his voice shaky. "Don't you know that Gorath is scared of nothing?"

Gorath thought it very strange that the birds seemed to disappear into thin air. He was tempted to turn around and try to find his way home, but he reminded himself why he had come this far: "Revenge! I want revenge!" Forgetting about the birds, he stomped into the forest, angrily using his sword to hack off branches that blocked his path. He turned and looked behind him. He noticed that while it was bright inside the forest, night had fallen outside. None the wiser, he shrugged and marched forward, content that he could clearly see the trail of Meadow and Starglow.

Deeper in the forest, the trail divided in two. Gorath stopped and studied both paths. When he saw fresh tracks on the one that angled to the left, he rubbed his sweaty palms together and licked his lips. "It won't be long now," he said. He started to follow the path to the left. But suddenly a strong gust of wind knocked him off balance and pushed him toward the other path.

He tightened his fingers around his sword and looked about suspiciously. All seemed calm. Was the forest playing tricks with him?

Looking in all directions, Gorath stealthily moved toward the path to the left. But he never made it. A second, much stronger gust of wind came howling and twisting toward him. It nearly lifted the big man off the ground. Before Gorath knew what hit him, he was being blown at great speed down the path to the right. Because his legs were thick as tree trunks and rubbed together whenever he moved, it was difficult for him to stay on his feet. But each time he fell, the wind swept him up and forced him to continue.

The wind ceased as quickly as it had begun, leaving Gorath sprawled on the ground with his boots twisted together. The dazed warrior spat dust and struggled to catch his breath. Then he slowly rose and, still quite bleary-eyed, looked around.

He was facing a small, crumbling black shack. It had no windows, just a crooked black door. A walkway of broken stones led from the path to the door. Tall weeds filled a garden to the left, and strange, twisted vegetables grew on the other side. Gorath thought the shack deserted until he noticed that thick black smoke curled upward from a crooked chimney on the dilapidated roof. Suddenly it blew in Gorath's direction, carrying with it a ghastly aroma. Gorath's stomach became queasy. He could have sworn someone was cooking a stew consisting of spoiled meat and rotten vegetables.

Gorath prided himself on his bravery, but his instincts urged him to get away at once. Without understanding why, Gorath walked briskly past the house and farther down the path. But he didn't get very far. An angry gust of wind grabbed him, spun him around, and hurled him through the air toward the house, causing him to crash into the door and bounce off with a loud thud.

Again, the wind quickly subsided. The large man staggered to his feet, rubbing his bull neck and bruised left arm. He was only a few feet from the door. He started to back away, but it was too late. The door creaked open.

An old woman peeked out. Gorath had never seen anyone uglier. She had a hatchet-face, with sharp bones pushing through the skin, a needle-shaped nose, and tiny, pointed ears. Her hair was white and wild, yet her thick eyebrows were black. Her eyes were pale yellow, her thin lips were colorless, and her complexion was as pale as a fish's belly. It would have taken Gorath a lifetime to have counted the deep wrinkles that lined her face.

The tiny woman looked the big man up and down. She wiggled her nose as if she were smelling him. Her scowl gave way to a smile. Her heart, which had so long ago resigned itself to eternal loneliness, began to pound. Her chest began to rise and fall. Her eyes looked at the stranger hungrily. Women had always been repulsed by Gorath's appearance, but he left this one breathless. At last she spoke.

"You're so handsome, I must hold you," she said brazenly. As the stunned Gorath backed up, she moved toward him out of the shadows. That's when Gorath saw how she was garbed.

"Ah, I . . . I see you are a black-robed magic-user," he said, somewhat relieved. "Then we are both servants of the Queen of Darkness."

The old woman stopped in her tracks upon hearing Gorath's remarks. "You are mistaken, my darling," she replied humbly, her teeth chattering annoyingly. "I am just Zorna, a poor and forgotten old woman. This robe was discarded in the forest by a sorceress who was passing through. I took it because I had nothing to wear."

"You don't know how to perform magic?" asked Gorath skeptically.

"I swear I am no sorceress. But I have other talents, darling. I can cook the finest slug stew you've tasted in your life. Won't you be my guest?"

Gorath didn't know what to make of this weird woman. He wanted to laugh at her invitation, run her through with his sword, and ransack her shack for anything of value. But he kept his distance, not fully convinced she wasn't a black-robed magic-user. "I have no time to waste with you," he told her coldly.

"Now I must find the woman who betrayed me and slay the scoundrel who stole her from me."

"Forget your woman!" Zorna shrieked. "She doesn't love you. *I* love you. And I'll cook, and clean, and care for you for the rest of your life . . . *if* you will let me . . . darling."

"Enough, you batty crone," snapped Gorath, remembering how he had tried without success to force Meadow to say such words to him. "Only one thing matters: Revenge! I want revenge!"

Before Zorna could protest, Gorath wheeled around and walked down the path that brought him into her lonely life. He felt her sad eyes upon him and heard her pitiful, blood-curdling wail of anguish. He laughed.

Gorath returned to where the trail into the forest divided. This time there were no mysterious gusts of wind to prevent him from going in the direction he intended. So he followed the left path, the one Meadow and Starglow had taken.

He walked quickly, anticipating the kill. Soon he came to a large clearing. There he spotted Meadow and Starglow standing by a fallen vallenwood, about twenty feet from a deep ravine. The lovely young woman and handsome tribesman were locked in an embrace.

Drawing his sword, Gorath charged from the bushes toward the lovers. "Gorath!" Meadow screamed in terror. "He's found us!"

Starglow eyed his sword, which was resting on the ground near the far end of the fallen tree. He made a dash for it, but wasn't quick enough. As the fingers of his right hand touched the handle, Gorath's sword slashed his wrist, causing blood to spurt and the young warrior to grimace in pain. Meadow screamed and ran toward her stricken lover. "Meadow!"

Starglow shouted. "Stay back!"

Starglow's agony was great, but his desire to protect Meadow was much greater. So he again reached for the sword. Just as he lifted it, Gorath's heavy boot smashed into his hand. The sword flew out of Starglow's weak grip and landed by Meadow's feet. Without hesitating, she picked up the weapon and ran to Starglow's side. Surprised, Gorath backed up a few feet to contemplate the situation. He certainly hadn't expected Meadow to put up any physical resistance.

Starglow reached for the sword Meadow held. "No!" she said firmly. "You're hurt." When he started to protest, she calmly said: "I am a woman and your lover, Starglow. But don't forget that I am also a warrior like you."

Starglow nodded and smiled slightly. He kissed her trembling lips and placed a gentle hand on her shoulder. Together they bravely waited for Gorath to approach them. They were going to resist to the death even though they had little chance to defeat the mighty Gorath.

"We're ready," said Meadow boldly. As she looked at Gorath, revulsion showed clearly in her beautiful green eyes. She had withstood his drunkenness and savage nature long enough. She preferred to die here with her beloved Starglow by her side rather than return to Gorath's cabin. Never again would she be a slave to him, endure his beatings, or have him clutch her in his filthy arms.

Gorath's eyes were sour and mean. He laughed cruelly. "So you want to die together. How touching! I'll grant your wish as long as you die first, Starglow, so Meadow can watch the blood pour from your body. Revenge! I want revenge!"

Gorath began to drool as he walked toward the lovers, who pulled closer together. He lifted his sword higher and higher. Meadow dug her feet into the soil and held the sword in front of her, gripping it with both hands.

All at once Gorath noticed that an intruder sat between him and his intended victims.

He stopped and tried to figure out where this large, mangy dog had come from. There had been no dog in this clearing just a moment before. And what a strange dog it was. Gorath suspected it was a red-rover, but it was the only red-rover he'd ever seen sporting a shaggy tail with a snow-white tip.

The dog sat perfectly still, its tongue hanging out the right side of its mouth.

"Call off your dog, Starglow," Gorath threatened, "or I'll chop it into a million pieces!"

"But I have no dog," replied Starglow, puzzled.

"Wh . . . what dog?" asked Meadow, also bewildered.

"Very well, you had your chance!" Gorath shouted as he attacked the animal. He swung his sword with all his might at the dog's head, expecting to see it rolling in the sand. But the dog easily dodged the blow. Now Gorath aimed for the shaggy tail with the snow-white tip. Gorath's sword whistled through the air repeatedly. The dog moved from side to side, causing the brute to miss by a hair, a shaggy hair, each time.

Gorath's frustration increased because he could sense that the dog was actually enjoying itself, as if it were unaware its life was in danger. It barked happily and playfully nipped at Gorath's feet. When Gorath raised his sword above his head, the dog jumped up, put its front paws on his chest, and licked his face several times.

Gorath lost all patience. He shoved the dog away and simultaneously swung the sword with all his might. He missed badly. He also lost his balance. So when the big dog jumped back up on his chest to continue their game, it knocked Gorath back a few steps toward the ravine. Again the dog jumped up. Again Gorath was knocked backward, his curses shattering the quiet of the forest. This happened several more times. Each time, the force of the dog's paws increased, and Gorath was knocked farther back. Then came the mightiest blow of all.

Suddenly, Gorath found himself somersaulting backward through the air, falling helplessly into the deep, deep ravine. Gorath expected to see his life flash before his eyes, but for some reason he had a vision of Zorna's old, ugly face instead. He screamed. Then everything went black.

When Gorath opened his eyes, he was looking directly into Zorna's face. Only this time it was no vision. It really was Zorna. He screamed again.

She attempted to comfort him, wiping the sweat off his feverish brow with her icy hand. "There, there, darling," she whispered into his ear. "I'll make you feel better."

Gorath realized he was strapped to a chair. But where was he? He looked around. He was in Zorna's cold, musty house. It was as inviting as a tomb. It was too dark to see clearly, but he could make out some crooked furniture in the shadows, some heavy pots hanging from cobweb-infested walls, and a large bubbling kettle by the fireplace. There was a horrible stench in the air, and Gorath suspected Zorna was still preparing slug stew. "How did I get here, old woman?" he snapped.

"I brought you from the ravine."

Gorath looked at the frail woman. "How could *you* carry me all the way from the ravine?"

"I love you," she said simply.

"Then untie this strap before I lose my temper!"

"I've strapped you to the chair so you won't fall," she said tenderly. "I'm sorry, my poor darling, but when you landed in the ravine, you struck a boulder and snapped your spine. You're paralyzed from the neck down." A look of shock and anguish came over Gorath, terribly saddening Zorna. "But please don't worry, darling. I'll cook, and clean, and care for you for the rest of your life."

Upon hearing those words, Gorath could think of only one thing: "Revenge! I want revenge!"

That's when Zorna began to feed Gorath slug stew.

By the time Zorna shoved the final spoonful into Gorath's miserable mouth, he had figured out his only chance for exacting the revenge he desperately desired.

He batted his eyes at Zorna and sighed happily. "That was delicious!" he said.

Zorna nearly blushed. "I'm so happy you liked it, darling."

"Could you make it for me again some time, dear?" he asked hopefully.

Zorna nearly cried from happiness. "I make it *every* day, darling."

Gorath looked around the shack. "You know, dear, you have a lovely home. I think I'll enjoy spending the rest of my life here with you."

Zorna gushed. "We'll be so happy together!"

Gorath frowned. "But you wouldn't want to take care of *me*."

"Oh, darling, it would give me such pleasure!" Zorna objected.

Gorath shook his head. "That's so sweet, dear. But I could never be happy unless I could hold you in my arms . . . and I can't do that because I'm paralyzed." He closed his eyes as if he were trying to hold back a flood of tears.

Zorna was overwhelmed with pity. She kissed Gorath on his fleshy cheek. She felt him tremble. "My darling," she said softly, her voice quivering. "I understand your misery. I have lived alone, always. Eternity passed, and I almost gave up hope of finding a man I could open my heart to. Now that I have found you, it would be torture not to be able to express my love."

Gorath opened one eye. "If only you could help me. . . ."

"Darling, maybe I can."

Gorath opened his other eye, his hopes rising. "Only someone with magic powers could mend my severed spine. But you have said you are not a black-robed sorceress."

"This is true, but many years ago a black-robed sorceress traveled through the Forest of Wayreth and rewarded my hospitality by granting me the power to perform *one* feat of magic, only once."

Gorath immediately became worried. "Just *one* feat? Only *once?*" he asked nervously. "Have . . . have you performed it . . . y . . .yet?"

"I am a simple woman. I never had reason before."

Relieved, Gorath batted his eyes again. "Will you perform it now . . . dear?" he asked, trying not to sound too anxious.

"First you must promise me something."

"Anything, dear, I promise."

"If I heal you, I want you to promise that you will stay with me forever and that you will forget that other woman and your quest for revenge."

"Of course, dear," Gorath said sincerely. "I long only to hold you in my strong arms."

Zorna nearly swooned. She was so happy. "Very well, darling. I'll do as you ask."

The old woman stood in front of Gorath. He

expected her to call on the Queen of Darkness, recite a lengthy chant, and go into contortions. But she merely pointed a lone finger at him and wiggled her sharp nose a couple of times.

Gorath immediately felt a wave of heat deep in his back. He felt bones shift and fuse together. Then his chair started spinning, faster and faster. The strap broke, and Gorath was propelled to his feet. He stretched his arms and legs. He smiled broadly. He was no longer paralyzed.

Zorna moved toward him with arms spread, expecting Gorath to draw her to his powerful chest. Instead Gorath shoved her aside, knocking the feeble woman to the ground. "Out of my way, foolish woman," he said, taking broad steps toward the door. "Too bad you wasted your only feat of magic on *me*," he said mockingly.

"So you lied to me," said Zorna, showing no emotion. "You *betrayed* me."

Gorath laughed. "Be thankful that I don't throw you in the kettle with your wretched stew. But I have no time."

"Your sword is next to the door," said Zorna quietly, her eyes closed.

Gorath retrieved his weapon and needlessly kicked open the door on his way out. As he raced into the forest, he shouted: "Revenge! I want revenge!"

It didn't take long for Gorath to find his way back to the large clearing. Once again, he found Meadow and Starglow by the fallen vallenwood, about twenty feet from the deep ravine. Again they were locked in an embrace.

He was surprised that they hadn't traveled further. But then he figured they thought they were out of danger after he'd fallen into the ravine and become paralyzed.

However, he couldn't figure out why Starglow showed no sign of injury. He remembered distinctly striking Starglow's wrist with his sword and seeing blood spurt. What was going on?

Drawing his sword, Gorath charged from the bushes toward the lovers. "Gorath!" Meadow screamed in terror. "He's found us!"

Starglow eyed his sword, which was resting on the ground near the far end of the fallen tree. He made a dash for it but wasn't quick enough. As the fingers of his right hand touched the handle, Gorath's sword slashed his wrist, causing blood to spurt and the young warrior to grimace in pain. Meadow screamed and ran toward her stricken lover. "Meadow!" Starglow shouted. "Stay back!"

Although in obvious agony, Starglow again reached for the sword. Just as he lifted it, Gorath's heavy boot smashed into his hand. The sword flew out of Starglow's weak grip and landed by Meadow's feet. Without hesitating, she picked up the weapon and ran to Starglow's side. Surprised, Gorath backed up a few feet to contemplate the situation.

He was bewildered. Why was this experience so similar to the earlier one, when he first found Meadow and Starglow at this clearing?

Starglow reached for the sword Meadow held, just like before. "No!" she said firmly. "You're hurt." When he started to protest, she calmly said: "I am a woman and your lover. But don't forget that I am also a warrior like you." Just like before.

As before, Starglow nodded and smiled slightly. And again, he kissed her trembling lips and placed a gentle hand on her shoulder. Together they bravely waited for Gorath to approach them. Just like before.

"We're ready," said Meadow boldly. As she looked at Gorath, revulsion showed clearly in her beautiful green eyes.

Just like before.

"Revenge! I want revenge!" Gorath demanded, but he seemed only mildly interested in either Starglow or Meadow. He didn't approach them but instead looked around the clearing. "I'll deal with you two later," he said at last, searching for the one creature he hated more than Starglow and Meadow, the creature that had been the last to hurt him and had hurt him worst of all. "*First*, Starglow," he announced, "I must kill your *dog!* Revenge! I want revenge!"

"But I have no dog," said Starglow, puzzled.

"Wh . . . what dog?" asked Meadow, also bewildered.

"You know very well what dog!" Gorath bellowed. "The dreadful beast that tried to kill me! The one that caused me to be prisoner of an ugly crone and eat her awful slug stew. The one that pushed me into that ravine. . . ."

Meadow and Starglow seemed to be completely baffled.

"When did you fall into that ravine?" asked Starglow incredulously.

"You know very well it happened when I last confronted you at this clearing."

Meadow and Starglow looked at each other as if they were dealing with a madman.

"But, Gorath," said Meadow slowly, "this is the first time we've seen you since we fled your tent. . . . The Forest of Wayreth must be playing tricks with your mind."

Gorath snarled. He didn't know what to think. Was this indeed the first and only time he'd found Meadow and Starglow in this clearing? While standing here facing them, had he blanked out and imagined that horrible red dog? And falling into the deep, deep ravine?

And being paralyzed? And returning to Zorna's shack? Had the Forest of Wayreth indeed played tricks with his mind?

Suddenly Gorath heard growling. He turned toward the ravine. The red dog sat by the ledge, wagging its shaggy tail and whipping the snow-white tip into the ground as if it were issuing a challenge. "Ah, ha! There's the *dog!*" howled Gorath, thrilled to have proof that his story was true.

Meadow and Starglow looked at each other, then at Gorath. "What dog?" they both wondered aloud.

But Gorath wasn't listening. He was slowly stepping toward the ravine, hoping to exact the most satisfying revenge of his entire life. He did not even notice that Meadow and Starglow had seized the opportunity to escape in the opposite direction. They would not halt their anxious flight until they were out of the Forest of Wayreth and safely back in their Que-shu village.

Hiding his unsheathed sword behind him, Gorath approached the shaggy dog. He attempted a friendly, toothy grin. The shaggy dog responded by growling and baring its teeth. This time it was not in a playful mood.

Gorath stopped smiling. He lifted his sword high in the air. He charged and took a mighty swing at the dog. Amazingly, the dog slipped out of the way. Gorath turned around, the heels of his boots touching the edge of the cliff. "Oh, no!" cried Gorath as the dog jumped at him, striking him a mighty blow in the chest with its entire body.

Again Gorath found himself somersaulting backward through the air and helplessly falling into the ravine. This time it seemed even deeper.

When Gorath regained consciousness, he was not surprised to find himself paralyzed from the neck down and strapped to the chair in Zorna's shack. And there was Zorna, busily preparing slug stew. He yelled: "Revenge! I want revenge!"

Zorna turned toward him, her eyes blazing with anger. "I've heard enough about *your* revenge! After you deceived and deserted me, it's *me* who wants revenge!"

Gorath's eyes showed fear. "But I . . . I . . . I love you, dear," he stammered.

Zorna pointed a finger at Gorath and wiggled her nose. Instantly, he lost his ability to talk. "That will teach you never to betray a black-robed sorceress!" she sneered, causing sweat to pour down Gorath's unhappy face. "I hope a few years without speech will help you learn your lesson."

She pointed toward her terrified guest, and his chair slid toward her. She waved her hand slightly, and the chair rose into the air so their noses nearly touched. "I'll never forgive you or let you forget your cruelty toward me!" she shouted. Then, as she looked into his eyes, she calmed down and even smiled slightly. "But I do love you, darling," she said thoughtfully. "And I'll cook, and clean, and care for you for the rest of your life. You'll see. We'll have such a happy time together."

Leaving Gorath in midair, Zorna turned back to the kettle. The black-robed magic-user caused the fire to rise underneath just by raising her finger. She then leaned over the kettle to stir the stew, putting her hand directly into the boiling water without feeling any discomfort. The folds at the back of her black robe separated slightly.

Gorath's frightened eyes bulged from their sockets. Even if he still had the ability to talk, he couldn't have uttered a sound. He stared in disbelief at what was sticking out from Zorna's black robe.

It was a shaggy red tail with a snow-white tip.

Lord Toede's Disastrous Hunt

By Harold Bakst

---

*T*he Pilgrim's Rest was a pretty old tavern, having been started by the great grandfather of its owner, a gnarly old dwarf by the name of Pug. But the place looked even older than it was because it was built into the hollow of a huge and truly ancient oak tree near the Darken Wood.

Following the shape of the trunk, the room was basically round and soared up into the dark heights of the tree's interior. Up there, unseen, were woodpeckers, bats, a few squirrels, and various other critters. Occasionally one of them would fly or creep down along the wall to steal food from the round, rough-hewn tables, and old Pug was constantly chasing them back up again with a broom. "Don't feed the animals!" he kept telling his patrons. "It only encourages them!"

Business at the Pilgrim's Rest was usually good, thanks to the forest paths that crisscrossed all around it. On any given day, there was likely to be an assortment of many peoples—elves, dwarves, humans, and such—all traveling to and from the four corners of Krynn.

On one particular evening, this crowd was joined

by a kender. Old Pug kept an eye on the little, slight-boned fellow, for he knew a kender was likely to slip away without paying his tab. True to form, the kender, dressed in red leggings and tunic, sat at a table near the door.

But this kender, apparently a bit inebriated, was talking loudly, and this reassured Pug, who could at least turn his back and hear him.

" . . . I tell you," the kender was saying, "Kronin and I *did* kill him!"

"You expect us to believe," said a squat, black-bearded dwarf sitting at the kender's table, "that two puny kender killed Toede, a Dragon Highlord?"

"Why, Kronin isn't just *any* kender! He's our leader!"

"Even so," said another patron, a lanky human who was walking over with his beer stein, "kender are no match for a hobgoblin lord."

The kender's pointy ears turned red. "Do you think I'm lying?" he shouted.

"Yes!" came back all the patrons as they gathered around the boaster's table.

"And how did you two kill Toede?" asked a tall, willowy elf, a fair eyebrow arched incredulously. "With that silly what-do-you-call-it you kender carry?"

"The hoopak," said the dwarf, picking up the pronged stick from under the table for everyone to see.

"Leave that alone!" shouted the kender, snatching the weapon back.

"What's this?" said the human. "A kender getting angry? Where's your usual sense of humor?"

"He's had too much ale," suggested the dwarf with a smirk.

"Yes, that explains his ridiculous claims," agreed the elf, waving the story away with his long, slender hand.

"Phooey on you all!" shouted the kender. "Kronin and I are heroes whether you believe it or not!"

"Tell me," called old Pug from behind the counter, "did anyone actually see you do this deed?"

There was a brief silence.

"That's right," said the lanky human, resting his stein on the table. "Can anyone back you on this?"

The kender started to sputter in frustration, when, from across the room, someone shouted:

"I can!"

Everyone turned in surprise to see who had spoken.

Sitting at a table near the wooden wall was a hooded figure slouched over a stein. It was unclear what sort of being he was, but his robes were all in tatters.

"And who, pray tell, are you that you should know?" asked Pug, his thick eyebrows rising inquisitively.

"I was there," said the hooded stranger. "I saw it all. This kender's name must be Talorin."

The kender beamed, proud that news of his deed had reached another's ears and that this stranger actually knew his name. He crossed his slender arms. "Thank you, sir," he called to the stranger. "Perhaps you can tell these Doubting Trapspringers what you saw."

Everyone, still gathered around the kender's table, waited for the stranger to speak. But he didn't seem to care to continue, and he sipped from his brew mysteriously.

"Yes, why don't you tell us?" asked the dwarf, taking his stein and waddling over to the stranger's table.

"What difference does it make?" growled the stranger from beneath his cowl. "Toede was a sniveling, cowardly idiot. He had no business being a Dragon Highlord."

At this, Talorin's pointy ears grew red again.

"Maybe so," said the elf, also walking over. "But he caused much harm. If he's dead, then I for one would like to know how it came about."

From deep within his hood, the stranger seemed to be staring at the nearly empty stein sitting before him.

"Perhaps if someone were to buy me another ale—"

"Pug! Bring the gentleman another brew!" called the dwarf, settling himself on a chair at the stranger's table, his broad, leather-clad feet dangling. Soon everyone who had been around Talorin drew closer to the stranger. But the kender, not to be left out, squeezed himself back into their midst. Pug brought the stranger another stein of ale and clunked it before him, the foamy head spilling over and onto the table.

The stranger took a sip and cleared his throat. "I once served that wretch-of-a-hobgoblin," he said. "And, yes, I was there that day. . . ."

And so the stranger told a tale that, since then, has been retold many times throughout Krynn.

* * * * *

For many weeks Toede had been stewing in his somber manor in the decrepit port city of Flotsam, grumbling about how his subjects were not paying him the respect due to a Dragon Highlord. "They don't pay their taxes, they desert my army, they laugh behind my back!" he growled. Then he would just sit slumped on his throne, his two pink eyes squinting out of his flat, fleshy face as if he were hatching some plot that would make everyone realize he was not to be taken so lightly.

But all he did was put himself in a worse and worse mood. If anyone crossed him during those weeks—if an attendant so much as spilled something at the table—Toede fell into a rage. More than one such fellow was tossed off the docks to be eaten by sharks.

Naturally, his attendants were getting increasingly nervous. Finally one of them, Groag—a fat hobgoblin like Toede but who liked to dress in elegant, stylish robes and wear large, bejeweled rings—tried to divert his master from his self-pity. "Perhaps Lord Toede would like to disport himself," he said, standing by the squat, round-backed throne.

Toede glanced up and sideways at the dandified attendant. "Do you have anything in particular in mind?" he snarled. He always felt that Groag, like everyone else, showed him little genuine respect and always sounded snooty.

"There are many things," said Groag. He counted them off on each bejeweled finger. "You could take your ship out and harpoon dolphins, you could attend a dogfight, you could go hunting—"

"Hunting," snarled Toede, slumping even deeper into his throne. "How can I be expected to catch anything when my forest is full of poachers?" He began to stew again.

"Well," Groag shrugged, "perhaps you can catch a poacher."

At this, Toede's beady eyes lit up, and his broad fleshy mouth actually spread into a twisted smile. "Hmm," he began, drumming his stubby fingers on the throne's broad armrest. "Wouldn't that be fun . . ."

Now, Groag hadn't really been serious about catching a poacher, but the idea did seem to catch his master's imagination. So he said, "Say no more, my lord." Whereupon he hastily arranged a hunting party.

For the hunt, Toede left behind his faithful amphi dragon, Hopsloth, who was much too clumsy on land (pity the terrorized servants who had to comfort the disappointed beast!) and, instead, he rode his fastest, furry-legged pony, Galiot. He also took a large pack of black hunting hounds, each of which was held on a leash by an iron-collared slave who ran along on foot. The hounds were vicious, long-fanged beasts, and sometimes, out of impatience to be let loose, they nipped at the slaves holding them. All the hapless slaves could do to defend themselves was keep the mongrels at bay with sticks found along the way.

Also for the hunt, Toede surrounded himself with half a dozen pony-backed, spear-carrying body-guards—hobgoblins all—just in case he came upon a particularly nasty poacher. Toede himself wore his armor, which, of late, had become an especially tight fit, causing his flab to squeeze out of the chinks. Only Groag, preferring to remain in his fancy, flowing robes and rings, went unarmored. As he rode beside Toede, however, he did carry his master's bow and arrows.

It was late morning when the hunting party paraded through the crooked, filthy streets of Flotsam. Soon they entered a large, grassy field, at the far end of which was a somber fringe of dark pine forest. Not surprisingly, no poachers were quick to reveal them-selves, but Toede did spot a great big stag at the perim-eter of the woods. As the party approached, the animal raised its magnificently antlered head and sniffed the air suspiciously.

"Shh," hissed Toede as Groag handed him his bow and an arrow. "No one make a sound."

From atop Galiot, Toede nocked the arrow and pulled back on the bowstring, his red tongue poking out the corner of his mouth as he concentrated on his aim.

But before he could release the arrow, a sudden screaming whine pierced the air, startling the stag. The creature spun around, crashed into the outlying underbrush of the woods, and disappeared. Then ensued a series of muffled, skittering noises that receded into the distance.

"Damn it!" shouted Toede, his pink eyes reddening. He spun in his saddle toward his bodyguards. "Who did that? Come on! Speak up!"

The hobgoblin guards shrugged and looked at each other stupidly.

"The noise did not come from our party," said Groag, sounding typically haughty.

"Oh? Then who from?" asked Toede.

"A kender," said Groag. "Perhaps more than one. The sound was made by a hoopak, of course."

"Kender!" snapped Toede, his eyes darting about the field and woods. "I should have known! I bet they're the ones who've been poaching in my forest!"

"I wouldn't be surprised," said Groag, though in fact he was indeed surprised to learn that their quest for poachers might have real results.

"All right, then," said Toede, handing the bow and arrow back to the know-it-all attendant, "let's keep our eyes open for damned kender!"

With that, Toede and his hunting party continued on, searching for kender. They saw none. Soon they were skirting the edge of the dark pine forest, whose lower, horizontal branches were dead, gray, and bare.

Of course no kender showed, but Toede did spot a second stag just within the gloomy woods, drinking at the near bank of a purling brook. "Shh," whispered Toede, sticking out his hand for his bow and arrow; Groag handed them over. Toede acted faster this time, quickly nocking the arrow and pulling back on the bowstring.

But, once again, before he could even take proper aim, another whining scream pierced the air.

"Damn it!" roared Toede as the stag darted off, splashing to the other side of the brook and disappearing deeper into the woods. Toede stood straight up in his saddle and scanned all around him. "Where are they? Where are these blasted kender?"

"They are quite good at hiding," said Groag as if it were too obvious to even mention. "You won't spot them so easily."

"I won't, won't I?" said Toede, straining his eyes even harder. "We'll see about that!" He turned to his bodyguards. "You there," he hissed at one of them, "circle around with some slaves! We'll use them as beaters!"

"Yes, sire!" snapped back the hobgoblin, excited at the idea. He took several slaves and dogs, and off he went, spurring his pony and hoping to encircle the kender, wherever they were.

Toede glared at Groag, who averted his eyes. The rotund Highlord led the hunting party back into the center of the field so that he'd have a wide view of the forest perimeter. Grumbling to himself, he waited atop the impatient Galiot, who kept snorting and pawing at the ground with his small, front hooves.

When at last Toede heard the yelling of the distant beaters deep in the forest, he muttered, "Now, my little kender, the tables are about to be turned. . . ."

The shouts of the beaters and the dogs barking got louder. In trying to flee these beaters, plenty of other game now burst forth from the forest: rabbit, fox, grouse, even another stag, all hurried past Toede and his hunting party. Toede ignored them all, intent and filled with malicious glee. But two of his hobgoblin bodyguards couldn't resist. They chased and felled the dashing stag with thrusts of their spears.

"Stop that!" shouted Toede, waving them back. "Prepare yourselves for the kender!"

The two hobgoblins looked at each other, then, if a little reluctantly, let the dead deer lay where it fell. They rode obediently back to Toede's side.

Suddenly the dark hounds around Toede began barking furiously and straining at their leashes, testing the strength of the scrawny slaves holding them. Straight ahead, breaking from the forest with the other game, were two small beings running from the beaters and chattering to each other and not at all looking where they were going.

"What have we here?" Toede chuckled smugly, sticking his hand out for his bow and arrow; Groag handed them over. "The dogs shall have some kender meat tonight!" Toede nocked the arrow and drew back the bowstring. He squinted and aimed, sticking his red tongue out the corner of his mouth.

But just when the two kender were within range, Toede relaxed the bow. "No," he said as a contorted smile spread across his face. "No, I have a better idea—a much better idea . . ." He savored the thought a moment and nodded approvingly. He turned to his bodyguards. "Catch them!"

The bodyguards spurred their ponies and galloped off. They were almost on top of the kender before the little people knew what was happening. One of them had stopped to replace a button on his raiment, and the other was offering him a variety of choices from his pouches, so they were surprised by the onslaught.

But it wasn't so easy catching those kender. They were very spry, and one of them kept swinging his hoopak, eliciting that whining scream. This scared the ponies, which, in turn, nearly trampled over the beaters as they themselves came forth from the woods. In the confusion, the kender nearly escaped as they bolted across the field. But they were chased down by two hobgoblins who held an outspread net between their ponies. The two kender were swooped up, the hoopak flying—with a final whine—from the hand of the kender who had held it.

Toede, watching this from a distance, nearly fell out of his saddle from excitement. "Bring them here! Bring them here!" he shouted hoarsely. He settled back on his saddle and began rubbing his pudgy hands expectantly. He leered at Groag, who nodded, if begrudgingly, to acknowledge his master's accomplishment.

The two hobgoblins rode up to Toede, the snared kender dangling between their mounts. The dogs continued barking, straining at their leashes and snapping their jaws only a hand's length from the net.

"Now what have we here?" said Toede, leaning down. Suddenly his beady eyes widened. "What's this? Groag! Look who we've bagged!"

Groag leaned forward, and even he seemed impressed. "I do believe—goodness, could it be?"

"It could!" said Toede with great satisfaction. "The kender leader! Oh, won't this impress the other Highlords!"

It was, indeed, Kronin Thistleknot. Except for a certain regal bearing and minnow-silver hair, he looked like an ordinary kender, although slightly taller and sturdier. Also, he had twice as many pouches and ornaments slung around his slender waist. In his company was a more youthful kender with a gap-toothed smile, as thrilled as could be to find himself in the middle of such an unusual experience as being captured by the great Toede.

"Good afternoon," said Kronin casually, swinging in his net-hammock. "Fine day for hunting."

"Fine day, indeed," responded Toede with a sneer. "Mind you, my dear Kronin, the real hunting hasn't even begun!"

Toede quickly looked about until he spotted the

slain stag crumpled on the ground some dozen paces away. His eyes glinted with a notion. "Bring that here!" he ordered.

The two hobgoblins who had killed the animal hurried over to it on their ponies, chasing away some complaining jackals and buzzards that had already gathered there. They grabbed the buck by its antlers and dragged it back before Toede.

"Now," said Toede, gesturing impatiently in the direction of his highly prized prisoners, "release them."

The hobgoblins holding the net tilted it, and out plopped the two small beings. They dusted their similar red leggings and white tunics, and Kronin adjusted his furry vest.

"Now," continued Toede, slowly unfolding his plan, "chain them to the carcass!"

The kender looked at each other in some confusion as two hobgoblins quickly obeyed, chaining a slender wrist from each kender to a separate broad antler. The kender raised their arms questioningly, hefting the head of the dead animal.

Toede slapped his hands together. "Now, then, my pointy eared pests, I will give you a head start."

"A head start?" repeated Kronin.

"That's right," said Toede. "And when I feel you've gone a fair distance, I will release these hounds and hunt you down and kill you. What have you got to say to that?"

Kronin smiled broadly with realization. "Oh, I do love a good game," he said, looking up at the fat hobgoblin who regarded him with such contempt.

"Then you're in luck!" came back Toede, trying to sound as glib as the kender leader. "Now, you'd best be off, my friends. I won't wait *too* long."

"Oh, I'm sure of that," said Kronin. "Until we meet

. . ." He bowed deeply. The other kender, who was a bit smaller than Kronin, did likewise. It seemed the polite thing to do.

"Bah!" snapped Toede. "You won't be so smart-alecky when I get through with you!"

But Kronin ignored the Dragon Highlord and turned to his small friend. "Come, Talorin," he said. "We must be off."

The other kender grinned and jumped up and down in anticipation of the sport to begin. "Yes, sir, my liege!" he said. "Oh, I do love a good game, too!"

The two kender began to shuffle away, dragging the bloody stag carcass—which was bigger than both of them combined—across the field. At the edge of the forest they turned around, waved farewell to Toede, then disappeared through the underbrush, heroically tugging the deer carcass.

Toede drummed his fingers impatiently on his saddle pommel. Galiot snorted and pawed the ground nervously. The dogs yanked at their leashes. The slaves looked imploringly up at Toede, waiting for the command to release the beasts.

"Um, we shouldn't wait too much longer," said Groag, looking a bit concerned. "Kender are awfully tricky—"

"I know how long to wait!" snapped back Toede. And he waited still longer to prove it.

But finally he, too, got nervous, and so he shouted: "Release the hounds!"

The hounds bolted ahead, and the hobgoblins galloped behind them while the panting slaves, watched over by two rearguards, were forced to try to keep up on foot.

At the edge of the forest, the hounds slowed and began sniffing for the scent of the deer carcass, their dark muzzles sweeping feverishly across the ground, snorting now and then to clear dirt from their wet nostrils. After a few moments of this, one of them suddenly plunged into the woods, pulling the others after it, all of them yapping away. The hunting party followed, the riders forced to duck beneath the low, dead limbs of the pine tree.

"Whew!" said Talorin, pulling his chain with both hands, barely keeping up his share of the burden. "I think I'm actually beginning to sweat!"

The two kender were slowly making their way among the towering trees of the gloomy and silent inner forest where only flecks of sunlight broke through the branches above, dappling the forest floor.

"Good for you!" said Kronin as he also tugged away, taking care to show less strain, because, after all, he was the leader. "You don't get enough exercise."

"Oops!" said Talorin, turning his head. "I think I hear the dogs!" He paused to listen. "Yes, yes, that's them all right. You know, my liege, I think we ought to be making better time."

Kronin also stopped, and as he did the deer's head slumped to the soft bed of brown pine needles. "Well," he said, trying to catch his own breath, "these low branches should slow the riders down a bit." He pointed to the crisscrossing limbs, most of which were over the heads of the two kender. "But you're right, my friend—" he casually rested an elbow on one of the dead animal's upright antlers "—although I feel certain if we had enough time, we could pick these two locks." He looked thoughtful.

"Doubtless!" said Talorin, rattling his chain. "Only . . ." He hesitated to break into Kronin's meditation. "Only, the dogs are coming closer as we speak. . . ."

"No kender should be hobbled this way," continued Kronin philosophically, shaking his head. "It's *so* embarrassing. And then, of course, as far as the game goes, it doesn't seem altogether fair."

"True enough. Those dogs are getting rather loud, aren't they?"

"Perhaps," Kronin mused, "we ought to do something about those dogs. . . ."

"Yes, yes! Capital idea!" Talorin brightened. "And I even have an idea how to do it! We need only—oh. Darn. We'd need the hoopak for that." He furrowed his brow to think. "Of course!" said Talorin again, snapping his fingers. "We could take—ahhh—no, that wouldn't work, either. We'd need four more kender. . . ."

Kronin rolled his eyes upward.

"Hey! We could try to—darn it! That's no good! There are too many trees in here! Well, I suppose we could always—drat! I doubt even hobgoblins are that stupid." Talorin rubbed his slender face. "Say, how about—?"

"Um, don't trouble yourself, my friend," interrupted Kronin finally. He spat into his hands, rubbed them, and took up the chain again. "I do believe I already have an idea. . . ."

Toede and his hunting party had now been riding through those gloomy woods a long while—so long, in fact, that they eventually came to a groaning halt. The slaves collapsed to catch their breath. Toede scratched his broad, squat face. "It seems," he said, only slowly perceiving the truth, "that we've been returning to the same spot over and over."

"Yes, it does seem that way," said Groag, somewhat fatigued by the long search. "The kender apparently dragged the carcass in a circle."

Toede's pink eyes reddened. "So! Kronin thinks he's put one over on me, does he? We'll see about that! Leash the dogs!"

The slaves, who had only just gotten comfortable lying on the bed of pine needles, forced themselves to their feet with a moan. When the dogs were leashed, the hunting party, at Toede's orders, proceeded more slowly and methodically along the scent trail. Toede kept some dogs on the outside of the circle the kender had made, hoping to catch the spot where Kronin and Talorin had veered off. Sure enough, the dogs ranging the perimeter soon grew wild and loud, snorting at the ground and tugging on their leashes.

"Do you see?" shouted Toede gloatingly. "They've only managed to postpone their end—and, may I add, not for very long!" He turned to the slaves. "Release them!"

The slaves were only too happy to obey. The dogs, once free, bolted deeper into the forest in the direction of the fresh scent, scaring up several grouse and other birds along the way.

"Oh, I've never felt such a thrill!" declared Toede gleefully as he galloped after his dogs, the needles on the ground kicking up under the hooves of Galiot. "We ought to hunt kender more often!"

"Yes, sire," responded Groag without much conviction, his robes fluttering. He was more concerned with trying to stay in the saddle.

"Oops! I hear them again!" said Talorin as he and Kronin sat on rocks by the purling stream that meandered among the trees.

Kronin was fumbling with a pin at the lock around his skinny wrist. His pointy ears perked. "You're right," he said, distracted. "I think they've caught on to our ruse."

Talorin rested his slender face in an open hand and sighed. "Boy, I really do hate being chained. I really do."

"It's no picnic for me, either," said Kronin, now standing, his attention focused on the barking. "My, they do make a racket, don't they? I'm glad we don't do this every day."

"They seem a little too . . . how would you put it?"

"Enthusiastic?"

"Yes, that's it: enthusiastic! Bad for us, huh?"

"Could be. Perhaps we ought to run in circles again."

"Frankly, I'm a bit bored with that."

"Well! Aren't we being finicky!" said Kronin. "Very well, I'll just have to think of another idea." So, with the distant barking getting ever louder, Kronin took a moment to reflect. He furrowed his brow and scratched his chin. He looked around. He thought harder.

"Um, my liege, could you think a bit faster?"

"Got it!" blurted Kronin, his eyes lighting. He sat down and began to untie the leather thongs of his shoes. "Come on," he pressed.

Talorin looked at him in confusion. "What on Krynn—?"

"And you'll want to roll up your leggings, too," said Kronin, rolling up his own.

Talorin, with a heavy sigh and clank of his chain, slowly pulled one foot onto his bony knee and began removing a shoe. "Well," he said wistfully, "at least the hounds seem to be having a good time. . . ."

The hounds snorted excitedly at the spot where the two kender had been sitting, but they grew frustrated because, once more, they had lost the scent of the kender. They searched frantically around the fern-covered bank, scaring the daylights out of a small green frog who jumped into the water.

"Apparently, my lord, the kender waded into the

stream," said Groag, squirming uncomfortably in his saddle and wishing desperately to return to the manor. "There's no telling which way they went."

"No telling?" came back Toede. "You think Kronin has won this little sport?"

"I'm only being practical," said Groag, massaging his rear. "You should have killed them when you had them in hand."

"Bah!" came back Toede. "You give up too easily!" He turned to the rest of his hunting party. "All right, comb the banks!"

The hunting party split up and covered both sides of the stream in each direction. Toede, more impatient than ever now, waited with Groag and drummed his fingers on his saddle pommel while Galiot took the opportunity to drink some of the cool, crystalline water. "We'll see," muttered Toede. "We'll just see . . ."

Before too long, the dogs upstream on the opposite side began barking furiously. A hobgoblin there blew his horn.

"Ha! Now what do you say, Groag?" called Toede as he splashed across the stream on Galiot. He hunched over to avoid some low branches. "Kronin is not as clever as he—or you—believes!"

An exhausted Groag, falling to the rear of the pursuing hobgoblins, didn't answer. A dead branch had torn the sleeve of his fancy robe.

"Uh oh, do you hear what I hear?" asked Talorin as he and Kronin dragged the dripping wet, impossibly cumbersome deer carcass through the woods. They stopped to listen. Talorin leaned against a large, rough-barked tree and slid to the ground to rest.

"Goodness, they are persistent," remarked Kronin.

"My poor wrist is starting to chafe," complained Talorin, "and I'm tired and hungry—"

"My, my, such a grumpy boy," said Kronin. "How do you think I feel? Is there a worse curse than for two kender to be chained together?"

But then Talorin, only half listening to the older kender, snapped his fingers. "Say, I have an idea!"

Kronin looked at him skeptically.

"No, really, I do! It's a good one!"

"Are we going to need anything special for this one?"

"No, no, just some muscle grease!" Talorin jumped to his feet. His face shone with eagerness.

"Well, that's too much. Mine requires only—ahh. Hmmm. No. We'd need lard for that—"

"You see? Our situation is dire. Please let me tell you my idea! Please, please, please—"

"All right, all right!" said Kronin, half covering his pointy ears. "Just keep your voice down. They're getting close."

Talorin beamed and rubbed his hands. He leaned toward Kronin and whispered, "That hobgoblin dunderhead will never figure this one out!"

"At last!" said Groag, wiping his forehead with a silk handkerchief and looking up into the high branches of an especially large pine. "We've treed them!"

"It would seem so," said Toede, peering up and rubbing his weak chin. He frowned grotesquely. "Although for the life of me, I don't see anyone up there."

All the guards looked up stupidly and scratched their heads. The dogs, which had led the party to the tree, continued jumping up onto its trunk and sliding back down again—though one of them had actually managed to jump onto a particularly low limb and now stood upon it on jittery hind legs, barking furiously.

"You're right," said Groag over the din. "I don't see them either. Can kender fly?"

But even as Groag suggested this, a smile spread slowly across his master's face. "Sire?" Groag prodded dimly.

"Fly, Groag?" blurted Toede. "Ha! Fly, you say? Is that your theory?"

"Well, no. I was only wondering—"

"Don't you see what they did?"

"Um, let me see—"

"And you think you're so smart!" Toede pointed with a stubby finger at the various heavy limbs jutting from the tree. "It's obvious! They climbed along one of those upper branches, crossed to another tree, down they came, and—" Toede turned to the rest of his party. "Everyone! Spread out!"

The hunting party radiated from the tree. Toede, more confident than ever, waited with Groag. Every so often he smirked at his uppity attendant. Sure enough, one of the dogs started yapping at the base of a neighboring pine.

"Oh, I do love it!" shouted Toede as he galloped off behind his noisy black dogs. "We'll show Kronin yet!"

"I'm sure we will, my lord," sighed Groag, mostly to himself as another limb tore at his robe.

"Darn! I almost had it!" said Kronin, hunkered down before a large cave at the base of a rocky hillside. His own reddened wrist was at last free of the chain, and he was now working on Talorin's. From the rim of the cave, the two kender had a good view across a clearing of the surrounding forest.

"Will you please hurry, sir?" asked Talorin, sitting on the glassy eyed deer carcass. "Those dogs are getting awfully close."

Kronin rose to his feet. "You're right." He looked

pensive for a moment. "Say! Why don't we split up? That would confuse them!"

"What? Me lug this deer all alone?"

Kronin's face showed that he did not think it was such a terrible idea. "You could always hide in this cave—"

"Sire!"

"Hmm. I suppose not." But he looked unconvinced.

"Sir, perhaps it would help you to think if you pretended you were still chained."

"You may be right," said Kronin. "Let me pretend I'm still chained. Hmmmm . . ."

And while Kronin pondered, the dogs' barking got steadily louder.

Talorin cleared his throat and held out his wrist, rattling his chain. "Um, in all due respect, sir, maybe you should continue picking the lock." Of course, Talorin could pick the occasional lock, but Kronin was better at it, and besides, he was the leader.

"Maybe," said Kronin vaguely, taking Talorin's shackled wrist. "But I can't pick locks and think at the same time."

"That's all right, my liege. I'll think for us. In fact, I've already got an idea. Why don't we—rats! We already tried that. Or, maybe . . ."

The barking got louder; in addition, the pounding of the ponies' hooves could be heard along with Toede's own hoarse shouting as he frantically barked orders at his hunting party.

"This is going to be just a bit too close for comfort," said Kronin, fumbling at the lock.

Talorin, still sitting on the carcass, squinted in deep thought. Every so often he brightened, but then quickly shook his head and fell back to his cogitating. "Well, that does it!" he finally announced, slapping his thigh with his free hand. "I'm fresh out of ideas!"

Suddenly Kronin stopped picking the lock. His ears twitched. "Say, did you hear something?"

"Hear something?" repeated Talorin, who was busy scooping up pebbles and inspecting them to see if any might, accidentally, be jewels. "Yes, but I thought it was you tugging at the lock—"

"No, no—" said Kronin. His ears twitched again. He turned to face the cave behind them. "I think it came from in there."

Talorin directed his attention to the cave as well. He leaned toward it to listen better, dropping his pebbles. "You're right! Hmm! Someone's an awfully loud snorer!"

The two kender stared at each other a moment. Their eyes lit up with recognition. Kronin resumed picking the lock more feverishly than ever. Talorin was almost giddy with excitement. "Hold still, will you!" said Kronin.

"Oh, this will be a good one!"

The dogs soon came to the cave and barked furiously at its dark entrance, refusing, however, to go in.

"At last!" shouted Toede, pulling up on the reins of Galiot and stopping behind his dogs. He slid off. "They're trapped!"

"I hope so, sire—" groaned Groag.

"Oh, they're in there, all right," said Toede. He stuck out his hand for his bow and arrow.

"Yes, but every time—"

"Come, come! Be quick about it!" shouted Toede, snapping his fingers impatiently.

Groag handed the weapons over. "They've been very sneaky so far—"

"That's right! Very sneaky, indeed!" said Toede, nocking his arrow. "And look where it's gotten them! They're doomed!"

"All the same, my lord, I would proceed carefully—"

"Bah! You just don't like seeing me outwit a kender," came back Toede, turning his back on Groag and peering eagerly into the darkness of the cave.

"You're wrong, my lord," said Groag, sliding his bulk clumsily off his pony. "Nothing would please me more. But—"

"Never mind 'but,'" said Toede, turning back. "Just follow your orders. Stay by the trees and watch the mounts and dogs. I'll leave you the slaves and the two rearguards. If Kronin and that other pointy eared pipsqueak should sneak by us, kill them at once! Understand?"

"Yes, sire," said Groag, grateful at least for the respite.

"The rest of you follow me!"

While four of the hobgoblins eagerly dismounted, Groag retreated back across the clearing to the trees with the slaves, dogs, ponies, and the two rearguards. Toede peered once more into the cave, but this time more tentatively. His faithful attendant had given him second thoughts. "Damn that Groag," he muttered. "Always ruining my fun! Well, not this time!" Bow and arrow nocked at the ready, Toede padded stealthily into the cave, followed closely by his guards. Soon they disappeared in the blackness.

There was a moment or so when nothing much happened, except that the dogs kept barking and yanking at their leashes, pulling some of the exhausted slaves from the trees into the clearing. Groag himself settled against a tree and sat down on a bed of pine needles. He gently fingered the tatters of his robe and sighed.

Suddenly, several prolonged hobgoblin screeches echoed from the cave. They were followed almost immediately by none other than Toede himself and his four guards, all squealing like pigs at the top of their lungs and bolting out of the cave as fast as their fat, armor-clad bodies would carry them.

"My lord, what happened?" called Groag, jumping to his feet.

The answer came quickly enough. Out of the cave emerged a huge, very angry, reptilian head. Right between its flaring nostrils was stuck Toede's puny arrow. The emerging head was quickly shown to be attached to a long, thick serpentine neck that slid out and out until the entirety of an enormous green dragon stood before the cave.

"Attack! Attaaaack!" screamed Toede, his hands flailing the air as he retreated across the open ground, his bodyguards clanking after him. Meanwhile, the dogs had reversed themselves and were now lunging in the opposite direction, yelping and dragging some of the slaves with them back into the forest.

The dragon sat back on its haunches before its cave, its head soaring above the surrounding pine trees, its leathern wings opening like two green sails of a great ship. Around the dragon's thick rear ankle, looking like nothing more than a bracelet and charm, were attached the chain and deer carcass.

"Attaaaack!" screamed Toede, continuing his dash toward the forest.

The two hobgoblins who had remained with Groag stepped forward uneasily, their little pig eyes widening, their spears trembling. "Kill it! Kill it!" Groag squealed. "Protect your master!"

The two seemed inclined to head for the rear, but they were pressed forward by Toede. Planted behind them, he was grabbing at the arms of the other fleeing hobgoblin guards, trying to spin them around. "Where are you going, you cowards? Stop! Stop!"

By now most of the guards, dogs, and slaves—with

Galiot leading the way—had scattered into the woods.

The dragon kept its glare fixed on the fat hobgoblin Highlord who stood at the edge of the forest, jumping up and down, waving his fists, and barking orders at the two quivering guards he had pushed into the clearing. Groag was frozen to his spot.

"Get him! You idiots! What are you waiting for?" Toede shrieked.

At last the angry dragon, tired of the squealing, opened its great maw, rolled its pink tongue out of the way, and released a great, thunderous discharge of flame that caught Toede right in the middle of one of his jumps. The flames passed right over the heads of the two hobgoblins edging their way backward. Tossing their spears in the air, they fled in opposite directions.

The dragon's flames were so loud that they drowned out Toede's squeals.

Groag, standing several paces away from Toede, could only watch in horror, his torn robes slowly being singed. And when at long last the flames stopped, all he could see remaining of his master was his red-hot, glowing armor, partly melted, lying on the ground.

The dragon roared victoriously, causing pine needles to rain from the trees. Then, using a front claw, the dragon swatted the irritating arrow from between its nostrils and slowly crawled back into its cave, the deer-carcass bracelet disappearing with it, followed by the dragon's own tapering, spiked tail.

In the ensuing silence, Groag, pine needles covering his head and shoulders, stood alone, gawking at where Toede had been ranting only moments before. After a moment more, he was finally able to move his legs a bit. About to slink back into the forest, he heard an odd sound—a sort of high-pitched, squeaky laughter. He stopped and looked to see where it was coming from.

His eyes fell upon two small beings perched on the rocky hill, just over the entrance to the cave. So hard were they laughing that they had fallen right over onto their backs and were holding their aching stomachs. . . .

* * * * *

And that, more or less, was the tale that was told in the tavern and came to be retold over and over throughout Krynn.

When the hooded stranger had finished speaking, the other patrons looked first at him, then at Talorin, who was smiling proudly from pointy ear to pointy ear. "Kender can sneak up on any sleeping dragon," he added unnecessarily.

Old Pug scratched his curly hair. "Well, I'll be," he said. "So it's true about Kronin."

Another patron, the lanky human, patted the proud kender on the back.

"And now, kind stranger," continued Talorin expansively, "perhaps you would like to offer thanks for your liberation. I would be most happy to relay your gratitude to the great Kronin himself."

"Gratitude?" grumbled the hooded stranger. "Gratitude? For my *liberation*?"

"Why, of course. Everyone knows Toede was a horrible tyrant, and ever since that day—"

"Ever since that day," broke in the stranger, "I have sure enough been free—but free to what? To wander aimlessly? To go hungry? To find no shelter? Gratitude, you say? Look! Look upon my gratitude!" And, with that, the stranger tossed back his hood. The once elegant and haughty, once well-fed minion of the

Highlord was now gaunt-faced and clothed in rags.

"Groag!" yelped the kender, sitting up straight.

And before anyone knew it, the crazed hobgoblin brought forth from under the table a rusty double-edged battle-ax, which he immediately swung overhead. Down he came with it, just as the inebriated kender jumped away, his abandoned chair cracking in two. Everyone else around the table jumped back, knocking over their chairs.

"Stand still!" cried the enraged hobgoblin, jumping to his feet and hefting the heavy axe once more. "I want to show you how damned grateful I am!"

"Some other time, perhaps!" called back Talorin, springing lightly back toward the door.

Groag rushed him and swung the axe, smashing a row of clay steins on the counter.

"Oops!" cried Talorin. "I think maybe it's time I take my leave!" And, with that, he hopped out a round window. "Farewell!" he called, his voice already distant in the woods. "I'll give Kronin your best!"

"Come back!" raged Groag, holding the axe aloft and dashing out the tavern door. "Come back and let me thank you and all your meddling race!"

The remaining patrons pressed back to the circular tree-trunk wall for safety and looked at each other in disbelief. Then the elf, a twinkle coming to his eye, began to chuckle. His cheeks reddened merrily. The others slowly joined him, and soon everyone was laughing.

"Well, how do you like that?" said the elf, wiping a cheerful tear from a pale blue eye as he returned to pick up his chair. "Some people just don't know how to say thank you."

Everyone was now roaring heartily and shaking their heads in amusement as they resettled themselves into their chairs to resume their drinking.

All, that is, except old Pug. He only sighed deeply as he returned to his counter to sweep away the shards of his broken clay steins. Once again, as he knew would happen, a kender had left without paying his tab.

DEFINITIONS OF HONOR

Richard A. Knaak

They called the village DRAGON'S POINT. It was a grand name for a tiny human settlement located at the tip of a peninsula northeast of Kornen. Fishtown might have been more appropriate. All who lived in Dragon's Point played some part in the fishing trade. Young and old, men and women.

Visitors were rare in this part of the world: a few traders, a wandering soul, even a minor cleric now and then. A Knight of Solamnia, then, should have been a sight rare enough to make every villager cease his work and stare in astonishment. At least that was what Torbin had believed. Yet, they did little more than eye him suspiciously and then disappear into their respective homes. They seemed more frightened than surprised.

Those standing nearest to him—those that did not run or sneak away—watched him with narrowed, covetous eyes. His personal wealth amounted to little, but it must have seemed a king's treasure to these folk. His hand strayed to his sword just long enough to warn potential bravados. The message shot home with the swiftness of an arrow. Torbin soon found himself alone in the midst of the very village he had come to protect.

A young knight, he had a tremendous desire to prove himself to the world. He wanted to make a name for himself, something that would gain him the respect of the elders of his order, something that would make the common folk gaze at him in wide-eyed admiration. In short—though he would not have admitted it to himself, much less to anyone else—Torbin wanted to be a hero.

Most of his fellows had chosen to go south toward the more populous regions. They would fight a few bandits, stare down a few peasants, and come back boasting of their great struggles. Torbin wanted much more than that. He wanted a real struggle, a worthy adversary. That was why he had chosen to head toward Kornen and then up the peninsula. The minotaurs lived near here. Savage man-beasts with their own code of honor.

A commoner, making his ways to the more hospitable lands to the southwest, had spoken of the village held in a grip of terror by a great band of minotaurs. The man-beasts prowled the woods and marched along the shore. Any day now they would surely overrun the helpless settlement.

Torbin suspected the commoner of being a great embellisher, and further questioning proved him correct in that assumption. The great band was reduced to one lone minotaur and a few whispered but unaccountable incidents. The situation seemed ideal.

Two weeks later, Dragon's Point's new savior had reached his destination.

It stank heavily of fish.

Three slightly better-dressed men met him at the village center. By their continual bickering over which of them was to speak—none of the three seemed to want the actual honor—he assumed them to be members of the local governing power. As a matter of fact, they turned out to be the mayor, the chief fisherman, and the tax collector. Torbin took the choice out of their hands by steering his horse toward the mayor. The man looked ready to faint, but managed to sputter out a greeting. The knight removed his helmet and returned the greeting.

The three elders seemed a bit disappointed in his youthful appearance. Torbin was clean-shaven and rather handsome, though his nose hooked slightly. His eyes were a bright blue, which seemed to accentuate his lack of experience. His brown hair contrasted greatly with the blond locks that dominated in this village. The tax collector, a weed of a man who stared down his prominent nose at everyone, sniffed at the newcomer with open disdain. The others shushed him.

"My name is Torbin. I am merely seeking a place to stay for a night before I continue my journey." He had decided to play it dumb for the time being, the better to check the accuracy of his own information.

The mayor, a plump, bald man with the unlikely name of Hallard Boarbreaker, looked even more distressed. "Then you have not come to save us from the minotaurs?"

The knight stiffened. "Minotaurs? I vaguely remember hearing that the islands of the great man-beasts were said to be somewhere near here, out beyond the Blood Sea of Istar, correct?" He waited for them to nod. "I know nothing about your plight. How many? How near?"

Between the three of them, he eventually discovered that there was indeed only one such creature, though it had originally arrived in a boat with others. The rest had immediately turned around and headed for home, to plan more war strategy, no doubt. The remaining minotaur had situated itself somewhere on the shore, though from their inconsistent accounts, the exact location could be anywhere within an hour's to a day's ride. The one thing all three agreed on was that this minotaur must be an advance scout for an invading army. Those brave enough to spy on the creature had reported that it sat in the same spot every day, cutting sharp sticks from wood it gathered and staring out at the sea in expectation.

A grand image was swiftly forming in the young knight's mind. He pictured himself standing over the gutted body of the horrific minotaur, his sword bearing the severed head of the beast on its point. A better trophy he could not have asked for. It did not occur to him that such a scene could easily be reversed. He was, after all, a Knight of Solamnia.

Looking as stern as possible, he nodded. "Very well. Come the dawn, I will ride out to deal with the minotaur. Before the sun sets, I will be back with its head. You have my word on it."

They looked rather dubious at this last statement, but thanked him nonetheless. If he succeeded, they would be all too happy to honor him with a feast. If he failed, they would be no worse off than if he had never come.

At Torbin's request, they found him a place to stay for the night. He was also served one of the finest meals the inn's cook had ever made, though the knight himself had never really been that fond of fish and thus did not realize the trouble the woman had gone through. As it was, he was barely able to down the foul dish. Torbin was also ignorant of the fact that she had outdone herself for the sole reason that she believed this young man was going out to die and deserved one last fine meal.

Torbin made no attempt to converse with those who drifted in and out of this poor attempt at a public inn. The few who stayed for very long only glanced his direction, that same hungry look in their eyes. The knight found himself anxiously awaiting the morrow.

He bedded down for the night—it could only loosely be called a bed, being more of a bug-ridden mattress on a piece of wood—and eventually drifted off into sleep despite his numerous tiny companions. In his dreams he finally found pleasure, skewering his hapless foe a thousand different ways, each one more daring and skillful than the one preceding it.

He rode quietly, hoping not to alert the minotaur. The tracks he had come across were fresh and spoke of a large beast. Torbin's pulse quickened. Legends said the minotaurs were crafty fighters, as skilled in their own way as the Knights of Solamnia. They also had their own code of honor of which some of the older knights had spoken with great respect.

For a short time, he was forced to ride around trees on a path that could be described as maddening at best. It twisted this way and that, and the knight even found himself momentarily facing the direction he had just come from. Abruptly, it turned toward the coastline and led him to a gritty, open area.

Off to the north, his left, he saw the lean-to; nearby sat the feared minotaur, his great horned head bent over some unknown task.

Using the natural curve of the land to hide him, Torbin readied his sword and shield and backed the horse up in order to give it more time to build up speed before he clashed with the minotaur. A smile flickered on his face. He took a deep breath, quickly searched his mind for any options he might have missed, and then spurred the horse on.

The warhorse's great speed quickly ate away at the distance between Torbin and the minotaur. The knight saw his adversary stand at first notice of the noise and turn quickly toward him. The minotaur was unarmed, but there were a large number of long wooden shafts beside it. The man-beast could easily reach one of them long before Torbin came close enough to strike.

Nevertheless, the minotaur made no move toward its weapons. Torbin's grim determination gave way to puzzled indignation. He had never struck down an unarmed foe. It went against everything he considered honorable, even when fighting a creature such as the minotaur.

They would close soon. The minotaur had still not reached for a weapon and, in fact, looked ready to die. With a sudden curse, the young knight pulled sharply on the reins of his horse, trying desperately to go around the creature rather than run into it. He did not think even a minotaur could survive the blows of a trained warhorse if the victim had no intention of defending itself.

The horse finally allowed itself to be turned. For several seconds, man and steed whirled wildly around as the horse fought to rebalance itself. Torbin lost his sword in an attempt to keep the reins from slipping from his hands. The horse snorted loudly and then slowed. The knight was able to regain his own balance and pull the horse to a halt. It was then that he first noticed the loss of his weapon.

He twisted around and locked gazes with the minotaur. The massive creature calmly walked over to the sword and picked it up. Turning it so that the hilt pointed toward Torbin, the minotaur returned it to him. The knight blinked, then accepted the blade. The minotaur returned to its carving, staring once more out at the Blood Sea while it worked.

Torbin led his horse so that the minotaur's view would be blocked. The creature looked up at him. Torbin pointed the sword at the minotaur.

"Will you stand and fight? I've always been told that minotaurs were courageous, fierce warriors, not cowards!"

The man-beast's nostrils flared, but it made no attempt to attack. Instead, it put down one stick and began work on another. Torbin grew angrier. How was he to prove himself if his adversary refused to fight? His sense of honor prevented him from striking an opponent who refused battle.

The minotaur chose that moment to talk. Its voice was deep and tended to rumble like thunder. "I would rather talk than fight, Knight of Solamnia, who is too far from home. Please, join me."

It took several seconds for the words to sink in. Torbin stared at the minotaur. With those first words the minotaur became a person, not an "it" like so many people, including Torbin, considered the individual members of the minotaur race to be. Torbin accepted the invitation without thinking. It did not occur to him until he had dismounted and sheathed his blade that the minotaur could have easily skewered him several times.

"Sit here." His unusual host indicated a spot next to his own. Torbin followed his lead.

"Who are you? Why do you disturb me? I have done nothing save sharpen a few sticks." The minotaur was genuinely annoyed, as if this were his personal beach and no one else's. He paused in his labors to inspect the latest stick. Grunting, he threw it away.

Torbin, who had not expected to play question games with a full-grown minotaur, took some time in answering. He was still not sure that he was not sitting in some sort of elaborate trap. Minotaurs were highly intelligent creatures who enjoyed proving their superiority over other races.

The minotaur repeated his questions. Torbin saw no reason not to relate the truth. The creature nodded as he listened to him go over the story of his arrival in Dragon's Point, the fears of the people there, and what the town elders had asked of him.

The creature shook his head. "Humans! So ready to fall prey to the shadows of fear. Your race has a mind; it should learn to use it."

Torbin did not disagree, but felt the case was rather overstated. Men, he told the minotaur, were not all the same. Some were brave, some were fools, some had honor, some were thieves.

"Let us talk of honor." The minotaur's gaze was oddly intent. He had completely abandoned his woodwork.

Having never studied the minotaurs or their way of life, Torbin allowed the man-beast to go first. The creature turned his eyes once more to the sea. Torbin looked, but could see nothing but the eternal motion of waves rolling toward the shore.

"Minotaurs, like some men, believe that honor is first and foremost."

The knight nodded. "Without honor, a man's life is worthless. He is damned. The tale of Lord Soth is legend among the Knights of Solamnia."

"I have heard the tale. The knight who abandoned his mate for an elf woman, condemned now to haunt the halls of his castle, reliving his crimes to his family and friends."

"That is essentially correct."

The man-beast seemed to consider something. "Was he an honorable man before this great transgression?"

"To my knowledge. As I understand it, he was highly thought of by all among the orders. That is what makes his crime that much more terrible. To abandon honor so abruptly. It is unthinkable."

"Apparently not. Soth did so. I wonder what he felt?"

Torbin shrugged. Only Soth knew, and no one was going to take the risk to ask him.

The minotaur blinked. "On the islands, honor is everything. It sets us above the lesser races. The elves claim they are honorable, but they are perhaps the greatest tricksters other than kender. Worse yet, they will not fight. They run and hide, shouting all the while that it's none of their concern, they had nothing to do with it, it wasn't their fault. In the end, they are an old, cowardly people."

Torbin, who had never met an elf face-to-face and had heard a number of stories concerning them, could not judge how much truth the minotaur's statements contained. He did know, however, of the rather egotistical attitude of the minotaurs in general.

"One day, the minotaurs will swarm from the islands and conquer all of Krynn. Our leader claims that. His predecessor claimed that we are the supreme race."

Fearing the conversation was steering toward the blind rhetoric of superiority the minotaurs were famous for, Torbin dared to interrupt. "You were speaking of honor?"

The minotaur nodded. "On Mithas and Kothas, we fight for our place in society. In the name of honor, we slay one another. A minotaur who does not fight has no honor. He is a coward, a non-being."

"A cruel society. The Knights of Solamnia would never permit such useless bloodshed."

The minotaur gave a fierce snort. Torbin froze, sure that the man-beast was preparing to jump him. As the snorting continued, the young knight realized the minotaur was laughing. There was no humor in his laughter, though.

"I have heard many tales of the Knights of Solamnia. You are well respected by my people. There are stories of bands of knights who have fought on, refusing to yield their position, until all are dead. Forget that in many circumstances they could have retreated to better ground, to fight another day. I have heard of knights who have taken their own lives because they have shamed themselves before their fellows."

Torbin's hand went to the hilt of his sword. "What you say is true; there are such tales. Yet, you twist them so that they sound like acts of—"

"Blind pride and stupidity. Are honor and pride really so important to you, young knight? If a friend died because you were lax, would you leave the Knighthood?"

"A knight who fails in his duty is not worthy of his title." The quote by one of his instructors came to Torbin with little difficulty.

"Could you not make up for your mistake?"

"The friend would still be dead. It would still be my responsibility."

The minotaur sighed, a sound much like a roaring wind. "How long would you go on paying for that mistake? Ten years? Twenty? If you should save a dozen lives, would you still punish yourself for that one?"

"Your question is beyond the point of ridiculousness."

"Is it?" The man-beast studied his own hands. "Would you run a man through from the back? A man who did not even know there was a hint of danger?"

Torbin gasped. "A minotaur might slay a man in such a way, but a Knight of Solamnia would never do such a foul deed! I would challenge him!"

"Indeed? What if you knew this man could easily outfight you? What if you knew that, if he survived, he would cause the deaths of many?" The minotaur's eyes now bore deep into the young knight's. "I ask again, are honor and pride such good things? Must we always do 'the right thing'? "

Torbin did not answer. He was confused. The minotaur's words made some sense, yet, they could not.

The man-beast turned away from him, an almost sad look in his eyes. Torbin waited, but the minotaur would not speak. Instead, he commenced once more with his carving. The knight sat and watched him for a few minutes more, and then he stood up. The minotaur paid him no mind and went on carving another shaft. Torbin returned to his horse and mounted up.

He rode away without looking or speaking to the minotaur again.

The mayor, the chief fisherman, and the tax collector were all waiting for him. As he rode up to them, he noticed how their eyes kept returning to the sword in his sheath. He remembered his earlier promise and gritted his teeth. The mayor stepped forward.

"Is the beast dead, then? Would that I had been there! We feared for you—such a silly thing! Did you severe his head from his body? Campos!" The chief fisherman trundled forward, picking his yellowed teeth as he walked. "Have some of your boys drag the carcass back nere! We'll put it where all can see it!"

"The minotaur is not dead."

Torbin might well have demanded the mayor's first-born child by the look on the man's pudgy face. The chief fisherman looked grim and spat. The tax collector smiled knowingly.

"Not dead?! Wounded? Run off, has he?"

This part was even more difficult for Torbin to get out. "I did not fight him. We talked."

"*Talked*?!?" all three shouted in one voice. A number of villagers popped their heads out of windows and doorways to see what the noise was all about. A few began muttering and pointing in Torbin's direction. Someone laughed harshly.

"I do not think he will harm you."

"Coward!" The mayor raised his fist, though his distance to the knight did not shrink by even the minutest amount. "I should have you run out of Dragon's Point!"

Torbin was turning red with anger. On top of everything else, he did not need idiotic backwoods fishermen calling him a coward for no reason at all. He pulled out his sword with one swift motion and tucked the point neatly under the plump man's chin. The mayor let out a gurgle and froze. Villagers began pouring out of their homes, though none moved close enough to lend the stout, blustery man a hand.

"I did not come here to be insulted. You know very little about the situation as it really is. If it will satisfy you, I'll keep an eye on the minotaur. Should he attempt to cause any harm, I'll deal with him. Will that suit you?" In truth, he could not have cared less if it did or did not. This village, this whole region could be damned for all he cared. It stank. The people stank even more.

The chief fisherman whispered something into the mayor's ear. The mayor nodded as best he could, considering the circumstances. The tax collector joined in. Breathing a little slower now, Torbin removed the point from the mayor's throat. After several seconds of swallowing, the man was able to speak.

"It—it has b-been decided that your suggestion is quite reasonable—" He paused as Torbin's grip grew tight around the hilt of the sword. "—I mean *really* reasonable. Therefore, we will let you deal with the situation as it stands. Provided—" The mayor hesitated again until he felt it safe "—provided that you give us your oath that you will kill the creature at the first sign of hos-hostility."

Torbin sheathed his sword and eyed the three in disgust. "Agreed."

The meal he received that evening was far inferior to the one the night before, though Torbin was unaware of it. He had a great desire to leave this village. He was sick of fish already and sick of these people. The minotaur was better company than these thieving worm-diggers, despite his maddening questions. Were it not for his pride, the young knight might have ridden out of the village there and then. As it was, he merely retired early, relieved to be away from the inhabitants of this godforsaken village and anxious to see what the next day would bring.

Sunrise saw him far from the village, nearing the shore where the minotaur made his home. The man-beast was there; in fact, he looked as if he had not budged from the spot since yesterday. As usual, he was carving. Torbin wondered why the ground was not littered with short spears from his previous efforts. Perhaps the minotaur used them for hunting at night, the knight reasoned.

He steered the horse toward the minotaur. The animal snorted its displeasure at being forced to go peaceably toward what it considered a major threat. Training won out, though. Torbin was master and must be obeyed. The minotaur continued to gaze out at the sea so intently that the young knight was unsure whether the creature knew of his presence.

As if on cue, the minotaur spoke. His gaze remained

fixed on the Blood Sea. "Welcome back, Knight of Solamnia. You're early."

Torbin had not been aware that he had had an appointment, but he chose to say nothing. Today, he wanted to talk to the minotaur, find out more about the man-beast's homeland. By his manner, the minotaur was unlike many of his race. The tales of blood-thirsty, arrogant monsters was too consistent to be entirely false.

Buried in his subconscious, hidden by a number of excuses, lay the true reason for his visit; Torbin's mind was now riddled with doubts about himself and that which he had believed in until now.

"I have come to a decision today."

The knight blinked. "A decision?"

The minotaur spoke as if Torbin's words had gone unheard. "I have come to a decision today. Honor and pride are nothing without reason. It is not an abrupt decision; in fact, it is the same decision I made long ago. There is a time to fight, a time to give up one's life for another, and a time to run. Tomorrow, the run will be over."

"Run?" Torbin climbed off his horse very quietly lest he destroy the minotaur's chain of thought. The man-beast ignored him. He seemed to be watching every wave, marking every turn of the breeze.

"Minotaurs must fight for their place in society. A minotaur who does not fight does not exist. He shames his family. They call him 'kenderwhelp' or 'elf-bastard.' Even 'manling.' He is shunned by those who know him and cursed by those who do not. Might makes right; honor is all."

The minotaur abruptly turned to Torbin, who had forgotten to sit, so intent was he on following the oth-er's words. "Tomorrow, honor will be returned. No longer will they hold their heads in shame." The final word sounded almost like a curse. The minotaur threw his latest effort far into the sea. He watched it hit with an unruly splash and then vanish from sight.

Torbin found himself oddly concerned. "What happens tomorrow?"

"Is it pride or love? Is it honor or fear?" The man-beast stood. For the first time, Torbin noticed the small, neat stack of short spears. Each point had been finely honed. The best of the minotaur's work. "Forgive me if I leave you so soon. I have preparations to make which must be made in private. I ask you not to follow me. I will harm no one."

Torbin protested, but the minotaur held up one massive, clawed paw. "I know what the village thinks. They are humans, after all, with human idiocies. Let them believe what they wish to believe. Come the morrow, they will know the truth of things."

The minotaur chose two of the sharpened sticks and hefted them, his skill and knowledge evident as he dropped one in favor of another. Eventually satisfied with two, he trudged off toward the woods, his huge feet leaving deep holes in the soft ground. Torbin estimated him to be well over seven feet when standing upright, seven feet of fighting minotaur, undoubtedly a champion among his race if he so chose.

Yet, he had not. Torbin could only guess at the twisted turn the other's life must have taken.

He returned to the village shortly thereafter, refusing to acknowledge the mocking stares of the inhabitants. Most of the day was spent checking and rechecking his equipment, running through his exercises, caring for his horses. It was all done half-heartedly, like some sort of stalling maneuver. Torbin could not find it in himself to push on, but at the same time could not stand the thought of staying any longer. He could feel the eyes at his back, hear the whispers and curses.

He stayed the night at the inn again, this time completely avoiding any meal even remotely smelling of fish. He had long ago learned to live off the land. He did not even consider eating something else; food prepared in the village left a bitter taste in his mouth.

He woke at first light, the decision to leave this place firmly planted in his mind. Despite such grand determination, however, he still found himself packing as the sun neared midday. That was when the decision was taken away from him.

The minotaur had entered the village.

The people were in a panic. Women were pulling children off the streets. Men rushed to the town elders, demanding that something be done. The town elders, once again led by the less-than-eager mayor, in turn rushed to Torbin, demanding that he do as he promised or suffer the consequences. Torbin idly wondered what sort of consequences the mayor could have in mind if he really thought the minotaur was there to destroy the village. Did he expect the minotaur to wait his turn?

The man-beast did not slink into the village. Despite being realistically outnumbered should the villagers discover their backbones, he walked straight and tall. Even the tallest man in the village came no higher than his shoulder. There was disdain in the minotaur's eyes; Dragon's Point was no argument for the strengths of man. It smelled. The people were dirty, cowardly. Among all of them, only the Knight of Solamnia, an outsider, deserved respect. The others deserved nothing—not even notice.

Minotaur and knight met just before the center of the village. Torbin forewent meeting the other on horseback, which would have given the knight a psychological edge. The minotaur had given no indication that he had come to fight. Torbin could do no less.

Revealing empty hands, the man-beast acknowledged the knight. Torbin returned the greeting. The villagers had mostly vanished by this time; a few hardy souls dared to stand in the shadows and watch. The mayor and his allies, more out of fear for their positions than their lives, actually remained out in the street, only a few yards from the encounter itself. The minotaur did not even glance in their direction.

"I have come to you because you are the only one worthy of notice amongst this rabble." The minotaur's breathing was ragged, as if the man-beast had been running or was anxious about something. Torbin studied the other's form. With the exception of a loincloth, the minotaur was bare of any sort of clothing. Though the fur-covered skin glistened slightly, it was not the sweat of heavy movement. The knight's curiosity deepened.

"What is it you wish of me?" Torbin did not bother to whisper. No one was close enough to hear him.

The words were difficult for the man-beast to get out. "I ask that you follow me back to the shore. Today things will come to a proper conclusion. The village will have no need to fear me anymore."

The knight wanted to know more, but his trained eye could see that the minotaur was under heavy strain and wanted to be away from those he still considered his lessers, despite his rather peaceful ways. "I'll need to get my horse."

"One hour. No later." As an afterthought—"Please hurry. Time is short."

The minotaur turned to leave and again noticed how the villagers scurried out of sight whenever he turned toward them. He turned back to Torbin and glared, not at him, but at the village and what it represented. "They live in constant fear here, yet they will not leave. A stupid lot. One more thing you can tell them: should they even come near the shore this day, they will bring the wrath of the supreme race down upon them. There will be nothing but ashes to mark where this village once stood. Understand that I do not threaten; what I say is merely fact."

Torbin stood there and absorbed the full impact of the minotaur's words as he watched him stalk off, purposefully noticing every human on his way out. The knight doubted any warning was necessary. It was more stubbornness than bravado that kept the villagers at the tip of the peninsula. What their ancestors had been like Torbin could only guess. The present inhabitants of Dragon's Point, however, were not the adventurous type.

He relayed the minotaur's message to the mayor and those villagers who had already dared to step foot out of their homes and was more than pleased by their reactions. Torbin had almost as little love for these people as the minotaur had; it was his duty, though, to protect them in spite of themselves. For that reason alone—not his chief reason, assuredly—he would be at the minotaur's dwelling by the time of the deadline.

Returning to his restless steed, he mounted up. Though it would have been to his preference if the horse had charged, he forced himself to keep the animal under control and make it trot slowly through the village street. The mayor, who seemed to have nothing better to do than to stand in the streets, wished him the best of luck in what the people of Dragon's Point had now assumed was at long last the great battle. Torbin focused his eyes straight ahead and remained silent. He would explain the truth when it was all over.

The minotaur was at the shore when Torbin arrived. The huge man-beast was startlingly swift. He was sweating and breathing heavily, but he was far from exhausted. He greeted the knight with a slight nod of his massive, horned head. Torbin dismounted and sat down beside him. The minotaur waited until his breath returned to him before speaking.

"The village is in no danger from my people. It probably never will be. Dragon's Point is nothing— a foul-smelling pool of your people's dregs. In fact, its presence may very well be important to us. It lets us point at humans and say 'see them—see how weak and pathetic they are.' "

The dark brown eyes shifted to the familiar horizon. Torbin automatically followed suit and thought he saw something in the distance. A speck, little more.

Letting loose an animalistic snort, the minotaur said, "My people. Despite their prowess, their disdain for the 'lesser' races, they are less than gully dwarves in some ways."

The man-beast's words startled Torbin. From what he understood of the race, such words were nearly treason. The minotaur gave his equivalent of a smile, one filled with more mockery than humor.

"We are blind to our faults. The lesser races have no need to fear us. We will continue to kill and maim one another in order to prove our individual superiority and gain ourselves rank. We have done so for as long as memory has existed and will do so until the Final Day. It is our way; it has become . . . habit."

The minotaur's eyes never strayed from the Blood Sea. Now, they widened ever so little. Torbin, trained to notice such minor things, turned his attention back to the sea. The speck was still there, but it was now just close enough to be identified.

It was a boat.

He heard the minotaur groan softly and looked at him. The massive creature stood up and stretched. His animallike features contorted in an attempt to frown. "Thus it begins again. For their sakes."

The words did not seem directed to Torbin. Rather, they were unconscious thoughts accidentally spoken out loud. The minotaur peered intently at the incoming craft, as if assuring himself that it was really there. He then bent over and began selecting the best of his woodwork.

Torbin reacted instantly. If the passengers on the boat meant trouble, he was more than willing to lend his strength to that of the minotaur, whom he had come to think of as a kindred spirit. To his surprise, however, a hand prevented him from drawing his blade. He turned to find himself staring into the bottomless, dark eyes of the man-beast.

"The feeling is appreciated, human, but I cannot permit you to risk yourself. This is my battle. I ask that you only observe." The minotaur would not remove his hand until the knight had sworn an oath.

With incredible speed, the boat made its way toward the shore. Though he should have expected it, Torbin was still taken aback by the crew's appearances. They were all minotaurs, to his eyes varying only slightly in appearance; they wore some armor and carried swords or tridents. He noted that as a group they stared at the first minotaur whenever able.

As the boat ran aground, four of the creatures jumped out and helped drag it farther to shore. Watching them work, Torbin could not help being awed by the strength in their arms and legs. He tried to imagine a large, coordinated force of minotaurs and shuddered. Better that they should continue to kill one another than turn on the world itself. If not for their brutal ways amongst themselves, they would have swarmed over the eastern part of the continent long ago.

Torbin's friend muttered, "I tried to convince them of the idiocy of fighting one another. Only later did I realize what that would result in. Fortunately, they were too ashamed of me to listen."

There were six all together. None seemed as tall as the original minotaur. They saluted him solemnly. The minotaur saluted them back. The leader of the new band glanced at the knight.

Torbin's companion spoke. "A Knight of Solamnia, here to observe. The rules permit—no, demand—such a witness."

The leader snorted. His voice was even deeper than the first minotaur's. "We greet you, Knight of Solamnia. The honor of your order precedes you." He paused, considering the other minotaur's statement. "I also accept you as witness, though I believe it may very well be the first time that one other than our race has stood for a possible condemned."

Torbin forced himself to utter an empty, formal greeting. Like and unlike fish, it left a bad taste in his mouth.

The leader turned back to the original minotaur. "Have you come to terms?"

"I still remain the same. My thoughts have not changed."

The newcomer seemed almost sad. He tightened his grip on the sword he carried. "Then there is nothing more to say."

"Nothing. We may begin whenever you wish."

Turning to his own companions, the leader said, "Form the circle. Alternate order."

There were three minotaurs armed with tridents. An equal number, including the leader, carried huge broadswords. Each minotaur, barring Torbin's companion, wore a breastplate and arm and ankle guards. The six formed a circle and held their weapons before them in ceremonial style.

The original minotaur, carrying two of his best hand-crafted stakes, stepped into the middle. He saluted the others. They returned the salute. The leader gave a shout in some tongue Torbin could not understand. The six dropped into fighting stances. The single figure in the center copied their actions almost immediately.

A trident flashed toward the encircled minotaur.

Armed with only the two stakes, the entrapped minotaur ducked below the jab and thrust. The attacker backed away, but two others moved in. A great gash appeared in the right arm of the condemned man-beast. He showed no sign of pain and fended off both weapons.

The battle began in earnest.

As one, they moved in with swift thrusts, jabs, and counterattacks. Blood flowed freely. At least one attacker went down. A sword fell near the condemned. He made no move toward it. A trident point caught him in the side of the chest. He grunted and stumbled to one knee. The over-eager executioner charged into the circle, expecting to bring an end to the fight. He was greeted with a stake to his throat, which the trapped minotaur threw with amazing power.

The loss of that weapon, though, was the condemned man-beast's undoing. He was not allowed time to reach any of the weapons that had been dropped. Nor could he defend himself completely with only the stake in his left hand. The edge of a blade cut into his good arm. A trident sank deep into his chest. The minotaur fell back, still clutching the simple weapon in his hand.

Three of the other minotaurs backed away. A single executioner, armed with a trident, stepped toward the bleeding, slumping form. The minotaur on the ground closed his eyes.

Torbin remembered shouting something at that point, but the exact words would forever be lost. One of the minotaurs turned toward him and made sure he did not interfere. His emotions screamed for him to interfere—to stop the final blow—but the Training and the Oath held him back. The empty words made him pause that one initial moment.

The trident came down with terrible speed.

It was over quickly. The outcome had never been in doubt, though the possible damage was. Blades had thrust, tridents had jabbed. All the while, two simple, sharpened sticks had attempted to hold them off while also trying to reach targets of their own.

The condemned lay crumpled in a large heap, the broken points of a trident sticking out of the side of his chest. The owner of the trident would not care about the loss of his weapon; he lay sprawled no more than a foot away, blood flowing from the opening which had once been his neck. Slightly away from the two, a third limp form lay spread across the ground, a gaping wound in the stomach his undoing.

Of the remaining four minotaurs, not one had escaped some sort of injury. The leader sported a jagged cut on his right arm, made just before the final thrust of his own weapon. Two of the others, covered with minor cuts, were attempting to remove part of a wooden stake from the leg of the third. Torbin's companion had more than accounted for himself.

After assisting the minotaur with the leg wound aboard the boat, the other three quietly turned to the task of picking up the dead. They carried both of their fallen comrades to the vessel, but completely ignored the remaining corpse.

Torbin could stand no more. He had sworn that he would not interfere, and he had not. The pure callousness of the man-beasts, however, had shaken him completely. He pulled forth his sword and stepped forward, shouting such violent curses at them that they could not possibly pretend to not hear.

At first he thought they would all come charging at him. The leader, though, raised his good arm and prevented any movement by his warriors. Alone, he walked calmly over to the knight.

"We have no quarrel with you, Knight of Solamnia. You are here as witness, no more. Do not force disaster upon yourself." The minotaur eyed Torbin's weapon as if it were a child's toy. Compared to his own massive weapon, it might have been.

"You can't leave him there! He fought against impossible odds and fought admirably!"

The minotaur glanced coldly at the remaining body. "It was to be expected of him . . . to make up for his cowardice. He brought shame upon his family, so great and strong . . . until now." The cold stare fixed on Torbin. "You would not understand. You are still only a human, even if one of the Knights of Solamnia."

Torbin's grip tightened on his sword hilt. "Then explain it to me. Please."

The man-beast sighed. "His family is great and powerful. For ten generations, they have had a champion, a living symbol of our superiority. He was to be the symbol of this generation." The voice lowered. The coldness slipped away without warning, revealing a figure silently fighting anguish. "Some say he must have met a cleric on one of his journeys to the continent. They are known to seek out our kind, subvert them to the weak gods of the humans and the other races. No one would have expected it of him. Not the preaching of peace, of dwarves and kender being our equals—ha!—or of us abandoning the games! How else can we find our place in society? Who would we choose for our leaders? An unblooded cow?"

The minotaur stiffened, his mask on once more. "Thus he was given the choice. His family was disgraced. Combat was their only hope. We would see if his cowardice was so great that he would pull his family down with him, for they would have suffered if he had refused combat. Such weakness can only be inherited."

Torbin sheathed his weapon, but did not otherwise move from his place. "This? This is combat?"

"He could have run. We gave him days to prepare or flee. The choice was his."

"That is no choice."

The minotaur sighed once more. "As I said, you would not understand our way of honor. It is not your fault. Forget it and return to your kind. The scales have been balanced; honor has been returned to his family."

"He deserves burial."

"His honor has been vindicated. His crimes can never be. It is forbidden to bury criminals on home soil."

One of the other minotaurs came up behind the leader and whispered something. The leader thought for a moment and nodded. "This one would speak to you alone. He is kin to the condemned."

The leader returned to the boat. The newcomer sniffed in the direction of Torbin, apparently finding his odor offensive. He pointed at the body. "I have been given permission to make a request of you."

Puzzled, the knight allowed the minotaur to continue.

"Despite his weakness, I would have my kinsman buried with some sort of ceremony. He was good

---

173

before the madness overtook him."

Torbin mentally questioned who was actually mad. Aloud, he said, "What do you want of me?"

"You seem to be a fr—companion or acquaintance. I ask if you will give him burial. I will compensate you for your time. I know how much humans value m—"

The knight cut him off, shocked by the insinuation. "I will bury him. I want no money."

The minotaur blinked in confusion, then nodded slowly. "Thank you. I must return to the boat now."

Torbin watched while the creatures pushed the boat back into the water. Only then did he realize that the minotaur who had asked for the burial of his kin had also been the final executioner. He wondered briefly if this were another part of minotaur custom.

The leader glanced at him briefly, but made no attempt to communicate. Torbin continued to watch the vessel as it began its journey home. He did not turn away until it was no more than a tiny speck on the horizon.

The knight chose a spot near the site of the lean-to yet well hidden from the prying eyes of the locals. It was a shallow grave; the ground was too loose on top and too hard about four feet down. In addition, he was forced to use make-shift tools left behind by his friend, the minotaur.

The prayers lasted until the sun set. Torbin, his body stiff, rose and wandered over to the lean-to. He picked up the small, crude blade with which the lone man-beast had created his handiwork. After studying it, he put it into one of his pouches.

His mount greeted him energetically, inaction and the scents of the minotaurs having caused him no end of frustration. Torbin soothed the animal and then slowly climbed on. He did not look back.

* * * * *

His reappearance in the village caused a great commotion, despite the lateness of the day. Villagers pressed around him, asking if the beast was dead. The mayor and his cronies located him some five minutes later while he was packing the rest of his gear onto his horse.

"Is it true? Have you dispatched the beast?" The mayor's breath smelled of fish and beer.

"The minotaur is dead." Torbin continued to concentrate on packing his equipment.

The group let out a rousing cheer. The mayor declared the next day a holiday. A feast would take place, each villager bringing food or drink as a contribution. The victorious Knight of Solamnia would be the guest of honor. Various members of the town council began vying for spots at the main table. Others formed committees and subcommittees designed to coordinate the feast. A few talked of bringing the body back to the village. Eventually, most of the townspeople drifted off to plan the next day's events.

His own preparations complete, Torbin steadied his horse and then remounted and moved away at a trot. Villagers smiled or bowed in his direction as he rode; others looked at him with puzzlement. The knight kept his eyes on the path before him.

At the edge of town, a breathless mayor caught up to him. "Sir Knight! Where are you going? Will you not join us at our feast tomorrow? We wish to do you honor."

Torbin pulled the reins tight, bringing the trained warhorse to a dead stop. He turned the animal around and matched gazes with the round man for a full half-minute. The mayor shifted like a small child under his stare.

Then, as abruptly as he had stopped, Torbin turned his horse back around to the path and rode off at a trot.

He did not look back.

———

Hearth Cat and Winter Wren

By Nancy Varian Berberick

---

*T*he golden tabby eyed the caged squirrel with
sleepy interest. The squirrel panted miserably, not certain which was worse: the grim possibilities inherent
in the cat's white teeth or the aching reality of his own
imprisonment. The cage, he decided wretchedly.

The cage made his bones hurt and his heart race
hard in frightening fits and starts. But when he saw the
fire smouldering in the cat's almond-shaped, green
eyes, the squirrel thought that it might not be such a
bad thing that there were bars between them.

Tell me, squirrel, the cat murmured, *when do you
think he'll feed us again?*

Oh, soon, soon, I'm sure! the squirrel chattered.
*Very soon. But I can't imagine you're still hungry. You
ate two mice only a little while ago. . . .* The squirrel
winced, then flicked his tail and scrubbed at his whiskers with his small white paws. He didn't like to think
about the mice or their helpless scurrying. And he
especially did not like to think about the cool and
deadly look of the cat as he licked his lips with his
rough pink tongue, or the pitiful crunch of little
mousy bones.

And they had been small mice. The squirrel wondered whether the cage would hold if the tabby decided to knock it from the table.

Cat, he said, trying to be as friendly and amiable as he could through his fear, *I think there might be another mouse around here somewhere. Just in case you're hungry, that is.* In some place far back in his mind, he felt a little ashamed that he would so readily cast another luckless creature into the cat's jaws to save his own gray hide. But he ignored that. He was, after all, a squirrel. And what are mice to squirrels but cat food?

The tabby purred gently, the softness of the sound belied by the hard glitter of his eyes. He leaped gracefully to the table. *Squirrel*, he sighed. To the squirrel it sounded as though the cat might be remembering with fondness a meat he hadn't tasted in some time.

Oh, cat, oh, cat, why don't you nap a while in the sun? There's a lovely bit of sunshine there on the hearth. There haven't been too many warm days like this. I should think you'd want to take advantage of it. He'll be back to feed us both soon.

And, in truth, the squirrel was hungry. He could almost taste the sweet, chewy meat of a chestnut. Oh, for a nice pile of chestnuts now! Or even a few bitter acorns.

A soft paw tapped at the bars. Chattering and scolding, the squirrel made himself as small as he could and ducked into the farthest corner of his cage. He was caught between an instinctive need to be free of the confining cage and the understanding that only the bars kept the cat at bay. Frustrated, the squirrel flashed his tail once more.

The cat only purred again, the sigh of one who had decided it best to save a tasty snack for later. He dropped to the floor and went to preen in the golden splash of late afternoon sun. Now and then he looked up at the squirrel to yawn and grin.

The grin was deadly and dark and very confident.

Though the day had been warm, almost springlike, the weather, as it often did in late winter, had changed swiftly sometime just before night. Rain poured now from a dirty gray sky, pounded angrily against the snug roof and walls of Flint's house. The smell of the vallenwood's wet bark mingled comfortably with the scent of a cozy fire.

The old dwarf carved a last, feathering stroke on the small object he'd been whittling all afternoon. Not since he had started work had he looked at what it was he was making. There were times, when he was thinking hard about something, or when he was very peaceful, that he could simply let his hands take over. The result of his work then was not craft but art.

The talk that night was desultory and wandering, aimless paths of conversation that made for no goal but, more often than not, returned to Tasslehoff's sudden and urgent departure three days before. Urgent to Tas, at least.

It had to do with a talking wren. Tas had been certain that the bird had spoken, pleading for help. His long brown eyes had been bright with that certainty. No one had been able to convince him otherwise. So off he'd gone like some small knight on a quest.

And, everyone agreed, it was best to give Solace a chance to cool its collective temper and forget about Tas for a time. A winter-bound kender in Solace could do about as much damage as a skulk of foxes in a henhouse, or an invading army. Few folk had the patience for Tas's long and tangled explanations about how he had simply "borrowed" the missing item, truly meant to return it, and just couldn't understand how the pilfered goods ended up in *his* pouches.

Across the room Caramon's deep, bright laughter pounced and overrode the quiet voices of his friends.

"A talking wren!" He attempted to raise the pitch of his voice in imitation of the kender's piping insistence that he had, indeed, spoken with a wren. He failed utterly. "And one who asks for help, at that. Then off he goes with hardly a good-bye."

Raistlin murmured something, and Tanis smiled. Sturm only shook his head and continued to polish the already gleaming blade of his sword.

Flint closed his hands over the little carving, rubbing the edges of it with his thumbs. His home, these days, seemed always to be filled with these oddly assorted young comrades.

Tanis, the quiet, seemingly young half-elf whose hazel eyes were alight now with good humor, seemed always to have been here, though the old dwarf could remember a time when he wasn't.

Caramon, all six feet of him, had made it his life's duty to keep Flint's larder as empty as possible. Raistlin, thin and as cloaked in uneasy mystery as he was now cloaked by the shadows of the corner he habitually inhabited near the hearth, was often so silent that one almost forgot he was there. Almost . . .

And then there was Sturm, taller though slimmer than Raistlin's brawny twin. This one should have matched Caramon's high spirits flash for shine. But he did not. Too grim by half! Flint thought now, watching the young man working intently over his sword. The weapon must be as perfect as its master strove to be.

"Tas'll be back," Caramon said, yawning. "How far can he follow a bird, anyway?"

Tanis, quiet through most of the conversation, got to his feet and stretched. "Likely not far. It's what catches his eye after he's lost the bird that will keep him away." He smiled and shook his head. The kender's attention was like a feather on the wind. "Still, I don't doubt you're right, Caramon. This rain will be snow before morning. We're not done with winter yet, and Tas likes a warm fire and a good meal as well as anyone. I don't think Solace is going to have a chance to miss him before he's back."

"Miss him?" Raistlin left his seat by the fire and gave his brother a quick look and Tanis a dour smile. "He could be gone for a year and go unmissed around here. The hour is late. Are you coming, Caramon?"

Caramon nodded, bade his friends good night, and followed his brother from the room. Sturm was up and gone a moment later, and the house was silent but for the drumming rain on the roof.

Tanis poked up the fire in the hearth and poured himself a last cup of wine. He settled down on the floor next to Flint's chair and watched the flames dance.

"Talking wrens," he said, after a time. "I think it was more boredom and restlessness. I can understand that. It has been a long winter."

Flint snorted. "Long winters are fine, peaceful things when they're not plagued by kender."

"And old dwarves are solemn, grim creatures when they've no kender to be plagued with. You've had little enough to say tonight, Flint."

"I've been working, and listening to your chatter."

Tanis eyed the little carving still nestled in Flint's hands. He reached for it, asking permission with a questioning smile. Flint reluctantly gave it over.

Tanis always met Flint's work with his hands first. "Know what it is with your hands," the old dwarf had taught him, "before you see what it is with your eyes."

Now the half-elf traced the careful detail, the artful

evocation of wing and feather. "Nice. A wren, is it?"

With a scowl he hoped was forbidding, Flint snatched the wooden bird away. "Don't you have a home to go to? Off with you now, and let me get some sleep."

Tanis rose gracefully and dropped a hand to his old friend's shoulder. "Well, get some then, and don't spend the night worrying about Tas. He'll be fine."

"Worry? Not me! Not unless it's to worry about the person who is luckless enough to encounter him on his bird chase. Talking wrens, indeed. As likely as finding a kender with a brain that works. Good night, Tanis."

Tanis grinned. "Good night, Flint."

The hard, hollow scent of the cat's hunger filled the small cottage now. There was murder in the golden tabby's eyes.

You can't be nearly as hungry as I am, cat! the squirrel thought resentfully. Or at least he hoped not. The cat had killed a third time just as the setting sun's orange light gilded the windowsill. It was full dark now, and the squirrel was glad that clouds and rain hid the moons tonight. Lunitari's light might remind him too much of blood.

I'm so hungry! And so thirsty! If that cat knocks the cage off this table to get at me, I don't know if I'll have the strength to run. Then I'd really be up a tree. . . .

Almost the squirrel laughed. He wished he *were* up a tree, curled all safe and warm, his nose tucked into his thick gray tail. With a nice fire blazing in the hearth.

Hearth?

The squirrel shook himself and whipped his tail over his head. Where had that strange thought come from? What he really wanted was a nice leaf-lined nest, a hearty cache of nuts to nibble on from time to time, a little water from the puddles on the ground . . . *and some eggs and cheese, a little fresh bread and new honey . . .* He wondered if hunger was making him lose his wits. He wondered, too, when the man would return to feed him and the cat.

The cat leaped onto the table again, rubbing against the bars and making an ominous rumbling sound in his throat. The squirrel could smell dead mice on the tabby's breath.

Cat, he ventured, *you look like you need a nap.*

I've been napping all day, squirrel.

You've been eating all day.

I wouldn't mind eating all night.

The squirrel sniffed then and bared his teeth. *Be fair, cat! You've eaten every poor little mouse who was foolish enough to come into this cottage. I haven't had a thing to eat since I got locked up in this horrible cage. And I don't think you'd find me very palatable—I'll be skin and bones before morning.*

Bones, anyway, the cat purred, *if I have my way.*

He'll be back soon, he will.

He might be. Sometimes he stays away for days at a time.

The squirrel felt his belly rub up against his ribs. Days! Days in this dreadful cage with no food, no water, and a hungry cat! He had to get out!

He'd no sooner had the thought than the cat lifted his head, ears cocked, and glided silently across the table and to the floor. Man-scent filled the air; booted footsteps sounded outside the door. Twitching and trembling, the squirrel rose onto his hind legs. He smelled food!

The man had food, indeed, but he took his time about passing it out. He kicked off his boots at the door, sloughed cold rain from his black robes, and complained in his deep, rumbling voice about how the rain would soon turn to snow, and about some wren that couldn't be found.

Wren? The wren . . . The squirrel wanted to think about the wren, he knew he *should* be thinking about the wren, that the wren was somehow important to him. But all he could manage to concentrate on was the man as he went about poking up the fire in the cold hearth and dropping, from time to time, terrified mice from some hidden pocket in his robe.

To the man's great amusement, the cat promptly dispatched the first mouse, took his time with the second, and only knocked the third one witless.

Saving it for later no doubt, the squirrel thought sourly. He smelled acorns, bitter and likely woody and thin. All his patience fell away. Chattering furiously, berating the man for his cavalier attitude toward his starving condition, he threw himself against the wooden bars.

"Ah! Yes, yes, I was getting around to it, noisy one." The man reached into a pocket and pulled out a handful of winter-dull acorns. Dark eyes coldly alight in a craggy face, he slid them, one by one, into the cage.

Getting around to it! Getting around—! The squirrel dove for the acorns. He lashed his tail here and there, stopped once or twice to glare up at the man, and finally managed to get the nuts all into a pile.

"Hungry, eh!" the man said. There was a hard light in his black eyes that made the squirrel even angrier.

Hungry? Oh, yes, you hind end of a mule! I'm hungry! I'm starving! And I've had to spend all day trapped in here with that murderous villain of a cat!

The cat snarled and twitched the tip of his tail. Enjoying both the tabby's reaction and the squirrel's anger, the man laughed and stuck his finger between the bars of the cage to taunt the squirrel some more.

Gleefully, the squirrel sunk his sharp little teeth into

the soft flesh of the finger. He almost didn't care that his brains were nearly rattled out of his head when the man's fist knocked the cage into the wall.

Caramon was certain that if it had been Tanis who'd heard the wren's cry for help, or Raistlin, or Sturm, packs would have been out, provisions gathered, and swords and bows checked for readiness. As it was, he was the one the wren had chosen to cry to this time, and Flint was not having any of his story.

"But, I tell you," Caramon insisted, "I *heard* it!"

Flint sighed. He had been listening to this tale all morning, and he was growing more than a little tired of it. "Have done, now, won't you? It was barely a decent joke when Tas tried it."

The brawny youth was not noted for his patience or for any great skill at cunning or strategy in matters other than martial. But his instincts were often good, and they served him well now. He took a long breath, clamped his teeth down on the loud protest he'd meant to make, and poured another cup of ale. He looked around the deserted inn, heard only Otik in the kitchen, and sighed heavily.

"Flint, listen," he said in what he hoped was a calm and reasoning manner. "I was the first to laugh at Tas. I was still laughing at him last night. I'm not laughing this morning, because I heard the wren."

"The gods know," Flint muttered, "I will be more than glad when winter is over. You youngsters are like colts chasing the wind these days; you hear the call to run in every stray breeze."

"Flint, the bird was asking for help. That's what Tas said, and off he went. He's been gone for three days. And now the bird is back."

"And you can tell one wren from another, can you?"

Caramon could not keep the mischief from his grin.

"When they speak, I can."

"Hah! You're starting to sound like your brother now."

That stopped the young man short, left him wondering to what he must reply now: Flint's implied insult (though he wasn't quite certain that he *had* been insulted), or the dwarf's still patent disbelief. He was spared the need for any retort when the door to the inn swung slowly open.

"Caramon, I think you'd better find your brother."

Sturm's was not the voice to which Caramon responded. He heard, and from the corner of his eye he could see that Flint had, too, the small piping of the wren. She rode Sturm's wrist with serene confidence. The late morning light glinted along a chain of tiny gold links around her neck.

Help! Oh! Help!

All the morning's trial of disbelief was worth that one moment, Caramon thought as he bolted for the door, worth that one, stunned look on the old dwarf's face. Laughing, he clattered down the wooden steps from the inn built high in the mighty vallenwood to the bridgewalks.

Around the town women looked up from their washing and baking, merchants abandoned their customers to run to windows, and children came flying from their games, all wondering what it was that caused the big youth's bellowing summons of his brother and his friend Tanis Half-Elven.

When the squirrel awoke he was confused. He slept a lot, it being still winter and he having some deeply rooted *need* to sleep. But when he slept he dreamed. And there was the source of his confusion: no squirrel ever dreamed during long winter sleeps. And, as though the fact of the dreaming wasn't enough, the dreams themselves were decidedly odd.

He dreamed about people. Not the gray-furred, broad-tailed squirrel people. Humans walked in his dreams, and a dwarf, and a long-eyed half-elf with hair the color of a fox's pelt. In his dreams he knew who they were; sometimes he spoke with them and they with him. And when they spoke with him he knew—though he didn't quite understand how he knew—that they were not speaking to a squirrel.

It was almost as though he were having someone else's dreams.

Yawning now, stretching first his hind legs and then his front, he poked among the neatly piled acorn shells for some left-over tidbit. There was none.

He looked around the cottage, noted that the man was gone again, though his scent still clung to everything in the place, and then felt a sudden tightening of alarm: the cat prowled restlessly from window to door to window.

Not hungry again, are you?

Always, the cat murmured without looking around. *You sleep a lot, squirrel. He's off again, looking for the wren.*

The wren . . . Yes, well, I'd like to find her myself. I think I might have some unfinished business with her.

The tabby did look around then, his green eyes alight with a certain careful curiosity. *With the wren? And what business might that be?*

The squirrel wasn't sure, and said so. Again he felt confused and uncomfortable. He remembered thinking the night before that the wren meant something to him. Now, though, when he tried to recall what it might be, he could not. His attempts to remember were as distressing as his dreams had been.

The cat padded silently across the room and leaped easily onto the table. When the squirrel scolded and skittered to the back of his cage, the tabby only yawned and smiled.

Easy, squirrel, easy. He eyed the squirrel closely, and this time the squirrel had the impression that he was not being considered as dinner. After a moment the tabby twitched his tail and murmured, *I thought—maybe—but I suppose not. You're just a squirrel, aren't you?*

I—I guess so, responded the squirrel, *though sometimes I don't quite feel like one. Maybe it's just that I'm trapped in here, and I hate it. I should be grateful, I suppose, that there are bars between you and me, you being as hungry as you are all the time—oh! Well, I didn't mean any offense, of course—*

Of course, the cat murmured.

I didn't really, but you are a cat and I am a squirrel, and you cats do have a taste for squirrels from time to time and—

I am not a cat.

What? Well, of course you are. You're a cat, I can assure you. And you'd have a hard time convincing the mice you terrorize around here that you aren't.

I am not a cat. The tabby raised his head, and for the first time the squirrel noticed a small collar of braided leather clasped loosely around his neck. *Do you see that?*

The collar? Very nice.

Aye, the cat sighed, *it is, and so I thought when she gave it to me.*

She? Who?

The wren.

The wren. The squirrel was beginning to have a headache. He closed his eyes and burrowed his nose into his front paws. *Cat, I don't know what you're talking about.*

No, like as not you don't, being a squirrel.

And one who is too confused to worry about wrens and collars.

The tabby purred softly. *What confuses you, little one?*

Dreams, the squirrel sighed.

Dreams . . . The cat cocked his head. *Dreams?*

Yes, dreams. And squirrels aren't supposed to dream. I know that. I know that because I'm a squirrel. But I still dream.

And yet, the cat said, *you wear nothing.*

The squirrel blew his cheeks out indignantly. *Of course not, or nothing but my skin. And that only because there's a cage between you and me. What else am I supposed to wear?*

You'd be wearing something if you were more than a squirrel. The wren wears a golden chain. I wear a collar. It keeps us, despite your form, what we are.

The squirrel's headache was getting worse. *I don't understand.*

I am a man. My name is Pytr. The wren is a woman whose name is, well, Wren. Pytr stretched lazily, then curled up on the table next to the cage. It was a long tale he had to tell, and he thought he might as well be comfortable. It had begun to snow again, and the day was waning. He was hungry and restless and worried. It helped a little to have someone to tell his story to, even if it was only a squirrel with a headache.

. . . And so, the wren sighed, *when I wouldn't agree, when I refused to forsake Pytr for him, the mage laid an enchantment upon us both. "Wren," he said,* and she fluttered her wings a little, a small shudder, *"Wren you are called and wren you shall be." And—and Pytr he made into a cat. Then I escaped. I flew far and came to Solace where I found the little kender who heard me and came to help. And now the*

mage has him, too.

Oh, is there no way you can help us?

On the strength of that tale, Wren had led them far and long, flying ahead and darting back, making sure the five did not deviate from the way. All of her small strength was for leading, for bringing help. She had none to talk and so, though Caramon wondered and Sturm speculated, Tanis and Raistlin agreed that greater detail must be garnered later when Wren had recouped her strength. Flint neither speculated nor wondered. He feared. And, since he did not like to show it, he hid his fear behind a spate of grumbling in which stone-headed kender played a large part. He fooled no one.

They followed her through all of the snowy day and as much of the night as they could. When camp was made, Wren dropped again to her perch on Sturm's wrist. She was comfortable there, sensing a steadiness and kindness in the young man that gave her confidence. She only gripped him lightly and tucked her head beneath her stippled wing as though to rest.

"Wren," Sturm said gently. "Wren?"

She looked up, weary with flying and fear, and cocked her head.

"What happened to the kender, Wren?"

The squirrel was unharmed when I saw him last.

Sturm frowned, puzzled. They heard Wren's voice as a bird's song with their ears, but in their minds they heard the soft, gentle voice of a woman. This, at times, could be confusing. But Sturm suddenly understood Wren's reply when he heard Raistlin's dry, whispered laugh.

"What else?" the young mage asked. "What else would you make a kender? This mage, whoever he may be, understands kender as well as any it seems."

He's caged the squirrel. It amuses him, I think, as it

amused him to make a cat of Pytr and a bird of me.

Tanis winced at that. Flint growled low in protest. The soul of a kender caged or bound would wear the bruised colors of misery. "Who is this mage, Wren?"

Rieve is his name.

Raistlin lifted his head then, the way a man who scents smoke on the wind does. Tanis glanced at him. Caramon, silent till then, sat forward.

"Raist?" Caramon said, his hand moving reflexively to the hilt of his sword lying scabbarded at his feet. "You've heard of this mage?"

"He has an evil reputation, this Rieve. I've heard of him." Raistlin smiled slowly then, humorlessly, as though he understood the question his twin hesitated to ask. "But you need have no fear, brother mine. Though I would be foolish indeed if I did not acknowledge that Rieve's skills are greater than mine might be now, I think he has gone so far in his cruelty that he has given me a weapon against him."

"A weapon?" Tanis asked.

Raistlin's pale blue eyes glittered. Had there been light from the moons that night, its wash across the new snow would have been as cold. "A weapon. Or perhaps four."

But though they pressed him, the young mage only settled back into the warmth of his cloak and did not answer further. He stared into the fire.

As Tanis set the night watches he wondered what weapons Raistlin might be forging out of the silence and the flame.

Pytr knew that the squirrel was in trouble. This was not, he realized, a squirrel after all. The dreams said that. But what he might be, Pytr did not know. He did know, however, that whatever the squirrel might have been before now would fade and vanish one day.

———

191

With no piece of his real self to cling to, whoever he might have been, he would wake, dreamless, to find that he was indeed a squirrel. And likely, Pytr thought with a cold shudder, he would never know that there had been a time when he wasn't.

Come, squirrel, tell me your name.

My name? Squirrel, I guess.

No, tell me your real name. I don't think you are truly a squirrel. What is your real name?

I don't know.

Think, won't you?

The squirrel tried, but thinking only made his head throb worse. *Let it go, cat—Pytr. I think I'll nap.*

I don't think you should.

Why? Maybe I'll dream again, maybe . . .

Ah! The dreams. Pytr purred softly, nudged the squirrel through the bars, and managed to ignore the cat-hunger that reminded him just how tasty a squirrel could be. *Don't sleep, squirrel. Talk to me, eh? Tell me, how did he catch you?*

Right outside the door. The squirrel sighed. *Right outside the door.*

That's why I thought you were really a squirrel. I didn't see him change you. I thought—well, I'm sorry, but I thought you were dinner.

I can understand how you would. But I still think I am.

Dinner?

No. A squirrel. I don't remember being "changed." I think I've always been a squirrel.

Squirrels don't dream, remember?

Maybe crazy squirrels do.

No, no, you're not crazy, squirrel. Pytr made a sound low in his throat that might have been a chuckle. *You're not crazy.*

The squirrel looked up then, and Pytr thought he

saw the light of some memory shine in his black eyes.

Not crazy—stone-headed.

What?

A stone-headed . . . something. That's what he always calls me. I don't think he really means it, but that's what he always calls me.

Pytr purred his satisfaction. *Who? Who calls you that?*

But the light and the memory were gone. The squirrel curled up again, nose to tail, and sighed heavily. *I don't know. I can't remember. Won't you let me sleep now, Pytr? I need to sleep. It's winter. I need to sleep.*

Poor squirrel, Pytr thought. He slipped from the table and crossed the room to the hearth. He didn't see any way he could help, though he badly wanted to.

Rieve, he thought, growling at the moonless night and wondering if there were any mice to be had, *you are going to have so much to pay for.*

There was a certain elegance about Raistlin's plan. Tanis acknowledged it with a grin.

"What do you want us to do, Raistlin?"

"Eat."

Tanis frowned. "What?"

"Eat. Eat everything you can, all the provisions we brought along." The young mage's lips twisted in a wry smile. "That should be no trial for my brother, but everyone should eat until he is full."

"But—"

"Don't debate with me, Tanis. I know what I'm doing. But, I will tell you why. These are not the shapes of animals that you will be taking on. You will *be* these creatures. And the primary need of an animal in winter is to be sure that his belly is full. If that need is not satisfied, all of your other purposes will fall aside. You will have, to a degree, your own minds, but not your own bodies, nor your own instincts. And instinct to an animal is what your mind is to you. Do you understand?"

Tanis did, and he was not certain now that the plan was quite so elegant. "Raistlin, I—"

The young mage raised an eyebrow, offered a mild challenge. "Afraid, Tanis?"

"I'd be a fool if I wasn't."

"Yes, you would be. What does it come down to, then? Can you trust me? You'll have to answer that. For yourself and for the others. They will do what you ask of them."

Tanis knew that this was true. It had been proved many times before now. He looked away from the young mage to where his friends sat near the morning's dying fire. Caramon, he thought, would not require convincing. He trusted his twin completely. Sturm, speaking quietly with Wren who yet rode his wrist, could be made to understand. But Flint? There would be a problem. The old dwarf disliked and mistrusted anything that had to do with magic.

As though he heard the half-elf's thought, Raistlin leaned forward and spoke quietly. "Let Flint be the first. I'll do it quickly, before he knows."

"Why?"

"If you give him a chance to argue, we could be here until the day after tomorrow."

Tanis smiled without humor. It was true. "He'll be all right?"

"He'll be fine. You all will be. They trust you, Tanis. Do you trust me?"

Trust was a habit, gained slowly and lost quickly. The habit of trusting Raistlin was still on him, despite the unease Tanis felt now. "I trust you."

"Good. Then go tell them to eat. The last thing we need is one of us turning on another out of hunger.

Most particularly," he said, smiling as though over some private jest, "my brother."

I trust you, Tanis thought as he rose to leave, but you do make it hard sometimes.

Raistlin was kind with his choices. And kind in other matters. Tanis knew that when he saw the young mage step silently behind Flint as though the old dwarf was the last thing on his mind. The air around the two shivered, sighed softly, and before Tanis could draw a breath, Flint was gone.

In his place stood a dog who shook himself as though shaking off rain. Tanis grinned. This was no lean-shanked mongrel, but a broad-chested, thick-furred shepherd's dog. Though the dog's muzzle was white with invading age, his long, tapered jaws were still powerful. Those jaws, Tanis knew, could tear the throat out of a marauding wolf. Or, under noble restraint, could lift a kitten carefully by the scruff of its neck to carry it out of harm's way. It was to this breed that shepherds had trusted their flocks and their families for generations.

Right now, though, Flint the dog looked dangerous. Ears back, he snarled and bared long teeth made for slashing.

Wren left Sturm's wrist and dropped to the ground before the dog. She whispered something that sounded like encouragement and the snarling faded to a familiar low grumbling. As he'd planned with Raistlin, Tanis dropped to his knee beside the dog—*Flint!* he reminded himself—and tied around his neck a bright blue square of cloth torn from the spare shirt in the dwarf's pack. There was a look in the shepherd dog's eyes that made Tanis glad he resisted the urge to ruffle the silky ears.

Caramon drew a breath to speak—to laugh or question, Tanis didn't know—and suddenly a tawny panther, muscles rippling, tail switching restlessly, stood where once Raistlin's twin had sat.

Well done! Tanis thought. Across the panther's thick chest and shoulders he strapped Caramon's belt in the form of a harness. He looked around for Sturm but saw neither the young man nor a beast to which he might have been changed.

"Raistlin?"

The mage pointed upward to the trees. A black-headed, gray-bodied peregrine falcon sounded a long, high wail and spread its wings with unconscious grace.

He knows them, Tanis thought, he knows them well to choose so fittingly. He offered his wrist, and the falcon glided down, gripping with sharp talons.

"Easy, Sturm, easy!"

The grip relaxed a little; when the falcon lowered his head Tanis slipped a tightly knotted thong and the signet ring from which Sturm was never parted over the peregrine's head.

"Only one left, Tanis," Raistlin said softly.

"I'm ready."

Raistlin met the half-elf's eyes and held them. "I'll be with you," he assured. "I'll be right with you to bring you back."

"I know."

Once more the air shivered, then sighed. Raistlin was alone in the clearing with Wren, the shepherd dog, the panther, the bright-eyed falcon, and a quick, red-pelted fox.

"What else?" Raistlin said to Wren when she cocked her head as though to question his choice. "A fast and far hunter." He collared the fox with another square of cloth, this garnered from Tanis's pack, and sat back on his heels. "Follow the wren and the hunt well, fox. Use all your cunning. And remember, do not harm the mage, for I can only undo those spells of my own working."

Pytr smelled danger in the wind. Rieve, back since the afternoon from another fruitless search for Wren, brooded darkly before the fire. The danger smell did not come from him. In him Pytr noted only the hard, bitter scent of anger. This smell was different. It was a combination of odors, woven together to send a fearful message of disparate creatures banded for some common purpose. Dog, he smelled—and fox. Pytr lifted his head and caught the scent of a bird, large and bold and bright: a deadly raptor. Over them all rode the thick, musky scent of a far-removed cousin; a mountain panther prowled near. They hunted, their scents told him, but they were not hungry.

In the cage on the table the squirrel roused and sniffed the air.

Cat! Pytr! Do you smell it?

I do. The scent of enemies.

Enemies? The squirrel's tail danced. Yes, these were the scents of enemies. And yet the dream from which he'd just woken was not one of enemies.

Cat—Pytr, I thought when I was dreaming that I scented friends.

Pytr's tail switched impatiently, then slowed to a considering wave. *Friends?*

Well, it's hard to explain. It's . . . I smell the dog and the fox, the falcon and the panther. And my nose tells me to be afraid. But . . . in my mind I don't see the beasts the smells are supposed to show me. I . . . I don't know how else to explain it.

Pytr wondered then if maybe the squirrel *was* crazy. He sighed and left his place by the window. He gave Rieve wide berth and leaped to the table. *What do you see in your dreams, then, squirrel?*

I don't know. I don't see anything that I can tell you about for sure. I just don't see a dog. Or a fox, or the rest of them. What about the man?

Rieve? He's nose-blind, like all his kind.

The squirrel sighed. *I don't know how I know this, Pytr, being a squirrel as I am, but I have a feeling that friends are coming.*

The long, eerie howl of a dog cascaded through the night. The hackles rose on the back of Pytr's neck. A fox's sharp yipping followed, and a falcon wailed high, then low. The panther was silent, but Pytr knew he was near.

Pytr rose, back arched, tail swollen to nearly the width of the squirrel's. Rieve was on his feet, his back to the fire. His fear scent, sour and urgent, filled the room.

Let us hope, squirrel, that these are friends, indeed. Though if they are, I will tell you now that you have some very strange friends for a squirrel.

Part of the squirrel agreed completely. Another part, however, the part that dreamed memories he knew he shouldn't have, laughed happily.

The falcon descended on a dropping air current and caught the tree's bare branch neatly to perch. He spread his wings, his dark eyes flashing, and screamed an imperious challenge.

Sturm! the fox thought, stretching his sharp-toothed jaws in a grin of acknowledgement. Behind him he heard the shepherd dog, Flint, just drifting down the hill. That path would take him right into the cottage's dooryard, shadowed now by night and trees. To his left and ahead, around the far side of the cottage, rumbled the low growl of the panther. Caramon was in place. It occurred to the fox—Tanis—that it was a very good thing that Caramon had eaten well before the change.

The fox tested the air carefully, identified the scents of his companions and of those within the cottage. Man-scent was strong, and so was the smell of cat and squirrel.

Squirrel. His mouth began to water in spite of himself. Squirrels, he knew from some heretofore untapped well of information, tasted nearly as good as rabbits. Tanis shuddered and shook himself.

He caught man-scent again, this time from a hill behind him. That scent he knew well, though he had only recently come to recognize it: Raistlin. Light and sweet, the small scent of a wren hovered near. All were in position.

Wren, he whispered, though to any who heard it might only have been the soft pant of a fox pausing to rest in his night hunting.

Here, here.

You know what to do?

Yes. I'm ready.

Go, then!

She stitched the night air gracefully, darting from the bushes where Raistlin was concealed, down through the shadows pooled beneath the trees near the cottage door where Flint crouched ready.

The panther, Caramon, had silenced his ominous rumbling, but Tanis scented him closer now and knew he was prowling, ghost-silent, along the side of the house. Above him the falcon took wing and landed on the roof above the door. Tanis caught his breath; had he seen the falcon anywhere he would have known him for Sturm by the proud lift of his head.

Wren alighted on the windowsill and fluttered her wings against the glass. In the voice of the bird she piped and lamented. She might only have been some night-caught creature seeking shelter.

A shadow crossed the glass. Tanis heard an indrawn breath. Man-scent rose on the air, stronger now. The panther's green eyes glittered dangerously in the light spilling from the window. It seemed to Tanis, with his heightened sense of smell, that Rieve must know what waited outside his door.

Wren left the sill, flew to the door, and came near to hitting Flint where he waited in the shadows.

Rieve's shadow left the window, vanished, then fell to block the line of light leaking from beneath the door. A red ghost in the night, Tanis glided down the hill, keeping to the shadows until he was aligned with Flint at the opposite side of the door. He heard the sound of the latch being lifted.

"Wren," a cold voice said from within. "So, you've returned?"

Yes! she piped. *Oh, please let me in!*

"Of course, little one, of course." There was silky threat in the mage's voice. "You've reconsidered?"

Yes! Only let me in! Please!

The door opened quickly, orange light spilled out into the night, and Wren shot past the mage like a small brown comet. He turned, then fell, breathless beneath the weight of a large black shepherd dog and a slim red fox.

The mage kicked hard at the fox and sent it tumbling across the floor. Before he could move to rise, however, the dog's teeth clamped onto his shoulder. Behind him the cat hissed and the caged squirrel scolded and chattered. He brought up his knee and drove it into the dog's stomach. Snarling, the beast fell away.

Rieve scrambled to his feet, kicked again at the dog, and missed. He spun toward the door and came eye to razor-sharp beak with a dark-eyed falcon.

"No!" he shouted, flinging up an arm to protect his eyes. The falcon's talons raked along the back of his hand. "No!"

As though in response to his protest, the falcon darted away, lifting high to take perch on the mantel. Rieve drew a shuddering breath and stumbled again to the door. A heavy, tawny paw hit him hard in the chest and dropped him where he stood. The panther's fangs shone like daggers in the fire's glow.

Standing at the panther's shoulder, one hand on the mountain cat's broad golden head, another extended in a parody of greeting, stood a light-eyed, pale young mage. His cold smile awoke a fear in Rieve that even the panther's gleaming fangs had not.

Rieve moaned. He wondered if he would have time to prepare for death.

Animals were turning into people all around him, and the squirrel didn't know where to look first. The falcon, that beautiful bird, became a tall, dark-haired young man. There was still something of the falcon's brooding about him. The squirrel thought that it must always have been this way. The fox, limping from having been kicked half-way across the cottage, was no fox at all but a red-haired half-elf who leaned against the wall, holding ribs that must truly hurt from the look in his long eyes.

The dog . . . ah, the dog! The squirrel almost knew that he would be a dwarf, brown-bearded and grumbling about a sore stomach even before he was changed.

There remained only the panther, crouched over Rieve, his heavy paw still planted firmly in the middle of the mage's chest. The slight young man scratched the big cat's ears idly, smiling as though he had only dropped in for a cup of something warm to take the chill out of the night.

"Four more changes we need, friend Rieve," the

young man murmured. "I will effect one after you effect three."

Rieve panted something, and the squirrel thought it must be hard getting enough air to speak with the panther leaning so heavily on him.

"Do I take that for agreement?"

"Do I—do I have a choice?" Rieve asked sourly.

"Well, yes. We always have choices. Yours, however, are limited."

Rieve swallowed hard, recognized the limits, and nodded. The squirrel flashed his tail and scurried around in his cage.

Cat! Pytr! Watch! Watch! They're going to do more changes! Pytr? Pytr, where are you?

Pytr was gone. Or the cat was gone, anyway, replaced by a stocky, golden-haired man who wore around one wrist a slim bracelet of braided leather.

And the wren, who had clung so fearfully to the edge of the table near the squirrel's cage during the whole splendid attack only moments ago, was gone as well. Instead, a small, pretty girl, her hair the color of the wren's brown feathers, rested her hand on the cage.

"One more," she said, "And this, perhaps, the most important."

The panther, of course, the squirrel thought. *He looks fierce enough to eat the mage for dinner and still come away hungry. They'll change the panther next.*

But to the squirrel's surprise, the panther remained a panther, rumbling and growling deep inside his broad chest. The girl leaned over his own cage and undid the latch. She gathered him carefully into her hands and lifted him out.

No more cage! As though he hadn't breathed in days, the squirrel drew in a lungful of air and leaped from the girl's hands. He could smell the sweet night air. He could taste it, and it tasted like freedom.

The girl cried out, the dark-haired young man shouted something, and the half-elf leaped to kick the door shut. But squirrels can make themselves very small. Sucking in all the air that he could, the squirrel dashed between the closing door and the jamb and plunged into the night. He'd had enough of men and beasts and cages. He wanted trees, cozy nests, and sweet caches of chestnuts. And he was going to have those now, no matter what they shouted inside. . . .

"Come *back* here, you stone-headed kender!"

Halfway up the closest tree the squirrel stopped, frozen by the dwarf's cry. Not crazy, he'd told Pytr, but stone-headed. Stone-headed . . . something. Stone-headed kender! Kender?

Something strange happened to the cold night air. It shivered, the way it does under summer's heat, and then it sighed, the sound of a small drifting breeze. The squirrel tried to breathe but found that he couldn't quite draw in the air he needed. Suddenly he lost his grip and tumbled to the ground.

Kender!

"And where, in the names of all the gods, did you think you were going?"

"I—" Tas got his legs under him and climbed to his feet. Some of the squirrel feeling was in him yet. He had to swallow hard to ignore the imperative to run from the dwarf. "I—don't know. I don't even really know how I got here, wherever here is. I was following the wren, I think, and . . . well, then I was here, falling out of this tree. But I think I remember some dreams . . . strange ones, about squirrels and cats and—"

Flint snorted and pulled the kender to his feet. For all his scowling, though, his hands were gentle. "Come on, now, back inside. You can be sure Caramon is getting hungry by now. And Raistlin has some work to do yet."

"But Caramon is always hungry," Tas said, dusting himself off. "What's so important about that—oh, the panther?"

Flint nodded. Tas, remembering Pytr's intense and always sharp cat-hunger, grinned slyly. He was not unhappy that Rieve must be learning even now what it meant to be the object of that hunger. "It's just a thought, Flint, but perhaps they could just feed Caramon whatever's lying around the cottage?"

In the end, though Tas had not been alone in his wistful wish, they did not feed Rieve to the panther. Some oath or promise was extracted from him, though what passed between him and Raistlin none ever learned, for Raistlin banished all but the big panther from the cottage. If Caramon heard or understood, he was uncharacteristically silent about it. And a week later, when those who had been cat and squirrel, wren and falcon, fox, dog, and panther were gathered in Solace, it was yet a matter for speculation.

Wren watched Raistlin, who sat in the shadows of Flint's hearth. "Were truth told, I'm not sure that I want to know."

"I wouldn't mind knowing," Pytr muttered. He stroked her hair and sighed. "I'd like to know with what coin Rieve's debt has been paid."

The young woman shook her head and smiled. Small and cheerful, her brown eyes bright now when she looked at Pytr, she was, Flint thought then, very like the wren for which she'd been named and which she had, for a time, been.

Tanis, who at that moment had the same thought, glanced once at the dwarf and, when he received a slight nod, crossed to the hearth and took up one of

Flint's small carvings.

"For you," he said, taking a seat next to Wren.

"But—what is it? Surely you've given us enough?"

"One more thing, but you must close your eyes now."

Curious, Sturm and Caramon leaned closer and Tas ducked under Pytr's arm to get a closer look. They saw nothing, however, for Tanis had the object hidden in closed hands. In the hearth's shadow, Raistlin stirred but did not rise to join his companions.

Wren closed her eyes, and Tanis placed the small object in her hands. "Now, this is something Flint has taught me: let your hands know what it is you hold before your eyes tell you. Our eyes, as we have lately learned, can too easily deceive us."

Wren let her fingers discover the wings first, then the carefully rounded back, the beak, and finally the deftly carved tail feathers. "A bird!" she cried. "A wren?"

A little breeze sighed, then wandered away.

Yet when she opened her eyes and saw the small carving, Wren wore a small, puzzled frown. "But . . . it *felt* like a wren. I don't understand."

Neither did Tanis. Nor did Flint. It was Tas, finally, who spoke.

"Flint! That's wonderful! That's the nicest miniature I've ever seen! When did you carve it?"

"I didn't," Flint said shortly. "I had nothing to do with this piece." He peered hard at the little carving and shook his head. It was Wren in every perfect detail, her soft hair pulled back low on her neck as it was now, her serene smile shown in lips and eyes, her hands quietly folded at her waist.

Flint shivered and looked across the room. Though he could not be sure, he thought he saw Raistlin smile from the hearth's shadow.

"Wanna Bet?"

Margaret Weis and Tracy Hickman

FOREWORD

(or Afterword, as the case may be)

"A fine mage you are little brother," muttered Tanin, standing on the dock, watching the ship sail away. "You should have known all along there was something strange about that dwarf!"

"Me?" Palin retorted. "*You* were the one that got us mixed up in the whole thing to begin with! 'Adventures always start in such places as this,' " the young magic-user said, mimicking his older brother's voice.

"Hey, guys," began Sturm in mollifying tones.

"Oh, shut up!" Both brothers turned to face him. "It was *you* who took that stupid bet!"

The three brothers stood glaring at each other; the salt breeze blowing the red curling hair of the two elder into their eyes and whipping the white robes of the younger about his thin legs.

A ringing shout, sounding over the dancing waters, interrupted them.

"Farewell, lads! Farewell! It was a nice try. Perhaps we'll do it again some day!"

"Over my dead body!" all three brothers muttered fervently, raising their hands and waving half-heartedly, sickly grins on their faces.

"That's *one* thing we can all agree on," said Sturm, beginning to chuckle. "And I know another." The brothers turned thankfully away from the sight of the sailing vessel lumbering through the waters.

"And that is . . . ?"

"That we never tell another living soul about this, as long as we live!" Sturm's voice was low. The other two brothers glanced about at the spectators standing on the docks. They were looking at the ship, laughing. Several, glancing at the brothers, pointed at them with stifled giggles.

Grinning ruefully, Tanin held his right hand out in front of him. Sturm placed his right hand on his brother's, and Palin put his right hand over the other two.

"Agreed," each said solemnly.

CHAPTER ONE

Dougan Redhammer

"Adventures always start in such places as this," said Tanin, regarding the inn with a satisfied air.

"You can't be serious!" Palin said, horrified. "I wouldn't stable my horse in this filthy place, let alone stay here myself!"

"Actually," reported Sturm, rounding the corner of the building after an inspection tour, "the stables are clean compared to the inn, and they smell a damn sight better. I say we sleep there and send the horses inside."

The inn, located on the docks of the seaside town of Sancrist, was every bit as mean and ill-favored in appearance as those few patrons the young men saw slouching into it. The windows facing the docks were small as though staring out to sea too long had given them a perpetual squint. Light from inside could barely filter through the dirt. The building itself was weather- and sand-blasted and crouched in the shadows at the end of the alley like a cutpurse waiting for his next victim. Even the name, The Spliced Jib, had an ominous sound.

"I expected Little Brother to complain," Tanin remarked sourly, dismounting and glaring at Sturm over the pommel of his saddle. "He misses his white linen sheets and mama tucking him in at night. But I expected better of you, Sturm Majere."

"Oh, I've no objection," Sturm said easily, sliding off his horse and beginning to untie his pack. "I was just making an observation. We don't have much choice anyway," he added, withdrawing a small leather pouch and shaking it. Where there should have been the ring of steel coins, there was only a dismal clunk. "No linen sheets tonight, Palin," he said, grinning at his younger brother, who remained seated disconsolately upon his horse. "Think of tomorrow night, though—staying at Castle Uth Wistan, the guests of Lord Gunthar. Not only white linen but probably rose petals strewn about the bed as well."

"I don't expect white linen," Palin returned, nettled. "In fact, bed sheets at all would be a pleasant change! And I'd prefer sleeping in a bed where the mattress wasn't alive!" Irritably, he scratched himself under the white robes.

"A warrior must get used to such things," Tanin said in his worldly wise Elder Brother voice that made Palin long to toss him in the horse trough. "If you are attacked by nothing worse than bedbugs on your first quest, you may count yourself lucky."

"Quest?" Palin muttered bitterly, sliding down off his horse. "Accompanying you and Sturm to Castle Uth Wistan so that you can join the knighthood. This isn't a quest! It's been like a kender outing, and both you and Father knew it would be when you decided I could go! Why, the most danger we've been in since we left home was from that serving wench who tried to cut off Sturm's ears with a butcher knife!"

"It was a mistake anyone could make," Sturm muttered, flushing. "I keep telling you!—I intended to grab her mugs. She was what you might call a buxom girl and, when she leaned over me, holding the tray, I wasn't exactly paying attention to what I was doing—"

"Oh, you were paying attention, all right!" Palin said grimly. "Even when she came at you with a knife, we had to drag you out of there! And your eyes were the size of your shield."

"Well, at least I'm interested in such things," Sturm said irritably. "Not like some people I could mention, who seem to think themselves too good—"

"I have high standards!" retorted Palin. "I don't tumble for every 'buxom' blonde who jiggles in my direction—"

"Stop it, both of you!" Tanin ordered tiredly. "Sturm, take the horses around and see that they're brushed down and fed. Palin, come with me."

Palin and Sturm both looked rebellious, and Tanin's tone grew stern. "Remember what Father said."

The brothers remembered. Sturm, still grumbling, grabbed the horses' reins in his hand and led them to the stables. Palin swallowed a barbed comment and followed his brother.

Although quick-tempered like his mother, Tanin appeared to have inherited few other qualities from his parents. Instead, he was in temperament more like the man in whose honor he had been named—his parent's dearest friend, Tanis Half-Elven. Tanin idolized his name-father and did his best to emulate his hero. Consequently, the twenty-four-year-old young man took his role as leader and elder brother quite seriously. This was fine with one younger brother. The fun-loving Sturm was almost the epitome of his father, having inherited Caramon's jovial, easy-going nature. Disliking to take responsibility himself, Sturm generally obeyed Tanin without question. But Palin, just twenty-one, possessed the keen mind and intellect of his uncle, the powerful, tragic archmage Raistlin. Palin loved his brothers, but he chafed under what he considered Tanin's overbearing leadership and was irritated beyond measure by Sturm's less than serious outlook on life.

This was, however, Palin's "first quest"—as Tanin never failed to remind him at least once an hour. A month had gone by since the young mage took the grueling Test in the Tower of High Sorcery in Palanthas. He was now an accepted member of the Order of Wizards on Krynn. But somehow that didn't satisfy him. He felt let down and depressed. For years, his greatest goal had been passing the Test, a goal that, once attained, would open countless doors.

It hadn't opened one. Oh, admittedly Palin was a young mage. He had little power yet, being able to cast only minor spells. Ideally, he would apprentice himself to some skilled archmage, who would take over his tutelage. But no archmage had requested his services, and Palin was shrewd enough to know why.

His uncle, Raistlin, had been the greatest wizard ever to have lived. He had taken the Black Robes of Evil and challenged the Queen of Darkness herself, intending to rule the world. An attempt that ended in his death. Though Palin wore the White Robes of Good, he knew that there were those in the Order who did not trust him and who, perhaps, never would. He carried his uncle's staff—the powerful Staff of Magius, given to him under mysterious circumstances in the Tower of High Sorcery at Palanthas. Rumors were already buzzing among the Conclave as to how Palin could have acquired the Staff. It had, after all, been locked in a room sealed with a powerful curse. No, whatever he accomplished, Palin knew deep within himself, he would accomplish as his uncle had—studying, working, and fighting alone.

But that was in the future. For the time being, he supposed, he must be content to travel with his brothers. His father, Caramon, who, with his own twin brother, Raistlin, had been a hero in the War of the Lance, was adamant on that point. Palin had never been out in the world. He'd been sheltered by his books, immersed in his studies. If he went on this journey to Sancrist, he was to submit to Tanin's authority, placing himself under his brothers' guidance and protection.

Palin swore a sacred oath to his father to obey his brothers, just as Tanin and Sturm swore to protect him. In point of fact, their deep love and affection for each other made the oath superfluous—as Caramon knew. But the big man was also wise enough to know that this first outing together would put a strain on brotherly love. Palin, the more intelligent of the brothers, was eager to prove himself—eager to the point of foolhardiness.

"Palin has to learn the worth of other people, to respect them for what they know, even if they're not as quick-thinking as he is," Caramon said to himself, remembering with regret the twin who had never learned that lesson. "And Sturm and Tanin have to learn to respect him, to realize that they can't solve every problem with a whack of their swords. Above all, they've got to learn to depend on each other!" The big man shook his head. "May the gods go with them," he muttered.

He was never to know the irony of that prayer.

It appeared, at the beginning of the journey, that none of these lessons was going to be learned easily. The two older boys had decided privately (certainly not mentioning this to their father) that this trip was going to "make a man" of their scholarly sibling.

But their views as to what constituted "manhood" didn't accord with Palin's. In fact, as far as he could see, "being a man" meant living with fleas, bad food, worse ale, and women of dubious character. Something Palin considered pointing out when Tanin muttered, "Act like a man!" out of the corner of his mouth as he and Palin entered the inn.

But Palin kept his mouth shut. He and his brothers were entering a strange inn, located in what was reputedly a rough part of Sancrist. The young mage had learned enough to know that their very lives might depend on presenting a unified front to the world.

This the brothers, despite their differences, managed quite successfully. So successfully, in fact, that they had met with no trouble whatsoever on the long trip northward from Solace. The two older brothers were big and brawny, having inherited Caramon's girth and strength. Experienced campaigners, they bore their battle scars proudly and wore their swords with practiced ease. The youngest, Palin, was tall and well-built, but it was the slender body of one accustomed to study rather than to wielding weapons. Any who might consider him an easy mark, however, could look into the young man's handsome, serious face, note the intense, penetrating gaze of the clear eyes, and think twice about interfering with him.

The Staff of Magius that Palin carried might have had something to do with this as well. Made of plain wood, adorned with a faceted crystal held fast in a dragon's claw made of gold, the staff gave no outward, visible sign of being magical. But there was a kind of dark, unseen aura around it, perhaps associated with its late master, that viewers invariably perceived with a sense of uneasiness. Palin kept the staff near him, always. If he wasn't holding it, the staff rested near him, and he often reached out to touch it reassuringly.

This night as on other nights, the sight of Tanin and Palin entering the inn did not particularly impress those within, except for one party. Seated at a grubby booth in a corner, this group immediately began to jabber among themselves, whispering and pointing. The whispering increased, growing even more excited, when Sturm came in and joined his brothers. Several members of the group nudged a figure who was sitting nearest the wall, his face hidden in deep shadows.

"Aye, I see, I see!" grumbled the figure. "You think they'll do, do you?"

The others at the table nodded and chattered among themselves enthusiastically. Smaller than the figure in the shadows, they were just as hidden. Muffled to the eyebrows in brown robes, their features and even their hands and feet were indistinguishable.

The figure in the corner gave the young men a shrewd, appraising scrutiny. The brown-robed creatures continued to jabber. "Shut up, you buggers," the figure growled irritably. "You'll attract their notice."

Those in the brown robes immediately hushed, falling into a silence so deep they might have all tumbled into a well. Naturally, this startling silence caused everyone in the common room of the inn to turn and stare at them, including the three young men.

"Now you've done it!" snarled the figure from the shadows. Two of the brown-robed creatures hung their heads, though a third seemed inclined to argue. "Be quiet! I'll handle this!" said the figure, getting to his feet.

Leaning forward into the light, he gave the three young men an amiable smile from the depths of a full, glossy black beard and, raising his mug, said cheerfully, "Dougan Redhammer, at your service, young gents. Will you take a drink with an old dwarf?"

"That we will, and with pleasure," Tanin said politely.

"Let me out," grunted the dwarf to the brown-robed creatures, who were so packed into the booth it was impossible to tell how many of them there might have been. With much groaning and swearing and "ouch, that's my foot, you widget-brain" and "mind my beard, gear-head," the dwarf emerged—somewhat

flushed and panting—from the back of the booth.
Carrying his mug and calling for the innkeep to bring
"my private stock," Dougan approached the table
where the young men were seated.

The others in the inn, sailors and local residents for
the most part, returned to their own conversations—
the subjects of which appeared to Palin to be of a sinister nature, judging from the grim and ill-favored
expressions on their faces. They had not welcomed the
brothers, nor did they seem interested in either the
dwarf or his companions. Several cast scowling
glances at Dougan Redhammer. This didn't disconcert
the dwarf in the least. Pulling up a high stool that
compensated for his short stature, the stout and flashily dressed (at least for a dwarf) Dougan plopped himself down at the brothers' table.

"What'll you have, gentlemen?" asked the dwarf.
"The spirits of my people? Ah, you're men of taste!
There's nothing better than the fermented mushroom
brew of Thorbardin."

Dougan grinned at the brothers expansively as the
innkeeper shuffled to the table, carrying three mugs in
his hand. Putting these down, he thumped a large clay
bottle stoppered with a cork down in front of the
dwarf. Dougan pulled the cork, inhaling the fumes
with a gusty sigh of contentment that caused Sturm's
mouth to water in anticipation.

"Aye, that's prime," said the dwarf in satisfaction.
"Hand your mugs round, gents. Don't be shy. There's
plenty for all and more where this came from. I don't
drink with strangers, though, so tell me your names."

"Tanin Majere, and these are my brothers, Sturm
and Palin," said Tanin, sliding his mug over willingly.
Sturm's was already in the dwarf's hand.

"I'll have wine, thank you," Palin said stiffly. Then
he added in an undertone, "You know how Father feels

about that stuff."

Tanin responded with an icy glare and Sturm laughed.

"Aw, loosen up, Palin!" Sturm said. "A mug or two of dwarf spirits never hurt anyone."

"Right you are there, lad!" said Dougan roundly. " 'Tis good for what ails you, my father was wont to say. This marvelous elixir'll mend broken head or broken heart. Try it, young wizard. If your father be the Hero of the Lance, Caramon Majere, then he lifted a glass or two in his day, if all the tales I've heard about him be true!"

"I'll have wine," Palin repeated, coldly ignoring his brothers' elbow-nudging and foot-kicking.

"Probably best for the young lad," said Dougan with a wink at Tanin. "Innkeep, wine for the youngster here!"

Palin flushed in shame, but there was little he could say, realizing he'd said more than enough already. Embarrassed, he took his glass and hunched down in his white robes, unable to look around. He had the feeling that everyone in the inn was laughing at him.

"So, you've heard of our father?" Tanin asked abruptly, changing the subject.

"Who hasn't heard of Caramon Majere, Hero of the Lance," said Dougan. "Here's to his health!" Lifting his mug, the dwarf took a long pull of the spirits, as did both Tanin and Sturm. When the three set the mugs down, there was no sound for the moment except slight gaspings for air. This was followed by three, satisfied belches.

"Damn good!" said Sturm huskily, wiping his streaming eyes.

"I've never had better!" Tanin swore, drawing a deep breath.

"Drink up, lad!" said the dwarf to Palin. "You'll

surely drink a toast to your own father, won't you?"

"Of course he will, won't you, Palin?" said Tanin, his voice dangerously pleasant.

Palin obediently took a sip of his wine, drinking to his father's health. After that, the others quickly ignored him, becoming absorbed in conversation about the parts of the world each had traveled recently and what was transpiring where. Palin, unable to take part in the conversation, fell to studying the dwarf. Dougan was taller than most dwarves the young man had known and, although he called himself "old," he couldn't have been much over one hundred years, an age considered to be just suitably mature for a dwarf. His beard was obviously his pride and joy; he stroked it often, never failing to draw attention to it when possible. Shining black, it grew thick and luxuriant, tumbling over his chest and down past his belt. His hair, too, was as black and curly as his beard, and he wore it almost as long. Like most dwarves, he was rotund and probably hadn't seen his feet below his round belly in years. Unlike most dwarves, however, Dougan was dressed in a flamboyant style that would have well become the Lord of Palanthas.

Outfitted in a red velvet jacket, red velvet breeches, black stockings, black shoes with red heels, and a silk shirt with puffy sleeves—a shirt that might once have been white but was now stained with dirt, spirits, and what may have been lunch—Dougan was an astonishing sight. He was remarkable, too, in other ways. Most dwarves are somewhat surly and withdrawn around members of other races, but Dougan was jovial and talkative and altogether the most engaging stranger the brothers had come across on their travels. He, in his turn, appeared to enjoy their company.

"By Reorx," said the dwarf admiringly, watching

Tanin and Sturm drain their mugs, "but you are lads after my own heart. It's a pleasure to drink with real men."

Sturm grinned. "There are not many who can keep up with us," he boasted, motioning the dwarf to pour the spirits. "So you better have a care, Dougan, and slow down."

"Slow down! Look who's talking!" The dwarf roared so loudly that all eyes in the common room turned on them, including the eyes of the small creatures in the brown robes. "Why, there isn't a human alive who can outdrink a dwarf with his own brew!"

Glancing at Sturm, Tanin winked, though he kept his face solemn. "You've just met two of them, Dougan Redhammer," he said, leaning back in his chair until it creaked beneath his weight. "We've drunk many a stout dwarf under the table and were still sober enough, Sturm and I, to guide him to his bed."

"And I," returned Dougan, clenching his fist, his face turning a fiery red beneath the black beard, "have drunk ten stout humans underneath the table and not only did I lead them to their beds but I put their night-clothes on them and tidied up their rooms to boot!"

"You won't do that to us!" vowed Tanin.

"Wanna bet?" roared the dwarf with a slight slur.

"A wager, then?" cried Sturm.

"A wager!" shouted Dougan.

"Name the rules and the stakes!" Tanin said, sitting forward.

Dougan stroked his beard thoughtfully. "I'll match you lads one on one, drink for drink—"

"Ha!" Sturm burst out laughing.

"—drink for drink," continued the dwarf imperturbably, "until your beardless chins hit the floor."

"It'll be your beard and not our chins that hits the floor, dwarf," Sturm said. "What stakes?"

Dougan Redhammer pondered. "The winner has the very great satisfaction of assisting the losers to their beds," he said, after a pause, twirling a long moustache around his finger.

"And loser pays the tabs for all," added Tanin.

"Done," said the dwarf, with a grin, holding out his hand.

"Done," said Tanin and Sturm together. Each shook Dougan's hand, then the dwarf turned to Palin, his hand outstretched.

"I want no part of this!" Palin said emphatically, glaring at his brothers. "Tanin," he said in a low voice, "think of our funds. If you lose, we—"

"Little Brother," Tanin interrupted, flushing in anger, "next journey, remind me to leave you home and bring along a cleric of Paladine! We'd get preached at less and probably have more fun."

"You have no right to talk to me that way—" Palin retorted.

"Ah, it must be all three of you," Dougan interrupted, shaking his head, "or the bet's off. There's no challenge in a dwarf outdrinking two humans. And it must be dwarf spirits. Why, the lad might as well be drinking his mother's milk as that elf water!" (*Elf water*—a name dwarves use for wine, which they can't abide.)

"I won't drink that—" Palin began.

"Palin"—Tanin's voice was stern and cold—"you are shaming us! If you can't have some fun, go to your room!"

Angrily, Palin started to rise, but Sturm caught hold of the sleeve of his robes.

"Aw, come on, Palin," his brother said cheerfully, "relax! Reorx's beard! Father's not going to walk through that door!" He tugged at Palin's sleeve until his brother slowly resumed his seat. "You've been studying too hard. Your brain's gone all cobwebby.

Here, try some. That's all we ask. If you don't like it, then we won't say any more about it."

Shoving a full mug over to his brother, Sturm leaned close and whispered in Palin's ear, "Don't make Tanin mad, all right? You know how he sulks, and we'll have to put up with him from here to Lord Gunthar's. Big Brother's got your own best interests at heart. We both do. We just want to see you have a little fun, that's all. Give it a try, huh?"

Glancing at Tanin, Palin saw that his brother's face was grim and unhappy. Maybe Sturm's right, Palin thought. Maybe I should relax and have some fun. Tanin was more than half serious when he said that about leaving me home. He's never talked that way before. It's just that I've been wanting them to take me seriously, to quit treating me like a kid. Maybe I *have* gone too far. . . .

Forcing a laugh, Palin lifted the mug. "To my brothers?" he said huskily, and was pleased to see Tanin's green eyes brighten and Sturm's face break into a broad grin. Putting the mug to his lips, Palin took a drink of the infamous brew known as dwarf spirits.

The taste wasn't bad. It was pleasant, in fact, a kind of dark and earthy flavor that brought visions of the dwarves' underground home of Thorbardin to his eyes. Rolling it on his tongue, Palin nodded in pleased surprise and swallowed. . . .

The young mage wondered suddenly if a fireball had exploded in his head. Flames shot through his mouth. Fire burst out his ears and nose, roared down his throat, and seared his stomach. He couldn't breathe, he couldn't see. He was going to die, he knew it . . . any moment . . . here, in this filthy, godforsaken tavern. . . .

Someone—Palin had the vague impression it was Sturm—was pounding him on the back and, at last, he was able to gasp for air.

"I do enjoy seeing a man enjoy his liquor," said Dougan seriously. "My turn now. A drink to the young mage!" Putting his mug to his lips, the dwarf tilted his head back and drained it in one long swallow. When he reappeared, his eyes were watery and his large, bulbous nose bright red. "Ahhh!" he breathed, blinking back his tears and wiping his mouth with the end of his beard.

"Hear, hear," cried both Sturm and Tanin, raising their mugs. "A drink to our brother, the mage!" They, too, drained their mugs, not quite as fast as the dwarf, but without stopping for breath.

"Thank you," said Palin, deeply moved. Cautiously, he took another gulp. The effect wasn't so awful the second time. In fact, it was pleasurable. Palin took another drink, then another, and finally drained the mug. Setting it down on the table amid cheers from his brothers and Dougan, the young man felt warm and good all over. His blood tingled in his veins. Tanin was looking at him with approval and pride, Sturm was filling his mug again. Dougan downed two more mugs in a row, Sturm and Tanin drank theirs, and then it was Palin's turn. He lifted the mug to his lips. . . .

Palin was smiling and he couldn't quit smiling. He loved Tanin and Sturm better than anyone else in the world, and he told them so, until he broke down and cried on Sturm's broad shoulder. But no! There was someone else he loved—that was the dwarf. He staggered to his feet and went round the table to shake the dwarf's hand. He even made a speech. Fast friends . . . firm friends, like his father and his father's friend . . . old Flint, the dwarf . . . He went back to his chair, only there seemed to be four chairs now, instead of just one. Picking one, Palin sat down, missed and would have ended up on the floor if Tanin hadn't caught him. He drank another mug, watching his brothers and his new friend with tears of affection streaming down his face.

"I tell you, lads"—Dougan's voice seemed to Palin to come from a long distance away—"I love you like my own sons. And I must say I think you've had a wee bit more to drink than you can handle."

"Naw!" Sturm cried indignantly, pounding his hand on the table.

"We can keep up with you," Tanin muttered, breathing heavily, his face beefy red.

"Damnrigh'," said Palin, striking the table—or he would have if the table hadn't suddenly and unaccountably leaped out of the way.

And then Palin was lying on the floor, thinking this was an interesting place to be, much safer than up there in four chairs, with tables jumping. . . . Glancing around blearily, he saw his staff on the floor beside him. Reaching out, he caressed it lovingly.

"Shirak!" he slurred, and the crystal atop the staff burst into light. He heard some commotion at this; high, shrill voices jabbering and chattering somewhere in the background. Palin giggled and couldn't quit giggling.

From somewhere up above, he heard Dougan's voice come floating down to him. "Here's to our beds," said the dwarf, "and a sound night's sleep!" And if there was a sinister note in the gruff voice or more than a trace of triumphant laughter, Palin discounted it. The dwarf was his friend, a brother to him. He loved him like a brother, his dear brothers . . .

Palin laid his head on the floor, resting his cheek on the staff's cool wood. Shutting his eyes, he slipped away into another world—a world of small creatures in brown robes, who lifted him up and ran away with him. . . .

———

by Margaret Weis and Tracy Hickman

CHAPTER TWO

A Really Bad Hangover

The world heaved and shivered, and Palin's stomach heaved and his skin shivered in agreement, misery loving company. Rolling over on his side, he was violently sick, and he wondered as he lay on whatever it was he was lying on—he couldn't open his eyes to see, they felt all gummed together—how long it would take him to die and end this suffering.

When he could be sick no more and when it seemed that his insides might actually stay inside, Palin lay back with a groan. His head was beginning to clear a little, and he realized suddenly, when he tried to move, that his hands were tied behind his back. Fear shot through his muzzy brain, its cold surge blowing away the mists of the dwarf spirits. He couldn't feel his feet, and he dimly knew that cords tied around his ankles had cut off his circulation. Gritting his teeth, he shifted his position slightly and wiggled his toes inside his soft leather boots, wincing as he felt the tingling of returning blood.

He was lying on a wooden plank, he noticed, feeling it beneath him with his hands. And there was a peculiar motion to the plank, it was rocking back and forth in a manner most unsettling to Palin's aching head and churning stomach. There were strange noises and smells, too—wood creaking, an odd whooshing and gurgling, and, every so often, a tremendous roaring and thudding and flapping above his head that sounded like a stampede of horses or, Palin thought with a catch in his throat, his father's description of attacking dragons. Cautiously, the young mage opened his eyes.

Almost instantly, he shut them again. Sunlight

streaming through a small, round window pierced his brain like an arrow, sending white-hot pain bouncing around the backs of his eyeballs. The plank rocked him this way and that, and Palin was sick again.

When he recovered sufficiently to think he might not die in the next ten seconds—a matter of extreme regret—Palin braced himself to open his eyes and keep them open.

He managed, but at the cost of being sick again. Fortunately or unfortunately, there was nothing left inside him to lose, and it wasn't long before he was able to look around. He was lying on a wooden plank, as he had surmised. The plank had been built into a curved wooden wall of a small room and was obviously intended as a crude bed. Several other planks lined the walls of the oddly shaped room and Palin saw his two brothers lying unconscious on these, bound hand and foot as he was. There was no other furniture in the room, nothing but a few wooden chests, which were sliding along the wooden floor.

Palin had only to look out the small, round window on the wall across from him to confirm his worst fears. At first, he saw nothing but blue sky and white clouds and bright sunlight. Then the plank on which he was lying dropped—it seemed—into a chasm. The wooden chests scraped across the floor, running away past him. Blue sky and clouds vanished, to be replaced by green water.

Shutting his eyes once more, Palin rolled over to ease his cramped muscles, pressing his aching head against the cool, damp wood of the crude bed.

Or perhaps he should say "berth." That's the nautical term, isn't it? he said to himself bitterly. That's what you call a bed on a ship. And what will they call *us* on the ship? Palin asked himself in despair. Galley slaves? Chained to the oars, subject to the overmaster with his whip, flaying the flesh from their backs. . . .

The motion of the ship changed, the sea chests skittered along the floor in the opposite direction, sky and clouds leaped back into the window, and Palin knew he was going to be sick again.

"Palin . . . Palin, are you all right?"

There was an anguished tone in the voice that brought Palin to consciousness. Painfully, he once again opened his eyes. He must have slept, he realized, though how he could have done so with this throbbing in his head and the queasy state of his stomach he had no idea.

"Palin!" The voice was urgent.

"Yes," said Palin thickly. It took an effort to talk, his tongue felt and tasted as though gully dwarves had taken up residence in his mouth. The thought made his stomach lurch, and he abandoned it hurriedly. "Yes," he said again, "I'm . . . all right. . . ."

"Thank Paladine!" groaned the voice, which Palin recognized now as Tanin's. "By the gods, you looked so pale, lying there, I thought you were dead!"

"I wish I was," Palin said feelingly.

"We know what you mean," said Sturm, a very subdued and miserable Sturm, to judge by the sound.

Twisting around, Palin was able to see his brothers. If I look as bad as they do, he thought, no wonder Tanin believed I was dead. Both young men were pale beneath their tan skin, their pallor had a faint greenish tinge, and there was ample evidence on the deck below that both had been extremely sick. Their red curls were tangled and wet and matted, their clothes soaked. Both lay on their backs, their hands and feet tied with rough leather thongs. Tanin had a large bruise on his forehead and, in addition, his wrists were cut and bleeding. He had obviously been trying to free himself and failed.

"This is all my fault," said Tanin glumly, with another groan as nausea welled up inside of him. "What a fool I was, not to see this coming!"

"Don't give yourself all the credit, Big Brother," said Sturm. "I went right along with you. We should have listened to Palin—"

"No, you shouldn't have," Palin mumbled, closing his eyes against the sight of the sea and sky constantly shifting places in the porthole. "I was being a superior, self-righteous twit, as both of you tried to point out." He was silent a moment, trying to decide if he was going to be sick or not. Finally, he thought he wasn't and added, "We're in this together now, anyway. Either of you know where we are and what's going on?"

"We're in the hold of a ship," Tanin said. "And, from the sounds of it, they've got some great beast chained up there."

"A dragon?" Palin asked quietly.

"Could be," Tanin answered. "I remember Tanis describing the black dragon that attacked them in Xak Tsaroth. He heard a gurgling noise and a hissing, like water boiling in a kettle. . . ."

"But why would anyone chain a dragon up on a ship?" argued Sturm weakly.

"All kinds of reasons," Palin muttered. "Most of them nasty."

"Probably keeps slaves like us in line. Palin," called Tanin in a low voice, "can you do anything? To free us, I mean? You know, your magic?"

"No," said Palin bitterly. "My spell components are gone— Not that I could get to them if I had them, since my hands are tied. My staff— *My staff!*" He recalled with a pang. Fearfully he struggled to sit up, glanced around, then breathed a sigh of relief. The

Staff of Magius stood in a corner, leaning up against the hull of the ship. For some reason, it did not move when the ship listed, but remained standing perfectly still, seemingly unaffected by the laws of nature. "My staff might help, but the only thing I know how to make it do is give light," he admitted shamefacedly. "Besides," he added, lying wearily back down, "my head aches so I can barely remember my name, much less a magic spell."

The young men were silent, each thinking. Tanin struggled against his bonds once more, then gave it up. The leather had been soaked with water and had tightened when it dried so that it was impossible for the big man to escape. Then Sturm gave a low whistle and twisted his body to face his younger brother.

"Palin," he said softly, "I remember a story about Uncle Raistlin, how he and Father were captured by bandits and he freed himself using a knife he had hidden on his wrist. Do you—"

"Yes," said Palin. "I've got a knife like his. Justarius sent it to me when I passed the Test. It's attached to my wrist with a thong." He paused, then said reluctantly, "And I have yet to figure out how the damn thing works."

Sturm and Tanin, sitting up hopefully at the beginning of this conversation, lay back down with groans at its conclusion.

"So, it looks like we're prisoners in this wretched hole—"

"Prisoners?" called a booming voice. "Losers, maybe. But prisoners, never!"

A trapdoor in the ceiling opened, and a short, stocky figure in bright red velvet with black curling hair and beard poked his head through. "My guests you are!" cried Dougan Redhammer lustily, peering at them through the hatch. "And fortunate beyond all humans, because I have chosen you to accompany me on my grand quest! A quest that will make you famous throughout the world! A quest that will make that minor adventure your parents were involved in seem like a kender scavenger hunt!" Dougan leaned down so far through the hatch that his face became quite red with the exertion and he almost tumbled through upside down.

"We're not going on any quest of yours, dwarf!" Tanin said with an oath. And, for once, both Palin and Sturm were in full agreement.

Leering down at them through the hatch, Dougan grinned. "Wanna bet?

"You see, lads, it's a matter of honor," said the dwarf, eyeing them complacently. Throwing down a rope ladder, Dougan—somewhat perilously—climbed down into the hold of the ship, his journey being hampered by the fact that he couldn't see his feet for his great belly. Finally, after several slips, he made it. Reaching the deck, he rested a moment from his labors, removing a lace-covered handkerchief from the sleeve of his coat and using it to mop his perspiring face.

"I tell you, lads," he said solemnly, "I'm feeling a bit under myself. By Reorx, but you can drink! Just like you said." Stumbling slightly as the deck listed beneath him, the dwarf pointed at Sturm. "You, especially! I swear by my beard"—he stroked it—"that I saw two of yourself, lad, and I was workin' on four before your eyes rolled back in your head and you crashed to the floor. Shook the foundations of the inn, you did. I had to pay damages."

"You said you were going to cut us loose," Tanin snarled.

"That I did," Dougan muttered, drawing a sharp

knife from his belt. Making his way around the sea chests, the dwarf began to saw away industriously at the leather thongs that bound Tanin's wrists.

"If we aren't prisoners," Palin asked, "then why are we bound hand and foot?"

"Why, laddie," said the dwarf, looking around at Palin with an injured air, "it was for your own safety! I had only your welfare at heart! You were so enthusiastic when you saw we were carrying you aboard this fine vessel, that we had to restrain your enthusiasm—"

"Enthusiasm!" Tanin muttered. "We were out cold!"

"Well, no, actually, you weren't," Dougan admitted. "Oh, he was." The dwarf jerked his head back at Palin. "Sleeping like he was in his mother's arms. But you two, as I saw the moment I clapped eyes on you, lads, are grand fighters. Perhaps you were wondering how you got that bit of a clout on your head—"

Tanin said nothing, simply glared at the dwarf. Sitting up, the young man gingerly put his hand to his forehead where there was a lump the size of an egg.

"Enthusiasm," said the dwarf solemnly, going over to cut Sturm loose. "That's one reason I chose you for my quest."

"The only quest I'd consider going on with you is to see you in the Abyss!" Tanin retorted stubbornly.

Lying back, Palin sighed. "My dear brother," he said wearily, "has it occurred to you that we have little choice in the matter? We're on a ship, miles away from land"—he glanced at Dougan, who nodded assent— "and completely at the mercy of this dwarf and his crew of cutthroats. Do you think he would release us from our bonds if we had the slightest chance of escaping?"

"Intelligent lad," said the dwarf approvingly, cutting Palin's ropes as Sturm sat up stiffly, rubbing his wrists. "But then, he's a mage. And they're all intelligent, at least so's I've heard. So intelligent," continued Dougan cunningly, "that I'm certain he'll think twice about casting any spells that might come to mind. A sleep spell, for example, might be very effective and give my *cutthroat* crew a rest, but can you three sail the ship? Besides," he continued, seeing Palin's grim expression, "as I said before—it's a matter of honor. You lost the bet, fair and square. I kept my part, I put you to bed. Now you must keep yours." Dougan's grin made the ends of his moustaches curl upwards. He stroked his beard in satisfaction. "You must pay the tab."

"I'll be damned if I'm going to pay," snarled Tanin. "I'll yank your black beard out by its roots!"

Tanin's voice literally shook with anger, and Palin cringed, watching helplessly as his hot-tempered brother made a lunge for the grinning dwarf—and fell flat on his face in the muck and filth.

"There, there, lad," said Dougan, helping Tanin stagger to his feet. "Get your sea legs first, then you can yank out my beard—if you refuse to honor your bet. But from what I've heard of Caramon Majere, I'd be disappointed indeed to see his sons turn out to be welchers."

"We're no welchers!" said Tanin sulkily, leaning weakly against the berth and clinging to it with both hands as the ship rocked out from underneath him. "Though some might say the bet was rigged, we'll pay it just the same! What do you want of us?"

"To accompany me on my quest," said the dwarf. "Where we're bound is perilous in the extreme! I need two strong, skilled fighters, and a wizard always comes in handy."

"What about your crew?" Sturm asked. Carefully, he edged himself off his berth and dropped to the deck just as the ship listed, sending him crashing backward into the hull.

Dougan's grinning face went abruptly sober. He glanced up above, where the strange roaring sound could be heard again, mingled this time, Palin noted, with shrieks and cries. "Ah, my . . . um . . . crew," said the dwarf, shaking his head sadly. "They're . . . well, best you come see for yourselves, lads."

Turning on the heel of his fancy shoes, Dougan made for the rope ladder, stumbling awkwardly as the ship canted off in the other direction. "Ouch! That reminds me," he said, cursing and rubbing his leg where he had come up against one of the roving sea chests. "We stowed your equipment in here." He thumped on the lid. "Swords, shield, armor, and such like. You'll be needing them, where we're headed!" he added cheerfully.

Catching hold of the swinging rope ladder, the dwarf scrambled up it and pulled himself through the hatch. "Don't be long!" they heard him shout.

"Well, what do we do now?" Sturm asked, standing up cautiously, only to fall forward with the motion of the ship. The young man's face was decidedly green, beads of sweat stood on his forehead.

"We get our swords," Tanin said grimly, stumbling toward the sea chests.

"And we get out of this foul place," said Palin. He covered his nose and mouth with the hem of his sleeve. "We need fresh air, and I for one want to see what's going on up there."

"Wanna bet?" Tanin mocked.

Smiling ruefully, Palin managed to make his way to the Staff of Magius, which was still standing up against the hull. Whether it was any magical property of the staff, or whether just holding it gave him confidence, the young mage felt better the moment his hand wrapped around the smooth wood.

"Think of the danger this staff has seen and led its masters through safely," Palin whispered to himself. "Magius held it as he fought at Huma's side. My uncle held it as he entered the Abyss to face the Dark Queen. This situation probably doesn't bother it at all."

Gripping the staff in his hand, Palin started up the rope ladder.

"Hold on there, Little Brother," Tanin said, catching Palin's sleeve. "You don't know what's up there. You admitted yourself you weren't feeling up to spellcasting. Why don't you let Sturm and me go ahead?"

Palin stopped, looking at Tanin in pleased astonishment. His older brother had not ordered him, as he would have done earlier. He could almost hear him, "Palin, you fool! You wait below. Sturm and I will go first." Tanin had spoken to him respectfully, presented his argument logically, and then left it up to Palin to decide.

"You're right, Tanin," Palin said, stepping back away from the ladder—only it was back a little farther than he had intended as the swaying ship threw him off balance once again. Sturm caught hold of him and the three stood, waiting for the ship to right itself. Then, one by one, they climbed up the rope ladder.

Sturm's strong hand hauled Palin up on deck. Thankfully, the young mage breathed the fresh air, blinking in the bright sunlight and doing his best to ignore the throbbing in his head. His eyes were just adjusting to the glare when he heard the roaring behind him—a frightful sound, a combination of howling, shrieking, creaking, and hissing. The deck below his feet thrummed and shivered. Alarmed, he started to turn and face whatever horrible beast was attacking when he heard Tanin cry, "Palin, look out!"

His brother's weight struck Palin, knocking him off his feet and onto the deck just as Something dark and awful thundered overhead with a wild flapping noise.

"You all right?" Tanin asked anxiously. Standing up, he offered Palin his hand. "I didn't mean to hit you quite so hard."

"I think you broke every bone in my body!" Palin wheezed, trying to catch his breath. He stared at the prow of the ship, where the Thing was disappearing over the edge. "What in the name of the Abyss was that?" He looked at Dougan. The dwarf was also, somewhat shamefacedly, picking himself up off the deck.

His face as red as his velvet breeches, Dougan was brushing off bits of wood, strands of rope, and sea foam when he was suddenly surrounded by a horde of jabbering, small creatures, endeavoring to help him.

"Ahoy there!" Dougan roared irritably, flapping his hands at the creatures. "Stand off! Stand off, I say! Get back to your tasks!"

Obediently, the creatures ran away, though more than a few took a second or two to eye the three brothers. One even approached Palin, an eager hand stretched out to touch the Staff of Magius.

"Get back!" Palin cried, clutching the staff to him.

Sniffing, the creature retreated, but its bright eyes lingered hungrily on the staff as it returned to whatever it was doing.

"Gnomes!" said Sturm in awe, lowering his sword.

"Uh, yes," muttered Dougan, embarrassed. "My . . . um . . . crew of cutthroats."

"The gods help us!" Tanin prayed fervently. "We're on a gnome ship."

"And that Thing?" Palin's voice failed, he couldn't ask.

"That's the . . . uh . . . sail," Dougan mumbled, wringing water out of his beard. He made a vague gesture with his hand. "It'll be back again in about ten minutes, so . . . um . . . be prepared."

"What in the Abyss is a dwarf doing on a gnome ship?" Tanin demanded.

Dougan's embarrassment increased. "Ah, well, now," he muttered, twirling his long moustache around his index finger. "That's a bit of a long story. Perhaps I'll have time to tell you—"

Balancing himself on the heaving deck with the aid of the staff, Palin looked out to sea. An idea had occurred to him, and his heart was beginning to sink at about the same rate it appeared this vessel was sinking. The sun was behind them, they were heading west, riding on a gnome ship with a dwarf captain. . . .

"The Graygem!" Palin murmured.

"Aye, laddie!" Dougan cried, clapping the young mage on the back. "You've womped the lizard in the gullet, as the gully dwarves say. *That* is the reason I'm on this . . . um . . . somewhat unique vessel and *that*," continued Dougan, rocking back on his feet, his belly thrust out in front of him, "is my quest!"

"What?" asked Tanin suspiciously.

"My brothers," said Palin, "it appears we are bound on a voyage in search of the legendary lost Graygem of Gargath."

"Not 'in search of'," Dougan corrected. "I have found it! We are on a quest to end all quests! We're going to *recover* the Graygem and—Ahoy, lads, look out." Casting an uneasy glance behind him, Dougan threw himself down on the deck.

"Here comes the sail," he grunted.

CHAPTER THREE

The Miracle

The gnomish sailing vessel was a true technological wonder. (The wonder being, as Sturm said, that it managed to stay afloat, much less actually sail!) Years in design (longer years in committee), and centuries of craftsmanship later, the gnome ship was the terror of the high seas. (This was quite true. Most ships fled in terror at the sight of the gnome flag—a golden screw on a field of puce—but this was because the steam-generating boilers had an unfortunate habit of exploding. The gnomes claimed to have once attacked and sunk a minotaur pirate ship. The truth of the matter was that the minotaurs, rendered helpless by laughter, negligently allowed their ship to drift too close to the gnomes who, in panic, released the pressurized air stored in casks used to steer the vessel. The resulting blast blew the minotaurs out of the water and the gnomes off course by about twenty miles.)

Let other races mock them, the gnomes knew that their ship was years ahead of its time in practicality, economy, and design. The fact that it was slower than anything on the water—averaging about half-a-knot on a good day with a strong wind—didn't bother the gnomes. They know that nothing is perfect. (A committee is currently working on this problem and is confidently expected to come up with a solution sometime in the next millennium.)

The gnomes knew that all ships had sails. This was requisite, in their opinion, of a ship being a ship. The gnome's ship had a sail, therefore. But the gnomes, upon studying vessels built by other, less intelligent races, considered it a waste of space to clutter the deck with masts and ropes and canvas and an additional waste of energy hoisting sails up and down in an effort to catch the wind. The gnome ship, therefore, used one gigantic sail that not only caught the wind but, in essence, dragged it along with it.

It was this sail that gave the ship its revolutionary design. An enormous affair of billowing canvas with a beam the size of ten stout oaks, the sail rested upon three greased wooden rails, one on either side of the ship and one down the middle. Huge cables, running the length of the ship and driven by steam generated in a giant boiler down below operated this miracle of modern naval technology, pulling the sail along the greased wooden rail at a high rate of speed. The sail, moving from front to back, manufactured its own wind as it roared along and thus propelled the ship on its course.

When the sail had completed its impressive sweep across the deck and reached the ship's prow at the rear. . . . (There *was* one tiny problem. It was impossible to turn the ship around. Therefore the stern looked just like the prow. The gnomes had solved this slight hitch in design by fixing the sail so that it could go either forward or backward, as needed, and had given the ship two figureheads—buxom gnome maidens, one on either end, each holding screws in their hands and staring out to sea with resolute intensity.) . . . Where were we? Ah yes. When the sail reached the prow at the rear, it rolled itself up neatly and traveled under the ship through the water until it reached the prow at the front. Here it leaped out of the water, unfurled itself, and thundered along the deck once more.

At least, that is what the sail did on the drawing board and in numerous gnomish bathtubs. In actuality, the gears that controlled the winding-up mechanism rusted almost immediately in the salt water, and the sail often hit the water either completely or partially open. In this manner it swept under the ship, creating a tremendous drag that occasionally pulled the vessel back farther than it had gone forward. This small inconvenience was considered to be fully outweighed, however, by an unlooked-for bonus. When the open sail came up from the sea, it acted as a net, hauling in schools of fish. As the sail lifted up over the prow, fish rained down upon the deck, providing lunch, dinner, and the occasional concussion if one had the misfortune to be struck by a falling tuna.

The ship had no tiller, there being nowhere for a tiller to go, since the boat had, in essence, two prows and no stern. Nothing daunted, the gnomes designed their vessel to be steered by the use of the aforementioned pressurized air casks. Located at either side of the hull, these were kept filled with air by giant, steam-driven bellows. Letting the air out of one or the other allowed the ship to be whooshed along on a different tack. (We have said earlier that it was impossible to turn the ship around. We were in error. The gnomes had discovered that the ship *could* be turned by means of releasing the air in both casks simultaneously. This caused the ship to revolve, but at such an alarming rate that most of the crew was flung overboard and those that remained could never afterward walk a straight line. These unfortunates were promptly hired by the gnome Street Designers Guild.)

The name of this remarkable vessel was *The Great Gnome Ship of Exploration and Questing Made of Wooden Planks Held Together by the Miracle of Gnome Glue (of which the less said the better) Instead of that Paltry Human Invention the Nail Which We Have Designed More Efficiently Anyway and Driven by Steam Created by Bringing Water to a Rapid Boil* and so forth and so on, the full name taking up several volumes of text in the gnomes' library. This name, or rather a shortened version, was carved upon the hull and, when the gnomes ran out of room, the deck as well.

Needless to say, traveling upon the *Miracle* (the shorter human version of the name) was not conducive to either peace of mind or keeping one's dinner down. The ship wallowed in the water like a drunken sea elf when the sail was underneath it, surged forward with a stomach wrenching jolt when the sail was sweeping along the deck, and rocked sickeningly when the sail hit the water behind. The bilge pumps were at work constantly (due to the wonders of gnome glue). Fortunately, the gnomes were heading in a straight direction—due west—so that it was not necessary to turn the ship, thus avoiding the need to open the air casks (a thrill akin to being caught in a cyclone)—a blessing rather lost upon Tanin, Sturm, and Palin during the mercifully short voyage. This, then, was the *Miracle* with a crew of gnomes, a dwarf for its captain, and three sea-sick, hung-over adventurers (though Dougan assured them solemnly that they should thank their respective gods for it!).

Night was falling. The sun sank down into the sea in a blaze of red, as though trying to outshine the gaudily dressed dwarf. Crouching miserably on the foredeck, the brothers were glad to see night come. They had spent a wretched day, forced to duck every time the sail raced overhead. In addition, they were pelted by fish and drenched with water streaming down from the sail. There was little for them to eat except fish (plenty of that) and some sort of gnome biscuit that looked suspiciously like the miracle glue. To take their minds off their troubles and prepare them for the quest ahead, Dougan proposed to tell them the story of the Graygem of Gargath.

"I know that story," Tanin said sullenly. "Everyone on Krynn knows that story! I've heard it since I was a child."

"Ah, but do you know the *true* story?" Dougan asked, gazing at them intently with his bright dark eyes.

No one replied, being unable to hear themselves think as the sail—with much flapping of canvas and creaking of winches—leaped out of the water and hurtled along the deck. Fish flopped about their feet, the gnomes hopping here and there after them. The sail's traversal along the deck was punctuated by shrieks and screams as certain unlucky gnomes forgot to duck and were swept overboard by the beam. Since this happened almost every time the sail made a pass, several gnomes were stationed permanently along the sides of the ship to yell "Gnome overboard!" (which they did with great gusto) and heave their floundering fellows life-saving devices (which also doubled as anchors when in port).

"How should we know whether or not it's the true story?" Tanin said grumpily when he could be heard again.

"I know that there are differing accounts depending on whether one hears the tale from a dwarf or any other race," Palin added.

Dougan appeared extremely uncomfortable. "Aye, lad," he said, "and there you've touched on a sore point. But, for now, you go ahead and tell it, young mage. Tell it as you heard it. I assume you've studied it, since it involves the bringing of magic into the world."

"Very well," said Palin, rather pleased and flattered at being the center of attention. Hearing that the human was going to tell their favorite story, many gnomes left their duties (and fish chasing) to settle down around Palin, regarding the mage with varying expressions ranging from eager assurance that he was going to get it wrong to downright suspicion that he might accidentally get it right.

"When the gods awakened from Chaos and took parts of it to rule, the Balance of the Universe was established and Chaos subdued. The pendulum of Time swung between Good and Evil, with Neutrality watching to see that neither grew stronger. It was at this time that the spirits of the races first began to dance among the stars, and the gods decided to create a world for these races to inhabit.

"The world was forged, but now the gods fought over the spirits of the races. The Gods of Good wanted to give the races power over the physical world, nurturing them toward Good. The Gods of Evil wanted to enslave the races, forcing them to do their evil bidding. The Gods of Neutrality wanted to give the races physical power over the world, but with the freedom to choose between Evil and Good. Eventually, the later course was decided upon, the Gods of Evil believing that they would have little trouble gaining the upper hand.

"Three races were born, then—the elves, beloved of the Gods of Good; the ogres, willing slaves of the Gods of Evil; and the humans, the neutrals, who—of all the races—had the shortest life span and therefore were easily drawn to one side or the other. When these races were created, the god Reorx was given the task of forging the world. He chose some humans to help him in this task, since they were the most willing workers. But Reorx soon grew angry at the humans. Many were greedy and worked only to gain wealth, taking little pride in what they created. Some sought to cheat, others stole. Furious, Reorx cursed his followers, turning them into gnomes—small creatures doomed—I don't really mean *doomed*," Palin interrupted himself hastily, seeing the gnomes begin to frown—"I mean . . . uh . . . *blessed* to be tinkers"—the gnomes smiled—"and to spend their entire lives tinkering with mechanical devices that would never, er, I mean, rarely work. . . ."

The sail rumbled overhead, and Palin paused thankfully.

"Getonwiththegoodpart!" shouted the gnomes, who always speak extremely fast and jamtheirwordstogether. Deciding that this was good advice (once he understood it), Palin continued.

"Soon after this, Reorx was tricked by one of the evil gods into taking the vast power of Chaos and forging it into a gem. It is generally believed that the god behind this was Hiddukel, god of corrupt wealth—"

"No, lad." Dougan sighed. "It was Morgion."

"Morgion?" repeated Palin in astonishment.

"Aye, the God of Decay. But I'll go into that later." The dwarf waved his hand. "Carry on."

"At any rate," continued Palin, somewhat confused, "Reorx made the Graygem and set it into the moon, Lunitari the Red, the moon sacred to the Gods of Neutrality."

The gnomes were all grinning, their favorite part was coming up.

"During this time, the gnomes had built a Great Invention, designed to take them off the world and out into the stars. This Invention lacked only one thing to make it operational, and that was a force to propel it. Looking into the sky at night, they saw the Graygem shining from the heart of Lunitari and knew, instantly, that if they could capture the power of Chaos that resided in the Graygem, this would drive their Invention."

Much nodding of heads and wise looks among the gnomes. Sturm yawned. Tanin stood up and leaned over the railing, where he was quietly sick.

"One extremely gifted gnome built an extension ladder that actually worked. It carried him up to the moon and there, with a net he had brought along for the purpose, he captured the Graygem before the gods were aware of him. He brought the gem down to the world below, but there it escaped him and sailed off to the west, passing over the lands and trailing chaos behind. Chaos entered the world in the form of magic. Beasts and creatures were transformed by the gem in its passing, becoming wondrous or hideous as the gem chose.

"A band of gnomes followed the Graygem across the sea, hoping still to catch it and claim it for their own. But it was a human, a man named Gargath, who trapped the stone and held it in his castle by certain magical means. Reaching the castle, the gnomes could see the light of the Graygem illuminating the countryside. They demanded that Gargath give the stone up. He refused. The gnomes threatened war—" shouts and cheers among the gnomes here—"Gargath welcomed the battle. He built a high wall all around the castle to protect it and the gem. There was no way the gnomes could get over the wall, so they left, vowing, however, to return."

"Hear! Hear!" cried the gnomes.

"A month later, a gnome army arrived at Castle Gargath with a huge, steam-powered siege engine. It reached the wall of the castle, but broke down just short of its goal. The gnomes retreated with heavy losses. Two months later, the gnomes returned with an even larger steam-powered siege engine. This engine plowed into the first, caught fire, and burned. The gnomes retreated with even heavier losses. Three

---

months later, the gnomes were back with a colossal, steam-powered siege engine. It lumbered over the ashes of the first two siege engines and was thundering toward the wall when the drive mechanism broke down. The engine, with a mighty groan, toppled over on its side, smashing down the wall. Although not quite what they'd had in mind, the gnomes were delighted."

More cheering.

"But, as they rushed through the breech in the wall, a steel gray light beamed forth from the stone, blinding everyone. When Lord Gargath could see again, he saw—to his astonishment—that the gnomes were fighting among themselves!"

Frowns here and cries of "Liar! We were misquoted!"

"One faction of gnomes was demanding that they be given the Graygem to carve up and turn into wealth. The other faction demanded that they be given the Graygem to take apart and see how it worked.

"As the two sides fought, their aspect changed. . . . Thus were born the races of the dwarves, who carve rock and think constantly of wealth; and kender, driven by their insatiable curiosity to roam the world. The Graygem escaped during the confusion and was last seen heading westward, a party of gnomes and Lord Gargath in pursuit. And that," finished Palin, somewhat out of breath, "is the story of the Graygem— unless you ask a dwarf, that is."

"Why? What do the dwarves say?" demanded Tanin, looking at Dougan with a somewhat sickly grin.

Dougan fetched up a sigh that might have come from the tips of his black shoes. "The dwarves have always maintained that *they* are the chosen of Reorx, that he forged their race out of love, and that gnomes and kender came about from trial and error until he got it right."

Boos. The gnomes appeared highly indignant, but were instantly subdued by Dougan whirling around and fixing them with a piercing stare. "According to the dwarves, Reorx created the Graygem to give them as a gift and it was stolen by the gnomes." More boos, but these hushed immediately at a glower from Dougan.

"Well, it seems to me," said Sturm, with another yawn, "that the only one who knows the true story is Reorx."

"Not quite, lad," said Dougan, looking uncomfortable. "For, you see, *I* know the true story. And that is why I'm on this quest."

"Which is right, then?" asked Tanin, with a wink at Palin.

"Neither," said Dougan, appearing even more uncomfortable. His head drooped down, his chin buried itself in his beard, while his hands fumbled at the golden buttons on his sopping-wet velvet coat. "You . . . uh . . . you see," he mumbled, making it extremely difficult for anyone to hear him over the splashing of the sea and the flapping of fish on the deck, "Reorx . . . uh . . . losttheGraygeminagameofbones."

"What?" asked Palin, leaning forward.

"Helostit," muttered the dwarf.

"I still didn't hear—"

"HE LOST THE DAMN GEM IN A GAME OF BONES!" Dougan roared angrily, lifting his face and glaring around him. Terrified, the gnomes immediately scattered in all directions, more than a few getting clonked on the head by the sail as it whizzed past. "Morgion, God of decay and disease, tricked Reorx into making the gem. Morgion knew that if Chaos were loosed in the world, his evil power would grow. He challenged Reorx to a game, with the Graygem as the stakes and . . ." The dwarf fell silent, scowling down at his shoes.

"He gambled it in away in a *bone game?*" Sturm finished in amazement.

"Aye, lad," said Dougan, sighing heavily. "You see, Reorx has one little flaw. Just a tiny flaw, mind you, otherwise he is as fine and honorable a gentleman as one could hope to meet. But"—the dwarf heaved another sigh—"he does love his bottle, and he does love a good wager."

"Oh, so you know Reorx, do you?" Sturm said with a yawn that cracked his jaws.

"I'm proud to say so," said Dougan seriously, stroking his beard and curling his moustaches. "And, with his help, I've managed after all these years to locate the Graygem. With the assistance of these lads here"— he smote a passing gnome on the shoulder, completely bowling the little fellow over—"and with the help of you three fine young men, we'll recover it and . . . and . . ." Dougan stopped, seeming confused.

"And?"

"And return it to Reorx, naturally," the dwarf said, shrugging.

"Naturally," Tanin responded. Glancing over at Sturm, who had fallen asleep on the deck, the big man caught a gnome in the act of making off with his brother's helm. "Hey!" cried Tanin angrily, collaring the thief.

"Ijustwantedtolookatit!" whined the gnome, cringing. "Iwasgoingtogiveitbackhonest. You see," he said, talking more slowly as Tanin released his grip, "we have developed a revolutionary new design in helms. There's just a few problems with it, such as getting it off one's head, and I—"

"Thank you, we're not interested," Tanin growled, yanking the helm away from the gnome, who was admiring it lovingly. "C'mon, Little Brother," he said, turning to Palin. "Help me get Sturm to bed."

"Where is bed?" Palin asked tiredly. "And, no, I'm not going back into that foul-smelling hold again."

"Me either," Tanin said. He looked around the deck and pointed. "That lean-to-looking thing over there seems to be about the best place. At least it'll be dry."

He indicated several wooden planks that had been skillfully and ingeniously fit together to form a small shelter. Leaning against the hull, the planks were beneath the sail as it rumbled past, and protected those lying within from water and falling fish.

"It is dry," said Dougan smugly. "That *my* bed."

"It *was* your bed," returned Tanin. Leaning down, he shook Sturm. "Wake up! We're not going to carry you! And hurry up, before that god-cursed sail decapitates us."

"What?" Sturm sat up, blinking drowsily.

"You can't do this!" roared the dwarf.

"Look, Dougan Redhammer!" Tanin said, bending down and staring the dwarf grimly in the eye. "I'm hung over, seasick, and I haven't had anything to eat all day. I've been doused with water, hit by fish, run over by a sail, and bored to death by kids' bedtime stories! I don't believe you, I don't believe your stupid quest." Tanin paused, seething, and raised a finger, shaking it at the dwarf's nose. "I'm going to sleep where I want to sleep and tomorrow, when I'm feeling better, I swear by the gods I'm going to make these little bastards turn this ship around and take us back home!"

"And if I stop you?" Dougan threatened with a leer, not at all disconcerted by Tanin's rage.

"Then there'll be a new figurehead on which ever

end of this stupid boat is the front!" Tanin hissed through clenched teeth. "And it'll have a long, black beard!" Angrily, the big man stalked over to the lean-to and ducked inside. Sleepily, Sturm followed.

"If I were you, Dougan," Palin muttered, hurrying after them, "I'd keep out of his way! He's quite capable of doing what he says."

"Is he, lad? I'll keep that in mind," the dwarf replied, tugging thoughtfully at his beard.

The shelter was crammed with the dwarf's possessions—most of which appeared to be gaudy clothes. These Palin shoved unceremoniously out onto the deck with his foot. Tanin stretched out on the floor, Sturm collapsed next to him, and both were asleep almost as quickly as if their younger brother had cast a spell over them. Palin lay down in the small remaining space, hoping sleep would come to him as swiftly.

But he was not the campaigner his brothers were, he realized bitterly. Sturm could sleep in full armor on the sands of a desert while Tanin had been known to snore blissfully as lightning cut down a tree standing next to him. Soaked to the skin, shivering with cold, Palin lay on the deck and gave himself up to misery. He was hungry, but every time he thought of food, his stomach lurched. His muscles ached from the sickness, the bitter taste of salt water filled his mouth. He thought with longing of his bed at home; of clean, sweet-smelling sheets; of hours of peaceful study, sitting beneath the sheltering limbs of the vallenwood, his spellbook in his lap.

Closing his eyes, Palin tried to keep back the tears of homesickness, but it engulfed him like a wave. Reaching out his hand, he touched the Staff of Magius. And suddenly the memory of his uncle came to him. From where? Palin had no idea, Raistlin had died long before Palin was born. Perhaps it was from the staff . . . or maybe he was recalling some tale of his father's and it had become real to him now in his weakened state. Whatever the reason, Palin saw Raistlin clearly, lying on the ground in a dismal, rainswept forest. Huddled in his red robes, the mage was coughing, coughing until it seemed he could never draw breath again. Palin saw blood upon the ashen lips, he saw the frail body wracked by pain. But he heard him speak no word of complaint. Softly, Palin approached his uncle. The coughing ceased, the spasm eased. Lifting his head, Raistlin looked directly into Palin's eyes. . . .

Bowing his head in shame, Palin drew the staff nearer to him, resting his cheek upon its cool, smooth wood and, relaxing, fell into sleep. But he thought he heard, in the final moment before he slipped over the edge of unconsciousness, the voice of the dwarf, and he thought he saw a head peering into the lean-to.

"I've a deck of cards here, lads. . . . What do you say? High card sleeps here tonight? . . ."

CHAPTER FOUR

The Isle of Gargath

Both brothers knew that Tanin was quite capable of carrying out his threat to take over the ship, though just how he was going to force the gnomes to sail it was another matter entirely. During the night, the gnomes, just as firmly determined to continue the voyage, began to organize a supply of weapons. Since most of these weapons were of gnomish design, there was every possibility that they would do as much or more damage to the wielder as to the intended victim, and thus the outcome of the battle—two warriors and a mage against numerous gnomes and a dwarf—was open to question.

The question was, fortunately, never answered. The next morning the brothers were awakened by a tremendous crash, the heart-stopping sound of splintering wood, and the somewhat belated cry of "Land Ho!"

Staggering to their feet, they made their way out of the lean-to and across the deck, not an easy task since it was listing steeply to port.

"What is it? What's happened? Where are we?" demanded Tanin, rubbing his eyes.

"We've arrived!" announced Dougan, smoothing his beard in satisfaction. "Look!" He made a grand, sweeping gesture toward what was—at this time—the prow. "The Isle of Gargath."

The brothers looked. At first all they could see was a confused mass of split sail, dangling ropes, broken beams, and gnomes waving their hands, arguing furiously, and shoving each other about. The motion of the ship through the water had ceased, due, no doubt, to the presence of a cliff, which had bashed in the figurehead, part of the hull, and snapped the mast of the sail in two.

His face grim, Tanin made his way through the wreckage, followed by Sturm and Palin, several bickering gnomes, and the dwarf. Reaching the prow, he clung to the side and stared out past the cliff toward the island. The sun was rising behind them, shedding its bright light upon a stretch of sandy beach that curved out of sight to the north, vanishing in a patch of gray fog. Strange-looking trees with thin, smooth trunks that erupted in a flourish of frondlike leaves at the top surrounded the beach. Beyond the wide sandy strip, towering above the trees and the cliff face upon which the boat now rested, was a gigantic mountain. A cloud of gray smoke hung over it, casting a pall upon the beach, the water, and the ship.

"The Isle of Gargath," Dougan repeated triumphantly.

"Gargath?" Palin gaped. "You mean—"

"Aye, laddie. The Lord himself followed the Graygem, if you remember, when it escaped. He built a ship and sailed after it as it vanished over the western horizon, and that was the last anyone on Ansalon ever heard of him. His family figured he had dropped off the edge of the world. But, a few years back, I happened to be drinking with a group of minotaurs. One thing led to another, there was a game, as I recall, and I won this map off of them." Reaching into the pocket of his red velvet coat (now much the worse for wear and salt water), Dougan pulled out a piece of parchment and handed it to Tanin.

"It's a minotaur map, all right," Tanin said, setting it down on the listing rail and smoothing it out, trying to keep his balance at the same time. Sturm lurched over to see, and Palin crowded next to him, bracing himself on the Staff of Magius. Though it was written in the

by MaRGaRet Weis anD TRacy HickMan

uncouth language of the man-beasts, the map was
drawn with the precision and skill for which minotaurs are grudgingly renowned by the civilized races
of Krynn. There was no mistaking the continent of
Ansalon or, much farther to the west, a tiny island
with the word "Gargath" written out to the side.

"What does that mean?" Sturm asked, pointing to
an ominous-looking symbol next to the island. "That
thing that looks like a bull's head with a sword stuck
through it."

"That?" repeated Dougan, shrugging nonchalantly.
Snatching the map from Tanin, he rolled it up hastily.
"Some minotaur doodle, no doubt—"

"The minotaur 'doodle' for danger," Palin said grimly. "Isn't that right?"

Dougan flushed, thrusting the map back into his
pocket. "Well, now, laddie, I believe you may be onto
something there, although I personally don't put
much stock in what those savage creatures might take
it into their heads to draw—"

"Those 'savage creatures' have marked this island
with their strongest warning!" Palin interrupted. "No
minotaur ship will land anywhere bearing that mark,"
he added, turning to his brothers.

"And there are few things in this world or the next
that minotaur fear," Tanin said, staring at the island,
his face dark.

"What more proof do you need?" asked Dougan in
a soft voice, following Tanin's gaze; the dwarf's dark,
bright eyes were filled with hunger. "The Graygem is
here! It is its power the minotaurs feel and fear!"

"What do you think, Palin?" Tanin turned to his
youngest brother. "You're the magic-user. Surely you
can sense it."

Once again, Palin felt the thrill of pleasure, seeing
his older brothers, the two people he looked up to in

this world most with the exception of his father—or
maybe even more than his father—looking at him
respectfully, waiting his judgment. Gripping the Staff
of Magius, Palin closed his eyes and tried to concentrate and, as he did so, a chill feeling clutched his heart
with fingers of ice, spreading its cold fear through his
body. He shuddered, and opened his eyes to find
Tanin and Sturm regarding him anxiously.

"Palin—your face! You're as pale as death. What is
it?"

"I don't know. . . ." Palin faltered, his mouth dry. "I
felt something, but what I'm not sure. It wasn't danger
so much as a lost and empty feeling, a feeling of help-
lessness. Everything around me was spinning out of
control. There was nothing I could do to stop it—"

"The power of the gem," Dougan said. "You felt it,
young mage! And now you know why it must be captured and returned to the gods for safekeeping. It
escaped man's care before, it will escape again. The
gods only know," the dwarf added sorrowfully, "what
mischief it has wrecked upon this wretched island."

Wagging his black beard, Dougan held out a trembling hand to Tanin. "You'll help me, lads, won't
you?" he asked in heartfelt, pleading tones, so different from his usual braggadocio that Tanin was caught
off guard, his anger punctured. "If you say no," continued Dougan, hanging his head, "I'll understand.
Though I *did* win the wager, I guess it was wrong of
me to get you drunk and take you prisoner when you
were weak and helpless."

Tanin chewed his lip, obviously not welcoming this
reminder.

"And I swear by my beard," said the dwarf solemnly, stroking it, "that if you say the word, I'll have the
gnomes take you back to Ansalon. As soon as they get
the ship repaired, that is."

"*If* they get the ship repaired!" Tanin growled at last. (This appeared unlikely. The gnomes were paying no attention whatsoever to the ship, but were arguing among themselves about who was supposed to have been on watch, who was supposed to be reading the gnomes' own map, and the committee that had drawn up the map in the first place. It was later decided that, since the cliff hadn't been marked on the map, it wasn't there and they hadn't bashed into it. Having reached this conclusion, the gnomes were able to get to work.)

"Well, what do you two say?" Tanin turned to his brothers.

"I say that since we're here, we ought to at least take a look around," Sturm said in low tones. "If the dwarf is right and we could retrieve the Graygem, our admittance into the Knighthood would be assured! As he said, we'd be heroes!"

"To say nothing of the wealth we might obtain," Tanin muttered. "Palin?"

The young mage's heart beat fast. Who knows what magical powers the Graygem possesses? he thought suddenly. It could enhance *my* power, and I wouldn't need any great archmage to teach me! I might become a great archmage myself, just by touching it or . . . Palin shook his head. Raising his eyes, he saw his brothers' faces. Tanin's was ugly with greed, Sturm's twisted with ambition. My own face—Palin put his hand on it—what must it look like to them? He glanced down at his robes and saw their white color faded to dirty gray. It might just be from the salt water, but it might be from something else. . . .

"My brothers," he said urgently, "listen to us! Think what you just said! Tanin, since when did you ever go in search of wealth and not adventure!"

Tanin blinked, as if waking from a dream. "You're

right! Wealth! What am I talking about? I never cared that much for money—"

"The power of the Graygem is speaking," Dougan cried. "It's beginning to corrupt you, as it corrupted others." His gaze went to the gnomes. The shoving and pushing had escalated into punching and tossing one another overboard.

"I say we should at least investigate this island," Palin said in a low voice so that the dwarf would not overhear. He drew his brothers closer. "If for no other reason than to find out if Dougan's telling the truth. If he is and if the Graygem *is* here and if we could be the ones to bring it back . . ."

"Oh, it's here!" Dougan said, eagerly poking his black-bearded face into their midst. "And when you bring it back, lads, why the stories they tell of your famous father will be kender lies compared to the legends they'll sing of you! To say nothing of the fact that you'll be rescuing the poor people of this island from their sad fate," continued the dwarf in solemn tones.

"People?" Tanin said, startled. "You mean this place is inhabited?"

"Aye, there are people here," the dwarf said with a gusty sigh, though he was eyeing the brothers shrewdly.

"Yes," said Sturm, staring intently at the beach. "There are people, all right. And it doesn't look to me, Dougan Redhammer, like they want to be rescued!"

Tanin, Palin, Sturm, and the dwarf were ferried across the water from the *Miracle* by a party of gnomes in a dinghy. Bringing along the dinghy had been the dwarf's idea, and the gnomes were enchanted with something so practical and simple. The gnomes had themselves designed a lifeboat to be attached to *Miracle*. Roughly the same weight and dimensions as the ship, the lifeboat had been left behind, to be studied by a committee.

As the boat drew nearer shore, surging forward with the waves and the incoming tide, the brothers could see the welcoming party. The rising sun glinted off spears and shields carried by a crowd of men who were awaiting their arrival on the beach. Tall and muscular, the men wore little clothing in the balmy clime of the island. Their skin was a rich, glistening brown, their bodies adorned with bright beads and feathers, their faces were stern and resolute. The shields they carried were made of wood and painted with garish designs, the spears were handmade as well—wooden with stone tips.

"Honed nice and sharp, you can believe me," said Sturm gloomily. "They'll go through flesh like a knife through butter."

"We're outnumbered at least twenty to one," Tanin pointed out to Dougan, who was sitting in the prow of the boat, fingering a battle-ax that was nearly the size of the dwarf.

"Bah! Primitives!" said Dougan contemptuously, though Palin noted the dwarf's face was a bit pale. "First sight of steel, they'll bow down and worship us as gods."

The "gods'" arrival on the beach was something less than majestic. Tanin and Sturm did look quite magnificent in their bright steel armor of elven make and design—a gift from Porthios and Alhana of the United Elven Kingdoms. Their breastplates glittered in the morning sun, their helms gleamed brightly. Climbing out of the boat, they sank to their shins in the sand and, within minutes, were both firmly mired.

Dougan, dressed in his suit of red velvet, demanded that the gnomes take him clear into shore so he would not ruin his clothes. The dwarf had added to his costume a wide-brimmed hat decorated with a white plume that fluttered in the ocean breeze, and he was truly a wonderful sight, standing proudly in the prow of the boat with his axe at his side, glaring sternly at the warriors drawn up in battle formation on the beach. The gnomes obeyed his injunction to the letter, running the boat aground on the beach with such force that Dougan tumbled out head first, narrowly missing slicing himself in two with his great battle-ax.

Palin had often imagined his first battle—fighting at the side of his brothers, combining steel and magic. He had spent the journey into shore committing the few spells he knew to memory. As he drew toward shore, his pulse raced with what he told himself was excitement, not fear. He was prepared for almost any eventuality . . . with the exception of helping a cursing, sputtering, irate dwarf to his feet; trying to dislodge his brothers from the sand; and facing an army of silent, grim, half-naked men.

"Why don't they attack us?" Sturm muttered, floundering about in the water, trying to keep his balance. "They could cut us to ribbons!"

"Maybe they have a law prohibiting them from harming idiots!" snapped Tanin irritably.

Dougan had managed, with Palin's help, to stagger to his feet. Shaking his fist, he sent the gnomes on their way back to the ship with a parting curse, then turned and, with as much dignity as he could bluster, stomped across the beach toward the warriors. Tanin and Sturm followed more slowly, hands on the hilts of their swords. Palin came after his brothers more slowly still, his white robes wet and bedraggled, the hem caked with sand.

The warriors waited for them in silence, unmoving, their faces expressionless as they watched the strangers approach. But Palin noticed, as he drew near, that occasionally one of the men would glance uneasily back into the nearby jungle. Observing this happening more than once, Palin turned his attention to the trees. After watching and listening intently for a moment, he drew nearer Tanin.

"There's something in the jungle," he said in an undertone.

"I wouldn't doubt it," Tanin growled. "Probably another fifty or so warriors."

"I don't know," Palin said thoughtfully, shaking his head. "The warriors appear to be nervous about it, maybe even—"

"Shush!" Tanin ordered sharply. "This is no time to talk, Palin! Now keep behind Sturm and me, like you're supposed to!"

"But—" Palin began.

Tanin flashed him a look of anger, meant to remind the young man who was in charge. With a sigh, Palin took up his position behind his brothers. But his eyes went to the jungle, and he again noticed that more than one of the warriors allowed his gaze as well to stray in that direction.

"Hail!" cried Dougan, stumping through the sand to stand in front of a warrior who, by standing out slightly in front of his fellows, appeared to be the chief. "Us gods!" proclaimed the dwarf, thumping himself on the chest. "Come from Land of Rising Sun to Give Greeting to our Subjects on Isle of Gargath."

"You're a dwarf," said the warrior glumly, speaking excellent Common. "You've come from Ansalon and you're probably after the Graygem."

"Well . . . uh . . . now . . ." Dougan appeared flustered. "That's . . . uh . . . a good guess, lad. We are, as it happens, mildly interested in . . . uh . . . the Graygem. If you'd be so good as to tell us where we might find it—"

"You can't have it," said the warrior, his voice still depressed sounding. He raised his spear. "We're here to stop you."

The warriors behind him nodded unenthusiastically, fumbling with their spears and clumsily falling into some sort of ragged battle formation. Again, Palin noticed many of them looking into the jungle with that same nervous, preoccupied expression.

"Well, we're going to take it!" Tanin shouted fiercely, apparently trying to drum up some enthusiasm for the battle. "You'll have to fight us to stop us."

"I guess we will," mumbled the chief, hefting his spear in half-hearted fashion.

Somewhat confused, Tanin and Sturm nevertheless drew their swords, as Dougan, his face grim, lifted his axe. The words to a spell chant were on Palin's lips, the Staff of Magius seemed to tremble with eagerness in his hand. But Palin hesitated. From all he'd heard, battles weren't supposed to be like this! Where was the hot blood? the ferocious hatred? the bitter determination to die where one stood rather than give an inch of ground?

The warriors shuffled forward, prodding each other along. Tanin closed on them, his sword flashing in the sun, Sturm at his back. Suddenly, a cry came from the jungle. There was movement and a rustling sound, more cries, and then a yelp of pain. A small figure dashed out of the trees, running headlong across the sand.

"Wait!" Palin yelled, running forward to stop his brothers. "It's a child!"

The warriors turned at the sound. "Damn!" muttered the chief, tossing his shield and spear into the sand in disgust. The child—a little girl of about five—ran to the warrior and threw her arms around his legs. At that moment, another child, older than the first,

---

came running out of the woods in pursuit.

"I thought I told you to keep her with you!" the chief said to older child, a boy, who came dashing up.

"She bit me!" said the boy accusingly, exhibiting bloody marks on his arm.

"You're not going to hurt my daddy, are you?" the little girl asked Tanin, glaring at him with dark eyes.

"N-no," stuttered Tanin, taken aback. He lowered his sword. "We're just"—he shrugged, flushing scarlet—"talking. You know, man-talk."

"Bless my beard!" exclaimed the dwarf in awe. More children were running from the jungle—children of all ages from toddlers who could barely make their way across the sand to older boys and girls of about ten or eleven. The air was filled with their shrill voices.

"I'm bored. Can we go home?"

"Lemme hold the spear!"

"No, it's my turn! Dad told me—"

"Apu said a bad word!"

"Did not!"

"Did so!"

"Look, Daddy! That short, fat man with the hair on his face! Isn't he ugly?"

Glancing at the strangers in deep embarrassment, the warriors turned from their battle formation to argue with their children.

"Listen, Blossom, Daddy's just going to be a little longer. You go back and play—"

"Apu, take your brothers back with you and *don't* let me hear you using language like that or I'll—"

"No, dear, Daddy needs the spear right now. You can carry it on the way home—"

"Halt!" roared the dwarf. Dougan's thunderous shout cut through the confusion, silencing warrior and child alike.

"Look," said Tanin, sheathing his sword, his own face flushed with embarrassment, "we don't want to fight you, especially in front of your kids. . . ."

"I know," the chief said, chagrined. "It's always like that. We haven't had a good battle in two years! Have you ever"—he gave Tanin a pained look—"tried to fight with a toddler underfoot?"

Profoundly perplexed, Tanin shook his head.

"Takes all the fun out of it," added another warrior as one child swarmed up his back and another bashed him in the shins with his shield.

"Leave them at home with their mothers, then, where they belong," said Dougan gruffly.

The warriors' expression grew grimmer still. At the mention of their mothers, several of the children began to cry. The whole group began to turn away from the beach.

"We can't," muttered a warrior.

"Why not?" demanded Dougan.

"Because their mothers are gone!"

"It all started two years ago," said the chief, walking with Dougan and the brothers back to the village. "Lord Gargath sent a messenger to our village, demanding ten maidens be paid him in tribute or he'd unleash the power of the Graygem." The warrior's eyes went to the volcano in the distance, its jagged top barely visible amid the shifting gray clouds that surrounded it. Forked lightning streaked from the cloud, thunder rumbled. The chief shivered and shook his head. "What could we do? We paid him his tribute. But it didn't stop there. The next month, here came the messenger again. Ten more maidens, and more the month following. Soon, we ran out of maidens, and then the Lord demanded our wives. Then he sent for our mothers! Now"—the chief sighed—"there isn't a

261

woman left in the village!"

"All of them!" Sturm gaped. "He's taken *all* of them!"

The chief nodded in despair, the child in his arms wailed in grief. "And not only us. It happened to every tribe on the island. We used to be a fierce, proud people," the chief added, his dark eyes flashing. "Our tribes were constantly at war. To win honor and glory in battle was what we lived for, to die fighting was the noblest death a man could find! Now, we lead lives of drudgery—"

"Our hands in dishwater instead of blood," said another. "Mending clothes instead of cracking skulls."

"To say nothing of what *else* we're missing, without the women," added a third with a meaningful look.

"Well, why don't you go get them back!" Tanin demanded.

The warriors, to a man, looked at him with undisguised horror, many glancing over their shoulders at the smoking volcano, expressions of terror on their faces, as if fearing they might be overheard.

"Attack the powerful Lord Gargath?" asked the chief in what was practically a whisper. "Face the wrath of the Graygem's master? No!" He shuddered, holding his child close. "At least now our children have one parent."

"But if all the tribes fought together," Sturm argued, "that would be, how many men? Hundreds? Thousands?"

"If there were millions, we would not go up against the Master of the Graygem," said the chief.

"Well, then," said Dougan sharply, "why did you try to stop us back there on the beach? Seems to me you would be only too glad to rid yourselves of the thing!"

"Lord Gargath ordered us to fight any who tried to take it," said the chief simply.

Reaching their village—a scattering of thatched huts that had seen better days—the warriors dispersed, some taking children to bed, others hurrying to look into steaming pots, still others heading for a stream with baskets loaded with clothes.

"Dougan," said Tanin, watching all this in astonishment almost too great for words, "this doesn't make any sense! What's going on?"

"The power of the Graygem, lad," said the dwarf solemnly. "They're deep under its spell and can no longer see anything rationally. I'll lay ten to one that it's the Graygem keeping them from attacking Lord Gargath. But us, now"—the dwarf looked at the brothers cunningly—"we're not under its spell—"

"Not yet," mentioned Palin.

"—and therefore we stand a chance of defeating him! After all, how powerful can he be?"

"Oh, he could have an army of a couple thousand men or so," said Sturm.

"No, no," said Dougan hastily. "If he did, he would have just sent the army to attack the villages, kill the men, and carry off the women. Lord Gargath is using the power of the Graygem because that's all he's got! We must act quickly, though, lads, because its power will grow on us the longer we stay near its influence."

Tanin frowned, considering. "How do we get the Graygem, then?" he asked abruptly. "And what do we do with it after we've got it? It seems to me, we'll be in worse danger than ever!"

"Ah, leave that to me!" said Dougan, rubbing his hands. "Just help me to get it, lads."

Tanin kept on frowning.

"And think of the women—poor things," the dwarf continued sadly, "held in thrall by this wicked lord, forced to submit to his evil will. They'll undoubtedly be grateful to the brave men who rescue them. . . ."

"He's right," said Sturm in sudden resolve. "It is our duty, Tanin, as future Knights of Solamnia, to rescue the women."

"What do you say, Little Brother?" asked Tanin.

"It is my duty as a mage of the White Robes to help these people," Palin said, feeling extremely self-righteous. "*All* these people," he added.

"Plus it's a matter of honor, lad," Dougan said solemnly. "You *did* lose the bet. And it will be a few days before the gnomes have the ship repaired. . . ."

"And the women will probably be *very* grateful!" struck in Sturm.

"All right, we'll go!" said Tanin. "Though I'd rather face a dragon than fight the power of some sort of weird rock—"

"Ha, ha, dragon!" repeated the dwarf, with a sickly grin that Tanin was too preoccupied to notice.

The brothers and the dwarf walked up to the chief, who was hanging laundry out to dry and keeping an anxious eye on the stew pot to see that it didn't boil over.

"Listen to me, men!" Tanin called loudly, motioning the warriors of the village to gather around him. "My brothers and the dwarf and I are going to go to the castle of this Lord Gargath to take the Graygem. Would any of you like to come along?"

Glancing at each other, the warriors shook their heads.

"Well, then," Tanin continued in exasperation, "will any of you go with us as our guide? You can come back when we reach the castle."

Again, the warriors shook their heads.

"Then we'll go alone!" Tanin said fiercely. "And we will return with the Graygem or leave our lives in that castle!"

Spinning on his heel, the big man stalked out of the

camp, his brothers and the dwarf marching behind. As they left, however, they encountered dark looks from the warriors and heard muttered comments. More than a few shook their fists at them.

"They certainly don't look pleased," Tanin muttered. "Especially since we're the ones facing all the danger. What is it they're saying?"

"I think it's just occurred to them that the women will probably be *very* grateful," Dougan answered in a low voice.

by Margaret Weis and Tracy Hickman

CHAPTER FIVE

A Matter of Honor

Sturm later maintained that Tanin should have realized what was going on and kept the dwarf out of the game that night. Tanin retorted that Sturm should stay out of it since he slept through the whole thing. But Palin reminded them both that they were all under the influence of the Graygem at the time, so it probably wouldn't have made any difference anyway.

They had walked all day, moving easily through the thick jungle, following a trail that had obviously been there for years. The major problem was the heat, which was intense. Sturm and Tanin soon took off their armor and packed it away and finally convinced Palin to strip off his white robes, though he protested long against wandering the wilderness clad only in his undergarments.

"Look," said Tanin, finally, after Palin was on the verge of collapse, his robes dripping with sweat, "there aren't any women around, that much we know. Hang your spell bags around your waist. We can always get dressed again before we reach the next village." Palin reluctantly agreed and, other than taking some ribbing from Sturm about his skinny legs, was thankful he did so. The jungle grew steamier as the sun rose higher. Intermittent rain showers cooled the brothers and the dwarf occasionally, but in the end served only to increase the humidity.

Dougan, however, steadfastly refused to shed so much as his broad-brimmed hat, maintaining that the heat was nothing to a dwarf and ridiculing the humans for their weakness. This he did with perspiration streaming down his face until it dripped off the ends of his moustaches. He marched along with a defiant air, as if daring one of them to say something, and often grumbled that they were slowing him down. Yet Palin saw Dougan more than once, when he thought no one was looking, slump down on a rock, fan himself with his hat, and mop his face with his beard.

By the time they arrived at the next village, which was about a day's walk through the jungle, all of them—even the dwarf—were so limp and tired that they barely had the strength to put their clothes and their armor back on in order to make an impressive show. Word of their coming must have traveled in some mysterious way (Palin thought he knew, then, the reason for the strange drum beats they'd been hearing), for they were met by the men of the village and the children. The men regarded them coldly (though more than a few eyes flashed at the sight of the elven armor), gave them food and drink, and indicated a hut where they could spend the night. Tanin made a stirring speech about storming Gargath Castle and asked for volunteers.

The only response was dark looks, shuffling feet, and a muttered comment, "I can't, I got a chicken stewing. . . ."

This being no more than they had expected, the brothers stripped off their armor and their clothes and went to bed. Their night's rest was unbroken, save for slapping at some sort of winged, carnivorous insect that apparently had a craving for human flesh, and one other incident.

Around midnight, Tanin was wakened by the dwarf, shaking his shoulder and loudly calling his name.

"Whasit?" mumbled Tanin sleepily, fumbling for his sword.

"Nay, lad, put your weapon away," said Dougan, hurriedly. "I just need to know something, lad. You and me and your brothers, we're comrades, aren't we?"

Tanin recalled, as well as he could recall anything, that the dwarf had seemed particularly anxious about this and had repeated the question several times.

"Yeah, comrades," Tanin muttered, rolling over.

"What's mine is yours, yours is mine?" persisted the dwarf, leaning over to look the young man in the face.

"Yeah, yeah." Tanin waved a hand, brushing away a feeding insect and the dwarf's beard at the same time.

"Thank you, lad! Thank you," said Dougan gratefully. "You won't regret it."

Tanin said later that the dwarf's last words, "You won't regret it," lingered ominously in his dreams, but he was too tired to wake up and ponder the situation.

As it was, he had plenty of time for pondering the next morning when he woke to find a spear point at his throat and several tall warriors standing over him. A quick glance showed him his brothers in similar circumstances.

"Sturm!" Tanin called, not daring to move and keeping his hands in plain sight. "Palin, wake up!"

His brothers woke quickly at the sound of alarm in his voice, and stared at their captors in sleepy surprise.

"Tanin," said Palin, keeping his voice even, "what's going on?"

"I don't know, but I'm going to find out!" Tanin angrily thrust the spear point aside. "What is this nonsense?" he asked, starting to stand up. The spear point was at his throat again, joined, this time, by two more—one at his chest, the other jabbing him in the back.

"Tell them that no matter how grateful the women are, it won't matter to us!" said Sturm, swallowing and trying in vain to inch backward. The spear followed him. "We're going to be knights! We've taken vows of celibacy. . . ."

"It's . . . uh . . . not the women, lad," muttered a shamefaced Dougan, entering the hut and thrusting his head in between the warriors. "It's . . . uh . . . a matter of honor . . . so to speak. The truth of it is, lads," the dwarf continued with a heart-rending sigh, "I got into a wee bit of a game last night."

"So?" grunted Tanin. "What has that got to do with us?"

"I'll explain," Dougan began, licking his lips, his eyes darting from one to the other of the brothers. "I threw the bones well the first hour or two. Won the chief's feather head-dress *and* two cows. I was going to quit then, I swear it, but the old boy was upset, and so what could I do but let him try to win them back? My luck was going that good, I bet it all on one toss, plus threw in my axe and my own hat as well."

Tanin looked at the dwarf's bare head. "You lost."

Dougan's shoulders slumped. "I didn't miss the other so much, but I couldn't do without my hat, now could I? So I bet all my money against the hat and—" He looked at Tanin wistfully.

"You lost that, too," Tanin muttered.

"Snake eyes," said the dwarf sadly.

"So now you've lost your money and your hat—"

"Not quite," Dougan hedged. "You see, I just couldn't do without my hat. . . . And I didn't have anything left that the old boy wanted, my jacket not fitting him. And you *did* say we were comrades, share and share alike—"

"When did you say that?" Sturm demanded, glaring at Tanin.

"I don't remember!" Tanin growled.

"So, I bet your armor," said the dwarf.

"You what?" Tanin roared in fury.

"The chief had taken a liking to it when he saw it on you last evening," continued Dougan rapidly. Even with five spears pointed directly at him, Tanin looked extremely formidable and extremely angry. "I bet your armor against my hat, and I won." The dwarf was smug.

"Thank Paladine!" breathed Tanin, relaxing.

"Then—" said Dougan, looking uncomfortable, "since my luck was obviously turning, I decided to try for my money back. I bet the armor, my hat, and"— he pointed—"the magic staff against my money, the cows, and a goat."

This time it was Palin who sat forward (oblivious of the spears), his face deathly pale, his lips ashen. "You bet . . . my staff!" He could scarcely speak. Reaching out a trembling hand, he grasped hold of the staff which lay at his side even while he slept.

"Aye, lad," said Dougan, regarding him with wide-eyed innocence. "We're comrades. Share and share—"

"This staff," said Palin in a low, shaking voice, "belonged to my uncle, Raistlin Majere! It was a gift from him—"

"Indeed?" Dougan appeared impressed. "I wish I had known that, lad," he said wistfully, "I would have wagered more—"

"What happened?" Palin demanded feverishly.

"I lost." Dougan heaved a sigh. "I've seen a man roll snake eyes twice in a game only once before and that was when I— Well, never mind."

"You lost my staff!" Palin seemed near fainting.

"And our armor?" Sturm shouted, veins swelling in his neck.

"Wait!" Dougan held up his hand hastily. The warriors with the spears, despite their weapons and their obvious advantage, were beginning to look a little nervous. "I knew how upset you lads would be, losing all your possessions like this, so I did the only thing I could. I wagered your swords."

This time the shock was so great that neither Tanin nor Sturm could speak, they simply stared at Dougan in stunned silence.

"I put up the swords and my battle-ax against the magic staff and my hat—I truly wish"—Dougan glanced at the shaken Palin—"that I'd known the staff belonged to Raistlin of the Black Robes. Even here, they've heard of him, and I likely could have gotten the chief to throw in the armor. As it was, he wasn't all that impressed with what he'd seen of the staff—"

"Get on with it!" Palin cried in a choked voice, clutching the staff close.

"I won!" Dougan spread his hands, then sighed again, only this was a sigh of ecstasy. "Ah, what a throw that was. . . ."

"So . . . I have my staff?" Palin asked timidly, brightening.

"We have our swords?" Tanin and Sturm began to breathe.

"Finding that my luck had shifted," the dwarf said, plunging the brothers into gloom once more, "I decided to try for the armor again. Figuring what good were swords without armor, I bet the weapons and—" He gestured bleakly toward the warriors with the spears.

"You lost," Tanin said glumly.

"But I still have my staff?" Palin asked nervously.

"Aye, lad. I tried to use it to win back the swords, my axe, and the armor, but the chief didn't want it." Dougan shook his head, then gazed at Palin intently, a sudden, cunning expression twisting his face. "But if you were to tell him it belonged to the great Raistlin Majere, perhaps I could—"

"No!" snarled Palin, holding the staff close.

"But, lad," pleaded the dwarf, "my luck's bound to

change. And we're comrades, after all. Share and share alike . . . "

"This is great!" said Sturm gloomily, watching the last of his armor being carried out of the hut. "Well, I guess there's nothing left to do now but go back to the ship—"

"The ship?" Dougan appeared astonished. "When we're so close! Why, Lord Gargath's castle's only a day's march from here!"

"And what are we going to do when we get there?" Tanin demanded furiously. "Knock on the door in our underwear and ask him to lend us weapons so that we can fight him?"

"Look at it this way, Big Brother," Sturm muttered, "he might drop over dead from laughter."

"How can you joke at a time like this?" Tanin raged. "And I'm not certain I'm ready to leave yet."

"Easy, my brothers," Palin said softly. "If all we've lost from this fool quest is some weapons and armor, I'm beginning to think we can count ourselves lucky. I agree with Sturm, Tanin. We better head back for the ship before the day gets much hotter."

"That's easy for you to say!" Tanin retorted bitterly. "You've still got your precious staff!" He looked over to the chief's hut, where the old man was happily decking himself out in the bright armor, putting most of it on upside down. Then he cast a dark glance at the contrite Dougan. "I suppose Palin's right," Tanin said grudgingly, glaring at the dwarf. "We should count ourselves lucky. We've had enough of this fool quest, dwarf. We're getting out of here before we lose anything else—like our lives!"

Turning, Tanin found himself, once again, facing a ring of spears and this time his own sword, held by a grinning warrior.

"Wanna bet, lad?" Dougan said cheerfully, twirling his moustaches.

"I thought as much," Palin remarked.

"You're always thinking 'as much' when it's too late to do anything about it!" Tanin snapped.

"It was too late when we first set eyes on the dwarf," Palin said in low tones.

The three, plus Dougan, were being escorted down the jungle trail, spears at their backs, the castle of Lord Gargath looming ahead of them. They could see it quite clearly now—a huge, misshapen building made entirely of shining gray marble. All three brothers had visited the Tower of High Sorcery in Wayreth Forest, and they had been impressed and overawed by the magical aura that surrounded it. They felt a similar awe approaching this strange castle, only it was an awe mingled with the wild desire to laugh hysterically.

None of them could tell afterward what Castle Gargath looked like, since the appearance of the castle shifted constantly. First it was a massive fortress with four tall, stalwart towers topped by battlements. As they watched in amazement, the towers swelled out and spiraled upward into graceful minarets. Then the towers melted together, forming one gigantic dome that separated into four square towers once more. While all this was going on, turrets sprouted from the walls like fungi, windows blinked open and shut, a drawbridge over a moat became a bower of gray roses over a still, gray pond.

"The power of the Graygem," Dougan remarked.

"'The power of the Graygem,'" Tanin mimicked sarcastically. He shook his fist at the dwarf. "I'm getting so sick of hearing about that blasted rock that I—"

"I meant that I've figured out what's going on!" Palin interrupted.

"Well, what?" Sturm asked miserably. "They don't want us to go, apparently. Yet they threaten to kill us if we try to turn back! They take our clothes . . ."

In addition to losing their armor and their weapons, he and Tanin had been stripped of their clothes; the chief having discovered that the armor chafed without anything underneath it. Sturm and Tanin, therefore, were now approaching Gargath Castle clad only in loin cloths (having coldly refused the offer of breast-plates made of bone).

Palin and Dougan had been more fortunate, the mage having kept his robes and the dwarf his red velvet jacket and breeches (minus the hat). The reason for this leniency on the chief's part was, Palin suspected, Dougan's whispered remarks to the chief concerning the staff. Contrary to what the dwarf had anticipated, the fact that the staff belonged to Raistlin Majere caused the chief to open his eyes wide in terror. Palin also suspected Dougan of continuing to try to drum up a game (the dwarf wanted his hat back badly), but the chief obviously wanted no part of an object of such evil. The members of the tribe kept a respectful distance from Palin after that, some waving chickens' feet in his direction when they thought he wasn't watching.

It didn't stop the warriors from marching him off down the trail at spear point toward the castle with his brothers and the chagrined Dougan, however.

"Put yourself in the place of one of these warriors," said Palin, sweating in his hot robes but not daring to take them off for fear the warriors would grab them. "You are under the influence of the Graygem, which is literally Chaos personified. You hate the Graygem more than anything, yet you are ordered to guard it with your life. Because of the Graygem, you've lost your women. Strangers come to take the Graygem and rescue your women, who will undoubtedly be grateful to their saviors. You don't want strangers saving your womenfolk, but you'd give anything to have your women back. You must guard the Graygem, but you'd do anything to get rid of it. Are you following me?"

"Sort of," Tanin said cautiously. "Go on."

"So you take the strangers," Palin finished, "and send them to the castle naked and weaponless, knowing they're bound to lose, yet hoping in your heart they'll win."

"That makes sense, in a weird sort of way," Sturm admitted, looking at Palin with undisguised admiration. "So, what do we do now?"

"Yes, Palin," Tanin said gravely. "I can fight minotaur and draconians . . . I'd *rather* be fighting minotaur and draconians," he added, breathing heavily, the heat and humidity taking its toll on the big man, "but I'm lost here. I can't fight chaos. I don't understand what's going on. If we're going to get out of this, it's up to you and your magic, Little Brother."

Palin's eyes stung with sudden tears. It had been worth it, he thought. It had been worth this whole insane adventure to know that he had finally won his brothers' respect and admiration and trust. It was something a man might willingly die to achieve. . . . For a moment, he did not trust himself to speak, but walked on in silence, leaning on the Staff of Magius, which felt oddly cool and dry in the hot, humid jungle.

Glancing over at the dwarf, Palin was disconcerted to find Dougan regarding him with a wolfish leer on the black-bearded face. The dwarf didn't say anything aloud but, giving Palin a wink, he formed words with his lips.

"Wanna bet?"

CHAPTER SIX

Castle Gargath

It was nearing sundown when they reached the outer walls of Castle Gargath. The walls shifted aspect just like the castle. Sometimes they appeared to be built of bricks. When the brothers looked again, however, the walls were hedges, then iron bars.

On reaching the base of the shifting walls, the warriors left them, returning to their villages despite another recruiting speech from Tanin. The speech was a half-hearted attempt at best. The fact that he was giving it practically naked lessened his enthusiasm, plus he was fairly certain it was bound to fail.

"Come with us! Show this evil lord that you are men! That you intend to stand up to him and fight! Show him you are willing to risk your lives in defense of your homes!"

He was right. The speech had not worked. The moment the shadow of the shifting castle walls fell over them, the warriors backed away, looking up at it in terror. Shaking their heads and muttering, they fled back into the jungle.

"At least leave us your spears?" Sturm pleaded.

That didn't work either.

"They need their spears," Tanin said, "to make certain we don't hightail it back to the ship."

"Aye, you're right, lad," said Dougan, peering into the trees. "They're out there, watching us. And there they'll stay until—" He stopped.

"Until what?" Palin demanded coldly. He could still see the dwarf's leer and hear the unspoken words, and he shivered in the jungle heat.

"Until they're certain we're not coming back. Right?" Sturm said.

"Now, laddie, we'll be coming back," Dougan said soothingly, stroking his beard. "After all, you have me with you. And we're comrades—"

"Share and share alike," Tanin and Sturm both said grumpily.

"The first thing we have to do is make some weapons," Tanin continued. He looked around. Thick jungle vegetation grew all around them. Strange-looking trees of various types and kinds festooned with hanging vines and brightly colored flowers grew right up to within a foot of the wall that was now made of thorny rose-bushes. And there it stopped. "Not even the jungle comes near this place," he muttered. There were no animal noises either, he noticed. "Palin, give me your knife."

"Good idea," said the young mage. "I'd forgotten about it." Rolling up his white sleeve, Palin fumbled at the dagger in its cunning leather thong that held it to his forearm and was supposed to—at a flick of its owner's wrist—release the dagger and allow it to drop down into Palin's hand. But the cunning thong was apparently more cunning that its master, for Palin couldn't get the dagger loose.

"Here," he said, flushing in embarrassment and holding out his arm to Tanin, "you get it."

Keeping his smile carefully concealed, Tanin managed to free the dagger, which he and Sturm used to cut off tree branches. These they honed into crude spears, working rapidly. Day was dying a lingering death, the light fading from the sky, leaving it a sickly gray color.

"Do you know anything of this Lord Gargath?" Tanin asked Dougan as he worked, whittling the point of the green stick sharp.

"No," said the dwarf, watching in disapproval. He had refused to either make or carry a wooden spear.

"A fine sight I'd look if I'm killed, standing before Reorx with a stick in my hand! Naw, I need no weapon but my bare hands!" the dwarf had snarled. Now he was rubbing his chin, pacing back and forth beneath the strange walls that were now made of shining black marble. "I know nothing of this present Lord Gargath, save what I could find out from those cowards." Dougan waved his hand contemptuously at the long-gone warriors.

"What do they say?"

"That he is what you might expect of someone who has been under the influence of the Graygem for years!" Dougan said, eyeing Tanin irritably. "He is a wild man! Capable of great good or great evil, as the mood—or the gem—sways him. Some say," the dwarf added in low tones, switching his gaze to Palin, "that he is a wizard. A renegade, granting his allegiance to neither White, nor Black, nor Red. He lives only for himself—and the gem."

Shivering, Palin gripped his staff more tightly. Renegade mages refused to follow the laws and judgments of the Conclave of Wizards, laws that had been handed down through the centuries in order to keep magic alive in a world where it was despised and distrusted. All wizards, those who followed both the paths of Good and of Evil, subscribed to these laws. Renegades were a threat to everyone and, as such, their lives were forfeit.

It would be Palin's duty, as a mage of the White Robes, to try to reclaim the renegade or, if that failed, to trap him and bring him to the Conclave for justice. It would be a difficult task for a powerful wizard of the White Robes, much less an apprentice mage. Those of the Black Robes had it easier. "You, my uncle, would have simply killed him," Palin murmured in a low voice, leaning his cheek against his staff.

"What do you think he's done with the women?" Sturm asked anxiously.

The dwarf shrugged. "Used them for his pleasure, tossed them into the volcano, sacrificed them in some unholy magic rite. How should I know?"

Sturm looked grave; Tanin scowled; and Palin, truth be told, looked frightened.

"Well, we're about as ready as we'll ever be, I guess," Tanin said heavily, gathering up a handful of spears. "These look stupid," he muttered. "Maybe the dwarf's right. If we're facing an evil wizard gone berserk, we might as well die fighting with dignity instead of like kids playing at knights and goblins."

"A weapon's a weapon, Tanin," Sturm said matter-of-factly, taking a spear in his hand. "At least it gives us some advantage. . . ."

The three brothers and the dwarf approached the wall that was still changing its aspect so often it made them dizzy to watch it.

"I don't suppose there's any point trying to find a secret way in," Tanin said.

"By the time we found it, it'd likely be turning into the front door," Dougan agreed. "If we wait here long enough, there's bound to be an opening."

Sure enough, but not exactly the opening any of them anticipated.

One moment they were looking at a wall of solid stone ("Dwarvish make," remarked Dougan, admiringly) when it changed to a wall of water, thundering down around them out of nowhere, soaking them with its spray.

"We can get through this, I think!" Sturm cried above the noise of the waterfall. "I can see through it! The castle's on the other side!"

"Yes, and there's likely to be a chasm on the other

---

side as well!" Tanin returned.

"Wait," said Palin. *"Shirak!"* He spoke the magic word to the staff and, instantly the faceted crystal globe on top burst into light.

"Ah, I wish the chief had seen *that!*" said the dwarf wistfully.

Palin thrust the staff into the water, simply with the idea of being able to see something beyond it. To his amazement, however, the water parted the instant the staff touched it. Flowing down around the staff, it formed an archway that it seemed they could walk through, safe and dry.

"I'll be damned!" Tanin said in awe. "Did you know it would do that, Little Brother?"

"No," Palin admitted shakily, wondering what other powers Raistlin had invested into the staff.

"Well, thank Paladine it did," Sturm said, peering through the hole in the water. "All safe over here," he reported, stepping through. "In fact," he added as Palin and Tanin and Dougan—with a wide-eyed gaze of longing at the staff—followed. "It's a grass lawn!" Sturm said in wonder, looking around in the gray gloom by the light of the staff. Behind them, the water changed again, this time to a wall of bamboo. Ahead of them stretched a long, smooth sward that rose up a gentle slope, leading to the castle itself.

"Now it's grass, but it's liable to change into a lava pit any moment," Palin pointed out.

"You're right, Little Brother," Tanin grunted. "We better run for it."

Run they did; Palin hiking up his white robes, the stout dwarf huffing and puffing along about three steps behind. Whether they truly made their destination before the sward had time to change into something more sinister or whether the sward was always a sward, they never knew. At any rate, they reached the castle wall just as night's black shadows closed in on them, and they were still standing on smooth, soft grass.

"Now all we need," said Sturm, "is a way inside—"

The blank wall of gray marble that they had been facing shimmered in the staff's light, and a small wooden door appeared, complete with iron hinges and an iron lock.

Hurrying forward, Tanin tugged at the lock.

"Bolted fast," he reported.

"Just when a kender would come in handy," Sturm said with a sigh.

"Kender! Bite your tongue!" Dougan muttered in disgust.

"Palin, try the staff," Tanin ordered, standing aside.

Hesitantly, Palin touched the brilliantly glowing crystal of the staff to the lock. The lock not only gave way, but it actually melted, forming a puddle of lead at Palin's feet.

"Lad," said the dwarf, swallowing, "your uncle must have been a remarkable man. That's all I can say."

"I wonder what else it can do?" Palin muttered, staring at the staff with a mixture of awe, pride, and frustration.

"We'll have to worry about that later! Inside," said Tanin, yanking open the door. "Sturm, you go first. Palin follow him. We'll use your staff for light. The dwarf and I'll be right behind you."

They found themselves crowded together on a flight of narrow, winding stairs that spiraled upward. Walls surrounded them on all sides; they could see nothing save the stairs vanishing into darkness.

"You realize," said Palin suddenly, "that the door will—" Whirling around, he shone the light of the staff on a blank wall.

"Disappear," finished Tanin grimly.

"There goes our way out!" Shuddering, Sturm looked around. "These stairs could change! Any moment, we could be encased in solid rock!"

"Keep moving!" ordered Tanin urgently.

Running up the steep stairs as fast as they could, expecting to find themselves walking on anything from hot coals to a swinging bridge, they climbed up and up until, at last, the stout dwarf could go no farther.

"I've got to rest, lads," Dougan said, panting, leaning against a stone wall that was, unaccountably, remaining a stone wall.

"Nothing inside seems to be changing," Palin gasped, weary himself from the unaccustomed exercise. He looked with envy at his brothers. Their bronze-skinned, muscular bodies gleamed in the staff's light. Neither was even breathing hard.

"Palin, shine the light up here!" Sturm ordered, peering ahead.

His legs aching so that he thought he could never move them again, Palin forced himself to take another step, shining the staff's light around a corner of the stairwell. "There's a door!" Sturm said, in triumph. "We've reached the top!"

"I wonder what's beyond it," Tanin said darkly.

He was interrupted by, of all things, a giggle. "Why don't you open it and find out?" called a laughing voice from the other side of the door. "It's not locked."

The brothers looked at each other. Dougan frowned. Palin forgot his aching body, forcing himself to concentrate on his spell casting. Tanin's face tightened, his jaw muscles clenched. Gripping his spear, he thrust his way past Dougan and Palin to come stand beside Sturm.

Cautiously, both warriors put their hands on the

door.

"One, two, three," Sturm counted in a whisper.

On the count of three, he and Tanin threw their combined weight against the door, knocking it open and leaping through, spears at the ready. Palin ran after them, his hands extended, a spell of fire on his lips. Behind him, he could hear the dwarf roaring in fury.

They were greeted with peals of merry laughter.

"Did you ever see," came the giggling voice, "such cute legs?"

The mist of battle rage clearing from his eyes, Palin stared around blankly. He was surrounded, literally, by what must have been hundreds of women. Beside him, he heard Sturm's sharp intake of breath and he saw, dimly, Tanin lower his spear in confusion. From somewhere on the floor at his feet, he heard Dougan swearing, the dwarf having tripped over the door-stoop in his charge and fallen flat on his face. But Palin was too stunned, staring at his captors, to pay any attention to him.

An incredibly gorgeous, dark-haired and dark-eyed beauty approached Tanin. Putting her hand on his spear, she gently pushed it to one side. Her eyes lingered appreciatively on the young man's strong body, most of which—due to the loincloth—was on exhibit.

"My, my," said the young woman in a sultry voice, "did you know it was my birthday?"

More laughter sounded through the vast stone hall like the chiming of many bells.

"Just—just stay back," Tanin ordered gruffly, raising his spear and keeping the woman at bay.

"Well, of course," she said, raising her hands in mock terror. "If that's what you *really* want."

Tanin, his eyes on the dark-haired beauty, fell back

a pace to stand beside Palin. "Little Brother," he whispered, beads of sweat on his upper lip and trickling down his forehead, "are these women enchanted? Under some sort of spell?"

"N-no," stammered Palin, staring around him. "They . . . they don't appear to be. I don't sense any kind of magic, other than the force of the Graygem. It's much stronger here, but that's because we're closer to it."

"Lads," said the dwarf urgently, scrambling to his feet and thrusting himself between them, "we're in big trouble."

"We are?" Tanin asked dubiously, still holding the spear in front of him and noticing that Sturm was doing likewise. "Explain yourself, dwarf!" he growled. "What do you know about these women? They certainly don't appear to be prisoners! Are they banshees, vampires? What?"

"Worse," gasped the dwarf, mopping his face with his beard, his eyes staring wildly at the laughing, pointing females. "Lads, think! We're the first to enter this castle! These women probably haven't seen a man in two years!"

CHAPTER SEVEN
Our Heroes

Surrounded by hundreds of admiring women reaching out to touch them and fondle them, the confused and embarrassed "rescuers" were captured by kindness. Laughing and teasing them, the women led the brothers and the dwarf from the vast entry hall to a smaller room in the castle, a room filled with silken wall hangings and large, comfortable silk-covered couches. Before they knew quite what was happening, the men were being shoved down among the cushions by soft hands, the women offering them wine, sumptuous food, and delicacies of all sorts . . . *all* sorts.

"I think it's sweet, you coming all this way to rescue us," purred one of the women, leaning against Sturm and running her hand over his shoulder. Long blonde hair fell down her bare arm. She wore it tucked behind one ear, held back by a flower. Her gown, made of something gray and filmy, left very little to the imagination.

"All in a day's work," said Sturm, smiling. "We're going to be made Knights of Solamnia, you know," he added conversationally. "Probably for doing this very deed."

"Really? Tell me more."

But the blonde wasn't the least bit interested in the Knights. She wasn't even listening to Sturm, Palin realized, watching his brother with growing irritation. The big warrior was rambling on somewhat incoherently about the Oath and the Measure, all the while fondling the silky blonde hair and gazing into blue eyes.

Palin was ill-at-ease. The young mage felt a burning in his blood, his head buzzed—not an unusual sensation around such lovely, seductive females. He felt no desire for these women, however. They were strangely repulsive to him. It was the magic he sensed, burning within him. He wanted to concentrate on it, on his feeling of growing power. Thrusting aside a doe-eyed beauty who was trying to feed him grapes, Palin inched his way among the cushions to get nearer Sturm. The big man was enjoying the attentions of the attractive blonde to the fullest.

"Sturm, what are you doing? This could be a trap, an ambush!" Palin said in an undertone.

"Lighten up for once, Little Brother," Sturm said mildly, putting his arm around the blonde and drawing her close. "Here, I'll put your mind at ease. Tell me," he said, kissing the blonde's rosy lips, "is this an ambush?"

"Yes!" She giggled, wriggling closer. "You're under attack, right now."

"There you are, Palin. No help for it. We're surrounded." Sturm kissed the girl's neck. "I surrender," he said softly, "unconditionally."

"Tanin?" Alarmed, Palin looked to his oldest brother for help, and was relieved to see the serious young man getting to his feet, despite all efforts of the dark-haired beauty to drag him back down beside her. The dwarf, too, was doing his best to escape.

"Get away! Leave me be, woman!" Dougan roared, slapping at the hands of a lithesome girl. Struggling up from among the cushions, the red-faced dwarf turned to face the women.

"What about Lord Gargath? Where is he?" the dwarf demanded. "Using you women to seduce us, then capture us, no doubt?"

"Lord Gargath? Hardly!" The dark-haired beauty who had been making much of Tanin laughed, as did the other women in the room. Shrugging her lovely shoulders, she glanced at the ceiling. "He's up there . . . somewhere," she said without interest, caressing Tanin's bare chest. The big man shoved her away, glancing nervously about the room.

"For once you've made sense, dwarf. We better find this Gargath before he finds us. Come on." Tanin took a step toward a door at the end of the perfumed, candle-lit chamber, but the dark-haired beauty caught hold of his arm.

"Relax, warrior," she whispered. "You don't need to worry about Lord Gargath. He won't bother you or anybody." She ran her fingers admiringly through Tanin's thick, red curls.

"I'll see for myself," Tanin returned, but he sounded less enthusiastic.

"Very well, if you must." The woman sighed languorously, nestling her body against Tanin's. "But it's a waste of time—time that could be spent in much more pleasant pursuits. The dried-up old wizard's been our prisoner now for two years."

"He's *your* prisoner?" Tanin gaped.

"Well, yes," said in the blonde, looking up from nibbling at Sturm's ear. "He was such a boring old thing. Talking about pentagrams and wanting to know which of us were virgins and asking a lot of other personal questions. So we locked him in his old tower with his stupid rock." She kissed Sturm's muscular shoulder.

"Then who's been taking the women hostage all these months?" Palin demanded.

"Well, we did, of course," said the dark-haired beauty.

"You?" Palin said, stunned. He put his hand to his forehead and noticed his skin felt abnormally hot. He was dizzy, and his head ached. The room and everything in it seemed to be just slightly out of focus.

"This is a wonderful life!" said the blonde, sitting back, and teasingly rebuffing Sturm's attempts to pull her down. "The Graygem provides all we need. We live in luxury. There is no work, no cooking and mending—"

"No children screaming—"

"No husbands coming back from battle, bleeding and dirty—"

"No washing clothes in the stream day after day—"

"No endless talks of war and bragging about great deeds—"

"We read books," said the dark-haired beauty. "The wizard has many in his library. We became educated, and we found out we didn't have to live that kind of life anymore. We wanted our sisters and our mothers to share our comfortable surroundings with us, so *we* kept up the ruse, demanding that hostages be brought to the castle until all of us were here."

"Bless my beard!" exclaimed the dwarf in awe.

"All we lack are some nice men, to keep us from being lonely at night," said the blonde, smiling at Sturm. "And now that's been taken care of, thanks to the Graygem. . . ."

"I'm going to go find Lord Gargath," said Palin, standing up abruptly. But he was so dizzy that he staggered, scattering cushions over the floor. "Are the rest of you coming?" he asked, fighting this strange weakness and wondering why his brothers didn't seem afflicted.

"Yes," said Tanin, extricating himself with difficulty from the dark-haired beauty's embrace.

"Count on me, lad," said Dougan grimly.

"Sturm?" said Palin.

"Just leave me here," said Sturm. "I'll act as . . . rear guard. . . ."

The women broke into merry laughter.

"Sturm!" Tanin repeated angrily.

Sturm waved his hand. "Go ahead, if you're so keen on talking to some moldy old wizard, when you could be here, enjoying . . . "

Tanin opened his mouth again, his brows coming together in anger. But Palin stopped him. "Leave this to me," the young mage said with a twisted smile. Setting the staff down carefully among the cushions, Palin lifted both hands and held them out, pointing at Sturm. Then he began to chant.

"Hey! What are you doing? Stop!" Sturm gasped.

But Palin continued chanting and began raising his hands. As he did so, Sturm's prone body rose into the air, too, until soon the young man was floating a good six feet off the floor.

"Wonderful trick! Show us some more!" called out the women, applauding.

Palin spoke again, snapped his fingers, and ropes appeared out of nowhere, snaking up from the floor to wrap themselves around Sturm's arms and legs. The women squealed in glee, many of them transferring their admiring gazes from the muscular Sturm—now bound hand and foot—to the mage who could perform such feats.

"G-good trick, Palin. Now put me down!" Sturm said, licking his lips and glancing beneath him nervously. There was nothing between him and the floor but air.

Pleased with himself, Palin left Sturm in the air and turned to Tanin. "Shall I bring him along?" he asked casually, expecting to see Tanin regarding him with awe as well.

Instead, Palin found his older brother's brows furrowed in concern. "Palin," said Tanin in a low voice, "how did you do that?"

"Magic, my dear brother," Palin said, thinking suddenly how unaccountably stupid Tanin was.

"I know it was magic," Tanin said sharply. "And I admit I don't know much about magic. But I do know that only a powerful wizard could perform such a feat as that. *Not* one who just recently passed his Test!"

Looking back at the levitated Sturm hovering helplessly in the air, Palin nodded. "You're right," he said proudly. "I performed a high-level spell, without any assistance or aid! Not even the Staff of Magius helped me!" Reaching out, he took hold of the staff. The wood was cold to the touch, icy cold, almost painful. Palin gasped, almost dropping it. But then he noticed that the dizziness was easing. He felt his skin grow cool, the buzzing in his head diminished. "My magic!" he murmured. "The Graygem must be enhancing it! I've only been here a short while, and look what I can do! I have the power of an archmage. If I had the gem, I'd be as strong as my uncle!" Palin whispered to himself. "Maybe stronger!" His eyes glistened, his body began to tremble. "I'd use my power for Good, of course. I would seize the Tower at Palanthas from Dalamar and cleanse it of its evil. I would lift the curse from the Shoikan Grove, enter my uncle's laboratory." Thoughts and visions of the future came to him in a swirl of wild colors, so real and vivid he literally reeled at the sight.

Strong hands held him. Blinking, clearing the mist from his eyes, Palin looked down to see himself reflected in the bright, dark, cunning eyes of the dwarf. "Steady, laddie," said Dougan, "you're flying high, too high for one whose wings have just sprouted."

"Leave me alone!" Palin cried, pulling away from the dwarf's grip. "You want the gem yourself!"

"Aye, laddie," said Dougan softly, stroking his black beard. "And I have a right to it. I'm the *only* one who has a right to it, in fact!"

"Might makes right, dwarf," Palin said with a sneer. Picking up his staff, he started to walk toward the door. "Coming?" he asked Tanin coldly, "or must I bring you along as I'm carrying that great oaf!" Gesturing toward Sturm, he drew the young man toward him with a motion of his hand. Twisting his head, Sturm gazed back at Tanin in fear and alarm as he drifted through the air.

"Oh, no! Don't leave! Do some more tricks!" cried the women in dismay.

"Stop, young mage!" Dougan cried. "You're falling under the spell!"

"Palin!" Tanin's quiet voice cut through the buzzing in his brother's head and the laughter of the women and the shouts of the dwarf. "Don't listen to Dougan or me or anyone for a moment. Just listen to yourself."

"And what's *that* supposed to mean, my brother?" Palin scoffed. "Something wise that suddenly struck you? Did a brain finally make an appearance through all that muscle?"

He leered mockingly at Tanin, expecting—no, *hoping* that his brother would become angry and try to stop him. Then I'll *really* show him a trick or two! Palin thought. Just like my uncle showed my father . . .

But Tanin just stood there, regarding him gravely. "I— I— Name of the gods!" Palin faltered, putting his hand to his head. His cruel words came back to him. "Tanin, I'm sorry! I don't know what's come over me." Turning, he saw Sturm, hanging helplessly in the air. "Sturm!" Palin snapped his fingers. "I'm sorry! I'll let you go—"

"Palin, don't—!" Sturm began wildly, but it was too late.

The spell broken, the young man fell to the floor with a yell and a crash, to be instantly surrounded by cooing and clucking women. It was a few moments before Sturm made his appearance again, his red hair tousled, his face flushed. Getting to his feet, he pushed the women aside and limped toward his brothers.

"I was wrong," Palin said, shivering. "I understand now. These women *are* being held in thrall. . . . "

"Aye, lad," said Dougan. "Just as you were yourself. It's the power of the Graygem, trying to take hold of you, exploiting your weaknesses as it did theirs—"

"—by giving us what we want," Palin finished thoughtfully.

"That's what we'll turn into, the longer we stay here," Tanin added. "Slaves of the Graygem. Don't you see, these women are guarding it just as effectively *inside* this castle as their men are *outside*. That's why nothing changes in here. The Graygem's keeping it stable for them!"

The women began sidling nearer, reaching out their hands once more. "How boring . . . Don't go . . . Don't leave us . . . Stupid rock . . ."

"Well, let's go find this Lord Gargath then," Sturm muttered, shamefaced. Try as he might, his gaze still strayed toward the blonde, who was blowing kisses at him.

"Take your spears," said Tanin, shoving aside the soft hands that were clinging to him. "These women might or might not be telling us the truth. That old wizard could be laughing at us right now."

"They said he was 'up there.' " Palin gazed at the ceiling. "But where? How do we get there?"

"Uh, I believe I know the way, laddie," Dougan said. "Just a hunch, mind you," he added hastily, seeing Tanin's dark look. "That door, there, leads upstairs . . . I think. . . ."

"Humpf," Tanin growled, but went to investigate the door, his brothers and the dwarf following behind.

"What did you mean, *you're* the only one who has a right to the Graygem?" Palin asked Dougan in an undertone.

"Did I say that?" The dwarf looked at him shrewdly. "Must have been the gem talking. . . ."

"Oh, please don't go!" cried the women.

"Never mind. They'll be coming back soon," predicted the dark-haired beauty.

"And when you do come back, maybe you can show us some more of those cute magic tricks," called the blonde to Palin politely.

CHAPTER EIGHT
Lord Gargath

Dougan was right. The door led to another flight of narrow stairs carved out of the stone walls of the castle. It was pitch dark; their only light was the burning crystal atop the Staff of Magius. After another leg-aching climb, they came to a large wooden door.

"Would you look at that!" Sturm said, stunned.

"What in the name of the Abyss is it?" Tanin muttered.

It was a fantastic mechanism, sitting on the doorstoop in front of the door. Barely visible in the shadows, it was made of iron and had all sorts of iron arms and gears and rope pulleys and winches extending from the stone floor up to the ceiling.

"Hold the light closer, Palin," Tanin said, stooping down beside it. "There's something in the center, surrounded by a bunch of . . . mirrors."

Cautiously, Palin held the light down near the device and the room was suddenly illuminated as if by a hundred suns. Tanin shrieked and covered his eyes with his hands. "I can't see a thing!" he cried, staggering back against the wall. "Move the staff! Move the staff!"

"It's a sundial!" Palin reported, holding the staff back and staring at the device in astonishment. "Surrounded by mirrors . . ."

"Ah," said Dougan triumphantly, "a gnome timelock."

"A timelock?"

"Aye, lad. You wait until the dial casts the shadow of the sun on the correct time, and the lock will open."

"But," pointed out Palin in confusion, "the way the mirrors are fixed, there could never be a shadow! It's always noon."

"Not to mention," added Tanin bitterly, rubbing his eyes, "that this place is pitch dark. There're no windows! How's the sun supposed to hit it?"

"Small design flaws," said Sturm sarcastically. "I'm sure it's in committee—"

"Meanwhile, how do we open the door?" Tanin asked, slumping back wearily against the wall.

"Too bad Tas isn't here," said Palin, with a smile.

"Tas?" Dougan scowled, whirling around. "You don't mean Tasslehoff Burrfoot? The kender?"

"Yes, do you know him?"

"No," the dwarf growled, "but a friend of mine does. This crazy dwarf under a tree near my for— near where I work, day in, day out, whittling his endless wood and muttering 'doorknob of a kender this' and 'doorknob of a kender that.' "

"A friend?" Palin said, mystified. "Why that sounds like a story our father told about Flint—"

"Never you mind!" Dougan snapped irritably. "And quit talking about kender! We're in enough trouble as it is. Brrrrr." He shivered. "Makes my skin crawl . . ."

The faintest glimmering of understanding lit the confused darkness of Palin's mind. Dimly he began to see the truth. But though the light shone on his thoughts, they were such a confused jumble that he couldn't sort them out or even decide whether he should feel relieved or more terrified.

"Maybe we could break the mirrors," Tanin suggested, blinking in the darkness, trying to see beyond the sea of bright blue spots that filled his vision.

"I wouldn't," Dougan warned. "The thing's likely to blow up."

"You mean it's trapped?" Sturm asked nervously, backing away.

"No!" Dougan snapped irritably. "I mean it's made

by gnomes. It's likely to blow up."

"If it did"—Tanin scratched his chin thoughtfully—"it would probably blow a hole in the door."

"And us with it," Palin pointed out.

"Just you, Little Brother," Sturm said helpfully. "We'll be down at the bottom of the stairs."

"We have to try, Palin," Tanin decided. "We have no idea how long before the power of the Graygem takes hold of us again. It probably won't be a big explosion," he added soothingly. "It isn't a very big device, after all."

"No, it just takes up the whole door. Oh, very well," Palin grumbled. "Stand back."

The warning was unnecessary. Dougan was already clambering down the stairs, Sturm behind him. Tanin rounded the corner of the wall, but stopped where he could see Palin.

Edging up cautiously on the device, Palin raised the end of the staff over the first mirror, averting his face and shutting his eyes as he did so. At that moment, however, a voice came from the other side of the door.

"I believe all you have to do is turn the handle."

Palin arrested his downward jab. "Who said that?" he shouted, backing up.

"Me," called the voice again in meek tones. "Just turn the handle."

"You mean, the door's not locked?" Palin asked in amazement.

"Nobody's perfect," said the voice defensively.

Gingerly, Palin reached out his hand and, after removing several connecting arms and undoing a rope or two of the gnome timelock that was not locked, he turned the door handle. There was a click, and the door swung open on creaking hinges.

Entering the chamber with some difficulty, his robes having caught on a gear, Palin looked around in awe.

He was in a room shaped like a cone—round at the bottom, it came to a point at the ceiling. The chamber was lit by oil lamps, placed at intervals around the circular floor, their flickering flames illuminating the room brightly as day. Tanin was about to step through the door past Palin, when his brother stopped him.

"Wait!" Palin cautioned, catching hold of Tanin's arm. "Look! On the floor!"

"Well, what is it?" Tanin asked. "Some sort of design—"

"It's a pentagram, a magic symbol," Palin said softly. "Don't step within the circle of the lamps!"

"What's it there for?" Sturm peered over Tanin's broad shoulders, while Dougan jumped up and down in back, trying to see.

"I think . . . Yes!" Palin stared up into the very top of the ceiling. "It's holding the Graygem! Look!" He pointed.

Everyone tilted back their heads, staring upward, except the dwarf, who was cursing loudly about not being able to see. Dropping down to his hands and knees, Dougan finally managed to thrust his head in between Tanin's and Sturm's legs and peered up, his beard trailing on the polished stone floor.

"Aye, laddie," he said with a longing sigh. "That's it! The Graygem of Gargath!"

Hovering in the air, below the very point of the cone, was a gray-colored jewel. Its shape was impossible to distinguish, as was it size, for it changed as they stared at it—first it was round and as big as a man's fist; then it was a prism as large as a man himself; then it was a cube, no bigger than a lady's bauble; then round again. . . . The jewel had been dark when they entered the room, not even reflecting the light from the lamps below. But now a soft gray light of its own began to beam from it.

Palin felt the magic tingle through him. Words to spells of unbelievable power flooded his mind. His uncle had been a weakling compared to him! He would rule the world, the heavens, the Abyss—

"Steady, Little Brother," came a distant voice.

"Hold onto me, Tanin!" Palin gasped, reaching out his hand to his brother. "Help me fight it!"

"It's no use," came the voice they had heard through the door, this time sounding sad and resigned. "You can't fight it. It will consume you in the end, as it did me."

Wrenching his gaze from the gray light that was fast dazzling him with its brilliance, Palin stared around the conical room. Across from where he stood was a tall, high-backed chair placed against a tapestry-adorned wall. The chair's back was carved with various runes and magical inscriptions, designed—apparently—to protect the mage who sat there from whatever beings he summoned forth to do his bidding. The voice seemed to be coming from the direction of the chair, but Palin could not see anyone sitting there.

Then, "Paladine have mercy!" the young man cried in horror.

"Too late, too late," squeaked the voice. "Yes, I am Lord Gargath. The wretched Lord Gargath! Welcome to my home."

Seated upon the chair's soft cushion, making a graceful—if despairing—gesture with its paw, was a hedgehog.

"You may come closer," said Lord Gargath, smoothing his whiskers with a trembling paw. "Just don't step in the circle, as you said, young mage."

Keeping carefully outside the boundaries of the flickering oil lamps, the brothers and Dougan edged their way along the wall. Above them, the Graygem gleamed softly, its light growing ever brighter.

"Lord Gargath," Palin began hesitantly, approaching the hedgehog's chair. Suddenly, he cried out in alarm and stumbled backward, bumping into Tanin.

"Sturm, to my side!" Tanin shouted, pushing Palin behind him and raising the spear.

The chair had vanished completely beneath the bulk of a gigantic black dragon! The creature stared at them with red, fiery eyes, its great wings spanning the length of the wall, its tail lashing the floor with a tremendous thud. When the dragon spoke, though, its voice held the same sorrow as had the hedgehog's.

"You're frightened," said the dragon sadly. "Thank you for the compliment, but you needn't be. By the time I could attack you, I'd probably be a mouse or a cockroach."

"Ah, there! You see how it is," continued Lord Gargath in the form of a lovely young maiden, who put her head in her hands and wept dismally. "I'm constantly changing, constantly shifting. I never know from one moment to the next," snarled a ferocious minotaur, snorting in anger, "what I'm going to be."

"The Graygem has done this to you?"

"Yessssss," hissed a snake, coiling around upon itself on the cushion in agony. "Once I wasssss a wizzzzard like you, young one. Once I wassss . . . powerful and wealthy. This island and its people were mine," continued a dapper young man, setting in the chair, a cold drink in his hand. "Care for some? Tropical fruit punch. Not bad, I assure you. Where was I?"

"The Graygem," Palin ventured. His brothers could only stare in silence.

"Ah, yes," burbled a toad unhappily. "My great-great-great—well, you get the picture—grandfather followed the damn thing, centuries ago, in hopes of retrieving it. He did, for a time. But his power failed as he grew old, and the Graygem escaped. I don't know where it went, spreading chaos throughout the world. But *I* always knew that . . . someday . . . it would come within my grasp. And I'd be ready for it!" A rabbit, sitting up on its hind feet, clenched its paw with a stern look of resolve.

"Long years I study," said a gully dwarf, holding up a grubby hand. "Two years. I think two years." The gully dwarf frowned. "I make pretty design on floor. I wait. Two years. Not more than two. Big rock come! I catch . . .

"And I'd trapped the Graygem!" shrieked an old, wizened man with a wild cackle. "It couldn't escape me! At last, all the magic in the world would be mine, at my fingertips! And so it was, so it was," squeaked a red-eyed rat, chewing nervously on its tail. "I could have anything I wanted. I demanded ten maidens— Well, I was lonely," said a spider, curling its legs defensively. "You don't get a chance to meet nice girls when you're an evil mage, you know."

"And the Graygem took control of the women!" said Palin, growing dizzy again, watching the transformations of the wizard. "And used them against you."

"Yes," whinnied a horse, pacing back and forth restlessly in front of the chair. "It educated them and gave them this palace. *My* palace! It gives them everything! They never have to work. Food appears when they're hungry. Wine, whatever they want . . . All they do is lounge around all day, reading elven poetry and arguing philosophy. God, I *hate* elven poetry!" groaned a middle-aged bald man. "I tried to talk to them, told them to make something of their lives! And what did they do? They shut me in here, with that!" He gestured helplessly at the stone.

"But the women are getting restless," Palin said, his

thoughts suddenly falling into order.

"One can only take so much elven poetry," remarked a walrus, gloomily waving its flippers. "They want diversion—"

"Men . . . and *not* their husbands. No, that wouldn't suit the Graygem at all. It needs the warriors to guard the gem from the outside while the women guard it from inside. So, to keep the women happy, it brought—"

"Us!" said Tanin, rounding upon the dwarf in fury.

"Now, don't be hasty," Dougan said with a cunning grin. He glanced at Palin out of the corner of his eye. "You're very clever, laddie. You take after your uncle, yes, you do. Who was the gem guarding itself from, if you're so smart? What would it have to fear?"

"The one person who'd been searching for it for thousands and thousands of years," said Palin softly. Everything was suddenly very, very clear. "The one who made it and gambled it away. It has hidden from you, all these centuries, staying in one place until you got too close, then disappearing again. But now it is trapped by the wizard. No matter what it does, it can't escape. So it set these guards around itself. But you knew the women were unhappy. You knew the Graygem *had* to allow them to have what they wanted—"

"Good-looking men. They'd let no one else in the castle," said Dougan, twirling his moustache. "And, if I do say so myself, we fill the bill," he added proudly.

"But who is he?" said Sturm, staring from Palin to the dwarf in confusion. "*Not* Dougan Redhammer, I gather—"

"I know! I know!" shouted Lord Gargath, now a kender, who was jumping on the cushion of the chair. "Let me tell! Let me tell!" Leaping down, the kender ran over to embrace the dwarf.

"Great Reorx!" roared Dougan, clutching his empty

money pouch.

"You told!" The kender pouted.

"My god!" whispered Tanin.

"That about sums it up," Palin remarked.

CHAPTER NINE
Wanna Bet?

"Yes!" roared Dougan Redhammer in a thunderous voice. "I am Reorx, the Forger of the World, and I have come back to claim what is mine!"

Suddenly aware of the presence of the god, aware, now, of the danger it was in, the Graygem flared with brilliant gray light. Trapped by the magic of the wizard's symbol on the floor, it could not move, but it began to spin frantically, changing shape so fast that it was nothing more than a blur of motion to the eye.

The aspect of the wizard changed too. Once again, the black dragon burst into being, its great body obliterating the chair, its vast wingspan filling the cone-shaped room.

Palin glanced at it without interest, being much more absorbed in his own internal struggles. The Graygem was exerting all its energy, trying to protect itself. It was offering Palin anything, everything he wanted. Images flashed into his head. He saw himself as Head of the Order of White Robes, he saw himself ruling the Conclave of Wizards. *He* was driving the evil dragons back into the Abyss! *He* was doing battle with the Dark Queen. All he had to do was kill the dwarf. . . .

Kill a god? he asked in disbelief.

I will grant you the power! the Graygem answered.

Looking around, Palin saw Sturm's body bathed in sweat, his eyes wild, his fists clenched. Even Tanin, so strong and unbending, was staring straight ahead, his skin pale, his lips tight, seeing some vision of glory visible only to himself.

Dougan stood in the center of the pentagram, watching them, not saying a word.

Palin held fast to the staff, nearly sobbing in his torment. Pressing his cheek against the cool wood, he heard words forming in his mind. *All my life, I was my own person. The choices I made, I made of my own free will. I was never held in thrall by anyone or anything; not even the Queen of Darkness herself! Bow to others in reverence and respect, but never in slavery, nephew!*

Palin blinked, looking around as though awaking from a daze. He wasn't conscious of having heard the words, but they were in his heart, and he had the strength now to know their worth. *No!* he was able to tell the Graygem firmly, and it was then that he realized the black dragon behind him was undergoing similar torture.

"But I don't *want* to flay the skin from their bones!" the dragon whimpered. "Well, yes, I wouldn't mind having my island back the way it was. And ten maidens who would act like maidens and not turn into poets."

Looking at the dragon in alarm, Palin saw its red eyes gleaming feverishly. Acid dripped from its forked tongue, burning holes in the polished floor; its claws glistened. Spreading its wings, the dragon lifted itself into the air.

"Tanin! Sturm!" Palin cried, grasping hold of the nearest brother and shaking him. It was Tanin. Slowly the big man turned his eyes to his little brother, but there was no recognition in them.

"Help me, wizard!" Tanin hissed at him. "Help me slay the dwarf! I'll be the leader of armies. . . ."

"Dougan!" Palin ran to the dwarf. "Do something!" the young mage shouted wildly, waving his arms at the dragon.

"I am, laddie, I am," said Dougan calmly, his eyes on the Graygem.

Palin could see the black dragon's eyes watching him hungrily. The black wings twitched.

I'll cast a sleep spell, Palin decided in desperation, reaching into his pouches for sand. But as he drew it forth a horrible realization came to him. His fingers went limp, the sand trickled from them, spilling down upon the floor.

His magic was gone!

"No, please, no!" Palin moaned, looking up at the Graygem, which appeared to sparkle with a chaotic malevolence.

The wooden door to the room burst open, banging against the wall.

"We have come as you commanded us, Graygem!" cried a voice.

It was the voice of the dark-haired beauty. Behind her was the blonde, and behind them all the rest of the women, young and old alike. But gone were the diaphanous gowns and seductive smiles. The women were dressed in tiger skins. Feathers were tied in their hair, and they carried stone-tipped spears in their hands.

And now Tanin's voice rang out loudly as a trumpet call, "My troops! To my side! Rally round!" Raising his arm, he gave a battle cry and the women answered with a wild shout.

"Bring me wine!" cried Sturm, executing an impromptu dance. "Let the revelries begin!"

The blonde's eyes were on him and they burned with lust. Unfortunately, it was lust of the wrong kind. She raised her spear, her eyes looking to her leader—Tanin—for the order to attack.

"You promise me?" said the black dragon eagerly, its forked tongue flicking in and out of its dripping mouth. "No more gully dwarves? I didn't mind the rest so much, but I *won't* be changed into a gully dwarf again!"

"The world's gone mad!" Palin slumped back against the wall. He felt his strength and his sanity draining from him as the sand fell from his nerveless fingers. The chaos around him and the loss of his magic had overthrown his mind. He stared at the Staff of Magius and saw nothing more than a stick of wood, topped by a glistening bauble. He heard his brothers—one dispersing his troops for battle, the other calling for the pipers to strike up another tune. He heard the dragon's great wings creak and the intake of breath that would be released in a stream of acid. Shutting his eyes, Palin cast the useless staff away from him and turned his face to the wall.

"Halt!" thundered a voice. "Halt, I command you!"

Chaos whirled wildly an instant longer, then it slowed and finally wound down until all was silence and stillness in the room where before had been a blur of noise and motion. Raising his head, Palin looked fearfully around. Dougan stood on the pentagram in the center of the room, his black beard bristling in anger. Raising his arm, he cried out, "*Reorx Drach Kalahzar!*" and a gigantic warhammer materialized in the dwarf's hand. The huge hammer glowed with a fierce red light that was reflected in Dougan's dark, bright eyes.

"Yes!" shouted the dwarf, staring up at the flaring Graygem. "I know your power! None better! After all, you are my creation! You can keep this chaos going eternally, and you know that I cannot stop you. But you are trapped eternally yourself! You will never be free!"

The Graygem's light flickered at instant, as though considering Dougan's words. Then it began to pulse, brighter than before, and Palin's heart sank in despair.

"Wait!" Dougan cried, raising one hand, the other

grasping the handle of the burning red warhammer. "I say we leave everything up to chance. I offer you . . . a wager!"

The Graygem appeared to consider, its light pulsed more slowly, thoughtfully.

"A wager?" the women murmured, lowering their spears.

"A wager," said the dragon in pleased tones, settling back down to the floor once more.

"A wager!" Palin muttered, wiping his sleeve across his sweating brow. "My god, that's what started all this!"

"We agree to it, " said the dark-haired beauty, striding forward, the shaft of her spear thumping against the floor as she walked. "What will be the stakes?"

Dougan stroked his beard. "These young men," he said finally, pointing at Tanin, Sturm, and Palin, "for yourselves. Freedom for the Graygem."

"What?" Both Tanin and Sturm came back to reality, staring around the room as though seeing it for the first time.

"You can't do this to us, dwarf!" Tanin shouted, lunging forward, but two of the larger and stronger women caught him and, with strength given them by the brightly burning Graygem, bound the struggling man's arms behind him. Two more took care of Sturm. No one bothered with Palin.

"If I lose the wager," Dougan continued imperturbably, "these young men will stay with you as your slaves. I'll break the magic spell that holds the gem trapped here, and it will be free once more to roam the world. If I win, the Graygem is mine and these men will be released."

"We agree to the stakes," said the dark-haired beauty, after a glance at the Graygem. "And now what is the wager?"

Dougan appeared to consider, twirling his moustaches round and round his finger. His gaze happened to rest on Palin, and he grinned. "That this young man"—he pointed at the mage—"will throw my hammer in the air and it will hang suspended, never falling to the floor."

Everyone stared at the dwarf in silence, considering. What was the angle?

Then, "No! Dougan!" Palin cried frantically, pushing himself away from the wall. One of the women shoved him back.

"This young man?" The dark-haired beauty suddenly caught on. "But he is a magic-user—"

"Only a very young one," Dougan said hastily. "And he won't use his magic, will you, Palin?" the dwarf asked, winking at the young mage when the women weren't looking.

"Dougan!" Palin wrenched himself free from the woman's grasp and lurched across the floor, his knees so weak he could barely walk. "I can't! My magic—"

"Never say 'can't,' laddie," Dougan said severely. "Didn't your uncle teach you anything?" Once again, he winked at Palin.

It seemed the dark-haired beauty suddenly realized Palin's weakness, for she glanced about at her fellows and smiled in pleased fashion. "We accept your wager," she said.

"Dougan!" Palin said desperately, grabbing hold of the dwarf, who was looking up at him with a sly grin. "Dougan! I *can't* use my magic! I don't have any! The Graygem drained it!" he whispered urgently in the dwarf's ear.

Dougan's face crumpled. "You don't say now, laddie," he muttered, glancing at the women and rubbing his bearded chin. "That's a shame," he said sadly, shaking his head. "A real shame. Are you sure?"

"Of course, I'm sure!" Palin snapped.

"Well, give it your best shot, lad!" the dwarf said, clapping Palin on the arm with his hand. "Here you go!" He thrust the handle of the warhammer into Palin's hands. Feeling the unfamiliar touch, the hammer's red glow faded, turning an ugly, lead gray.

Palin looked around helplessly at his brothers. Tanin regarded him gravely, his expression grim. Sturm averted his head, his big shoulders heaving in a sigh.

Swallowing, licking his dry lips, Palin wrapped his hands around the handle of the hammer, uncertain, even, how to hold the weapon. He tried to lift it. A groan escaped his lips—a groan echoed by his brothers.

"By Paladine!" Palin gasped. "I can barely move this thing, Dougan! How can I throw it?" Leaning closer, staring into the dwarf's eyes, the young man murmured, "You're a god . . . I don't suppose . . ."

"Of course not, laddie!" The dwarf looked shocked. "It's a matter of honor! You understand . . ."

"Sure," Palin grunted bitterly.

"Look, lad," Dougan said, positioning Palin's hands. "It's not that difficult. You just hold the hammer like this . . . there . . . Now, you pick it up and began spinning round and round in a circle. Your momentum will help you lift the hammer and, when you're going good, just give it a heave, like so. Nature will do the rest."

"Nature?" Palin appeared dubious.

"Yes," answered the dwarf gravely, smoothing his beard. "It's called Centrifug's Force or some such thing. The gnomes explained it to me."

"Great!" Palin muttered. "Gnomes!"

Drawing a deep breath, the young man lifted the hammer. A groan of pain escaped his lips, sweat stood out on his forehead from the strain, and he heard several of the women giggle. Gritting his teeth, certain that he had ruptured something inside him, Palin began to turn in a circle, the hammer in his hands. He was startled to notice that Dougan was right. The momentum of his motion made the hammer seem lighter. He was able to lift it higher and higher. But the handle began to slip in his sweaty palms. . . .

"He's losing it! Get down! Everyone!" Tanin called out, falling flat on his face. There was a clattering of spears as the women followed suit. Even the black dragon—seeing Palin spinning about in the center of the room, out of control, the hammer starting to glow a fiery red—crouched on the floor with a whimper, attempting to fold its wings over its head. Only the dwarf remained standing, his face split in a broad grin.

"I . . . can't . . . hold . . . it!" Palin cried and, with a gasp, he let the hammer fly.

The young mage fell to his knees, in too much pain and exhaustion to even bother looking to see what happened. But everyone else in the room, lying flat on the floor, raised their heads to watch the hammer. Round and round it whizzed, flying over the heads of the women, buzzing over Tanin and Sturm, whisking past the cowering dragon. Round and round it flew and, as it flew, it began to rise into the air. Dougan watched it placidly, his hands laced across his great belly.

Glowing now a fiery red, the hammer circled higher and higher and, as it rose, the Graygem's light began to waver in sudden fear. The hammer was aiming straight for it!

"Yes, my beauty," murmured Dougan, watching the hammer in satisfaction. "You forged it. Now, bring it home."

Desperately the Graygem sought to dim its light, realizing, perhaps, that it was its own power that was drawing the hammer to it. But it was too late. The hammer flew to the Graygem it had helped create as a lass flies to her lover's arms. There was a shattering sound and a blinding flare of red and gray light, so brilliant that even Dougan was forced to shade his eyes, and no one else could see anything for the dazzling radiance.

The two energies seemed to strive together, the red light and the gray, and then the gray began to dim. Peering upward, tears streaming from his eyes in the bright light, Palin thought he caught a glimpse of a gray, sparkling jewel tumbling from the air to land in Dougan's hand. But he couldn't be certain because, at that moment, the red glowing hammer fell from the air as well, plummeting straight down on top of them!

Clasping his aching arms over his head, Palin hugged the floor, visions of his head being split open and his brains splattering everywhere coming to him with vivid clarity.

He heard a resounding clang.

Timidly raising his head, he saw the hammer, glowing red in triumph, lying on the floor at Dougan's feet.

Slowly, trembling, Palin stood up, as did everyone else in the room. He was hurting and exhausted; Tanin had to come help him or he would have collapsed. But Palin smiled up at him as his big brother clasped him in his arms. "My magic's returned!" he whispered. "It's back!"

"I'm back, too," said a voice. Glancing around, Palin saw the dragon was gone. In its place, crouched on the floor, his hands over his head, was a thin, middle-aged wizard dressed in black robes. The wizard sat up, staring around him as if he couldn't believe it. "I'm back!" he cried out joyfully, patting his head and his neck and his shoulders with his hands. "No rabbit ears! No dragon's breath! No minotaur muscles! I'm me again!" He burst into tears.

"And you lost the bet, dwarf!" the dark-haired beauty cried out suddenly, getting to her feet. "The hammer fell!"

"Yes!" shouted the women. "You lost the bet! The men are ours!"

"Dougan . . ." growled Tanin ominously.

The women were closing in on them, eyes burning with the fire of love instead of the fire of battle.

Dougan raised the hammer above his head. His face was stern, his black eyes flashed as red as the glowing hammer. The voice that spoke was no longer the voice of the dwarf with the flashy clothes, but a voice as ancient as the mountains it had carved, as deep as the oceans it had poured.

"Women!" the god called out in stern tones. "Listen to me! The power of the Graygem over you is broken. Remember now your children and your husbands. Remember your brothers and your fathers! Remember your homes and those who love you and need you!"

One by one, the women looked around in dazed fashion, some putting their hands to their heads, some blinking in confusion.

"Where are we?" asked one.

"Why are we dressed like this?" asked another, staring at the tiger skin.

"How dare you?" cried the blonde, slapping Sturm across the face.

Only the dark-haired beauty seemed sad. Shaking her head, she said with a sigh, "I miss my family," she said softly. "And I remember him that I love and am betrothed to marry. But it will start all over again. The eternal wars. The fighting, the bleeding, the dying . . ."

She turned to the god, only to find no one but a flashily dressed dwarf, who smiled at her in understanding.

"Think a moment, lassie," said Dougan kindly, patting her hand. "You've read the books, remember? And so have they." He pointed at the others. "You have knowledge now. No one can take that from you. Use it wisely, and you can stop the senseless wars. You and the others, with the help of your menfolk and your children, can make this island a paradise."

"I don't know who you are," the dark-haired beauty said, gazing at the dwarf in wonder, "but you are wise. We will do as you say. And we will honor you always, in our hearts and our prayers." (And so the islanders prayed to a dwarven god, becoming the only humans, as far as any one knows, to once again worship Reorx, the Forger of the World.)

Bending down, the woman kissed Dougan on his cheek. The dwarf's face flamed red as his hammer.

"Go along with you now!" he said gruffly.

Arms linked around each other's waists, the women ran, laughing merrily, from the room, and the brothers soon heard their joyful voices outside the castle walls.

"As for you—" Dougan turned upon the black-robed wizard.

"Don't scold me!" begged Lord Gargath meekly. "I've learned my lesson. Truly. I will never have anything to do with gems as long as I live. You can believe me!" he said, glancing up at the empty ceiling with a shudder.

"And we'll expect to see you at the Conclave," said Palin severely, retrieving the Staff of Magius. "You'll be a renegade no longer?"

by Margaret Weis and Tracy Hickman

"I'm looking forward to the next meeting!" Lord Gargath said eagerly. "Is there anything I can bring? A cake, perhaps? I make a marvelous devil's food . . ."

AFTERWORD

(This time for real)

Dougan and the brothers returned to the gnome ship without incident. In fact, the warriors were so happy to have their women back with them, their families once more reunited, that they returned the armor and their swords. (The chief had decided the armor was too hot anyway, and he thought the sword a primitive weapon compared to a spear.)

The gnomes had repaired the damage to the ship. Indeed, they discovered that having one end smashed in improved the steering immeasurably, and they were quite excited at the prospect of returning home to Mount Nevermind and smashing in the prows (or sterns) of the remainder of the gnomish fleet.

One small incident marred an otherwise idyllic cruise (not counting constantly ducking the sail, being hit by falling fish, and wondering whether or not they were going to sink before they reached land, due to the leaking of the smashed-in prow . . . or stern . . .).

Dougan was lounging on the deck one night, contemplating the stars (the constellation, Reorx, was missing) when suddenly he was accosted by the three brothers.

"Sturm, get his arms!" Tanin ordered, leaping on the dwarf from behind. "Palin, if his beard so much as twitches, send him to sleep!"

"What is this outrage! How dare you?" Dougan roared, struggling in Sturm's strong grasp.

"We risked our lives for that rock," Tanin said grimly, glaring down at the red-faced dwarf. "And I want to see it."

"You've been putting us off for days," added Palin, standing beside his brother. "We at least want a look at it before you take it back to your forge or wherever."

"Let me loose!" Dougan swore an oath. "Or you'll see nothing ever again!"

"Do you agree to show it to us?"

"I promise!" muttered the dwarf.

Sturm, at a nod from Tanin, let go of the dwarf's arms. Dougan glanced around at them uncomfortably.

"The Graygem?" the brothers said, gathering around.

"Well, now, lads." The dwarf appeared highly uncomfortable. "That's going to be a bit of a problem."

"What do you mean?" Palin asked nervously, not liking the expression on the dwarf's face. "Is it so powerful that we can't look at it?"

"Nooo . . ." said Dougan slowly, his face flushing in the red light of Lunitari. "That's not it, exactly. . . ."

"Well, then, let's see it!" Tanin demanded.

"The . . . uh . . . the fact is, lads," stammered Dougan, winding his black beard around his finger, "that I've . . . I've misplaced it. . . ."

"Misplaced it!" Sturm said in amazement.

"The Graygem?" Palin glanced around the boat in alarm, fearing to see its gray light beaming out at them.

"Perhaps, 'misplaced' isn't quite the word," the dwarf mumbled. "You see, I got into this bone game, the night before we left the island and . . ." His voice trailed off miserably.

"You *lost* it!" Tanin groaned.

Palin and Sturm stared at the dwarf, too stunned to speak.

"Aye, lad." Dougan sighed heavily. "It was a sure thing, too. . . ."

"So the Graygem's loose in the world again," Palin murmured.

"I'm afraid so. After all, I *did* lose the original wager, if you will remember. But don't worry, laddie," said the dwarf, laying his hand on Palin's arm. "We'll get it back! Someday, we'll get it back!"

"What do you mean *we?*" Tanin growled.

"I swear by Paladine and by Gilean and by the Dark Queen and by all the gods in the heavens that if I ever in my life see you even looking my direction, dwarf, I will turn around and walk—no, run—the opposite way!" Sturm vowed devoutly.

"The same goes for me," said Palin.

"And me!" said Tanin.

Dougan looked at them, downcast for a moment. Then, a grin split the dwarf's face. His beady eyes glittered.

"Wanna bet?"

Into the Heart of the Story

The True Authorship of the Dragonlance Songs

by Virumsortiticorporafurtimincludum[1]

I. Introduction

The recent publication of the book *Leaves from the Inn of the Last Home* should still, for the moment, all other argument among the distinguished members of the Philosophers Guild; once again, we are united, and the ongoing quarrel between the eminent Doctor Sicfatusdeindecomantemandrogeigaleam and the equally eminent Doctor Vitaquecumgemitufugitindignatasubumbras[2]—a dispute as to whether long abandoned armor still retains the thoughts and words of those who have worn it, and whether we would want to listen to it anyway—has been suspended in the interest of patriotism.[3]

---

1. An assumed name, for the danger I undergo in writing this will be apparent to all but the most unenlightened reader.

2. With all due respect to the distinguished professors involved in the dispute touched upon above, the editors have insisted that I use abbreviated names in order to condense the present document from its unwieldy (but certainly more courteous) length of approximately 3,000 pages.

3. Details of the present state of the discussion may be found by the interested reader in *Philosophika Gnomikon* MMXVII (323 A.C.), pp. 675,328 - 682,465. I have my own opinion, but shall not give it here, for I am equally patriotic.

For again the dignity of this Guild—indeed, the dignity of gnomes everywhere—has been insulted by outsiders. A Gnomish philosopher once said (and in saying it, could rest assured that somewhere, some human would claim the saying as *his* own and nobody would know otherwise), "The history of a war is written by the victors." Not all of the victors, mind you, but only those who escape the war with the least carnage and the most coinage, a most unfortunate circumstance for Gnomish philosophers, writers, and artists, only recently righted by last month's publication of Volume I of the *Philosophika Gnomikon*, an eminent journal which I hope will soon publish this article in its entirety. Surely the first two thousand or so volumes of the *Philosophika* have already filled considerable blanks in the recorded history of Krynn, and surely they will continue to do so, barring censorship or organized neglect on the part of others I could name . . . but I digress from the issue at hand, from that most ungracious insult that is our present concern.

The recent War of the Lance has inspired endless commentary, memoirs, speculations, and apologies, but how many of these documents have thrown light upon the Gnomish contribution to the deliverance of Krynn from the hands of the enemy and the domination of the Dragon Highlord?

None![4] Ours, it seems, is a marginal people, foot-

---

4. None, that is, except for those contained in the *Philosophika Gnomikon*, from which the author would be grateful to hear of any advance payment and royalty arrangements that might be involved in publishing this article in full—untouched, as the saying goes, by human hand.

noted in history as a race of toymakers and tinkers. For again one of our foremost poets, visionaries, and military heroes is overlooked, drowned in a flood of self-serving ink. Nowhere in the pages of *Leaves*, or in the *Chronicles* for that matter, is there mention of Armavirumquecanonevermindquiprimusabpedibusfatoprofugif,[5] poet and philosopher, an equal and honored Companion in his own right, completely forgotten in favor of a large supporting cast of elves[6] and gully dwarves[7], in favor of the highly overrated Gemstone Man, who is said to have used his highly overrated Gemstone to plug up some metaphysical leak the Companions had imagined because it seemed like good mythology at the time.

But lest we sound nervous or bitter in our attempt to set history right, we shall emphasize the positive— the timeless contribution of Armavir, as we shall call him—the author of most, if not all, of the poetry and songs contained in the *Chronicles*. For the elves have assigned this poetry to the pen of one Quivalen Soth[8] (for me to imply any relation between this fictitious poet and the infamous Lord Soth might be libelous, so

---

5. See note 1 above. Henceforth in the text, I refer to our hero as "Armavir."

6. A race of tree surgeons and thieves. True history also has its footnotes.

7. A race unworthy of a footnote.

8. Not "Quivalen Sath," a deceitful (and typically elvish) name change. For evidence see "Song of Huma," as first printed in *Chronicles*, I, pp. 442-445.

I shall not do so); the kender are as indifferent to who wrote the poetry as they are to anything of honesty and high seriousness; the dwarves as indifferent as they are to anything nonarchitectural or nonmetallic; and the humans seem to be represented on the issue by Caramon Majere (who at last report believed an ode to be a form of salted cracker) and his wife Tika (of whom, alas, I thought better than this betrayal, this *insult!*). Surely, the poet deserves an account less treacherous, less indifferent, less ignorant. But I grow bitter again, galled by the fading light in my chambers and the endless dripping of the faucets on the south wall, placed there generations ago for Reorx knows what purpose but to gall me with their dripping. I shall fix them this instant; mine is a long and unbearable story, made even less bearable by the perpetual accompaniment of water torture.

As I sit again, I mistrust the passage above, the self-pity that you, my philosophical fellows, may well read into my complaints of neglect, of poor lighting, poor plumbing. I am not a self-pitying gnome, a whiner; my duty is to the name and reputation of Armavir, regardless of my discomfort, of the water knee-deep in these chambers, of the scant light in the chamber from the holes through which, in a far better time than ours, wires and helmets dangled with hope and promise. His biography and the notes toward an annotated text of his poetry will be my testament, the testament of our people that the tides of history shall not overwhelm us before we recover these songs as our own.

Michael Williams

II. Of Armavir The Poet

A poet is not born but made, as another Gnomish philosopher once said,[9] and our Armavir was no exception. Born in the midst of the great Gnomish Industrial Revelation (267 A.C.), he was a pampered and protected child who could have expected a Life Quest in keeping with those of his family—a career as an optical illusion inventor or a winch facilitator. Instead, as he said once in a playful moment, he became a topical allusion vendor and a wench facilitator—translated ungraciously by one human,[10] who never understood his sensitive and generous poetic soul, as "a gossip and a skirt-chaser."

As the youngest of three children, Armavir's life was scarred by early tragedy, his father entangled and dragged to death through a malfunctioning pulley system while facilitating a winch (rumors abounding that he was tied to the fatal rope by a jealous husband), an older brother mistaking the reflection of an onyx ornamental pool for actual water and, clad only in swimsuit and water wings, plunging to his death from atop a fifty-foot stalagmite, an older sister (who, alas, promised in her meager thirteen years to be the genuine beauty of the family) catapulted to her untimely end by an experimental steam-powered seesaw. Needless to say, it was the lad's mother (the charming and still active Quacumqueviamvirtutepetivitsuccessum-

---

9. And in saying so, assured another gem that would fall from the mouth of a human!

10. Otik Sandahl the Innkeeper. I quote not to give merit to what the innkeeper has said, but to show how petty and unforgiving prejudice can shape history. We historians strive to be generous; after all, I have forgiven Otik's watering the beer in the Inn of the Last Home.

---

feminadiranegat)[11] who removed him early from the
rough life of mirrors and exploratory physics, leaving
him forever with a mistrust of mirages (his poems, as
well the reader knows, circle obsessively, skeptically
around the image of foxfire) and an even greater mistrust of simple machines.

Isolated by circumstance, by maternal decision, the
lad found his chief source of delight in the conversations around him: the retelling of the legends of Krynn
we all remember from childhood, those stories beginning with the famous phrase, "The elves tell it otherwise, but this is how it happened"; the recitals of
name-histories and genealogies (it is rumored that
young Armavir went sleepless for a month to hear
three genealogies in their entirety, and that he was
"never quite right afterwards");[12] but most of all he
enjoyed the gossip, of which his mother was chief
author, editor, and judge.

Lest this sound like the standard autho-biography,[13]
the repetition of the same tired story in which a child

---

11. See note 1. Of all the indignities!

12. Six weeks sleepless and five genealogies, actually. History
foreshortens this achievement because history mistrusts the
precocious child.

13. "The lad found his chief source of delight in the conversations around him"—opening sentence of *Bard from Practice:
the Autobiography of Quivalin Sath*. "The lad found his chief
source of delight in the conversations around him"—opening
sentence of *Rime Amid Reason: The Autobiography of Rag-
gart, Poet of the Ice Barbarians*. "The lad found his chief source
of delight in the conversations around him"—opening sentence
of *Song of Solamnia: The Autobiography of Sir Michael Williams, Knight of the Rose*. It is ironic how these three minor
poets try to conceal their major vanity by writing of themselves
in the third person.

falls early in love with the sound and power of words,
I shall continue at once with the actual events that
sealed Armavir's poetic calling. For love of language
and stories makes for a punster or a tattletale in most
children, qualities that do not necessarily blossom
into verse unless somehow the child receives enlight-
enment, direction.

Indeed, Armavir might have lived his life unnoticed
in the large and intricate underground kingdom near
Mount Nevermind—a minor courtier, a fishwife without fishes—were it not for his brush with death by
electrocution, a near-disaster with a happy outcome,
for it galvanized his aimless wanderings in legend and
gossip into a genuine (if overlooked) poetic gift, and
charged him with a restless desire to see the outer
world.

It happened as such things often happen—a youthful invention that backfires, but backfires in a most
fortunate manner. One does not discard a Life Quest
lightly, and Armavir's quest was what the Guild had
pronounced as "Something To Do With Wires": tensile
strength, heat conduction, musical properties—a
world of circuit and filament lay before our young
hero. His heart in none of these sciences but the musical, Armavir explored first the variations of sound
one could evoke from wires of different thicknesses,
tensions, and metals, designing the forerunner of the
cello.[14] At first the experiments faltered, for Armavir
had not chanced upon the idea of making the instrument portable; chambers of the undercity were strung
with thin and taut copper wire, hazardous to children,
who took it upon themselves to run chickens into
those very chambers, thereby decapitating and slicing

---

14. An instrument which would later ennoble his lyrics with
music, an instrument later claimed to be of elven make!

the creatures in one frolicsome yet practical pursuit.[15]

Nonetheless, the chambers remained dangerous, and Armavir was instructed by the Mechanical Engineers Guild to remove these hazards. While dismantling one of the more complicated structures in an alcove of the main library at Mount Nevermind, Armavir stumbled across a surprising discovery—one that might well have brought about great technological advances had not the discoverer soon been distracted from his studies.

It seemed that one of the wires had been affixed between two ornamental copper helmets: one in the aforementioned alcove, the other in a similar chamber directly above. Sweating, entangled with wires, the young inventor began to detach the crucial strands and to his astonishment heard voices emanating from the helmet in the alcove. At first he imagined the accompanying ghost of the standard "speaking armor" legend,[16] but decided otherwise when he heard only giggling and the rustle of clothing that had been, like the helmet in question, long abandoned.

It seemed that wire could conduct sound as well as heat, and the thoughts of young Armavir were immediately patriotic: an elaborate early warning system of wires stretched taut from the undercity to the world aboveground, where they could be affixed to metallic bowls cleverly disguised as fruit or stars, and positioned in the huge vallenwood trees on the slopes of Mount Nevermind. Then below, in a place of safety, those in charge of the city's defense could hear any

---

15. See "Gnome Chicken" recipe in *Leaves from the Inn of the Last Home*, p. 246.

16. For related discussion of the "speaking armor" issue, see *Philosophika Gnomikon* MMXVII (323 A.C.), pp. 675,328 - 682,465.

---

threatening movement by those who dwelt beneath the sun and the moons, and could act accordingly, preventing surprise and possible ambush.[17]

Excited by his developing project (which he lovingly entitled "Star Wires"), Armavir decided to put his findings to the test before submitting them to the Mechanical Engineers Guild. Making his way to the upper world bearing a helmet, 100 feet of wire, an augur, and a detailed map of the undercity, he began by drilling into the earth beneath several of the more prominent vallenwoods on the slopes of the mountain—a task that, of course, took him several years, especially since, as both poet and engineer, his auguries occasionally misfired. But enough of the trial and error: it is not the dark night of labor that we wish to see in a work of genius, but the flawless and seamless fruit (or stars) of that work.

And so, when the elaborate connection was made— the first helmet safely in the upper branches of a large vallenwood, the second at the ear of our hero in a secluded library alcove (not the one mentioned before), the two connected by a copper wire stretched almost to the point of breaking—young Armavir knelt silently and listened to the world outside.

Where it was raining, the birdsong stilled and the clamor of thunder in the distance growing nearer as Armavir listened to the spatter of rain against the leaves, the gentle rustle of the branches in a rising wind. Lulling sounds, tranquil sounds, and soon the budding engineer, the proto-cellist, the youthful poet slept the sleep of the just and the absent-minded, until

---

17. Such an idea is scarcely more fanciful than others proposed by advocates of strong military defense. See, for instance, Theros Ironfeld, "Arms for Hostages," *War of the Lance Veteran*, IV, pp. 42-57.

louder claps of thunder awakened him, and he found that his head had become lodged rather tightly in the experimental helmet, entangled in copper wire that was itself uncomfortably tight beneath his chin, so that he thought of the ill-fated chickens and shuddered.

It was then that the lightning struck the laboratory of the vallenwood, and our lyrical hero discovered that not only did copper wire conduct heat and sound, but also the considerable energies of lightning itself— energies so violent that he could not remember the seven ensuing years except for fleeting images of sunlight and leaves, the brilliant amber bottoms of three half-filled ale glasses, something about a dwarf and a kender, and when the memory settled, himself seated at the Inn of the Last Home, having aimlessly wandered (as he would say in his immortal but flawed "Song of the Ten Heroes")[18] "into the heart of the story."

And the rest, my friends, was the story itself. From Solace to Sancrist to Palanthas and further, our hero recording, enshrining the Companions in numbers and song, himself the one who embodied most fully the Gnomish ideal of *balance*— of balance between action and thought, movement and reflection (in the words of his dear departed sister, "teeter and totter"). Owing to modesty, of course, many of Armavir's more heroic exploits never found their way into his poetry; but some—lines and stanzas and staves (sometimes entire passages) in which Armavir appeared as a Companion in his own right—began to find their way *out* of the story.[19] For strangely, unac-

---

18. Printed shamelessly as "Song of the Nine Heroes" in both *Chronicles*, II, and in *Leaves from the Inn of The Last Home*. See comments in Section III of this essay.

19. Indeed, the text of Armavir's poetry was twice the length of the prose account that makes up the greater part of the

countably, the Heroes grew distant as the War turned in their favor,[20] and even at this late time, though I have sent appropriate letters and pleas to several of the original Companions, I "have yet to hear their answer" (as Armavir concludes in the "Canticle of the Dragon").

How easily they forget, these Heroes, but in their theft of the poetry to ornament their edited and self-serving story (the water is rising even higher in the chamber: my brother's old water wings, scarcely damaged by the fall, should hold me up until I have finished writing), in their theft of the poetry they have stolen the clues to their own discovery, their own embarrassment, as a famous fragment shows, as I shall show in other publications—given time, given an audience,[21] given a purchase of dry ground in this rapidly drowning tunnel. As for now, my readers: here is the "Song of the Ten Heroes" with accompanying notes—the first true chronicle of the Dragonlance.

Chronicles as they currently stand. It was the elves—the elves and the humans—who saw fit to disregard much of the compelling verse (never, alas, to be printed, for water damage from last month's flood has destroyed the *one* remaining copy of the poetry in its original splendor. Here lies one whose name was writ underwater!)

20. Oh, they have claimed several reasons for these slights. Claimed that Armavir was overly fond of wine (which is Caramon Majere on his high horse [or on the wagon] I am certain!) and overly fond of young girls, who kept getting younger and younger, larger and larger, as the War continued (this clearly an accusation made by Tanis, who made an incredible fuss over some harmless keyhole observations [see commentary on lines 46-50, "Song of the Ten Heroes," in Section III of this essay. I wish that only once, someone would ask him who ghosted his "Dear Kitiara" letter, but he's elf enough—just barely—to get by without questioning]).

21. The *Philosophika Gnomikon*.

Michael Williams

III. The "Song of The Ten Heroes"

Out of that water a country is rising, impossible
When first imagined in prayer.
—Amarvir, "Crysania's Song"

For the dedicated reader, I would suggest the following procedure as the most effective way to understand the argument that follows: Go out immediately and buy three more copies of this book. Read the poem from the copy you have at hand, my comments (which follow the poem) from the second copy, and reserve the other two copies on a high shelf in case the waters rise in your living quarters or study, for there are mages aplenty left in Krynn (even if old Sandglass-Eyes has gone Reorx knows where), and the rising tides across the planet may not be the work of the moons. Here then, the poem[22] and commentary:

SONG OF THE TEN HEROES

From the north came danger, as we knew it would: 1
    In the vanguard of winter, a dragon's dance
    Unraveled the land, until out of the forest,
Out of the plains they came, from the mothering earth,
        The sky unreckoned before them. 5
      Nine they were, under the three moons,
        Under the autumn twilight:
      As the world declined, they arose
        Into the heart of the story.

---

22. First appeared as "Song of the Nine Heroes": *Chronicles*, II, pp. 5-7.

One from a garden of stone arising,   10
From dwarf-halls, from weather and wisdom,
Where the heart and the mind ride unquestioned
In the untapped vein of the hand.
In his fathering arms, the spirit gathered.
Nine they were, under the three moons,   15
   Under the autumn twilight:
   As the world declined, they arose
   Into the heart of the story.

One from a haven of breezes descending,
   Light in the handling air,   20
To the waving meadows, the kender's country,
Where the grain out of smallness arises itself
To grow green and golden and green again.
Nine they were, under the three moons,
   Under the autumn twilight: 25
   As the world declined, they arose
   Into the heart of the story.

The next from the plains, the long land's keeping,
Nurtured in distance, horizons of nothing.
Bearing a staff she came, and a burden   30
Of mercy and light converged in her hand:
Bearing the wounds of the world, she came.
Nine they were, under the three moons,
   Under the autumn twilight:
   As the world declined, they arose   35
   Into the heart of the story.

The next from the plains, in the moon's shadow,
Through custom, through ritual, trailing the moon
Where her phases, her wax and her wane, controlled
The tide of his blood, and his warrior's hand   40
Ascended through hierarchies of space into light.
Nine they were, under the three moons,
   Under the autumn twilight:
   As the world declined, they arose
   Into the heart of the story.   45

One with absences, known by departures,
The dark swordswoman at the heart of fire:
Her glories the space between words,
The cradlesong recollected in age,
Recalled at the edge of awakening and thought.   50
Nine they were, under the three moons,
Under the autumn twilight:
As the world declined, they arose
Into the heart of the story.

One in the heart of honor, formed by the sword,   55
By the centuries' flight of the kingfisher over the land,
By Solamnia ruined and risen, rising again
Where the heart ascends into duty.
As it dances, the sword is forever an heirloom.
Nine they were, under the three moons,   60
Under the autumn twilight:
As the world declined, they arose
Into the heart of the story.

The next in a simple light a brother to darkness,
Letting the sword hand try all subtleties,   65
Even the intricate webs of the heart. His thoughts
Are pools disrupted in changing wind—
He cannot see their bottom.
Nine they were, under the three moons,
Under the autumn twilight: 70
As the world declined, they arose
Into the heart of the story.

The next the leader, half-elven, betrayed
As the twining blood pulls asunder the land,
The forests, the worlds of elves and men.   75
Called into bravery, but fearing for love,
And fearing that, called into both, he does nothing.
Nine they were, under the three moons,
Under the autumn twilight:
As the world declined, they arose   80
Into the heart of the story.

The last from the darkness, breathing the night
Where the abstract stars hide a nest of words,
Where the body endures the wound of numbers,
Surrendered to knowledge, until, unable to bless, 85
His blessing falls on the low, the benighted.
    Nine they were, under the three moons,
      Under the autumn twilight:
    As the world declined, they arose
      Into the heart of the story.   90

Joined by the others they were in the telling:
  A graceless girl, graced beyond graces;
A princess of seeds and saplings, called to the forest;
    An ancient weaver of accidents;
Nor can we say who the story will gather.   95
    Nine they were, under the three moons,
      Under the autumn twilight:
    As the world declined, they arose
      Into the heart of the story.

From the north came danger, as we knew it would: 100
In encampments of winter, the dragon's sleep
Has settled the land, but out of the forest,
Out of the plains they come, from the mothering earth
    Defining the sky before them.
    Nine they were, under the three moons,   105
      Under the autumn twilight:
    As the world declined, they arose
      Into the heart of the story.

Michael Williams

IV. Commentary

> *Holy the air*
> *That carried his words of endearment, his forgotten songs.*
> —Armavir, "Song of Huma"

Line 1: *From the north came danger, as we knew it would.* Well, *some* of us knew, but Armavir is being very generous in using "we" in the first line of the poem. It was he, of course, who first made the inspired deduction that the draconians were indeed a horrid perversion of magic, not a race that "just naturally grew" up in the northern lands, as some of the other Companions maintained at first (and Caramon Majere, not noted for his insight, believed until the end of the war). They marked down the poet's observation as "another Gnome prejudice," in the pettiness so widespread among all of their races, not seeing that the prejudice was their own.

Line 4: . . . *from the mothering earth*. Though even the alert reader may take this to be a reference only to Flint, the poet meant for the line to refer not only to Flint, but to himself. This was one of his favorite phrases, as one can tell by his repeating it intact in the final stanza. At the time, "mother earth" was a fresh and original phrase, but the humans picked it up and, as the saying goes, ran it into the ground.

Line 5: *The sky unreckoned before them*. In this line a suggestion of not only the obvious fear of the future shared by all of the Companions, but also a wistful look back at the failed "Star Wires" experiment (see Part II of this essay) in which Armavir received illumination.

Line 6: *Nine they were, under the three moons.* Obviously, the original of this line reads "Ten they were, under the three moons," as it does throughout Armavir's original manuscript. See also the note to line 81.

Lines 10-14: *One from a garden . . . the spirit gathered.* This part of the stanza obviously refers to Flint Fireforge, whom Armavir rather liked. Flint always maintained that the Companions would never have gotten together had it not been for the gnome's charisma and influence. As in so many other cases, the story you read has tangled in translation, and alas, Flint is no longer around to set it straight.

Line 12: *Where the heart and the mind ride unquestioned.* A reference to the poet's "Lost Years" (see Part II of the essay) in which, dazed and electrocuted, he wandered the lands of Krynn. Armavir always suspected he was under Flint's care at the time.

Line 14: *In his fathering arms, the spirit gathered.* A punning reference to the dwarf's fondness for distilled spirits, a vice Caramon Majere (himself no teetotaller, as I recall) had the audacity to claim was Armavir's own. Flint in fact gathered the dwarf-spirits on the pretext that he was keeping them out of Armavir's hands, but indeed these particular spirits dwindled unexplainably in his care (however, see note to lines 19-23 below).

Lines 19-23: *One from a haven . . . and green again.* He *hated* Tasslehoff. That fake innocence and false cheeriness masked the fact that the kender was a coldhearted squirrel of a creature, Tanis's pet vole. *We* know who really found the Dragon Orb at the High

Michael Williams

Clerist's Tower, don't we, you plundering, pony-tailed little pipsqueak? We also know who it was that was nipping Flint's firewater and refusing to scold Armavir after the blame was passed elsewhere, not, as the others thought, out of a natural soft-heartedness, but because it suited him to *appear* naturally soft-hearted, and in doing so, to shift the blame more easily elsewhere, because the smarter ones—Raistlin and old Flint—would have thought a self-righteous lecture was strangely out of character.

In composing the "Song of the Ten Heroes" Armavir had to put this third stanza in to stave off the kender's hard feelings (yes, some poetry is most fanciful, most feigning), and perhaps it was even a sincere gesture on the poet's part to say that his own hard feelings he was willing to put aside? But what does Mister Minimus, everybody's favorite, do? Tries to steal this manuscript, readers—the very manuscript you're reading at this moment. Wanted to publish it under *his* name, change it a little to prove *he* wrote the Dragonlance songs, when even the "Kender Trailsong"[23] and "Kender Mourning Song"[24] were not his, and his "Song of Courage"[25] an insipid little number he twisted by

---

23. *Chronicles*, I, p. 75. Caramon deftly changed the name of this (though why he would choose "Trailsong" is beyond this humble writer). It was written some years after the war, in a moment of abject bitterness, for Caramon himself (Tika being the "one true love" of the poem). Reorx knows what Tasslehoff sang before the centaurs, but it wasn't this.

24. *Chronicles*, III, p. 261. He'd even claim this as his own, that bald-faced little graverobber of metaphor!

25. *Legends*, II, p. 86. The last two stanzas are Armavir's, the first two Tasslehoff's perversion. Side by side (or rather, one on top of the other) they produce an astonishing contrast in quality that is evident to this day.

changing some words from the original text! I stole back the manuscript (poetic justice!), all but 700 or so pages, none of which had anything to do with who wrote the songs but were simply a learned treatise on kleptomania, from which you should read and benefit, rodent!

Lines 28-32: *The next from . . . she came.* Goldmoon. The phrase "bearing a staff" refers not only to the Blue Crystal Staff that the original *Chronicles* fussed over so, but also to the Que-Shu princess's rather numerous personal staff of handmaidens, pages, and other attendants—a rather large group of Plainsmen who appear nowhere in the original *Chronicles.* Often the highly revered Priestess of Mishakal implored Tanis to give up the quest, complaining of muscle cramps, of Flint's and Caramon's (and Armavir's) tendency not to bathe (but given Armavir's tragic past, surely he feared water as that most powerful of electrical conductors, and would have stood, as I stand now, afloat on the writing table, dry and safe for the time being as the waters in this cell keep rising . . .), complaining loudly, upon first handling the disks of Mishakal, that she had broken a fingernail.

Plains tribes were scattered as much through vagrancy and underemployment as through anything the draconians were doing at the time, and the fact is that they were confined to a life of wandering and forage merely because so many of the more promising young people among them were hastened off to dance attendance on the various Chieftains and Chieftain's daughters. Those who were left were essentially scavengers, as evidenced below.

I have an additional paragraph regarding Goldmoon, which shall not be published until after Riverwind's death (see note to lines 46-50).

Lines 37-41: *The next from . . . space into light.* Riverwind. "Hierarchies of space" indeed, for the poor man
was completely boggled by his semi-successful quest
for the Blue Crystal Staff.[26] He was indeed "in the
shadow of the moon," and Armavir constructs a marvelous pun in line 37. In Goldmoon's shadow is the
obvious reading—he was slavishly devoted to her—
but in addition, Armavir means to suggest that the
Plainsman walked beneath the shadow of Lunitari,
the moon from which the common speech derives the
term "lunatic."

Frankly, the Plainsman was frightening, and
although Armavir hoped devoutly to wake one morning and find a kender topknot (complete with, possibly, kender noggin) dangling from Riverwind's belt,
the poet never really ventured to make acquaintance
with the hunter, who suffered from all kinds of delu-
sions, including one that he had been raised by leop-
ards, the only support for which was a slight lack of
personal cleanliness and a tendency to glaze over and
grow abstract when Goldmoon stroked the top of his
head (a condition that Armavir thought resembled
hypnosis, although the hypnotic suggestion "you are
now . . . a chicken!" had no visible effect on either the
Plainsman's humanity or courage).

Lines 46-50: *One within absences . . . awakening and
thought.* Kitiara. Through a keyhole, Armavir saw
her taking a bath once, and Great Reorx! she was
lovely and dark and glistening with waterdrops, but a

---

26. A longer poem of Armavir's about this adventure appears
elsewhere, conveniently pirated by that Solamnic Knight of the
Rose, Michael Williams, who should remember that the Order
of the Rose urges its knights to take pity on those less fortunate
rather than to steal their verses.

big thing for the likes of us. Nonetheless, only the fact that the door was locked kept the poet from donning his water wings (not yet remembering where they had come from, but knowing that somehow they were ambitious and tragic) and, as he says in the farewell note he wrote for Tanis[27] (who, characteristically, was completely at sea over how to begin the note) "take in the darkness/blessed and renamed by pleasure."

Armavir used the keyhole research method on several other occasions (see notes to lines 92 and 93).

Lines 55-59: *One in the heart . . . forever an heirloom.* Sturm. From this distance, it is sometimes difficult to understand the amount of posturing that went on among the Companions: Tanis wavering and serious and oh so tragic, like a moonstruck ship's captain; Tasslehoff's infuriating innocence (I remind you that, yes, a snake is innocent, too); Goldmoon and Laurana like princesses from old romances they probably never had time to read in their devout attention to hair, eye shadow, and manicure.

Sturm was different, and undeniably dangerous, for he believed all of that posturing. It was as though someone had made him up, had said, "We need a perfect, gentle knight to play a role in the story. How about this one?" As a result, some criticism of the *Chronicles* has arisen in cynical circles (primarily, those of the elves)—the suspicion that Sturm is, indeed, a fictional character, added to the *Chronicles* so that the humans might be represented even more overwhelmingly than they are now.

A fictional character? Only in the widest sense, for Sturm was among the Companions and met his death, as the story says, in the Siege at the High Clerist's Tow-

---

27. *Chronicles*, III, p.5.

er. Fictional he might have been, but only in the sense that he lived by fictions—by the notions of honor and duty and compassion that have since passed from the world of Krynn. For as you see, he was none too bright.

Yet Armavir remembered him fondly, for it was Sturm who insisted that the poet's role in the *Chronicles* should be championed, that the truth will out as to Armavir's discovery of the Orb at the Tower, as to the gnome's teaching the Solamnic Knights to use the dragonlances in that dismal and beleaguered fortress—truths that died with this silly, honorable man on the fortress wall. One might detect a conspiracy of silence in his death and that of Flint, but I am generous and far from such suggestions.

He was tiresome at best, but it is to be said for him that he was also tiresome at his worst. Receive this soul to Huma's breast, improbable as he was.

Lines 64-68: *The next in a simple . . . see their bottom.* Caramon. An amiable dunce, he was Armavir's drinking companion throughout the War of the Lance and for some time afterward. Though many of Armavir's exploits with Caramon have been forgotten by both parties, one of them must have involved the elaborate project (designed by the gnome and urged on by substantial quantities of dwarf spirits) of restoring the original Inn of the Last Home to its original height in a nearby vallenwood. The project involved a complicated system of pulleys and winches employing wires of incredible girth and tensile strength.

Needless to say, such an undertaking stirred old memories in the poet, and with those memories arose a series of increasingly severe depressions in which Armavir lay face down on the floor of the inn, paralyzed by spirits and listening in terror for the sound of distant thunder. The project was finally abandoned, and remained unacknowledged in Caramon's rather smug preface to *Leaves*. All in all, though, he wasn't a bad sort, only easily influenced.

It was for Caramon that the poet wrote "Three Sheets to the Wind,"[28] not to mention a few less successful lyrics thankfully forgotten. Line 68 contains a punning reference to one of these lesser songs—certainly Caramon's favorite of the lot, and composed while the poet himself was hoisting still another sheet at the site of the old inn:

> *Dragonlance, Dragonlance,*
> *I see Tika's underpants.*

Not immortal, but high art to Caramon, who was known to faint or suffer nosebleeds when cornered and badgered into listening to "The Song of Huma"[29] or "Crysania's Song."[30] Not immortal, but I fear durable enough to come back into memory and embarrass the maker. I include it only to caution those who tend to idealize historical figures: Armavir was certainly no saint, and of course the couplet was not merely a performance for Caramon's benefit, but also contained an element of truth (see note to lines 46-50).

Lines 73-77: *The next the leader . . . does nothing.* Tanis (Armavir preferred infinitely his elf name "Tanthalas," which derived from the same root as the verb "tantalize"; tantalized the half-elf was—by all the

---

28. *Legends*, I, p 94.

29. *Chronicles*, I, pp. 442-445.

30. *Legends*, III, p. 164.

options, all the pretty faces!). As indecisive on policy as he was on matters of women (see note to line 93), Tanis often came to Armavir for advice on both fronts. Without this counsel, the quest would have turned into a kender fire drill on a number of occasions, and a tangled romantic life could have brought all Krynn to destruction.

I still have Tanis's draft of his farewell note to Kitiara—a draft refined and expanded, as the reader knows, by more poetic hands—but the text, here printed for the first time in its entirety, will give the reader an idea of the shuttling way in which the leader of the Companions thought:

> *Kitiara, of all the days these days*
> *Are filled with waiting (but there were those days*
> *Four years ago, when I awaited you,*
> *And then again, those days at the Last Home*
> *I waited more than I had four years ago,*
> *But not as much as . . . maybe I should say,*
> *Of most of the days these days,*
> *Of some of the days, of few, oh never mind.*

His policy decisions were painful to watch. By the time the Companions had reached Solace, Tanis had taken to standing on battlements, dressed in black and holding a skull in one hand, discussing with the skull (or with Armavir, when the poet had nothing better to do or when it was not bath time among the Companions) as to which hamlet, which village the party should pass through next. But judging from the text of the letter above, the half-elf was, if possible, more pathetic in matters of the heart than in matters of the head. "Laurana or Kitiara," he would whine, to Armavir or the skull: "Tell me which one?" To which the poet, making Tanis a party to his secret observations (see note to lines 46-50), perhaps unwittingly planted the seed of resentment that was to grow into the ingratitude with which our esteemed leader would later conceal Armavir's contribution to history.

Line 81: After this line in Armavir's original text, the following stanza:

> The next from the intricate mountains, believing
> The deed the design of the word arising
> From the light on the sword, from the netted darkness,
> Called like the others, but called into memory
> So that the deeds rise like water from stone.
> *Ten they were, under the three moons,*
> *Under the autumn twilight:*
> *As the world declined, they arose*
> *Into the heart of the story.*

By this time, there should be no doubt in the reader's mind why this stanza was excluded from the *Chronicles*. It was the best stanza of the poem, to boot, for it was hard for a gnome of Armavir's natural humility to write about himself. The best stanza: no matter what the others say, I shall not compromise, shall not grovel!

Lines 82-86: *The last . . . the benighted.* Raistlin. Another odd fish whom the poet had little to do with at the time, having started the acquaintance on the wrong foot by making a mild joke about the eyes of this particularly humorless individual: the suggestion that if Raistlin stood on his head he could reverse the flow of Time and make us all young again was greeted with such a withering stare that for a while Armavir feared that the mage might transform him into something terribly ungnomelike—a roll-top desk or a chicken, perhaps, sent scuttling back amid the tunnels and chambers beneath Mount Nevermind, where doubtless lay many snares that had slipped from a memory damaged by both dwarf spirits and electricity. Surely Raistlin had something to do with my being here in this cistern of a cubicle, with what is now inevitably my fate as the water keeps rising, bearing the writing table higher and higher in the drowned room until I shall be crushed among table and water and stone. . . .

But again to abandon self-pity, for the truth must be championed (and shall make me free?). Raistlin *did* write the farewell to his brother that concludes Volume III of the *Chronicles*,[31] and if he did not, I should be a fool to say otherwise. (Could it be that as I say this the water ceases to rise? An old pulley on the north wall of the cell, in danger of being submerged only a minute ago, remains dry and untouched above the surface of the pool—the water is still and unruffled as onyx—and for the first time I can see my reflection on the surface!) Raistlin was . . . by far the best of them, a man of uncommon genius, whose break with the Companions stemmed mostly from his great quest for knowledge, but also, I trust, from his sense of outrage when he saw the others begin to cover Armavir's role in the story (and now the water stands motionless—calm, dark, and limpid, thanks be to Reorx!).

As a tribute to Raistlin—a genuine tribute, knowing his understanding and merciful nature—Armavir includes within this stanza another clue as to the cruel exclusion of the poet from the *Chronicles*. Line 83,

Where the abstract stars hide a nest of words,

---

31. pp. 380-381.

should be noted, for the pun on "stars" takes in the meaning of "celebrities," and six of the nine celebrities of the *Chronicles* (I exclude Sturm and Flint and, Dear Reorx! I exclude Raistlin) have done their best to hide the "nest of words," the poet who was the birthplace of the story.[32]

Line 92: *A graceless girl, graced beyond graces.* The lovely, the fickle Tika. Armavir saw her first, as a very young girl who worked hours far too hard and long for her tenderness. Closely he watched her grow and blossom into the beautiful woman she was to become (see note to lines 46-50).

Well, as a young girl might, she went for the muscles, for the job security, instead of the immortality bestowed by the poet's pen. Tika, the wedding song[33] was for us, sold at the last moment for a pittance to Goldmoon and Riverwind, when it became clear that in your eyes we were not to be! If you ever read this, return to me, forgiven of all adolescent attachments and your part in the conspiracy that left the poet's name unsung! This chamber is bathtub unto itself, my dear, my dove, and my eyes are keyholes!

Line 93: *A princess of seeds and saplings, called to the forest.* Laurana. Why Tanis would throw over a number like Kitiara for this little one was beyond Armavir, is beyond me (and an incident before the siege of the High Clerist's Tower was conclusive evidence: see notes to lines 46-50). Of course, humans *age* a lot

---

32. Obviously, the line also refers to the abandoned "Star Wires" project: a quest that, it should be evident, the poet never entirely forgot.

33. *Chronicles*, I, pp. 436-437.

more quickly than elves, and though Kitiara was impressively arrayed, Tanis might have been enough of an elf to look toward the long run. I don't think the decision was political, like the self-righteous little farewell note maintains. In fact, I cannot see how Tanis could even have made that decision—indeed, any decision—without consulting his accompanying skull or using (without payment or gratitude) Armavir's considerable ghostwriting skills.

Line 94: *An ancient weaver of accidents.* Fizban. Although not entirely unsympathetic, his was a figure blown completely out of proportion by the tendency of many of the Heroes to mythologize. Though far too taken in by Tasslehoff's deceptive charm, apparently he was a shrewd old con artist himself, managing to parlay a standard "wise old man" image and an equally standard (but cleverly engineered) disappearance and reappearance into a claim of godhood and, no doubt, all the benefits that might accrue from such a position, while conveniently missing most—if not all—of the danger.

About that disappearance: it has never been emphasized enough that Tasslehoff was the sole witness of the mysterious event; whenever it has been mentioned, the reliability of the source has (incredibly) never been questioned. Perhaps the greatest accident Fizban wove was his own.

I always thought that the little speech he gave at the end of the war (quoted at the end of the *Chronicles*) was rather lame: all that theological clap-trap did nothing but give the surviving Companions an inflated sense of their own self-importance (which, I suppose, is what mythology is for, and why they were so willing to enshrine him on the spot). But from his story we can draw one valuable lesson: sometimes an important individual drops out of a tale, out of history, through accident or design, but given time and the continual hunger for truth, he shall return with an immortality won by his own cleverness, his own ingenuity. It is the tale of the poet in brief, of the true "weaver of accidents," if I have ever heard that tale spoken.

Line 95: *Nor can we say who the story will gather.* Often taken to be a grammatical error on the poet's part, a line that *should* read "Nor can we say *whom* the story will gather." Not true at all! It was Armavir's last insurance, his last hedge against oblivion! For the line, as printed, means grammatically, "Nor can we say who will gather the story." The final version of the poem, marred by the neglect or ill intentions of the chroniclers, proves Armavir a prophet.

V. Conclusion

Spared again, as the waters of the cell begin to recede (could it, perhaps, be Raistlin's taunting, toying with me over the years and the miles, over Reorx knows what boundaries, for a comment made only in jest? If so, I am properly instructed, and beg forgiveness. Or could it all have been an illusion of light and onyx, a damaged memory from a damaged childhood?).

True to his premonitions, the poet fell from the story. In the interest of truth, I have returned him. For this service I ask only a small reward: that my name shall be remembered as his, and that the day shall come when pseudonyms are things of the past, and those who were truly at the heart of the story shall be remembered and revered, their names echoed throughout the upper world, through helmets in the vallenwoods, through the memories of all decent folk, gnomish or otherwise, and finally, that something can be done about these faucets. These things I ask for, and also that a sizeable sum of money be sent to the address I enclose with the manuscript, for I have more to say, and to adopt the common misreading of line 95 of the "Song,"

Nor can we tell *whom* the story will gather.

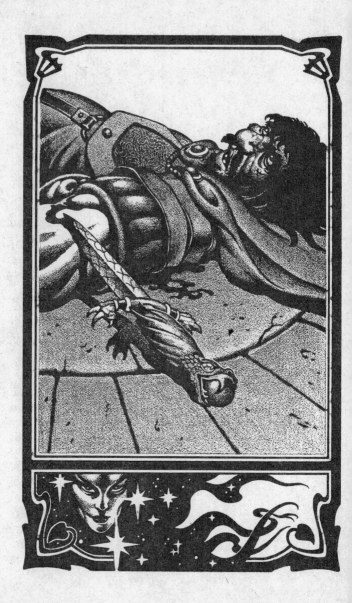

Dagger-Flight

Nick O'Donohoe

I

*I*t woke in warm darkness. A musical voice, not quite deep and not quite high, spoke. "I'll get it for you."

The weight rocked.

A higher, childlike voice said almost sadly, "No. I don't want it back. You can never get rid of the smell, you know."

The weight settled. Something wet and thick was dripping around it, seeping a little at a time in through tiny pits on the blade. "Blade," it thought, half-asleep. "I have a blade."

And a moment later, more sharply, "I taste blood."

The blood was rank and bitter, laden with strange salts. The thing knew, without knowing how, that it had tasted better blood than this—better than this goblin blood.

As more dripped on the blade, it suddenly thought clearly, "I'm a dagger. I'm a dagger, stuck through a goblin's heart."

A new voice that seemed to come from everywhere laughed, each word chiming like a falling icicle. *Poor pet. You hardly know yourself.* And it laughed again.

Though the voice sounded as if it could be

anything—rock, corpse, wind, or weapon—the dagger thought of it as "she."

You can't see yourself, can barely feel yourself, and don't know yourself at all. Her voice showed casual contempt for weakness. *You've only just fed, and it wasn't very good, was it?* She purred, *Soon you will feed again, perhaps many times.*

The dagger quivered with pleasure and fear; something about that voice . . . As the dagger moved, the surface of the congealing blood broke, and fresh drops fell all the way to the cross-piece. "Cross-piece," it thought uncertainly. "I *must* be a dagger."

The voice, colder than goblin corpse, said, *I hinted that you were not. Many have mistaken you for a dagger more times than you can dream of. Fools have died for that.*

The dagger strained to hear more, its slow mind uncomprehending. Movement was harder as the flesh around it stiffened.

She went on, *You look like worn, half-tarnished silver work. You have a pommel shaped like the head of a*—she hesitated—*a serpent, for one thing. Your cross-piece is a pair of talons, like a falcon's or an eagle's, and your tail is a scale-carved, six-inch blade. You feed through that, not through your mouth. You also do . . . other things with it, pet.*

She knows me, the dagger thought, and ever so slightly wagged its tail. The cooling blood stirred again. The dagger drank.

I know you well. You are not metal and were not forged by any hand, not even by my own. Long ago, your race was common. You were born to feed on those who used you, owned you, or had kinship. Blood stirred you; murder fed you; war multiplied you. In some autumn sunsets, the sky would darken early with your numbers, and the beating of your wings was like the roar of battle as you swept down on village after village.

Her tone changed. *Later there was . . . one who knew magic, though not as I knew it. I shall not name that name here. You and yours were put to sleep, without food, through the centuries. Most died. You are one of the last.*

A few years ago, a foolish peddler dug you up and carried you far south, hoping to trade you as a relic from some Pre-Cataclysm war. That was well, and was my bidding. But he sold you to a dwarf, a lumpish, sickly brute who does not do my bidding.

In the cold body, the dagger shivered at her voice. When the lady—she must be at least that—commanded, one did her bidding and hoped to live. Its little mind could not imagine disobedience, or its consequences.

Now I bid you, pet. The dwarf must die—partly to feed you, partly for disobeying, and partly, she added indifferently, *because he aids one who would be my enemy, if he but had the power. That is reason enough for the dwarf's death, if I needed reasons.*

But it was another who stabbed you into the goblin, who wielded you just now; I bid you to kill him, too— he and the dwarf—because I ask it. You need blood to do what you now must; I need all blood because I choose it. Find your owner, your user, your food; drink deep and do my bidding. Go. Now. The voice ceased.

The dagger strained to hear more. After a moment, slowly and painfully, it curled its talons on the crosspiece, grasping the flabby folds of the goblin's skin. Gradually it worked itself free and pulled itself out from under the body. Once in the open air, it crawled rapidly along the path, moving and looking as though it were an injured lizard.

Ahead it heard the high, childlike voice of the user—the dagger's next kill by right of use. The ruby eyes dimly made out curly brown hair, a fleece vest, and some sort of stick that the short creature was walking with, then spinning to make noise. The high voice was giggling. "Besides," he said, "That dagger was Flint's!"

The dagger swiveled its short stiff body, the hilt with wings, to peer at the squat figure who grunted in annoyance next. He had muscular arms and an age-lined silhouette, and he carried an axe bound to his belt.

"Flint," the dagger thought. "The dwarf who owned me. Owner and user. Both my food."

But the two, and a third one, their tall, bearded companion, turned and climbed the steps that wound up the trunk of a massive vallenwood tree. The dagger, attempting the first step, scuttled quickly aside as a great many people stepped past, going up and down.

A less simple, more wide-awake mind would have been frustrated. The dagger had slept more than a thousand years; it lay in the brush and waited patiently for the three to return.

II

After some time there was a great deal of noise: benches falling, bodies bumping or, more likely, striking the inn floor, a crowd gasping as a flare of blue light illuminated the night even through the stained glass of the inn's windows. A quavery old voice cried, "Call the guards! Arrest the kender! Arrest the barbarians! Arrest their friends!" The rest was lost in confusion. Someone ran down the long stairway, shouting for the guards and panting.

The dagger waited, but Flint and the others did not

appear. It heard a thump and muttering from under the kitchen of the inn, and then a ruckus nearby, but the dagger could not imagine anything so devious as a trapdoor.

Shortly, there was the sound of heavy, clumsy feet running. Armored goblins ran up the stairs and then back down; they dispersed. A pair of feet stopped in front of the dagger. "What's this?"

A voice as harsh said, "Somebody dropped an old knife. So what?"

The first voice chuckled. "You got no imagination, Grum." A horny hand lifted the dagger. "Nice piece." The dagger, after being flipped over twice, found itself tucked inside ill-fitting body armor.

The goblin's body was rank, but it was flesh. The dagger, still too weak to attack, lay hungrily beside the fat-laden rib cage, waiting.

It did not wait long. There was the sound of a door creaking open and of goblin voices. "The Seekers demand right of entry."

The second voice: "This place is empty. Let's move on."

"You got no imagination, Grum. Here's our chance to pick up a few pieces of silver."

Another light flared, seeping around the armor cracks. Both goblins screamed, and suddenly their bodies seemed to leap together, then collapse. From the floor, the dagger heard a muffled voice, then a deeper one say, "I'm afraid so. I hit them too hard."

After more muffled talk, the light died and there was the sound of feet running to and fro, furniture overturning, and finally silence. The dagger waited as long as it could bear, but even indoors the goblin's corpse was cooling.

With its talons stretched as far as they would go, it slid itself bit by bit under the body's ribs, into the goblin's black heart. This time it drank consciously, thirstily; each drop brought new awareness.

First came a greater sense of smell—no advantage just now, but a world of sensation. The ruby eyes glowed dimly, then grew brighter. Finally the entire dagger rippled with new life and knowledge.

"I am not a dagger," it thought. "She spoke the truth. I am a feeder."

Crawling out from under the body was easier, but a greater surprise waited as the feeder scuttled to the door. As it stumbled on the sill, its wings began to unfurl from the hilt, beating once, then lifting the creature off the wood.

The dagger flew tentatively back to the goblin body and dropped onto the neck with its full weight. After a moment it withdrew and flew strongly into the night, scanning and smelling for the dwarf, Flint, its owner, and—the kender, wasn't it?—its user.

The night was full of hurrying bodies; the feeder could smell their warmth, and its appetite was growing. Though it did not know why, the feeder knew it urgently needed blood, and afterward there was something it must do, something important. As it circled between the village and the lakeshore, suddenly a very old, familiar scent came to it: the smell of ownership. It flapped strongly toward the source.

But when the feeder reached the source, it wasn't the dwarf or the kender after all.

Parris the trader shouldered his duffel wearily, brooding over a bad night. First he had been abused and robbed by goblin guards. When he finally came to the inn, it was in chaos—something about a dwarf, a mixed-race company, and magic had the place upset. Then he was told to leave; the goblin guards had closed the inn to strangers. Solace had never been good luck for him; years ago he'd made a very bad bargain with a sharp-eyed dwarf here.

He rambled toward the lake, looking for a sheltered spot to spend the night. Suddenly, silhouetted against the water, he saw a strange group: slender man or elf, barbarian, knight, more humans, kender, dwarf. The dwarf was closest, hanging back from the water.

He squinted at the figure, who was arguing about a boat. The gruff voice was familiar; he squinted, trying to think where he had heard it before. He could almost hear it again, wheedling, grunting, bargaining over a dagger. . . .

"By all the gods the Theocrats sell," he breathed. "It's himself. It's Flint. What's he doing here, and that crew he's got with him?"

In a quick mental leap, he connected the grumpy dwarf and his party to the incident that had closed the Inn of the Last Home, and realized that the goblins were looking for Flint.

Parris smiled, not nicely. Surely he could talk Dragon Highlord Fewmaster Toede into giving him some reward. Solace might bring him luck after all.

Parris stretched his skinny neck, opening his mouth to call to the hobgoblin guards.

But something hit the back of his neck with an audible thud. A second mouth opened in Parris's neck, just below his chin. As it widened, a pointed silver tongue protruded from it. It looked as though the second mouth were screaming.

Above it, the real mouth was screaming. No sound came out. Parris dropped to his knees, then sprawled forward in the road. He just had time to grab at the back of his neck and feel a strangely carved hilt he thought he recognized. . . .

Hotter, thinner blood than the goblin's burst over

the blade and was absorbed. The ruby eyes burned brighter, and the feeder thought suddenly, clearly, "I know why I must do this. I am more than a feeder. I'm a mother."

And it remembered: the long-ago mating flight, once for a lifetime; the search for food, and for hosts; the red-filled nights of circling, seeking, diving into a host body, drinking deep, and laying its young in the corpse. It remembered, dimly, its own long weeks in rotting flesh, eating and absorbing, growing until one day it and its brothers and sisters crawled out of the hollowed body and into the night, looking for fresher and more lively food. There had been many brothers and sisters. . . .

The feeder felt a rush of warmth from hilt to blade. There would be many again. It was time to seek a host. Soon the race of feeders would darken the sky.

Suddenly from the shoreline came cries and the twang of bows. The feeder rose, its eyes blood-bright, and flew straight for the noise, gaining height for another dive.

On the shore were goblins, shouting and shooting arrows. The feeder ignored them, moving over the boat and its occupants. The kender, crouched at the oars, was too well covered by the others, and Flint was struggling in the water. The feeder hovered, waiting for a sure target.

"That does it!" The large one, the deep voice the feeder had heard before, pulled the dwarf halfway into the boat. Flint hung onto a seat, but his lower half was sticking out over the edge of the boat, unprotected.

A vague memory surfaced in the feeder: inside the biped's legs was a large, rich artery that could empty a body in moments. The feeder, not hesitating as a human might have for an enemy in such a vulnerable position, zeroed in, plummeted, blade flashing in the starlight.

At the last moment the one dressed as a knight grabbed the dwarf by the belt and dragged him aboard as the boat rocked wildly. The feeder, unable to stop, imbedded itself firmly in the seat of the vessel.

The one with the deep voice noticed the feeder, stuck and helpless. He grunted with surprise, then pulled it free. Before the feeder could move, the stranger had slid it into a thonged leather sheath, firmly binding the thongs around cross-piece, pommel, and hilt. He did it one-handed, as though from long practice; his other hand was embracing a cloaked man with strange, hourglass eyes. That one, who had been casting a spell as the feeder dove in, pulled away.

The feeder could see, bound as it was, that the one with the hourglass eyes was looking at it. The feeder struggled against its bonds, in vain. A skinny finger poked at the feeder, traced its outline in the sheath. The cloaked man made a small surprised noise in his throat, and coughed rackingly.

A moment before, this man had been casting spells, strenuous ones from the look of him; now, although he was exhausted, his eyes were lit with recognition. The feeder tensed. Any moment, the mage would tell the others. . . .

Just then there was a gasp of alarm from the only woman in the boat; the feeder heard her but could not see her. The big man, who now owned the dagger, poked the mage. "Raist, what is it? I don't see anything."

The mage stood up, out of the feeder's line of sight. A moment later he said, stricken, "Tanis . . . the constellations . . ."

The musical voice said, "What? What about the constellations?" So that was Tanis, the feeder noted.

The one who had shaken the feeder awake.

"Gone." The mage was racked with coughs, spasm after spasm shaking the boat slightly. The feeder relaxed; for whatever reason, the mage had forgotten about it for the present.

Then Raistlin said shakily, "The constellation known as the Queen of Darkness and the one called Valiant Warrior. Both gone. She has come to Krynn, Tanis, and he has come to fight her. All the evil rumors we have heard are true. War, death, destruction . . ."

The mage and the others said more, but the feeder did not hear. "The Queen of Darkness," it thought with certainty. "The voice I heard. The Lady who ordered me."

Then it thought as certainly, "These are the ones she bade me kill."

For now, however, there was nothing to be done until the boat reached shore and the company found shelter. All but those on watch slept. The feeder nestled patiently in its thong-bound sheath, dreaming of the blood and of its children while it waited for release.

III

The mage said nothing about the feeder, having forgotten it among more important things. In the morning the company of beings journeyed again through woods to a road. On the way they called each other by name, and the feeder linked names and voices: Riverwind, Goldmoon, Tasslehoff or Tas, Raistlin, Caramon, Sturm, Tanis, Flint. The way before them was hard, and the feeder smelled their sweat and, beneath it, their blood.

The feeder grew impatient, then frantic. Sometime in the night it felt the first movements of its brood, growing and dividing. By mid-day the feeder was flushed with new life from point to cross-piece, and the tiny bodies were expanding even into the hilt. It had fed well, and this would be a large brood—if it found a host in time.

Squirming uncomfortably against the thongs, the feeder discovered new urgency, the reward of feeding and the necessity of birthing. Its jaws on the snake's-head pommel were separating from each other, and it could feel its fangs growing, filling with venom.

Nature had provided well; once sated on dead flesh, its children could kill any being on Krynn. The feeder struggled helplessly, unable to control its need for birthing.

After some time on the road, Caramon ran suddenly and crouched in the brush. Tanis came and whispered to him. "Clerics!"

Caramon snorted and repeated the word, but brushed the feeder once with his hand. The feeder went rigid, willing with all its mind that Caramon would draw his dagger. There was a faint, wonderful scent in the air.

Several people on the road spoke. The feeder listened intently to the strange yet familiar voices of the clerics, but was distracted: Caramon was undoing the thongs that bound the feeder in the sheath. The feeder twisted its pommel-head around, trying to find free flesh to bite, but the man's chain mail left no gaps.

Still, sooner or later he would take the feeder in hand.

Tanis cried, "Caramon! Sturm! It's a tra—"

Faster than the feeder could react, Caramon whipped the dagger into his left hand and held it at guard, facing the clerics. The feeder opened its mouth wide, aiming its fangs at the underside of his thumb where the vein would be.

A cleric jumped forward and Caramon slashed him, leaving behind a sickly green stain on the cleric's robe following the line of the cut. There was a violent smell, and Caramon gasped.

The feeder rolled helplessly in Caramon's hand, overwhelmed and on fire with the taste. It was ecstasy. It was the blood of life. It was—the feeder trembled— it was like its own blood. The many children inside the feeder struggled, aroused by the taste.

Preparing a spell, Raistlin called out, "Don't stab them! They'll turn to stone!" Caramon dropped his sword and the dagger.

The feeder, dizzy with the strange green blood so like its own, lay on the ground, its mouth opening and closing. Dimly, it saw clawed hands and reptilian faces. Before the dagger could collect itself, the big man picked it back up and threw it at the clerics. The feeder braced for the rush of green blood.

It heard the warning in its mind again: "Don't stab them. They'll turn to stone." The children would die in stone. At the last moment, it flipped a wing and wavered past the clerics—draconians. They were draconians. The dagger opened its wings and soared up, fast as a hawk, circling for prey. It would never be more alive, more desperate and deadly, than it was now.

Tanis was on the road. He was no user, no owner, but he had blood and a body for children, and the Queen would want him dead. The dagger circled once and dove straight down, its whole body humming with the force of the dive.

Flames from Raistlin's spell flared out. Tanis flung himself to the ground.

The feeder slammed into a boulder beyond Tanis and gave a sharp, angry cry. Tiny flames came from its mouth. In all the confusion, Tanis saw and heard nothing.

The feeder shook its head, then peered left and right. Tanis had run on. The feeder spread its wings, rose, and circled, trying to pick out its prey in all the confusion. The clerics were distracting it.

Flint and Tasslehoff, each standing over Sturm, were open and exposed; the dwarf's attention was riveted by an oncoming draconian. The feeder raised itself up, folded its wings, and stooped toward the dwarf, who had his eyes on the sword-swinging, man-like creature.

The draconian's wicked, curved sword lashed out in a flashing arc, aimed for the dwarf's neck. Flint swung his axe, but at that moment Tasslehoff, his eyes on Sturm's sword, rose to his feet. The kender's hoopak staff struck the dwarf in the back of the knees, causing Flint's legs to buckle beneath him. The draconian's sword whistled harmlessly overhead as the dwarf gave a startled yell and fell over backward on top of Sturm.

The feeder shot helplessly past with the sword swing, moving too quickly for sight. By the time it stopped, it was even with Tanis, who had caught up with Riverwind and Goldmoon. Hissing with frustration, it beat its wings swiftly and aimed at Tanis's heart.

Tanis leaped toward the draconians and smote one of the creatures from behind, using the flat of his sword, then made a backhand swing at another.

The feeder missed Tanis's heart but caught in his clothes. Its red eyes glowed brighter as it twisted its head sideways and back, ready to expose its fangs and sink them into Tanis's side.

As Riverwind, low on arrows and lacking a sword, bounded toward Tanis, the half-elf's hand brushed the smooth back of the feeder's head.

Tanis let his enemies get past him, fending off the

---

creatures with the flat of his sword. "Here, take this dagger!" he shouted to Riverwind. Riverwind grabbed it.

Pulled from Tanis's waist just prior to its final deadly thrust, the feeder strained to reach Riverwind's intruding hand. The fangs were out; the Plainsman's thumb was in reach. After all, now Riverwind had possession . . .

. . . He reversed it and struck one of the creatures on the jaw . . .

Too greedily, the feeder sank its teeth into the draconian flesh. The taste was tangy, yet frighteningly familiar; there was a bond here. The feeder's body struck against a neck ornament on a thong, a silver copy of its own head.

The draconian jerked forward in a poison-induced spasm, and the feeder's fangs sank deeper. Even in the frenzy of feeding, it thought calmly; there was plenty of time to withdraw its fangs and pull back before the draconian turned to stone . . .

. . . Jabbing upward with the hilt, Riverwind broke its neck.

The Plainsman grunted with the effort as the draconian gasped and died. The feeder, trapped by its own bite, spasmed in Riverwind's hand. Startled, the Plainsman dropped it. The stone draconian fell forward heavily, shattering the blade of the feeder. Tiny replicant daggers the size and softness of earwigs flopped on the ground, dying before birth.

The Queen's voice sighed across the broken feeder, all but freezing it.

You have failed, she said indifferently, *but I shall not, and if I need these lives, I can take them elsewhere. Die, then.* The voice was still, and the feeder knew it would hear no more from her.

Even so, the light in the pommel's eyes lasted some time.

ABOUT THE WRITERS

HAROLD BAKST, a resident of New York City, is a long-time student and fan of traditional folk and fairy tales. His most recent novel, *The Legend of Whiskey Stop*, is a Western ghost story. His next novel, *The Strange Voyage of Kian the Mariner*, will be published as a WINDWALKER™ Book in the fall by TSR, Inc.

NANCY VARIAN BERBERICK lives in a small rural town in the west New Jersey hills with her husband and sixteen-year-old Rooney, two dogs, and a computer. Her work has appeared in AMAZING® Stories, DRAGON® Magazine, *The Magic of Krynn*, several small press publications, and has been excerpted in J.N. Williamson's *How to Write Tales of Horror, Fantasy, and Science Fiction*. Novels? Of course! One is being readied for publication, another is cooking in the computer, and several are patiently awaiting their turns for attention.

RICHARD A. KNAAK, a contributor to DRAGONLANCE® Tales I, *The Magic of Krynn*, makes his home in Schaumburg, Illinois. Among his obsessions are a fierce dislike for long-haired cats and the desire to write as many novels as he has in his own collection, which presently numbers some seven hundred books.

NICK O'DONOHOE writes the Nathan Phillips detective series (*April Snow, Wind Chill*, and *Open Season* so far), and has published in DRAGONLANCE® Tales I, *The Magic of Krynn*. He also plays mumbledy-peg, but never with flying knives.

DANNY PEARY is a film/television/music critic and sportswriter. His most recent book is *Guide for the Film Fanatic. Cult Movies 3* will be published in 1988. He lives in New York with his wife, poet Suzanne Rafer.

BARBARA SIEGEL and SCOTT SIEGEL are actually time travelers from Krynn. They have come here to study our modern world, and we are pleased to publish their findings: "What a place. These newfangled wizards are clever; you can get your fortune told by merely opening a cookie in a Chinese eating establishment. Even more surprising, there is